Backstage Pass

A Novel

By Ronald R. Hanna

<u>Dedication</u>

To all of those who entertain us, in music, in film, in life, realizing that the glamour we see is necessarily the result of a lot of extremely hard work and, in many instances, hard living.

Chapter One

It seemed that everyone was doing cocaine. The powdered type, which was being snorted by everyone from the roadies handling the band's instruments and equipment to the technicians responsible for ensuring that the sound was exquisite. Siren started snorting coke long before she became an international superstar, but inhaling the powder through cosmetically narrowed nostrils had long since grown tiresome. She liked her stuff raw now, cooked up and smoked. As pure as possible and with a high exhilarating in its immediacy. It kept her motivated, she believed, and enabled her to keep up with the torturous schedule required when on tour.

Her abettors consisted of a tight-knit group: Alverez was on payroll specifically to ensure that voluminous amounts of the powder were always available, though for fiduciary reasons he was identified on the payroll as a lighting technician. He did not know a damn thing about lighting, but was an expert in securing cocaine almost anywhere in the world and secreting it, in bulk, somewhere among the tons of musical equipment, costumes and show materials where even the keen nose of the best-trained drug-sniffing dog could not find it.

Not that the touring entourage of Siren Lavesque ever came under any type of law enforcement scrutiny. She was, after all, the multi-platinum songstress whose appearance in any city, and on any continent, bought with it hundreds of millions of dollars in revenue and residual attention. The lithe, beautiful, powerful songstress was a cocaine addict who was also an industry unto herself.

Her payroll supported 67 musicians, technicians, wardrobe people, dancers and security personnel. Every one of them knew that she was a cokehead, but certainly no one challenged her on her excessive use. Indeed, many among them participated in consumption with her, but few to the extent to which Siren partook of the substance. Few could afford to, and many, most snorters, knew that excessive use could lead to their own falling down on the job and an as quick dismissal from the entourage.

Siren though…. That damn Siren….

"What kind of shit is that?!" she blasted, strutting across the stage in the massive, 50,000 seat arena. "Billy? What key was that supposed to be in?"

She was in jeans, the arena empty at this hour. Her hair was wrapped in a massive, colorful scarf and she wore nothing under the tight blue leather jacket, zipped only a measure above the navel and generous breast poking out for all to see. Her small feet were stuck in a pair of $400 clogs, and they made a hollow clapping noise as she stormed across the stage.

"Y'all get this shit right!" she screamed. "I don't have time for all this! You know I have to hit two television talk shows and three radio stations before the first show tonight, then put up with that damn bitch from that fucking magazine tailing me all along this goddamn tour like some nosey little shit all into my personal business! I don't have time for this y'all! Get your shit together or I'll find somebody who can!"

The threats were constant, and few doubted Siren did not mean what she said. Only seven legs into this tour and the road behind was littered with the corpses of electricians, lighting technicians, stagehands, a dancer and one musician who had all failed to measure up to Siren's critical standards. She was on coke all right, and had been for seven years. But for a long time she remained the consummate perfectionist most knew when she was but an 18-year-old starting out in an often-cutthroat business. She was a young professional, surprising to many who viewed her business acumen, her balance, her drive.

Until she began having the almost pure powdered cocaine cooked up for her, and began smoking it.

Now, at 25, Siren was a tornado in search of a place to touch down. She was still driven, but most days now seemed on autopilot. The raw coke was having a noticeable affect on her voice, and her demeanor had grown from sweet to caustic, silky smooth to abrasive. She had fired so many associates on the tour even her own addled mind had lost count. Marvella Stanton, her personal assistant for seven years and guardian since she was a preteen, had been canned prior to the last concert in Milwaukee. Yet Siren stormed around the stage now, preparing for the show in Baltimore and screaming for Marvella to come and take hold of the myriad problems that were mostly perceptions of her own befuddled imagination.

"Where in the hell is Marvella?" she screamed at the top of her lungs, voice coarse, attitude equally needling. "I'm going to fire that bitch if she don't help us get this shit right! And I mean it! Marvella?! Marvella?!"

While seated on the aisle chair of the last row in the extreme rear of the massive auditorium, her longtime friend and as close to a mother as she'd ever had, Marvella, sat shaking her head at the train wreck on stage before her.

Marvella had been officially terminated, but even without pay was not about to let her girl go solo down a path of self-destruction. She paid her own way to Baltimore and maneuvered with friends still on the tour to gain surreptitious access to places where Siren would be rehearsing, appearing in public venues, sleeping and eventually performing.

"I just can't let my little girl go adrift like that," she told Georgia, the singer's manager, who had been with Siren since she had gained stardom. "I just can't."

Even before Siren was a star, Marvella Stanton had been legal guardian to Sirena Lavesque, a skinny little black figure whose natural parents had been drug addicts and had long ago abandoned her along with a number of her actual and step-siblings. Marvella was steaming, watching the fiasco of one who had been as close to a daughter to her as one of her very own.

She blamed it on the drugs, and of course had no love for Alvarez. She had even considered going to a relative who was a high law enforcement official and ratting out the drug supplier. But knowing Alvarez as she did and, of course, knowing what Siren would do if made aware of this, she thought better of the idea. Still she just couldn't watch her beloved Siren continue on what was certainly a death march. She arose, strode the long distance out of the darkness down the aisle and stood just before the stage.

"Oh, there you are!" Siren said when she noticed Marvella standing at the foot of the stage. "Mami, these guys seemed to not get it! Can you please do something about this? Messing up the arrangement and all, hours before the show. Please, Mami, get with Billy and make sure they have their act together."

She called her guardian the familial "Mami" whenever she really wanted to warm up to the woman, or when she knew that Marvella had been disrespected and was due an apology. But Siren was not one to apologize for her countless misdeeds, disrespects, malfeasances.

She was not only a star in the truest sense of the word, but a star within her own mind which outshined the one which graced the stage. There was no one greater than her on the entire planet, she truly believed, although her talents were surpassed by at least three of her backup singers. She'd simply impressed Cord Fredericks, the renowned impresario and head of Jupiter Solice Records, at the tender age of 16, was taken under his wing and groomed for the big-time before being surrounded by even greater vocal talents as a supporting cast.

Marvella shook her head in disgust but still couldn't suppress the in depth love for "that little girl," as she continued to mentally identify Siren.

"Child, you gonna get on my last nerve with your mess," the 55-year-old said, aged beyond her years over the past decade most certainly from having to see after the songstress/daughter she loved more than anyone else in the world.

She strode on knees paining with arthritis quite premature for one who'd lived fine and eaten well, and had barely had more than a chest cold before assuming the task of rearing Sirena Lavesque. She was met at the gateway leading backstage by Billy, the bandleader and, at 60, the only one in the entourage even close to her in age. He got in a few whispered words to Marvella before anyone else could hear their conversation.

"That girl is a mess, Miss Marvella. I swear she's going to be the death of me before we gets halfway through this tour."

Out of respect, he always addressed her as "Miss Marvella," an acknowledgement of their common background in black Baptist churches and both having been raised in stern, Christian families in Washington, D.C.

"She don't leave that mess alone," Marvella said in response, easing down the shadowy corridor which ended at stairs leading to the stage, "it's gonna be the death of her!"

Siren met her at the top of the stairs, appearing as if nothing had gone amiss between them.

"Mami! I'm so glad you're here! You don't know: It's been so hard to get these people motivated, with my new materials and all." They were side by side now, Siren looping an arm in one of Marvella's and escorting her to mid stage. "Billy knows the music, the girls know the music, but stuff just don't sound right, Mami! I don't want to go out here tonight and be embarrassed! The press reporting all nasty about me like they've been doing lately. Marvella, help me please! Help me get these people on key! Help me, Mami! Please?"

The band members, and Billy and Marvella, all looked at Siren as if for some directions. What did she want from them? They were, to a man, to a woman, at her beck and call. But she issued no instructions, only complained when she'd start a song, the band in its common precision, and she faltered, halted and nearly broke down in tears.

The cocaine was even now beckoning her, setting in crystalline abundance in the case that posed as a jewelry box. Her mind even pictured it, readily available for worn nostrils, but mind knowing too that a few snorts would only spark her to summon Toni, or Alvarez, to cook up a good measure of the substance for her so that she might experience the cocaine in an exhilarating, mind-bedazzling specter. Again and again. Until she'd blown off the bulk of her commitments, made a mess of the present performances, and devolved into a two-day period of additional consumption.

"I don't know what you want me to do, child," Marvella said exhaustively. "From what Billy here tells me, everything is on target and everybody on note. It's you girl, you child, who needs to get her act in order. And if you don't remember, you fired your 'Mami' again just days ago. I told you to not take on this tour till you got yourself some help. You know you need some help child, don't you?"

"I don't need shit!" She was fired up now, reminded of her sickness, her illness, her addiction, a mention of which had gotten Marvella and three other close associates fired before. "You don't know what the fuck I need anyway! And anyway, who told your ass you could

come back up in this camp? Don't nobody need your ass!
Get the hell out of my face!"

      Tears welled in Marvella's eyes as she watched Siren
storm off the stage, surely off to where the deadly drug
awaited her. The woman started kneading her fingers, her
knuckles, an unconscious habit she had which reflected the
stress injected into her heart, into her body and soul, as she
watched the child she'd raised go about destroying herself.

      "Well," Billy said to the band, stagehands, backup
singers and dancers. "I guess that's a wrap for now."

Chapter Two

"How much do you want me to do up for you, Baby girl?"

Alvarez was grinning, the gold front tooth glistening in the light of the flame of the torch he held under the test tube, the mixture of cocaine, water and baking soda being brought to a slight, gurgling boil. He took the broken off piece of a coat hanger and twisted it between thumb and forefinger, stuck one end in the test tube, the flame set aside for now. A globule of raw coke formed on the end of the coat hanger, and he carefully moved it to the napkin on the vanity in her dressing room.

"Cook up all of that shit," she said, pausing only long enough to answer and then again putting flame to raw coke in the end of the glass pipe she was using. "All of that shit..."

She had blown off the writer from Black Diamond magazine, and her publicist was none too pleased. The first show was in an hour, and no one had had access to Siren but Alvarez since she'd stormed out of rehearsal. The arena was already filling with fans, and members of the press afforded backstage passes were clamoring for access to her. But Siren had begun with an initial blast of the powder, which only sated her during the three minutes it had taken for Alvarez to be located and rushed to her dressing room.

Now she was on it like a fly on fresh dog droppings, sucking in the heated fumes and directing pure cocaine to a brain addled and entertained at the frontal lobes and temples with that tingling sensation that made her feel as if tiny ballerinas clad in little silky slippers were dancing on the rears of her eyeballs.

The rushes were immediate and impacting with each intake, and the dancers were growing in number and would not let her be.   The gypsies in little tutus were accompanying the ballerinas, skirting about her brain in patterns that would confound air traffic controllers, and the landing lights for her internal armada were seriously askew. They were directing the invading forces in all sorts of directions, and they crashed throughout her brain in cataclysmic wonderment even as she fed them additional fuel from the service ramp.

"Baby girl! You must slow your roll now," Alvarez said in his heavily-accented voice. "You got the show! That's your bread and butter, baby girl!"

A greasy, no-account leech. That was how most in the retinue described Alvarez Santonio Gomes. But there was no detaching him from Siren once he'd invaded her bloodstream.

Few could recall exactly how he had gained entrance into the tight little arena that was Siren Lavesque Inc. Yet he'd slithered in like a water moccasin during rainy season, and Siren would have had anyone's head who even dared suggest that the "lighting technician" be fired.

"I'm going to…be…alright," she stuttered. "It's all….cooked….up?"

"All I brought out of the stash, baby girl. That oughta be enough to hold you, you save some of this till after the show." He arose and headed to the door. "Be safe, baby girl. Knock 'em out!"

Her heart, however, was not into the two-hour performance scheduled to kick off in less than half an hour. She could hear the opening act rocking the crowd when Alvarez opened the dressing room door and quickly exited. She saw through slit eyes Billy and Marvella attempting to enter the dressing room, even as Alvarez tried to block them from even gaining sight of the increasingly bedazzled superstar.

"She's just getting ready, main man, Mami!" he said, standing just outside the still-ajar door.   "She asked me to ask you all to give her a few minutes alone."

"Man, you better get the hell out of my way, you low-down no-account motherfucker!" Billy said, his short stature having him tilting his head back near torturously to look directly up into the Mexican immigrant's eyes. "Get the fuck outta the way!"

"Aye,   Popi!   You   don't   have   to   be so….so….disrespectful, man!"

"You heard him, Alvarez," Marvella said, stepping up beside Billy.   "You get your ass on out there and do…what ever it is you do!"

They were the only ones among the entourage who ever challenged Alvarez; a long-time dancer in Siren's troupe, Contee Jamison, had two years ago threatened to sic law enforcement on Alvarez, and although he was thought to be among Siren's most beloved presences on the stage with her, Contee had been summarily dismissed from the entourage.   Three cities later on that particular tour, word was whispered around backstage that Contee had been slain shortly after his dismissal during what law enforcement officials said was an apparent robbery.

Flashing his gold tooth, Alvarez sneered at Marvella and Billy, but stepped out of the way just as Siren struggled to the door in an attempt to lock it.

"Girl, you're a goddamn mess!" Marvella blasted, pushed her way into the dressing room while Billy secured the door behind them and assisted in guiding Siren over to a sofa.   "How in the hell you expect to put on a performance, you in here smoking that goddamn shit?!"

"I'm gonna make it….alright," Siren sang, smiling, eyes half closed. She continued singing the bridge to one of her most popular songs.   "I'm…..gonna make it …..all…..all…right…."

"See if somebody got some coffee going in one of the supporting staff's dressing rooms," Marvella asked Billy. "Bring a whole damn pot if you have to."

She hadn't had a hit in over five minutes, and the little ballerinas in her head were fighting with the little gypsies and tearing off their tutus while the air traffic controllers were shouting warnings that the planes were out of gas and about to crash unto a darkened tarmac. The floodlights were shining torturously on the backs of her retinas while her microscopic vision keyed in on the chunks of cocaine rock on the vanity, sparkling just before the mirror and the glass stem and lighter. Respect, and any thought of formality, gave way to the need for another hit.

"Marvella! Leave me alone for another few minutes, OK?"

Although the cocaine had such a vicious hold on her and she could hardly put down the pipe at this particular moment, she'd never, ever done the drug before "Mami," and her heart was racing at a pace she wished would be mirrored by Marvella's exit.

She struggled to her feet, took Marvella in a grip that was solid, firm, almost vicious.

"You gotta go, Mami! You gotta go now!"

"Sit down! Sit back down, child!" Marvella said, taking over. She outweighed Siren by a good 100 pounds, and although she had never confronted Siren physically, she was certainly well capable of subduing her. And now was surely a time to do so, as Siren looked to the quite visible drugs and paraphernalia and then went limp in Marvella's arms and began sobbing uncontrollably.

"Sit down, child," Marvella whispered, again the comforting guardian. "Sit down, child. We're going to get you some coffee and see if the doctor's around. You just stay away from that shit for now."

Chapter Three

The opening act played an additional 40 minutes, and $2700 worth of cocaine was now costing Siren an additional $5000. Venus and Mars was quite an expensive accompanying act on this tour, and the very popular band had written into its contract the exact amount of time they'd be required to perform and, quite aware of Siren's erratic behavior, specific clauses as to how much they would be paid for additional stage time and an exorbitant fee tacked on should any part of this tour be cancelled. The band continued to play over scheduled time, as Siren was made to sip coffee and given a shot by the physician, who had been on call in anticipation of just such a measure of overconsumption by the star.

"How are you feeling," Dr. Samuelson asked, his thumb to one of her wrists as he timed her pulse.

"Kinda jittery, doc," she said, the common embarrassment felt when caught overindulging making her response weak, her voice meek. "Think I can go on for an hour and a half?"

"You can. But Ms. Lavesque, you really need to consider my earlier suggestion that you put this career on hold for a while and seek treatment."

"I don't need no goddamn treatment!" she blasted, her nasty, evil high persona reemerging with the quickness. "We don't pay you all this fucking money to be judging my career moves! I gots my goddamn treatment! And you better bet it I'm gonna ....treat....myself after I finish with this damn show!"

She pulled away from the doctor, moved to a vanity emblazoned with lights and dabbled at her makeup.

"Marvella? Get Shonda in here to fix my face, will you?"

Besides the doctor, Marvella was the only other one in her dressing room at the moment. Dr. Samuelson took

Marvella to the side, whispered to her even as Siren cast cold eyes at him warning him not to do so. But he insisted that Marvella convince Siren to seek treatment, before, as he put it, it was too late.

"Fuck you too, doctor," Siren said, but almost in a whisper, and then began attempting to fix her face.

The cocaine was still calling out to her, but in a calmer, almost subdural voice. What the doctor had given her, she did not know. But it served to keep her mentally alert and in realization of the fact that she had at least 45,000 fans anxiously awaiting her in the arena. She could even hear their chants for her, and their derogatory catcalls aimed at the present band playing, although the stage and main arena area were at least 1000 yards away.

The doctor left, followed by Marvella. Her guardian returned immediately, with the sinewy, petite woman who made $20,000 monthly working exclusively as Siren's makeup artist.

"Girl, get me hooked," Siren demanded, put down the implements she was haphazardly using to apply her own makeup and leaned back in the leather lounge, allowing Shonda to go to work.

In minutes, she was ready, and the fine dress, the upright stance, the finely done hair and lightly applied facial mask had the leggy woman ready for the stage. She was in character, the cocaine addict all but disappeared, the multi-platinum artist in full form.

She strode out of the dressing room in a scented air, greetings and shouts from those with backstage passes ignored, the instructions being hurriedly disseminated by a posse of handlers going in one ear, pausing to gain momentary consideration, then out the other. She was still high, but no longer "geeking," no longer in that state where further consumption seemed all but mandatory.

"Let's do this shit!" she shouted, nearing the stairs to the stage.

Supportive shouts surrounded her, grew into a bellowing crescendo as the professional at the top of the stairs motioned to the announcer, alerting the audience, the band, which began a common, low-keyed refrain familiar to any who was familiar with Siren, superstar, voice of an angel, and on occasion, the voice of a devilish siren, casting spells, casting the occasional aspersion, but always capturing her fans with the words, the wails, the sweet melodic deliverances that defined Siren Lavesque.

She only heard the final blasting announcement, the rise of the band, the shouts of the crowd and all around her closely issuing instructions and some warnings, many voices abuzz but most undecipherable. It was her time, and as the band blasted into the opening bars of her million-seller of four years earlier, she strode onto the stage, mike in hand, and did what it was that she did best.

Forty minutes, and Siren had the crowd pressing towards the stage, dancing in the aisles, in a fevered frenzy matched only by the one she was in prancing about the stage, dancing to her old tunes, belting out her latest, seemingly in a trance, a voice surprisingly prime, clear, reaching its highs with ease, its lows with a soothing tremor which brought tears to some eyes. She was in her natural form, unexpected by either the doctor or Marvella, who watched the performance from just off stage to the rear.

"She's marvelous!" Dr. Samuelson said. "Just marvelous!"

One hour, fifteen minutes, and Siren was exchanging a little banter with members of the band, with her backup singers, with those in the forefront of the audience. It was clear that the end was near, and as the first few bars of her most recent bestseller played, she moved to the front of the stage and grew serious, speaking directly to the audience.

"I know you all have been hearing a lot of mess about me, reading all that stuff about me in the tabloids,"

she said. "And I ain't gonna lie to you: A lot of that stuff?
Yeah, a lot of it is true. But I'm working on it, good people!
I'm working on it!   Like anybody else, I'm fighting my
demons. As quiet as it's kept, I haven't always had it so
easy. But I'm not going to let you down! I'm gonna stay
the course, baby! I'm gonna----"

    And the band took the cue. She segued into the
opening notes of "I'm Going To Be All Right," her latest
release and one which she penned herself with the thought
that the very words would inspire her to quit personal
destruction she long sensed could only end in disaster.

Chapter Four

She ended the show on a high note, and the relief was nearly palpable back stage; among the band, among her handlers, and particularly among the concert's promoters. Marvella was being enveloped in especially appreciative arms by Georgia Whitfield-Johnson, the artists and repertoire executive from Jupiter Solice Records who'd been credited with Siren's success and, to a point, held personally responsible for any of the star's failings. A Harvard Law School graduate who'd found more financial success in the A&R realm of the recording industry, Georgia was relieved that this leg of the tour had been completed without Siren devolving into one of her financially disastrous mishaps.

She had missed three performances over the past month, unable to wrench herself from the demands of her cocaine habit, and another such non-performance would surely have meant that Georgia's own contract with Jupiter would have been immediately extinguished.

"Great show!" Georgia said into Siren's ear, having summoned on-board security to dispatch any but Siren's closest associates away as they moved to the star's dressing room. "Damn good show, Siren! You showed your natural ass out there!"

"I was feeling it!" Siren said, draping an arm around Marvella, kissing her lightly on the cheek. "And, Mami, I don't know what you said to Billy, but the band was tight!"

Marvella was never one to bite her tongue, and the truths that she dispensed to her surrogate daughter were perhaps the only reasons Siren was still in the business.

"Ain't have to tell Billy nothing," Marvella said as she, Siren and Georgia entered the privacy of the dressing room. "Band is always tight. It's you that's always messing things up drinking that liquor and smoking that dope."

The very mention of smoking cocaine seemed to have a stimulating effect on Siren, and immediately she looked to the drawer where Alvarez had secreted a plentiful stash of cooked-up cocaine.

"Look Mami, Georgia. I need a few minutes of private time, to wind down, know what I'm saying?"

"Child," Marvella began, exasperation in her voice and an immediate alert to Siren that some form of chastisement was forthcoming. "You know you got about seven people from them magazines and newspapers and radio stations that's been allowed backstage to talk to you after the show. And the backup girls certainly want to talk to you before leaving for the night. And the band. Child, you can't be—"

"I can be!" Siren blasted. "Now Mami, Georgia. Give me about fifteen minutes to myself."

She moved to the secured door, stood by it and cast cold eyes at the two. Georgia moved slowly, Marvella took two steps behind Georgia, then paused and spoke just inches away from Siren's frowning face.

"You gonna have to get help, child. Go ahead and blow your mind some more on that mess. But after tonight, you don't get help, I'm finished with you!"

Georgia opened the door to a rush of hot air and a throng of shouting, pleading faces, voices, bodies clamoring to get to the star. When Marvella was out, she ensured that Siren had secured the door, twisted the knob to make sure it was locked, then began issuing her practiced plea to the media professionals and industry people in an attempt to again cover for the star who was even now, she was certain, putting flame to a dose of raw cocaine.

* * *

"Damn!"

There was a renewed circus being formed within her brain, and the little gypsies were back in full force accompanied by the ballerinas in pink tutus and a flagrant clown with an evil grin dancing on frontal brain lobes and telling her that the time was at hand.

"Damn!"

She took another toke, and her fluttering eyelids were now Monarch butterflies, their wings leaden, unable to take off yet insisting on tarrying on the taxiway.

Her breathing was now labored, and the heart was playing catch-up to a metabolism lost in the sauce, internal body parts functioning individually as they were designed to but seriously out of synchronicity, all awash in blood tainted with Alvarez's purest of concoctions, with some body parts confused in the way of functionality. The bladder wanted to release fluids but the brain was in conflict, directing the hands to place a powerful, yellow rock on the glass pipe before the Monarch butterflies which could barely move out of the way so that crystalline eyes could view and direct the activities.

"Oh, damn!"

She could see the flame of the lighter, its glow appearing too close to her face, but at least close enough so that she could slowly direct it atop the mound of cocaine rock. Her lungs said "NO!" but her mind said "BRING THAT SHIT ON!" and she inhaled greatly, filling the rejecting lungs with yet another powerful dose. So lungs did what they were supposed to do with only air, directing the caustic mixture into the blood stream while blood stream did its job of circulating the mixture throughout the body and particularly to the brain.

"Oh, shit!"

Those little ballerinas were having a field day, changing into blue tutus and scattering pixie dust all over the internal landscape that was Siren Lavesque but then was not, a playground for a dopefiend filled with scattered shards of glass and empty beer cans and that circus clown with the awry grin fanning at the Monarch butterflies before leaden eyes.

"Fuck!"

She placed yet another rock onto the smoking utensil, applied a flame and oversaturated body, brain, mind and soul.

The Monarchs ceased trying to fly, fluttered lifelessly to the tarmac and awaited death.

Chapter Five

"Siren?"

It had been half an hour since Marvella and Georgia had been asked to leave the dressing room, and the door remained locked from the inside.

"Siren!?" Marvella shouted now, trying the door, to no avail.

Those around her began to pay attention, silencing themselves in their individual conversations and, especially those in the media, turning to cast concerned eyes on the dressing room door.

Marvella and Georgia began to panic, both slamming palms on the door while shouting out for Siren. Billy, the bandleader, observed the commotion from a distance, as he stood in the hallway leading into the arena and to the stage. He summoned a man around his age, in a blue jumpsuit with the arena's logo ablaze in striking orange on the back, and the two rushed through the crowd gathered outside the dressing room.

"Make way! Make way!" Billy shouted, as the man accompanying him extended a chain of keys from a retracting device affixed to his beltline. "Make way!"

They arrived at the door as Marvella was weakening into a near panic mode, her anticipation of some tragedy on the other side of the door so acute that she leaned against a wall on weak knees and couldn't help but allow abundant tears to flow.

"Oh my Lord girl!" Marvella cried. "Oh, baby! Don't you do this to me!"

The janitor found the key to the door after trying three unsuccessfully, pushed the door open alongside Billy and Georgia and paused only for a split second to view the immobile form of Siren stretched out on the floor before the vanity. Billy rushed over to her, followed closely by the janitor and Georgia. Marvella, pulling herself off the wall outside the door as if she'd been affixed there, twisted into the doorway and stumbled into the room.

"Somebody see of Dr. Samuelson is still out there somewhere!" Billy shouted, kneeling now beside Siren's body and again leaning into her face, ear to her nose, checking to see if the singer was still breathing. "Anybody! Any-damn-body! Somebody call an ambulance!"

Marvella regained her composure, rushed over and knelt beside Billy and Georgia, who continued to fuss over the body in ways indicating that neither had any idea of procedures required in treating a trauma case. Georgia just shook Siren, hands on her chest in a manner that only rocked the immobile body on the floor. Billy seemed to be trying to blow air into her mouth, but from a distance that only served to direct a breeze across her closed lips, across the closed eyes. Marvella, becoming more stoic, grabbed Georgia by a shoulder and pulled her away from the body, felt Siren's neck for a pulse, then pushed Billy's ineffective head away from Siren's face.

She opened Siren's mouth, pulling her chin down and, gripping her nostrils, leaned her head back in a common act in preparation to deliver CPR. A thumb went into Siren's mouth to secure the tongue, then Marvella leaned into her and blew in such an abundance of air that Siren's chest visibly expanded. It seemed as if Siren was arcing off the floor of her own volition, as Marvella leaned back, took in a deep breath, then bent to blow yet another volume into the still unmoving figure.

"Come on baby girl!" she whispered, leaning upright then applying pressure to Siren's chest. "Don't you leave me like this."

Again she blew into Siren's mouth, took another deep breath, and repeated the CPR maneuver.

"Baby girl! Baby girl! Come on, baby girl! Come on!"

All the while a phalanx of media, security and entourage personnel were clustered outside the door, some with a clear view of what was happening, others being given a summation by those closer to the front. No one paid attention to the lighter lying in Siren's limp left hand, nor the glass crack pipe lying inches from her right. The mound of partitioned cocaine rocks on the vanity were scarcely a subject of attention to those who were watching the superstar stretched lifelessly on the floor, her matronly guardian struggling to bring the singer back to consciousness, the band manager Billy reduced to tears himself now, the A&R woman wringing her hands.

But all of the implements, the lighter, the pipe, the drugs, were within the frames of the lenses of the camera phones being held aloft just outside the door. And were certainly within the frames of the professional 35mm camera flashing chaotically atop the busting crowd.

"That's it, baby girl!" Marvella shouted, cradling Siren's head as the singer, seemingly as if coming out of a coma, began rocking her head back and forth on her own, and taking deep, labored breaths. "That's it, Siren! Come on, baby girl! Come on!"

With Marvella's assistance, Siren sat upright, opened her eyes slightly and began shaking her head slowly.

"Damn!" she said softly. "Damn that's some...that's some good shit!"

Chapter Six

The pictures were displayed in large, prominent form under blaring headlines not only on the front pages of the supermarket tabloids, but backed up news stories on network television and were widely used by a number of major daily newspapers. The words "overdose" and "brink of death" were used repeatedly, and even after Siren had refused medical treatment that night it was clear that the songstress had nearly died after a post-concert indulgence in cocaine. The number of photos clearly showed the crack pipe and mounds of cocaine in the dressing room. And if anyone wasn't astute enough to see them in long-shot photos, picture editors had enlarged the items to near fish-eyed magnification in many print editions, and additionally encircled them with a bold, black outline.

The record company went into crisis mode, gathering Georgia and Marvella into their New York City suites to map out a strategy to perhaps salvage what was left of a musical career, which had put millions of dollars into the coffers of at least five principles of Jupiter Solice Records. Siren was in seclusion, reportedly under the care of Dr. Samuelson, at her expansive estate in McLean, Virginia. She had purchased this property, just outside of her native Washington, D.C., with her initial earnings, and it was where Marvella and the Jupiter executives felt that she was most secure away from the leeches and drug merchants she'd been attracting over the past few years.

"I tell you, the child don't need to be thinking about no more tours right now," Marvella was adamant, telling the president and vice president of Jupiter her view on matters at hand. "All y'all want to do is keep on wringing money out of the girl until she ain't got no more to give!

Well, to hell with all of y'all! I ain't gonna see that child dead behind your greed!"

Jeremiah Ward Aikens, vice president of Jupiter, was now wishing he had allowed his less than upright partner Marcus get rid of Marvella when he'd suggested doing so a few years back. Siren was destined not only to be one of the nation's most prominent female artist then, but was certainly going to be the prime meal ticket for a then-fledgling record company being formed by Jeremiah Ward Aikens and Marcus Elliot.

"Now, come on, Mrs. Stanton," Jeremiah said, addressing Marvella formally in an effort to emphasize his seriousness. "Siren is going to be alright. We've agreed to a period of rest for her, and she should be out of the public spotlight for, oh, at least a month."

"You've agreed?!" Marvella said, pushing back from the extensive conference table and standing threateningly over the short, balding executive. "How in the hell you think a recording contract gonna allow you to manage the girl's time? You've agreed my ass! I agree that you keep your claws off that child till she...till we decide she's healthy enough to go back out there! Far as I'm concerned, with her nearly dying like that? Don't matter to me if she don't never sing another note! And you can talk all you want to about her 'contractual obligations'! I ain't studying your 'contractual obligations'!"

She had never liked either of them, but held an exceptional contempt for Marcus Elliot. Raised by a grandmother who worked as a domestic in the homes of wealthy white Marylanders and Virginians, Marvella had been taught from a child to distinguish between "good people" and those deemed scoundrels. Marvella considered Jeremiah Ward Aikens a good person, or at least a man with good intentions. But Marcus Elliot, whose sneering grin reminded one of a cartoon villain, could not be trusted as far as she could throw him, Marvella had long ago decided.

Marcus had allowed Jeremiah to do most of the talking this afternoon, in the ornate conference room along with Georgia, Marvella, and his equity partner, Jeremiah. He knew well that Marvella didn't hold him in high regards, to say the least. And he knew innately that the middle-aged black woman could somehow read his every intent like a dime store novel. So he kept his own counsel whenever she was around; his goal, after all, was the exploiting of Siren and all of Jupiter Solice Record's other artists, to the fullest. Be damned the consequences of their own weaknesses and lack of knowledge when it came to the vagaries, the ends and outs, the true cutthroat nature of the music industry.

Yet right now Marcus could not bite his tongue.

He was growing tired of the "old black bitch," in his personal caustic descriptive of Marvella, seeming to be running roughshod over plans for Siren he and Jeremiah had been working on for over five years. Of course he knew of Siren's cocaine addiction. Certainly, it was Marcus who had injected Alvarez Santonio Gomes into the entourage, not to get the company's stellar performer on cocaine but, after it was certain she was getting into it of her own volition, to make sure Siren didn't have to scrounge around outside of the "family" to score.

Marcus stood from his seat at the head of the long conference table, moved around to where Marvella stood above Jeremiah's seat at the opposite end.

"Mrs. Stanton. Marvella. Now, this is a meeting of the principles of Jupiter Solice Records. We're allowing you to sit in on this meeting out of your concern and your past history with Siren. But officially, you have no say in our business matters."

"This ain't no goddamn business matter, talking about Sirena's life," Marvella said, and her usage of Siren's birth name emphasized the seriousness of her concerns. "Now don't you be coming up here to me with none of your shit, Marcus. I used to diaper little punks like you when you were no more than a twinkle in your daddy's eye."

"Still," Marcus said. "It's a matter of Jupiter Solice Records! And as Siren is our premiere act, a matter of major concern to the principles."

"The principles can kiss my black ass!" Marvella said, and stormed out of the room.

Chapter Seven

On three acres of pristine land in McLean, Virginia, Sirena Renee Lavesque, the name on the property records, had had built one of the finest homes in the region. The location had been especially selected by Siren and Marvella after legal wrangling ensured that the songstress would be getting a good portion of the proceeds she generated for Jupiter Solice Records. Of course her meteoric rise had spurned Marcus to attempt to have her initial contract rewritten, a contract which, with Marvella's astute overseeing and after Marvella had also secured a most prestigious entertainment lawyer, would guarantee that Siren, unlike many artists with Jupiter Solice, received the lion's share of the net proceeds from record sales and concert gate receipts.

The home was impressive even by exclusive McLean standards. Set a quarter mile back from the main road and accessible only through a gated entrance, the two-story mansion was 10,500 square feet of luxury. A guesthouse the size of many expensive inner city homes sat 3,000 feet to the rear and left of the main home, and behind that a lining of mature spruce trees which marked the end of her property. On the main grounds, a six-car garage occupied a small parking area to the right of the mansion, and to the rear, beyond a patio of Italian marble, was a swimming pool which would be suitable for Olympic competition.

At 25, Siren was wealthy beyond all imaginings. The mere mention of a new recording by her would have fans worldwide anxiously awaiting the chance to purchase electronic versions of a single! Her albums sold in the millions globally within days of their release, and Marvella, attorney Franklin Cardova, and a phalanx of other attorneys and accountants ensured that Siren's earnings, and subsequent investments, continued to add massive sums to her diverse accounts.

Until recently she'd had a man in her life. But her devolution into rampant cocaine use had scared away even this well-off fellow entertainer. So now, for the most part alone, she occupied the massive home but for the help and her security detail. And Marvella, who maintained her own historic family home in Washington but kept a room at the mansion to be available when Siren, still considered as almost a daughter to her, needed her maternal oversight.

What Siren needed now though was more than even Marvella could provide.

Dr. Samuelson had been staying off and on in the guesthouse, and remained vigilant in seeing Siren through a most harrowing period of withdrawal. But as any alcoholic or addict knows, it is first up to the individual to want to recover from their addiction. The near-death experience in the dressing room had certainly frightened the singer, but after being rushed through the cascading mass of publicity, shielded from the creative snooping of paparazzi and taking a circuitous route to her well-protected Virginia estate, Siren spent but three days sober before telling all around her that she was fine and ready to resume her hectic schedule.

"I got this!" was her common statement when advised to take a break from the business. "I got this!"

At her record company headquarters, Jeremiah and Marcus were in conflict. Concerned about Siren's health, Jeremiah insisted that no further tour dates be scheduled and those already booked cancelled. Concerned about the millions he was missing out on even by the day, Marcus insisted that their cash cow be given no more than a week off before resuming her remaining concert dates and assuming the missed ones which he was already rescheduling.

"She's a strong, young black girl!" Marcus insisted in private conference with Jeremiah. "They're a resilient people! Hell, white girl had smoked as much coke as Siren has over the past year would have been dead long time ago."

"Are you keeping Alvarez away from her as she recovers?" Jeremiah asked, still afraid to show too much of the personal feelings he had for Siren yet determined that she get the help, the rest, that she so needed.

"He's away," Marcus said bluntly. "Has more…well, greater financial concerns to deal with at the moment."

Certainly the cocaine dealer kept on a substantial retainer had more pressing matters at present. Marcus had allowed him free reign when it came to supplying the number of musicians, stage hands and, surely, Siren with voluminous coke. It was done as a measure of ensuring that the tight-knit musical operation suffered little down time either through the need of a user to seek out drugs on their own, or God forbid, one of the label's prime artist or musicians or one easily connected to Jupiter Solice Records, be nailed in a public drug bust.

With the tour shut down unexpectedly, Alvarez had been forced to try returning to his old ways of drug distribution around the streets of Washington, D.C. and Baltimore. He'd been away from this distribution string for a few years now, his attachment to Jupiter allowing him to score and distribute with scant chances of being corralled by the law. His return to what he deemed low-level dealings had been met with stiff opposition, however; he was not selling a sparkling granule, and had attained the 14 grams he was stuck with on credit from a contact who was never, ever told that the check was in the mail.

While Marcus and Jeremiah were in conflict about Alvarez, Siren and drug use in general among the company's artist and employees, Siren was at home "geeking," experiencing the withdrawal effects of not having had any cocaine in close to a week.   With an unending access to plenty of cash, she was being needled by a wave of Gypsy moths and Monarch butterflies accompanied by a circus of dancing pixies in colorful raiment pulling her back towards the precipice of disaster. She'd called Alvarez's cellular number twenty-three times within the past two hours, only gaining his voice mail and pleading with him to make a delivery to her as quickly as possible. She didn't drive, although she'd purchased two Bentleys and a sporty red Corvette in anticipation of the day when she did. Still, there were motormen at her beck and call.

Usually.

It seemed somehow, after her near-death experience, that they too were unavailable by phone. Freddy Glover, her personal driver and prime bodyguard who stayed in the guesthouse when she was not on tour, had suddenly fallen ill and, according to Marvella, was hospitalized in a Washington facility. For all she knew she was alone in the massive home except for the servants Aileen and Maria, and she seemed alone too in cyberspace, the few trusted friends she communicated with on the social networks seemingly aware of her desperate need for solitude and recovery. They were apparently avoiding her as much as the army of Gypsy moths and Monarchs were conversely fluttering about ever present.

"Aileen!" she stepped out of her enormous bedroom into a hallway stretching 50 feet in either direction. "Maria!"

Right before her was an ornate gold railing, aligning the side of the hallway with a sweeping view of the arching staircases at either end leading to the main floor and a foyer shining with expensive Italian marble floors. The replica statues of Venus de Milo and one of the war god Zeus seemed forlorn standing in the massive vacancy, and a few of the Monarch butterflies seemed to be encircling the statues in torturous gestures, attempting to get Siren to hurl herself from the balcony. She was in just that much trauma, geeking like a crackhead with the misfortune of having just been jailed after scoring a most hefty hit.

"Maria?!!! Aileen?!!!!"

But there was no answer, and tears welled as Siren rushed to the left end of the hallway and stumbled down the stairs and towards the kitchen.

To her utmost surprise and disgruntled consternation, Dr. Samuelson, Marvella, her chauffer/bodyguard Freddy and both Maria and Aileen were seated around the elaborate mid-kitchen dinette counter, seemingly in conference, sipping coffee, other drinks, eating pastries and appearing to be having just a good old time.

"What the hell is this shit?!!" Siren blurted out, her addiction not even allowing for the sweet, cordial, acclaimed songstress to surface and give a modicum of consideration to niceties. "I'm up there sick as a dog, and you motherfuckers sitting around here like...like it ain't a goddamn thing going on but the rent! Marvella? I thought I made it clear I didn't want you always around me in the business after the last show and you ain't supposed to be up in my piece like this? I got you a damn home of your own to go to! And doctor...doctor...doctor what-ever-the-fuck your name is: You're supposed to be taking care of my...my...my illness! Get your goddamn medicine bag and hook a sister up! I'm illin' like a motherfucker! I'm...illin' like..."

But she couldn't finish, as the butterflies and moths cleared and she was afforded a good image of the words she'd just shouted and the disgraceful way in which she'd just carried herself. So she turned and wrapped herself in her own arms, hurried away from the embarrassment that was as much needling at her innards as were the circus clowns and ballerinas and the putrid gas that was forming in her gut.

"I don't want to be like this any more!" she sobbed, moving back up the spiral staircase on weak knees. "Please, God! I don't want to be like this any more!"

Chapter Eight

They were listening to the voice mail messages on Alvarez Santonio Gomes's smartphone, and were getting a kick out of the pleadings of the black girl they knew to be a superstar in America: Siren Lavesque. Alvarez couldn't come to the phone, a few among them joked, looking at the splattered remains stretched out on the garden's Kentucky bluegrass Salvadore was so proud of. While at the same time the boss, enjoying a moment of levity himself, was almost simultaneously devising a way to get another dealer of his product into the very bowels of Jupiter Solice Records.

"Alvarez was a good man, may he rest in peace," the boss with the enormous paunch said, looking down on the body from his throne-like perch. "The stupid fuck just overextended himself, and then you know, with the famous like the black girl: federales in America go ape-shit they find the source of her llello, and Alvarez" he paused, made the sign of the cross, "he not one of powerful cojones, rest his soul."

Salvadore took a sip of Xtabentun, the Mayan liquor he favored, threw his head back and took a puff on the cigar which was ever present when he conducted business. He looked to the stiff manservants standing about Alvarez's corpse, then nodded with a smirk which overemphasized his fat, bulbous cheeks.

"Get this dead fuck out of my presence," he said, struggled to his feet and returned to his spacious hacienda.

Salvadore Paz was not the only narcotics kingpin who sought to get his evil claws into the arena of America's social elite, but he was among the most ruthless and persistent. His income from the streets of the nation's cities was more than enough to supply him with wealth even a carelessly flagrant extravagant couldn't spend in two lifetimes. Yet he got a thrill which surpassed a sexual climax for him from knowing that personalities he viewed on the silver screen, personages he read about in the American newspapers he so loved, people whom he viewed everyday on television and in concert footage, were dependent on narcotics he was personally responsible for supplying.

Certainly there were other, and larger, drug dealers pumping cocaine and heroin into the American mainstream. But Salvadore specialized in weaving conduits to the stars, to the elite, and even with greater profits available on a larger scale in a more broader scheme, he just loved enslaving the rich and famous.

He moved into his elaborate den, the walls flush with signed photographs of Hollywood's elite, moved behind the massive, carved oak desk and again played the voice messages left on Alvarez's phone.

"I'll see someone gets to you shortly, sweetheart," he said in answer to Siren's pleading voice. "I'll see someone gets to you very, very shortly."

Salvadore not only reveled in the knowledge that he was personally responsible for the addiction of Siren and others, but he truly believed that his association with the artists somehow ensured that he could have personal access to them at some point in time. He was particularly enamored of young black women, especially those of the type he drooled over when looking at pictures and concert footage of Siren Lavesque: Tall, long dark legs, sharp African features, expansive, flowing locks, a smile which displayed teeth blindingly white.

Somewhere in his own personal history, a Portuguese settler onto land which would eventually become known as Brazil had taken up with a slave woman from Ghana, West Africa, and over hundreds of years his ancestors had come to populate regions from Honduras to Mexico.

"Yes," he said, stroking himself in the privacy of his office while remotely activating a video of Siren's last concert, a recording of which even officials at Jupiter Solice Records didn't have. "I'll be making sure you get your supply, young lady. And there's something else, something very, very special, I want to deliver unto you too. Personally."

Chapter Nine

Dr. Samuelson had just about had it with Siren. Not only was she keeping him away from his own beloved family, but was being a damn headache when it came to following the strict regimen he'd laid out for her to help with her recovery. The only reason he'd even considered taking on her attempt to beat the addiction was that she had finally convinced him that she was determined to quit. No one beat addiction strictly through external determinants, the doctor knew well. As in alcoholism and any other addiction, the addict must first determine, in the clichéd phrase, that they are sick and tired of being sick and tired.

She seemed determined to return to the stage, or at least to the city, summoning her driver/bodyguard without even consulting the doctor or Marvella. But Freddy had usurped the demands of secrecy from his young charge, informing both the doctor and Marvella of Siren's plans to have him secret her off the estate to some unidentified nightspot in Washington. It appeared now, after three weeks, that Siren's determination to quit cocaine was being overruled by the pull of the drug itself.

There must have certainly been a spark, something immediately reminiscent of her extensive highs and a present reminder that the same method of mind alteration was readily available. The doctor had no way of knowing it, but Siren had been getting a series of text messages from "Alvarez," or at least someone with access to his smartphone. And each time Siren anxiously answered, with both text and voice attempts, she'd been rebuffed with silence, and the caveat that she could get resupplied with her preferred "blocks" from the dealer, but only if she were to meet him at a club in a not-too-safe section of Northeast Washington.

"Please! Answer your damn phone!" she pleaded for the eighth time, setting on the edge of her massive bed, legs shaking, heels dancing a rhythmic patter on the carpet, her anticipation of the drug quite acute with each text message from "Alvarez." "Come on, man!"

Three weeks. Twenty-one days. If she believed Dr. Samuelson, in seven more days she'd be at a point where her physical addiction will have been brought under control. The mental addiction? That would be a lifelong process of recovery. She'd never be safe from addiction, and would always be a recovering addict. But she didn't have to use. Ever again.

Twenty-eight days.

"Where in the fuck are you, man?!" she cried, disconnecting for the twelfth time. "Got me all geeking and shit! Motherfucker!"

Someone was knocking on her bedroom door. She could barely hear it, eyes closed and the fluttering Monarchs swooping in psychedelic patterns before an airstrip awash in red lights and Gypsy moths flinging stinging arrows at her brain. And she didn't have to answer it but—

"What the fuck!" she said, arising and marching towards to door while leaving the circus atmosphere at the bedside.

The doctor, the driver and Marvella were standing stoic, having all conferenced minutes earlier regarding Siren's petition to the driver/bodyguard to sneak her out to some location in D.C. Freddy was all too familiar with.

"So?" Siren said, fist on slender hips.

"So, young lady," Marvella said, leading the contingent into the room, "you're still determined to further ruin yourself, play with the Devil again, trying to get Freddy here to sneak you out to get some more of that...that coke mess after the doctor here done got you halfway clean and sober."

It was a statement of fact, and Marvella, regardless of her oft dismissal by Siren, remained the only person on the entire planet who was known to have the wherewithal to put the songstress in her place.

"You just a snitching-ass motherfucker, Freddy!" she said directly to the suited, muscular man standing beside the doctor. "That's some cold shit!"

"You're almost there, Siren," Dr. Samuelson said pleadingly, as Siren moved back to her massive bed and plopped down forlornly. "Hang in there, young lady! Just...hang in there!"

"Hang shit!" Siren said, dropping her head to near between her legs. "I ought to hang my foot up your ass, Dr. Dread! Hang in there my ass!"

Freddy, at six-feet seven-inches in height and a former sparing partner for a professional heavyweight boxer, was a commanding presence in any room. He was also responsible for Siren's well being, and took the job for which he was handsomely paid quite seriously. He moved over to a bedside table, reached for Siren's personal cellular phone while at the same time Siren noticed his move and struggled to block him.

"Give me my damn phone, man! What the hell you want with my phone?"

While easily blocking her away from the device he hit keys to display her recent incoming and outgoing calls. Immediately he recognized Alvarez's name and number, went further and read a series of stored text messages.

"It's that goddamn dope dealer, ain't it?" Marvella asked, setting down exhaustively in a richly embroidered Queen Anne chair situated to the side of the bedside table.

"He's been hollering," Freddy said. "I ever get my hands on his tired ass again, either I'm going to jail and he's going to hell or both."

Siren had meanwhile sat back down on the edge of the bed and begun weeping uncontrollably. Shaking her head and appearing weary and worn, Marvella struggled to her feet and moved over to take Siren in a warm embrace, began rocking her back and forth.

"Baby girl," Marvella said, "Doc here say you gonna be alright you just hang in there a little longer without that mess."

Dr. Samuelson just stood there, not sure of what to say, or if saying anything in this familial setting would be appropriate. He had a few powerful prescription drugs in his carrying case, and had given Siren a liberal amount of the drugs during the first week of her withdrawal. Right now though he was worried that the legal narcotics might become another crutch the 25-year-old would become dependent on. Changing seats on the Titanic, AA members described it as, whereby an alcoholic might use marijuana to get off drinking, or a heroin addict might use alcohol to stop his heroin addiction.

"Your physical pull for the cocaine is over," Dr. Samuelson said peevishly. "It's the mental aspect, the callings from your former dealer and the mental dwelling on that fact that more is within reach, that's getting at you."

"I wish that damn Alvarez was within reach," Freddy said, still looking at the text messages. "Girl, I'm gonna tell you now: I have some of my...my less...legit fellas, going out to that club he mentioned here to see if they can get hold of his ass. And Siren, I'm gonna do the doc here one better: More is not within reach. My boys got a picture of Alvarez. They find him, girl, I'm gonna tell you the truth, you won't be getting none of that mess from him ever again."

Chapter Ten

He was determined to meet personally with Siren, and although a Who's Who of underground figures from Washington to New York to Miami were feting Salvadore on his rare visit to America, the only satisfaction he was seeking was a meeting with the songstress. She'd teased his loins from afar in video and song over the past few years and damn if there was anyone on the planet whom Salvadore Paz wanted to have a meet with who didn't abide him.

Especially not one who was also addicted to his prime product.

He decided to do as the last text message had requested, used Alvarez's phone and called Siren's private number. The husky male voice that answered took him aback.

"Yeah. Let me speak with Siren," he said finally.

"Siren's unavailable, Alvarez," Freddy replied.

After a brief pause, Salvadore decided to use his well-regarded interrogation skills to find out a little more about the person on the other end of the phone, and about Siren's whereabouts.

"So," he began again, "if the broad is unavailable, then you must be a very, very close associate of the young lady. So may I ask to whom I'm speaking?"

"Look, Alvarez, let me—"

"This is not that Alvarez piece of shit! You want Alvarez, you find him providing grub meal for dirt worms, you hear? Alvarez no longer….in the loop, so to speak."

Seated on a bar stool in the kitchen of Siren's mansion, Freddy grew cautious. If it was not Alvarez on the other end of the call, and if, as hinted at by the caller, Alvarez was dead, then it was more than likely that he was speaking with someone higher up in the drug organization Alvarez had been a part of. And without a face or name to put with the coarse voice, he too felt it was paramount that he use all of his skills to find out as much about the caller as possible.

"So, if this is not Alvarez, and you seem to know that Alvarez is not available, or no longer 'in the loop' as you say, I take it you were part of his...business. And that's why you're calling Siren?"

"Look...whoever you are: I have some personal...something personal in the way of Siren's business with Alvarez. I'm taking over his...associative needs...that Siren required. Now, can you put her on the phone or what?"

"No, I can't put her on the phone. And in fact, she'll no longer be using this number as a contact number. Simply because folks such as you...and Alvarez, have it!"
There was a good period of silence, but Freddy wasn't hanging up.
"Well, I guess Siren's....needs...have been met through other means," Salvatore said slowly, peeved that he apparently wasn't going to lure the songstress into his lair. "Then I guess I have no further need for her number, nor this particular phone."
He disconnected, handed the phone to a trusted assistant.
"Destroy it. The card. Everything."
He then pulled out his personal cellular, made a call to a high-ranking official within Jupiter Solice Records.

* * *

Freddy moved into the "Brown Parlor," a small room adjoining the spacious kitchen, expecting to find Marvella. He passed through the room and out another door to the far side of the room, into a hallway that led to an office situated in a rear corner of the mansion. Marvella often used this office to undertake business related to Siren's career when she wanted solitude.

It was recognized by staff and all close to Siren, and even Siren herself, as Marvella's personal space. Everyone knocked before entering, and it was so personalized for Marvella that, besides her generous room upstairs and complete and total control of a guesthouse, it comprised living, working and occasional sleeping quarters for the 55-year-old.

Freddy knocked on the door lightly, having seen the glow of a light shining from beneath the door as he approached from down the hall.

"Come on in, Freddy."

She was expecting him, having discussed matters with him earlier out of earshot of the doctor and Siren. He eased the door open, moved to a leather chair he often occupied when the two spent time here discussing business matters, security, Siren's future, or theirs.

"I'm probably going to have to transfer all of her legit contacts out of this phone into a new one with a new number," he said, holding up the cellular as if to emphasize his point. "Talked to a fellow using that fellow Alvarez's phone, and from what I gather Alvarez has...seems like he's...met with some sort of misfortune."

"No better for him," Marvella said, seated behind an ornate teak desk in a leather, high-back chair which seated her slightly overweight girth comfortably. "I don't know how them boys who run that record company allowed that man to dig his claws into a legitimate business such as theirs anyway. Selling that mess to all of his peoples, all over the States and overseas and such. Just didn't never make no sense to me. But who am I to say..."

"Well, Marvella," he leaned forward, impacting the seriousness of his message, "what I'm going to try to do is make sure that girl is kept away from any and all who want to get into her pockets through cocaine or anything else that's not only detrimental to her health, but, hell, illegal as hell! Been a task over the past few years keeping her and some of them others around her from coming under the eye of the law. Though I have to tell you the truth, Marvella:

Was a time I was tempted to let some of my associates with the Feds and a few local boys know about some of the mess that damn Marcus has had his hand in. You know he's the one allowed Alvarez to be peddling coke on the tours and supplying Siren, don't you?"

"I know that scheming, money-grubbing scoundrel wasn't never up to no good," she said, shaking her head at the very thought of the label's co-owner. "He's got Jeremiah all fooled, and probably skimming a little excess money under the table and in them backroom deals he's always making. I never trusted that fool as far as I could throw him."

"I never trusted either one of 'em."

"Well, Jeremiah is an upright fella, far as I can tell. Honest type. Wasn't comfortable with some of the contract things Marcus tried to get Siren to abide with. I put her with some good entertainment lawyers from the outset. That's partially why Marcus ain't never had no use for me, I suspect."

"He never took a hankering to me neither," Freddy said, laughing lightly. "Fools wanted to wrap ol' girl up in so-called security peoples associated with Alvarez. You know how that would have turned out."

They looked to one another, each breathing in audibly, a measure of further calm being felt in one another's presence.

The two had grown close after an initial bumping of heads. Marvella thought initially that Freddy, though nearly twice Siren's age, was maneuvering to get very, very personal with the girl he was then charged with protecting. But even at 22 when Freddy came aboard, Siren was as flirtatious as she'd been since a pre-teen. Marvella blamed it on her dopefiend mother and father, who had surrounded the child with nothing but the worse of personalities and especially men who tended to favor fresh, young meats to savor.

Eventually though Marvella came to recognize Frederick J. Glover as the consummate professional, and in the three years that he'd been responsible for Siren's safety, she could see that he cared enough for the singer that on many occasions he'd placed his own personal safety at risk to ensure Siren met no harm. Yet there was little Freddy could have done to keep Siren away from cocaine, especially since her prime abettor, it appeared, was none other then one of the men responsible for her very lucrative career.

"I just don't see why Jeremiah put up with Marcus and his mess," Marvella said, shaking her head in pure disgust. "He knowed that heathen Alvarez was selling that damn dope to Siren, to them boys in that group Keepin' It Easy, to musicians and techs and the like. If I had my way, him and Alvarez would have both been turned over to the law."

"Well it don't seem that Alvarez will be coming back, from what the guy on the phone hinted at," Freddy said, arising and heading for the door. "But the place they wanted Siren to meet them at, over there in Northeast? Soon as I got a hold of the message I had some of my friends on the D.C. police force check the place out. They have video cameras inside and out. I'm going out there and review them, see if anybody on there might be a match to the guy I was talking to. I think they're still trying to get that large money Siren was spending with Alvarez, not to mention some of the musicians and tech people. Those are large money dealers, Marvella. They have people specialize in finagling their way into music groups, into Hollywood even. All that bank that Siren was spending, I don't think they're going to give up on her that easily."

Chapter Eleven

It was not as if Jenkins didn't have other sources for the drug he preferred. It was just that he enjoyed getting high with Siren, and since both were major artists on the same record label, it had been quite easy for the lead singer of the boy band to hook up with the sultry songstress when she and his group, Keepin' It Easy, were on tour together. But now the tour had been put on hold, all because of Siren, and his repeated calls to her, and to Alvarez, had been met with silence at best, the fearful voice of the security guy Freddy at one time.   And after a short conversation with Freddy, Jenkins was convinced to seek his drugs, and his female companionship, elsewhere.

They had been hanging together ever since Marcus and Jeremiah signed the group and introduced them to the label's most productive artist. Five young black men fresh out of the Barry Farm public housing projects of Washington, D.C., Siren's own city of birth and a community which she was intimately familiar with. Her father had grown up in Barry Farm, and indeed Jenkins immediately reminded her of the tall, dark-skinned man who occasionally showed up at the home she and her mother occupied when she was a child. They called him Raymond, and the astute 12-year-old, quite familiar with the mannerisms of a certain element in her Southeast Washington neighborhood, had always thought of Raymond as a "dopefiend." She knew one when she saw one, what with the nodding and fluttering eyes and constant scowl when under the influence. For Jocelyn, her own mother, was a heroin user also.

Jenkins was a snorter. He'd once confided in Siren that he and his boys on occasion inhaled heroin, and was truly surprised when Siren told him then that she too liked to engage in chemical mind alteration on occasion, but preferred snorting cocaine. They were both considerably fresh in the music business at the time, and after getting to know one another came to realize that their drug use was not something that came upon them when they entered the hectic business, but was something which had accompanied both from their lives in similar surroundings while growing up.

Many of their peers as teens either sold or used drugs, most users preferring marijuana, most sellers marketing crack cocaine and heroin. Theirs were backgrounds flush with illegal narcotics, and although hundreds of thousands of youths escaped the callings of instant money as well as instant gratification, there were always those who didn't have the mental fortitude to escape the callings.

After a period Jenkins grew lackadaisical, dormant in his involvement in the group and was eventually called to task by his brother, among other group members, for excessive use of heroin. He was turned on to a "lighting technician," Alvarez, who convinced him that powdered cocaine was a more suitable drug for one in the entertainment business. Pretty soon Jenkins had put aside his minor heroin habit and was putting powdered cocaine into his broad nostrils. Siren was pleased with that, but was also a prime motivator in convincing her new lover that, after extended shows, cocaine cooked up into its "raw" form and smoked was the way to go.

In AA and NA meetings, Jenkins would be held forth as a prime example of one who exchanges one addiction for another, switching seats on the Titanic, in the common analogy. But if that scenario rang true in Jenkins's case, he was not satisfied with merely switching seats. By the age of 27 and with a sterling musical career before him, Jenkins got into smoking cocaine so deeply that he was nearly responsible for destroying the careers of his brother and childhood friends in Keepin' It Easy. He not only switched seats on the Titanic but, seeing the approaching iceberg, apparently viewed it as one, huge rock of cocaine. With that analogy in mind, Jenkins switched seats, jumped off the Titanic, took up passage on the iceberg, began chipping away at it and was continually feeding pieces of it into a crack pipe.

He was in a desperate mood now, unable to get in touch with Alvarez and unable to reach Siren by phone. He knew she had connections in the city, and from his own spacious home in Ft. Washington, Maryland decided to chance a drive over to McLean. For not only was he in desperate need of a considerable volume of coke, but he'd been cut out of the financial loop since the tour had been cancelled, and for all his riches on paper, couldn't put his hands on little more than a few hundred dollars in cash.

Siren was always good for a few thousand dollars. He pulled the luxurious Mercedes Maybach up to the entrance to Siren's McLean mansion, pressed the intercom in hopes of gaining entrance.

"Yes, can I help you?"

He recognized Freddy's voice, and knew that the security man was looking dead in his face from the camera that was pointed at his car from atop the ten-foot tall, remotely operated gate blocking the main entrance to the estate.

"Yo! Freddy! Jenkins Shorter here for Siren. Buzz me in, bro!"

There was a pause that seemed interminable to Jenkins, as he puffed hard on the menthol cigarette and took a swig from the bottle of Ciroc peach vodka which had kept his counsel during the drive over.

After what seemed to be a prolonged period, the mechanics could be heard struggling loudly, and the heavy, cast-iron gate began to slowly swing open. Sparkling bubbles of anticipatory waves coursed through Jenkins's forebrain, his habit automatically assuming that at lease a good measure of cocaine was somewhere on the grounds of Siren's estate. He had been told that she was in recovery and not using. But his own addiction would not allow for such a scenario. He was after all a fellow addict, and like crabs in a barrel, he was not about to let Siren out while he wallowed in a sea of waste and angst, improbability at anyone escaping the grip of the substance which had such a firm hold on his own tortured existence the most acceptable scenario.

"I know that girl got some shit stashed somewhere," he said to himself, as he pulled around the arching driveway and before the massive, pillared entrance to the main home.

One of the huge, oak front doors swung open, and Freddy stood in the doorway, leaning on the other side, on the unopened door, and pinning Jenkins with a not-too-welcoming gaze.

"Main man!" Jenkins said, stepping up the three stairs to the main entrance and extending a hand.

Hesitantly, Freddy took the hand, motioned with his head for Jenkins to enter, stepped in behind him and closed the door.

"You know Siren's in recovery," he said to a smiling yet antsy Jenkins.

"Yeah man yeah," Jenkins said, looking around the spacious yet empty foyer. "I was just, like, you know, since the tour's been cancelled, wanted to holler at ol' girl for a minute, you know, on a kind of personal note, know what I'm saying?"

"I know what you're saying, young buck." He moved towards one of the spiral staircases leading to the upper level. "Have a seat over there, or in the living room over there, and I'll let Siren know she has a visitor."

Wishing he'd had the nerve to bring the Ciroc in the house, Jenkins nodded to Freddy and moved to a door to the left of the foyer, looked back at Freddy who was looking back at him as he ascended the stairs.

Jenkins moved into an anteroom. With a measure of relief, he found a fine cedar and glass cupboard which clearly contained a wide assortment of alcoholic beverages. He moved over to it, wrenched a knob on one cabinet and retrieved a bottle of vodka and a crystal glass. Without hesitation, he poured a drink, downed it and poured another. When the door opened Jenkins turned expecting to see Siren, and was visibly crestfallen when only the large form of Freddy shadowed the doorway.

"The girl is resting," Freddy said. "She asked that you call the offices of her agent before just dropping by, and also wanted me to give you a personal message."

Jenkins frowned, took a huge swig from the glass and refilled it, feeling that he was surely about to be ejected and remained quite antsy for his lack of his preferred mind alterative. He looked at the silent bodyguard, who didn't seem as if he was going to say anything more. Just standing there, and pinning him with a cold, chilling gaze.

"So," Jenkins asked, visibly unnerved now. "What's the personal message?"

"Girl said while the tour is down, and she's in a period of recovery herself, might be a good time for you to think about taking...and these are her words, 'taking a chill pill' yourself."

Jenkins felt dejected, and a world-renowned star in his own right, considered that no one, not Siren, not this..chauffeur...had a right...had the nerve...to speak to him in such a manner.

He stomped towards the door, past Freddy and headed towards the exit.

"Man, fuck that bitch!" Jenkins spat, struggling to wrench open the massive wooden front door. "She ain't all that! Fuck her! And fuck you too!"

Chapter Twelve

They certainly had no idea that the club was fitted with unobtrusive security cameras, or they never would have held the meeting there. But Salvadore Paz had been assured that this night spot, in a nondescript building in a section of Washington almost completely populated by African-Americans, would be the perfect place to meet with the record company executive. And Marcus Elliot was quite secure in meeting the international drug dealer here. Unbeknownst to his partner Jeremiah, and certainly unknown to the hundreds of blacks who poured their dollars into this popular dance club, Marcus was majority owner of Sandy's Secret, although local go-go personality Sandy Rollins was publicly identified as the club's owner.

Marcus's stable of talents was growing uneasy. With Alvarez out of the picture, and three major tours still ongoing, the record company executive couldn't afford having any of his personnel who favored cocaine going out onto foreign streets to score. For over a decade he'd made sure that talents under the Jupiter Solice umbrella were protected from the whims of nosey paparazzi and gossip rags, and that those who were surely to indulge in sordid engagements of both drug and sexual natures kept these indiscretions in house, as it were.

Salvadore told Marcus straight out that Alvarez would never, ever again be available, and was meeting with him to discuss a new arrangement that would benefit the drug lord financially and would in addition salve one of his most pressing desires that had thus far eluded him.

"I want that black girl Siren," Salvadore said in his brusque, gravelly voice. He took a good pull on the $75.00 cigar, continued. "I'll see that you have a new...'lighting technician' placed in house and well supplied. But you got to do me this one thing that I haven't been able to do with my own people: Get the girl Siren to come to one of my...special gatherings...while I'm her in Washington. And I and my associates will take it from there."

Marcus was actually afraid to tell the drug lord that his superstar songstress was in rehab, even if it did consist of one that confined her to her own McLean estate with drug counselors and medical personnel flown in and put up on her property.

"Sal," Marcus began, feeling sweat moisten the collar of the hand-woven cotton shirt he favored when not in suit and tie. "We welcome the new...lighting technician. Matter of fact, as soon as possible.   That boy Jenkins...Jenkins Shorter that leads my group Keepin' It Easy, is just a measure away from getting his ass busted running around in D.C. and Maryland and Virginia trying to score. And our tour that's moving through Toronto and then Seattle: A few of the roadies with that bunch have been going to some unsavory sorts out West to get their fix. But Sal, about Siren: The girl is in seclusion, and from all reports   is   doing   well   at   overcoming   her...her little...flirtation with that...little...thing."

Freddy couldn't hear what was being said at the secluded table, but as he watched the monitor from within cousin Sandy Rollins's office, he could only shake his head at what he anticipated was being discussed between the record executive and drug lord.

"So, you're saying she's no longer interested in my product?" Salvadore asked, leaning onto the table and fingering a glass of Laurent-Perrier Cuvée Rosé Brut champagne.

"Urr, it seems she's...well, overcoming her illness, if you will," Marcus said, sweat now peppering his clean-shaven face, his armpits pockets of uncomfortable heat.

Salvadore leaned back, puffed on his cigar and looked to the ceiling retrospectively.

"There's something about that girl that just…just…moves me!" he said.

"I can understand it," Marcus said, feeling a measure of relief now. "Her stage presence is as vital to her popularity as is her voice. The young lady is—"

"Not available," Salvadore said, brusquely. "Not…even…available…"

Uncharacteristically, Marcus, the penultimate salesman, was at a loss for words.

"What can I say," he muttered. "Right. She's apparently….unavailable."

"Then I'm going to leave it up to you, my friend," Salvadore said, arising, "to make her available. To me!"

And he walked out of the club with a blanket of security men surrounding him.

Chapter Thirteen

When it came to his role as a protector, Frederick J. Glover, aka Freddy, did not play around. He had his hands full with Siren, whose exciting, almost tempestuous persona exuded sexuality to most every man, and some women, who were fortunate enough to be within emotive reach of her scented presence. At 21 she was beyond beauteous and exciting, at 24 a measure more following minor cosmetic surgery and presently, at 25, was still a striking beauty comparable to the highest-paid runway model. A few years into heavy cocaine use, one would have thought that the drug would have diminished her vitality, her warmth, her physical stature. She was only a considerably repulsive presence when in private and under intense influence of the drug. Freddy had been summoned when her rocket was just taking off, and often he had to let a subcontract to secure temporary services of some expert martial artists to supplant his security over the heralded songstress.

Instinctively, he knew that Salvadore Paz posed a threat to Siren. After receiving a copy of the video recording of the meeting between the record executive and drug dealer, Freddy engaged one of his contacts in the Federal Bureau of Investigation, was directed to a professional lip reader and within a day had a partial transcript of the conversation. The drug kingpin had mentioned Siren quite often, and Freddy further utilized FBI contacts to get good readings on Salvador's movements in the United States from both Customs and Border Patrol officials and Immigration and Naturalization offices. Agents from those organizations had already been monitoring his movements, along with the FBI and a few local law enforcement agencies.

With the information he had gathered Freddy ensured that Siren was sticking to her recovery regimen, told Marvella to call him at any hint of trouble, and began his own secretive program to secure Siren's future. Perhaps, he reasoned, he might also blunt potential trauma facing some of the other young acts with the record label. He thought of the recent encounter with Jenkins Shorter of Keepin' It Easy, felt that the young artist reminded him of his own son, and made a mental note to have some of his more street-wise associates engage an identical program to the one he was instituting for Siren to see that Jenkins's foray into cocaine use was similarly squelched.

Rebuffed by Siren, Jenkins meanwhile was cruising back into his childhood neighborhood, all alone and paying no mind to the warnings issued by record company officials that, being a millionaire (on paper) negated his ability to romp back onto the street of the Barry Farm housing project without a care in the world.

Yet he was pressed, and even though his manager, his immediate family, and members of his group had undertaken an intervention of sorts and blocked his access to hard cash, Jenkins just knew he could "get on" with a good measure of cocaine at "the Farms," as the SE Washington project was familiarly called. As a last resort he was sure some dealer would not mind "holding" the Maybach as collateral until Jenkins could finagle his was into some hard cash.

His numerous credit cards had been issued through an arrangement with the record company. He had never been one to manage money well nor indeed even maintain a bank account before hitting the big time, and with his well-known tendency to overindulge, first in alcohol, then other substances, his manager, family and company officials had agreed to give him credit cards which had no real ceiling. He could spend what he wanted, including his off-the-cuff purchase of the Maybach Landaulet convertible, which had cost well over a million dollars.

But the same ones who'd given him the cards also had the ability to cut him off, without notice, and at present he was cruising up the parkway abutting the housing project with barely enough gas in the expensive vehicle to make it back to his Ft. Washington, Maryland home.

He did have a good amount of valuable gold strung around his neck, and a Patek Philippe watch on his wrist which cost $69,000 brand new. Still swigging from the bottle he kept to somewhat calm his nerves while also puffing on a menthol cigarette, he was sure that he would get a good measure of coke in his old neighborhood, and certainly could visit a few old, trusted friends and borrow gas money too.

When he pulled into the squat, clapboard housing units, he was surprised to see that they were deserted, boarded up, not a soul in sight on the corner which was usually occupied every night by young men peddling their wares or just hanging out and smoking marijuana blunts. He'd not kept in touch with his old friends, and some kinfolk, who'd remained in the Farm, and couldn't have known that, with the Department of Homeland Security locating its headquarters on the grounds of the old St. Elizabeths Hospital just south of the Farm, the historic farmland, the nation's first public housing project, was sited for a tract of million-dollar townhomes.

In time there would be a plaque near the intersection where the Farm's northern border intersected Suitland Parkway, within spitting distance of the U.S. Capitol building which sat imposingly on the Hill, just across the river. The plaque would point out that Barry Farm was home to hundreds of thousands of blacks following the Civil War. It would not mention the dozens of black boys slain on the streets of a latter day "Farm" whose cash crop had, for years, been heroin and cocaine.

No one in official Washington wanted to remember that sordid aspect of Barry Farm and other public housing project's histories.

Chapter Fourteen

Freddy first returned to McLean to check on Siren and have a discussion with Marvella. In route he'd made a few calls, one to his friend at FBI headquarters, and another to a brother who was part of the Joint Terrorism Task Force that was among the many in law enforcement monitoring Salvadore Paz's movements. Another call had been made to a less austere personage, and this man was given the information culled from the Global Positioning Satellite service embedded in Jenkins Shorter's Maybach.

Siren was doing just fine, he found out upon arriving at the estate. Still Marvella had her concerns, and was glad to have a friend around her own age to sit and chat with. It was very late in the evening, but Marvella, often a night-owl who watched old episodes *of Sanford and Son* and *Good Times* on cable TV, had prepared coffee and sat in comfort with Freddy in one of two first-floor parlors.

"All I can ask of you, Freddy," she said, the nearby television alive but muted, "is keep that boy Jenkins away from her for a while. And if what you say about Alvarez is true, then make sure that some of his...how you say?...surrogates don't come up in the group with no more of that stuff."

Freddy knew more than he was willing to tell her, but was internally confident that he could keep his charge safe and drug free, if she indeed wanted to remain sober.

"Long as Siren wants to stay clean, then I'm certainly going to do my part to see that nothing is...well, not forced upon her, but put out in front of her by those people who just want to keep their hands in her pocket."

He sipped coffee, thought about the plans he'd put in motion to perhaps negate any reentry of the drug dealers into the ranks of musicians and artist waiting in the wings for Siren's return. From all the information he'd gathered, he was almost certain that Salvadore Paz's organization had placed others in parts of the myriad tours Jupiter Solice Records had underway. His contacts were even now working to lance these drug-dealing culprits from the artists and troupes, but Freddy was of the old-school leaning that you cut a snake off at the head. Marvella, sipping coffee also, seemed to be having similar thoughts.

"So," she said exhaustively, "what about the source of all of them drugs that girl and others were getting? From what I hear, the evil son-of-a-bitch is around now, in Washington or somewhere near abouts?"

Freddy was impressed by the knowledge Marvella seemed to always have access to, and simply smiled and shook his head lightly before responding.

"Marvella, you seem to have as good a set of contacts as I have. Yeah, the fella that's on top of the drug group is around now, down there in D.C.   But if what I hear…what I know…is planned for his ass, he's not going back to South America this time unless it's in a box."

He felt the vibration of his smartphone. Marvella sensed it and shook her head. She didn't "cotton to" the omnipresent devices, as she would say. She held her own council and awaited Freddy as he took the call or read the message. She had no way of knowing just what was emanating from the device.

Freddy put the phone to his ear.

"Yes, take him," he said bluntly, then immediately disconnected.

"That boy Jenkins who left here not long ago? He's been out there visiting some not-too-safe haunts in search of his get-high. One of my friends with Metropolitan Police got him at a place over in Southeast, big-ass million-dollar ride of his drawing attention around some who don't want no attention drawn to them. They're going to take him in

on some okey-doke stuff, get him safely out of the 'hood.
Some of my other people will get him from the precinct and
see him to his place in Ft. Washington. But you know,
Marvella, this is something the record company should be
handling. They don't care if one of their artists gets bad
press or even killed out there messing around with that
coke. Hell, I think they reason that if the artist does go
down in flames, that will boost record sales more than if
they were alive and kicking."

"That's the way I feel that they feel about it too
sometimes," Marvella allowed, then arose and bid her
friend a good night.

Chapter Fifteen

Salvadore Paz had security that almost rivaled that of the President. But he was in the camp of some who knew every nook and cranny of the landscape, some who had eyes in place wearing everything from maids' uniforms to the uniforms of at least seven different law enforcement agencies. He was on foreign soil, and even his well-known bravado and dedicated bank of bodyguards couldn't save him when some native to this present locale determined to have him eliminated.

He was his buoyant, robust self, lounging along the rooftop pool of the Alexandria condominium, the entire top floor of the fourteen-story building occupied by minions, or relatives of minions, who were solely responsible for plying his wares up and down the East Coast. No one had access to the area without his expressed permission, and no one from any of the nearby buildings could get a clear view of the drug lord, nor of the young blonde woman whose head bobbed up and down at his midsection.

They were only visible in the precision scope of the marksman a quarter mile away, in a building situated on a bluff in a less prestigious region of Alexandria. The gunman was directing a rifle with a most explosive round at the center of the drug merchant's bare chest.

Salvadore was nearing a climax, and still he put the expensive cigar to his mouth with one hand while cupping the back of the woman's head with the other. He never inhaled when smoking a cigar, so the smoke which burst from a sudden hole in his hairy chest somewhat dumbfounded the man, and the personal security guard who stood unobtrusively nearby.

There had been no sound, yet Salvadore's chest emitted a whiff of smoke before a hole was clearly visible, clean at first, then releasing an outpouring of blood. He came in the woman's mouth, explosively, and she eased back on the stiff rod with a satisfactory grin, knowing she'd earned the extra three-hundred dollars he'd promised if the "head" was exceptionally good. But then she saw the shocked look on his face, and then the gaping hole in his chest and the outpouring of fresh blood from the wound. She started to scream, but took a deep breath and fainted.

* * *

Jose Pena was doing as he'd been instructed to do: Staying out of the way backstage and watching as the rap artist Considerate Lil' Cathy pranced about the stage and moved her thousands of fans as the opening act of this particular leg of the tour. Although he was only there in support of the habits of the star attraction and a few of the roadies, his embedding in the tour, he felt, had all sorts of potential.

Mr. Paz had said that he would be officially employed as an "electronics technician," had the approval of Mr. Elliot with the record company, and was assured great profits on this, his first venture into the American music industry. But Jose had even grander ambitions, and was sure that he could get the group surrounding Considerate Lil' Cathy at first indulging in his volume of powdered cocaine and then, on down the line, into smoking it up in large quantities. He had already convinced a number of the roadies and members of the star attraction's group that that was the way to go, and as the cooked up coke required it in greater quantities, he immediately experienced a doubling of sales and profits.

The massive, 1,000-pound speakers had been situated on the stage of the Greensboro Coliseum, with two stacked atop one another on the corners of the stage and two equally huge ones hung from taunt, strong wires above the stage-mounted ones. Jose stood just to the rear of the speakers on the left rear of the stage, and was completely unaware of the man in the far rear rafters as he maneuvered one of the hung speakers to just above him.

Once sited, the man in a full-bodied black suit freed the wires holding the massive speaker, and it plunged down on Jose like a disgruntled child's foot crushing a cockroach.

*   *   *

It would have been advisable for Palmer Layton to at least have known a little bit about the power that was used to deliver a spectacular show to the 7,000 fans gathered to hear French Connection of Po' Boy perform. After all, he was on the payroll of Jupiter Solice as a lighting technician, and should have known that, when asked to handle the 10,000-voltage wires running from the amplifiers to the sound board, any astute electrician would have worn insulating gloves. Just in case.

The man in the black overalls didn't seem familiar, but Palmer was working on contract, and that didn't concern him. After all, he didn't know many of the operatives on the tour, and couldn't have cared less. His job was to ensure that those who wanted cocaine were supplied with it, and the money he was making didn't allow for frivolities. Mr. Paz and Mr. Elliot didn't abide the asking of too many questions. He took the cable, and was roasted like a pastry left in the toaster oven for much too long.

*   *   *

The apparent concert hall maintenance man in the black overalls had asked Fulton Del Homme to take his spot at the backstage entrance while he went to use the men's room. Only take a minute, the man had said. Just a quick piss. Fulton had nothing better to do; he'd already fed 24 grams of powdered cocaine to members of The Questions, the popular rock band which was among the few white groups on Jupiter Solice. Fulton was also new on the job, having been inserted into the tour by Mr. Elliot just days ago, when the 18-city tour kicked off. He was supposed to ensure that everyone who even approached the stage had the colorful backstage pass strung around their neck. But that wasn't actually his job, so he didn't give it much consideration that the man in black who asked him to take up this momentary task wasn't wearing a backstage pass himself.

When the man finally returned, members of The Question were then on stage, behind thick, floor-to-ceiling curtains, tuning up their instruments even as the gear from the opening act was still being cleared away. Fulton was glad the man was back, greeted him in a common embrace and handshake. He felt as if some ornament on the man's black uniform pricked him in his side, removed himself from the embrace and watched as the smiling man backed away into the rear stage darkness.

A few strums on the highest notes of Flash Royal's electric guitar seemed to reverberate in the thickest veins of Fulton's neck, and for some reason he was suddenly hit with a flashback of the time he'd dropped acid, Yellow Sunshine to be exact, some 30 years earlier, when he was but an 18-year-old roadie himself slogging along behind a rock band that would eventually become known worldwide. The tingling was just like that; as if he'd dropped a tab of acid. Or two. Or perhaps…too many….

He swooned for a moment, noticed a rush of stage hands passing by and could hear the bass guitar thrum and the clash of a symbol and in the semi-darkness and light, a flash, a red and then a green and psychedelic thoughts flowed out from an overtaxed brain and a nosebleed preceded his pitching forward to the floor and he needed to get the remainder of the cocaine off of his person for certainly he was going to need medical attention but the coke was just being secured into a sweating, wet palm when Fulton's heart jumped and pumped a final beat before the drug dealer had a massive coronary attack and as quickly died.

Chapter Sixteen

Keepin' It Easy tried replacing Jenkins Shorter for the first of seven shows, but word got out quickly after the Baltimore kick-off of the newly formed tour and through Internet word-of-mouth ticket sales for the remaining shows floundered to the point where it was certain that the tour would not be profitable. The tour was immediately cancelled, with word being leaked that Shorter was in rehab and that Keepin' It Easy would not return to live performances until its lead vocalist was better.

That wasn't setting well with Siren. After 28 days of sobriety, she was itching to get back on the road, back out before her admiring public. But her aborted tour had promised Siren as the headliner, with Keepin' It Easy, featuring Jenkins Shorter, as an added incentive for fans to dole out $125.00 minimum for tickets. The record company was willing to revamp the tour, but not without the initial lineup.

She was growing antsy, moving about the massive estate, busying herself with video games and dispatching Freddy to pick up a few of her childhood girlfriends from the city when she was on the verge of returning to Washington nightlife on her own. The doctor had recommended against it though, so she found solace in the presence of Genese Taylor, whom she'd known since both were in elementary school, and Sunshine Melody (her true birth name!), who had been a tight friend during a most tumultuous teenage period.

All three were the same age, all African-American, and all with similar backgrounds, having grown up in shattered homes and in the same Southeast Washington neighborhood. Both had been close with Sirena as she attained stardom (they still called her by her own birth name), and had accompanied her on the ride for a while.

But Genese and Sunshine shunned drug use, and after
calling Siren to task when they observed her devolving
further and further into cocaine use, they were callously
dispatched from her entourage with words so cold that
Sunshine, the more emotional of the trio, had been reduced
to tears.

Before even accepting the offer and being driven out
to her McLean estate, Genese and Sunshine had held a
private telephone conversation, and had hesitantly agreed
to return to meet with Sirena as she had requested.

"She can be a bitch sometimes," Genese had said to
Sunshine. "But you know, you saw how that stardom went
to her head there for a moment. Mostly though after she
started with that coke."

They were gathered in Siren's massive bedroom,
thrown about either on the huge bed or stretched about the
embroidered furnishing, laughing and reflecting on "the
old days," though each was all of 25-years of age.

"Girl, you was all over Jenky-Jenks!" Genese said,
laughing. "But that black motherfucker was so fine! Is so
fine, from what I see on All-Rap TV. You still hollering at
him, Sirena?"

Siren recalled the last time Jenkins had visited her,
and didn't want to tell mutual friends that the singer,
whom she'd helped get his professional musical footing,
was hard on crack cocaine.

"I've seen him not long ago, and him and Keepin' It
Easy were on the road with us before...before my last
time...just fucking things all up," Siren said. "But I think
my man Freddy and some boys from the record company
got with his ass not too long ago and I think they got him
into rehab. I don't know..."

"But y'all was tight like that though, wasn't you?"
Sunshine, the more reserved among them, asked.

"We was hanging for a minute," Siren said. "But
you know: Industry. And that drug mess. I fucked up, for

real though. And girls, I'm sorry about dissing y'all like I did..."

Siren and Genese were stretched out on her huge bed, and would appear to a stranger as if sisters. They had spent nearly all of their teenaged years together, along with Sunshine.   But the two were near identical in makeup: Tall, slender, dark, generous hair complimented by extensions expertly applied by fanciful and costly beauticians. Many remarked over the years that the two had grown so close growing up together that they took on each other's appearance. And although Sunshine had been a part of the trio for as long, she was a more reserved personality, a light-skinned African-American girl whose own generous locks were hers and hers alone.

"Yeah, you did show your black ass back then after Atlanta," Genese said, leaning on an elbow a few feet away from Siren. "But that's okay, girlfriend. We know you like a book."

"Knowed you just needed to slow your roll," Sunshine added, setting on a lush Victorian chaise a few feet from the bed. "We started not to come out here after you called, know what I mean? I mean, dag, like, you probably needed time to chill. Way you was on that cocaine a hundred miles an hour...."

"I know," Siren said. "I know..."

"You know girl," Sunshine said, growing serious, "It still ain't over. You been chilling, what? A month?"

"Twenty-nine days," Siren said.

"Quiet as it's kept, I've been through some rehab shit with my father. That Al-Anon program for the family of addicts and alcheys. From what I learned, my sister, it's a lifelong program. You have to watch out for them triggers that might send you right back to using."

"'Triggers' my ass," Genese, the lifelong smart mouth added. "Fool ass niggas! Niggas will send her ass back to using."

"Triggers, Genese," Sunshine continued calmly. "You know, Sirena. Drinking. Being all caught up in that high after your performances. Those are times you need to be vigilant, and have some good peeps around you for support. Like Miss Marvella."

"Yeah," Siren said. "Marvella. And Freddy. All them other....fools...especially them fools the record company have around they call part of A&R, ain't worth shit."

"A&R?"

"Artist and repertoire. Like that fool was supposed to be A&R...then his ass was a 'lighting technician,' and come to find out he wasn't doing nothing but dealing."

"And working right in your camp," Sunshine said. "I peeped his ass one time when you were down in Miami doing a gig."

"Alvarez," Genese said. "I knew that fool was a snake when I first laid eyes on him."

"But that's why I called my sisters from another mister together," Siren continued. "I really, really need your help with this thing. I want to go back out, but, you know, I got Marvella and Freddy. But only my girls, only y'all, been able to keep me in check. Make me feel a little...guilty...about messing up like I was, know what I mean?"

"Yeah, girlfriend," Genese said. "But what are you going to do when you get back out there and me and Sunshine got to get back to our own lives?"

Siren let a short smile crease her beautiful features, stood and moved to a vanity mirror, looking at herself and, through the mirror, to both her friends.

"Y'all could come on board with me. You know: Personal assistants. And I'll talk to Cord and Georgia, see that y'all paid quite handsomely. And for real, won't be no charity type shit if that's what you're thinking. I mean, with my girls along, you know, I'm quite sure y'all will keep me level-headed, you know, about that...little...thing...I was involved with."

"You mean that coke?" Genese said bluntly.

"Yeah...that mess," Siren answered, guilt ridden and still feeling a measure of remorse.

"Girl, you know we would have always had your back," Genese said, a measure of self-satisfaction prominent in that she'd been the closest friend to warn Sirena years earlier about the dangers prevalent in the drug world both had been quite observable of as teens. "But girl I'm gonna tell you what: You know I ain't messing around and not finishing up my medical assistance training and come all out there with you and ain't got no future myself. Know what I'm saying?"

Siren knew exactly what Genese was hinting at. The two had been together for the most part all of their young lives, and she knew well that Genese, whose talents were few and saw her fine looks and figure as about the most precious of her endowments, wanted a more meaningful, long-term position in the artist's career.

"Girl, I wouldn't ask you to do anything, make any commitment, unless I got my legal peoples to draw out and explain to you a contract and all the different aspects of what you're getting into...committing to," Siren said. "All on the up-and-up. You know you're my girls, like sisters, and I wouldn't do nothing with you, you with me, that didn't have in place some things to look out for your futures. I mean, I'm trying my best to stay sober, you know? With y'all around, I know I'm gonna make it. And got some things in the hopper about doing some films, getting back on the road with a nice tour, getting back in the studio. Y'all know I was a pure-D mess doing up that coke like I was, don't you?"

"You know that's right!" Sunshine and Genese said simultaneously, and they all had a good, heartfelt laugh

that had eluded this tight knit group of young women in recent years.

Chapter Seventeen

The catastrophes that had rained down in an unbelievable pattern on segments of the musical tours of Jupiter Solice Records did not go unnoticed by some in the entertainment industry, and was a whispered topic among a slew of artists filling venues across the nation. Some on other record labels were taking joy in the misfortunes of Jupiter Solice, particularly the challenges now being faced by Marcus Elliot, whom many knew to be one of the seediest characters in an industry which had been seriously contracting over the past decade.

There were certainly a number of drug dealers, mostly foreign nationals, itching to step into the well-regarded though now dormant shoes of Salvadore Paz. His demise did little to shake up a cocaine market which viewed America as its Wall Street, Hollywood its central bank, the recording industry its Fort Knox. The deaths of a few mid-level dealers wasn't going to stop a virtual feeding frenzy where cocaine was the omnipresent bait, although only a few moneyed dealers were attempted to embed yet other drug merchants into a music industry surely under the federal law enforcement microscope.

Freddy and his well-placed associates were comfortable in the knowledge that all those investigating the deaths of dealers implanted in Jupiter Solice Records' ranks were looking almost exclusively at foreign nationals. Most being sought were illegal immigrants, and most also, Freddy found, were being tied to the late Salvadore Paz. Even though the drug kingpin's own death remained unsolved, law enforcement officials were rounding up many who were merely associated with him, and since many were in America with papers that dissolved with but a cursory examination, both Freddy on one end, and Marvella on a more personal level with Siren, were convinced that the internal drug problems of the record label, at least, had been solved.

Siren asked Freddy to put his considerable skills to work seeing that her old flame Jenkins was seen after, while Marcus, breathing a sigh of relief after being suspect to even partner Jeremiah, found space in time to perhaps cover up his serious misdirection of funds from the record company.   Jeremiah knew, as did a few others, that Marcus's thievery was predominantly from the accounts maintained for artists' expenses, and a few of the more astute managers were beginning to do the math and find out that expenses supposedly covered by tour income were being siphoned off the monies which were supposed to go directly to the artists.

"I ought to steal that motherfucker!" Jenkins spat when advised by his agent about his serious lack of liquid assets, and why he was consistently short when profits were divvied up. "Punch him right in his goddamn jaw!"

He'd been reigned in for a few days from his drug quest, a series of manipulations by his agent, Freddy, Siren and Jeremiah serving to redirect the singer's misspent energies away from the search for cocaine. Now sober for the moment, Jenkins was reconnecting with his group, his friends in the industry, his family, and his still beloved Siren.   She, Marvella, Freddy, Jeremiah and Jenkins's mother were gathered at Jenkins's palatial home in Ft. Washington, Maryland, Jeremiah there to go over the present business situation of Keepin' It Easy, the aborted tour, and efforts to revive it. Jeremiah also let on that he was seeking to legally detach Marcus from the record company they'd jointly founded, and didn't hold back as to the reasons why.

"We've had representatives from the accounting firm of Hanford, Grace, Donnelly give our books a thorough going-over," Jeremiah said, seated on the long, sectional sofa in Jenkins's living room. "I wasn't going to trust it to our in-house accountants; they and Marcus have been close for oh too long. Indeed, Marcus had a good hand in hiring most of them."

Jeremiah's demeanor had long endeared him to the primarily black and young clients who were responsible for the success of Jupiter Solice Records. At 35, he had wealth which surpassed that of any among his roster of artists. But unlike partner Marcus, he was a beloved, even jovial presence when taking up business matters with his singers.

Short, nearly completely bald and rotund, he paid little attention to his appearance, often jostling around in off-the-rack suits a size too large, unpolished plain, black shoes and white dress shirts that could have used a good ironing. Marcus was the polished presence representing the multi-million dollar corporation, and when the two were together they appeared in comic contrast to one another.

"What about the drug dudes that were on the tours?" Freddy, seated directly across from Jeremiah, asked pointedly.

Jeremiah visibly popped a few beads of sweat, loosened his crumped collar before answering. "We've had a special investigator who's looking into the...accidents...studying the pattern of hirings in that vein. Mr. Glover, I know of your concerns about how that guy Alvarez was placed on the tour with Siren here. Siren? You knew the guy wasn't on the up and up for quite a while, didn't you?"

"I knew his ass was nothing but a damn dope dealer," Marvella said.

"He was..." Siren said, seeming to struggle to find words. "He was...just...in there! You know, Jeremiah. It was Marcus who introduced him....first as a 'lighting technician.' Then, Alvarez let it be known...you know..."

She trailed off. Jenkins, seated in a plush chair to the side of the sofa, leaned forward.

"Yeah. That mug ain't never had nothing to do but hang around backstage and wait...wait for fools to come to his ass...and the boy had mad coke! I mean, big-ass baggies of the shit!"

"And sometimes would hook it up into rocks, if you asked," Siren said peevishly.

"That's some crazy stuff you young'uns got into," Janice Shorter, Jenkins's mother, deigned to put her view in. "All you got going for you, Siren, Jenkins, and you want to throw it all away behind that stuff."

One of the reasons this diverse collective was meeting at Jenkins's home instead of at Jupiter Solice's New York headquarters was, one, due to Jenkins's shaky determination at sobriety and, two, because the meeting was informal, and meant to keep Marcus, primarily, and some other Jupiter Solice principles out of the loop. Janice, 45 years of age with a history of heroin use, was abided by most when she insisted on overseeing her son's career. But she'd proven quite astute of late when addressing the issue of drug and alcohol use among the artists, and even reminding anyone who'd listen that she had seven years and, counting up the exact moment, so many days sober. She thus pricked many a keen ear when she addressed the subject.

Short, of thick build with huge breast and blacker than the ace of spades, Janice exuded the sense that she was not one to be messed with. Indeed, it was whispered (but no legal charges existed anywhere) that she had shot three men to death. One, the rumor mill had it, was a D.C. "rap impresario" who'd dared attempted to manage Jenkins and Keepin' It Easy. Indeed, the man in question was gunned down, the shooter never caught, in what was reportedly a failed street robbery. Shortly thereafter, the group was signed to Jupiter Solice.

"I'm staying sober, Ma," Jenkins said. "Jeremiah hooked us up with this drug counselor, and we're going to start going to meetings soon. Me and Siren."

"Yes we are," Siren added. "And together we're going to beat this thing, never go back to doing that...shit...again."

"I'm going to hold you to that, guys," Jeremiah said.

"Me too," added Marvella.

"Well," Freddy said, "For my part, I'm going to be on the two of you like white on rice. You better bet it."

"And although it has cast an investigative light on us," Jeremiah said, "those tragic...accidents...as it were, pointed out something I've suspected for quite some time: Marcus had a...program....if you will, to see that our artists who used didn't have to go far to...score."

Freddy, who'd been directing his eyes at Jeremiah, suddenly threw his head back, looked to the ceiling and arose.

"Tragic," he said, looking between those gathered. "But as we used to say in Special Forces: You want to kill a snake, cut it off at the head. Jeremiah, you have some good people up there in headquarters. I hope you all do take care of...that...problem...with Marcus Elliot."

"Certainly," Jeremiah said. "I love him like he's kin, and I certainly wouldn't want any harm to come of him."

He and Freddy looked sternly to one another for what seemed an interminable period, and this wasn't lost on the others. Then Freddy headed for the door.

"If you all handle it, Jeremiah, I think Marcus will be all right."

"All right," Jeremiah said, and everyone else seemed to take this as a sign that the meeting was over, went about their individual endeavors elsewhere.

Siren and Jenkins left for his private quarters, smiling, arm in arm.

Chapter Eighteen

They were on the road again. Siren the star attraction, Keepin' It Easy on the undercard along with two other acts from Jupiter Solice. Jeremiah, along with the assistance of Freddy, had put together what amounted to a mobile Alcoholics Anonymous/Narcotics Anonymous group, and both Siren, Jenkins, and a few member of the house band who admitted to drug problems attended at least three meetings daily. Others in the entourage poo-pooed the idea, especially a few musicians and roadies who were content to continue consuming alcohol and drugs.

Silver Shadow, Siren's favored lead guitarists, was among the holdouts.

Shadow, as she was more often familiarly called, was a white woman, six-feet tall and thin as a rail, with a natural one-inch wide white streak running right through the middle of her lush mane of otherwise jet black hair. At present, Shadow was addicted to the hallucinogenic drug phencyclidine, known on the streets as PCP, Love Boat, Dippers, Butt Naked. Often hard to come by, especially for one who spent weeks on end on the road, Shadow had been afforded her own supply of the liquid, enough in fact to keep her tripping, psychotic but in a controlled manner, until there was a break in the tour and she could fly back to one of her few connections for a resupply.

Although her skills at the guitar never faltered and she remained among the best and most highly acclaimed in the music industry, the PCP was not kind to a brain that wasn't particularly literate from the get-go. When high, Shadow existed in a spastic haze of internal delirium, yet still played the hell out of her guitar. It was an extension of her delusions, and the shrill and strings painted a landscape before her which undulated with waves she and she alone controlled.

She knew Siren's catalogue, indeed, had been a key in many sessions where the songs were initially created. And even though everyone knew that she was smoking PCP before performances, they knew too that she never missed a beat, a stroke, and certainly was a force within herself in ensuring that the crowds were moved to seemingly undulate themselves at her command.

But any use of PCP can have uncertain consequences, and continued use can find a smoker dashed over the cliff and into a chasm of psychotic infinity at any unsuspecting moment. Shadow took flight sans wings half an hour before the opening act took stage in Houston, and Siren, Marvella, Freddy and Jenkins were all present to witness the disaster. New "entourage" members Genese and Sunshine were present, but had not attended the AA meeting the others were coming out of and were awaiting Siren in her dressing room.

The Silver Shadow was in rare form, many would say later, gliding about the stage behind lowered curtains and in full concert mode. Even the audience was being heatedly aroused by the pre-concert extravaganza Shadow was putting on, grazing through a riff that was partially Siren's popular "Living Life With You"-hit, and at the same time was a blazing, screaming guitar solo reminiscent of the late electric guitar master Jimi Hendrix.

Other musicians wanted her to pipe down, her solo performance completely out of context with the strict arrangement of the show and almost certain to overshadow all opening acts and maybe even making Keepin' It Easy's and Siren's premier acts pale in comparison.

"Somebody go get that crazy bitch off the stage," Georgia Whitfield-Johnson, the road manager of all things Jupiter Solice, demanded. "She's high on that shit again! Big time!"

But everyone appeared afraid to approach the Silver Shadow, her grimacing, goonie-like features, the swinging about of the guitar, appearing quite threatening. Siren was among the few who could talk to Shadow when she was high. Yet it was when under the influence herself that she most often was able to reason with the haphazard mind that was Shadow on PCP.

"I'll try and talk to her," Siren said, but Freddy, Georgia and Marvella were having none of it. The star of the show was not going to confront what appeared to be a particularly unorthodox madwoman, even if the two did have a brief but intimate history.

"I got her," Freddy said, and proceeded from offstage left where the intrigued mass of singers, musicians, handlers and company hands were gathered.

The former pro-heavyweight boxer hadn't lost much stamina since being retired 21 years earlier. Embellished with the heavy blast of electronic air Shadow forced from the speakers with her heavy-handed exhibition, Freddy took her by a shoulder before she knew it, and the sudden introduction of another human form into her addled, bedazzled mind sparked her into frenetic action.

Shadow swirled around at Freddy's touch and, without missing a guitar chord, stabbed at the massive form just a few inches taller than her. She chopped down at Freddy with the neck of the guitar, still striking strings and plucking individual high-pitched notes, all the while throwing her head back and hyperventilating, swirled a complete 360 degrees and chopped the ax down at the man before her.

Her fingers flew to the lower frets on the guitar, as Freddy saw a strength and a strangeness in her that he'd heard of from law enforcement friends as a sign that the person was on PCP. Indeed, she slashed a few notes in an eerie vibratory pitch, took a seemingly massive inhale and appeared as if she were about to levitate to the 200-foot ceiling.

Freddy decided to disconnect power to the amplifiers rather than risk having to subdue the madwoman. He moved over to a sound technician, shouted amidst the continued wail of the guitar and demanded that Shadow's power be cut off. The technician did as he was told, and immediately the wail of the guitar ceased.

Shadow looked at the now-silent instrument, took a look at the crowd gathered in the spaces off stage, took yet another deep, swelling breath, and crumbled stone cold dead to the rear stage floor.

Chapter Nineteen

The show must go on, the producers were quick to say, and although a fuss was made backstage about the sudden death of one of the world's leading guitarists, the 30,000 fans who filled the arena had no idea Rhees "Silver Shadow" Matrix had apparently decided to leave once her solo was completed, and were anxiously awaiting the main attractions.

Peaches, a 17-year-old from Atlanta who was burning up the charts with her combo rap/neo-soul hit, "Sensations," began the program. She performed a number of well-received tunes for her allotted 40 minutes and left the stage to a genuine show of affection by the crowd. Her ovation moved the crowd into performing themselves for the 15 minutes between Peaches's act and that of Fresh Flowers, another girl act on Jupiter Solice's rostrum which was a nominal draw on the upper East Coast. It was this group's guitarist who would cover for Silver Shadow when Keepin' It Easy and, lastly, Siren performed.

Members of Keepin' It Easy had committed to joining lead singer Jenkins in his quest for sobriety. Although the four tended to drink a bit too much after shows, none had devolved into the destructive use of powdered then crack cocaine that Jenkins had, and still considerably young with fresh, blossoming careers, were truly pissed at Jenkins when his drug use began to hamper their ability to perform. Some blamed Siren for Jenkins's devolution, for it was she who was more known to use coke and, since both she and Jenkins were from the same Barry Farm housing project in D.C., it was just assumed that she had reeled him into the drug use maelstrom.

That was hardly the case, however. Although Jenkins had fallen for Siren early on in both their budding careers, Siren had done all she could to shield the boy with the beautiful falsetto voice from the cocaine that was prevalent on the tours.   Over time though both were approaching the now-deceased Alvarez at the same time and, casual lovers, they began doing their mind alteration spiels together also.

At present though it was Jenkins trying to calm Siren before he and the boys took the stage. She was overly distraught over the passing of her friend Shadow and, in tears, had to be consoled by any and everyone close to her so that she would regain her composure and not leave the 30,000 fans wanting and, probably, due a refund.

"Come on, baby girl. Come on," he whispered into her ear, embracing her as Marvella, Sunshine and Genese stood close in on them. "You know Silver girl wouldn't want you to blow off all these people just because of her simple shit now, don't you?"

"I know," Siren sobbed. "I know…"

"Them dippers, yo," Sanford, a member of Keepin' It Easy and close friend of both Jenkins and Siren added. "Smokin' that Butt Naked, yo, and down for the count…"

"The way she kept at it," Freddy interjected, "that's the way she apparently wanted to go out. Flying. Girl was flying, I can say that much…"

"Look, baby," Jenkins said, holding Siren at arms length. "It's time for us to go on. Why don't you and your girls go in the dressing room and chill, take a little break. I know y'all want to watch me and the fellas show our natural asses out there, but I'm gonna forgive you this one time you don't watch me, OK?"

He smiled and gave her a look that had amused her so often in the past.

"OK, boo," she said, forced a smile and headed further backstage with Sunshine and Genese.

The atmosphere remained quite gloomy backstage, but musicians, technicians and singers moved about their preparations for the coming acts, clearly lacking any enthusiasm. Even though all knew that Silver Shadow was indulging in a substance whose history frightened most all who heard the tales, when sober she was among the most joyful and pleasant persons on the tour.

She'd been with Jupiter Solice since just after its founding, among the musicians who formed the "house band" that did studio work for a number of singers. She'd been with Siren since the fresh young 18-year-old entered the elaborate New York City studios, and even though it was widely rumored that Shadow favored women, Siren never saw the special attention Shadow gave to her and her music as anything other than a professional courtesy.

"I loved her, for real, though, y'all," Siren said, again weeping but in a comfortable room with only her two best friends. "That lady played the hell out of the guitar. I ain't never want no one else backing me up on guitar. We could always get a good drummer, bass player, the brass. But Shadow on guitar? Man!"

There was champagne in the room, an acquiescence by Siren to Sunshine and Genese. The two had never had a drug problem, were not alcoholics, but enjoyed a fine drink every now and then, especially the Dom Perignon Vintage 2003, which they'd only dreamed about after seeing rap artists in videos flaunt it.

And Siren knew she was not to have a drink herself; part of the recovery program to stave off her relapse into drug use emphasized that any drug use, including that initial drug for many, alcohol, could serve as a spark to the use of more deadly substances. Yet it was calling out to her, three bottles thrust down in ice in silver buckets.

"Why don't y'all drink some of this Dom?" she said, moving over to the dresser where champagne and glasses stood. "Shit! I'm 'bout to have some my got-damn self! In memory of my girl Shadow."

Sunshine and Genese stared hard at one another, both beginning to shake their heads as one as if in musical synchronicity.

"Girl, don't!" both said in unison.

Siren glowered at them, hand on one bottle whose cork had already been removed.

"What the fuck is this?" she said, turning and wiping a tear.

"You know," Sunshine, passive again, began. "What they said in them meetings about one drink being a spark."

"Girl," Genese said, always the more boisterous and take-charge of the three. "Just don't do the shit, that's all! Ain't no excuse you bringing that in here for …'your girls!' Hell, dude in the meeting say you relapse mentally before you do physically. Your ass had the mindset to get back rolling, at first with this, from the get-go. Don't be throwing that on us, Siren-a! Now sit your ass down and leave that right there alone! Get ready for your show!"

Siren sniffled, removed her hand from the bottle, slowly glided over to the plush seat before the vanity and eased into the settee. She looked at herself in the mirror, the 15 lights framing it giving her a sparkling, surreal glow. She wiped away the tears, began opening make-up containers.

"Sunshine, go tell Shonda it's time to get me ready, OK sis?"

"OK!" Sunshine said enthusiastically.

"And Genese? Bring your ass over her girl and do that thing you do with my hair!"

Genese laughed, a measure of relief in her gait as she moved up behind her dear friend, grabbed a teasing comb and began fussing with Siren's hair, the locks shimmering in a haze as tears began forming but not yet flowing.

"You know I got your back, girl," Genese said, then began to weep. Siren spun around in the settee, reached over its back and hugged Genese around the waist.

"Thanks, Genese," she said, tears flowing freely. "Thank you, girl…"

Chapter Twenty

"What a show!"

"Day---ummmm!!"

"Girl sang her ass off!!!"

"Man!!!!"

Laudatory comments were being issued by the thousands of fans filtering out of the arena, and more were accompanied by congratulatory plaudits being shouted amidst the flashes of camera lights and shouts of a fortunate few reporters who had backstage passes. Siren seemed to have put some emotions into her set which had previously been suppressed, many stated. Not only had she sang with seemingly added spiritual energy her entire catalogue of No. 1 hits, but had taken unrehearsed and unexpected moments to simply talk to her audience, to speak sincerely of personal trials many were aware of, and some even Marvella said later that she was unfamiliar with.

"Day---uummm that was one hell of a show!" Jenkins shouted, taking Siren in a bear hug while others clamored to get close to her. "Day----uuummmm, girl!"

She spoke for a minute to the familiar reporter from the gossip television station, Shonda close in upon her clearing away the sweat and trying to make Siren appear like the superstar who'd just performed and not an Olympic sprinter, which was how she appeared returning from the stage drenched in sweat.

"Even without your main guitarist, The Silver Shadow," Abby Vann, the "Hollywood Remote" television reporter asked. "And, Siren: Just what has happened to Shadow? Is she no longer with you?"

That brought Siren again to tears, and even as she was escorted out of reach of all and to her dressing room, the astute reporter managed to get word from a stagehand that Rhees Matrix, aka Silver Shadow, had died.

Another round of bad press followed, now with the more well-heeled reporters doing enough expansive research to make a case that Jupiter Solice had drug dealers embedded in its ranks. While at the same time, Jeremiah, true Jupiter Solice patriarch Cord Fredericks and other principles were examining the books with accountants and about to level charges against Marcus. And while they were at it and the spotlight was on them, they jointly reasoned, why not lay the drug dealing charges at his feet also.

A grey-haired 67-year-old of fine stature and with history on Wall Street, Cord Fredericks had provided a bulk of the initial investment capital to start Jupiter Solice. The record company was little more than a toy to the seasoned businessman though. Jeremiah was the son of Cord's beloved sister Corinne, and having no children himself (he claimed he was too busy to bother with parenting and had never married) he was quite willing to pour a considerable part of his vast fortune into the venture presented quite professionally to him by the young nephew and his talkative partner Marcus.

Indeed, the business model the two young men put forth ten years earlier was quite impressive. Cord would hold 51 percent of the voting stock in the record company, and the remaining percentage divided equally between the other two principles.

Jupiter Solice was a success within 18 months, as promised in the business model. Jeremiah proved quite astute at gauging talent, stocked the record company with some of the finest yet unknown musicians from New York City and Washington, D.C. "underground" music venues, and along with Marcus began signing fresh young talents which combined to flood a floundering music industry with recordings radio stations were virtually forced to play, if only because of demand from the public.

Profits soared, not in small part due to the contracts the labels finest artists were eager to ink while primarily under the guidance of entertainment attorneys whom Marcus had put on retainer.   They were greedily committed to Marcus's scheme, presenting to artists contracts he had, with his own legal background, ensured were flush with jargon which provided measly amounts to the artists and grand sums in actual and residual monies to the company.

In time Marcus became intimately involved in the private wishes of the company's artists, particularly their appetite for things grand.   Most having come from dire poverty, Marcus realized that when afforded previously unimagined luxuries, the artists tended to over consume.

Liquor, and later drugs, would become substances which not only served to addle the business senses of some of Jupiter Solice's artists, but in time would be central in another scheme in which the fortunes actually paid some artists were redirected into Marcus's personal accounts.

Cord was heading the meeting with Jeremiah and two accountants from the esteemed firm of Hanford, Grace, Donnelly, who'd already discovered that monies from Jupiter Solice had been funneled into a company whose sole owner was Marcus James Elliot.   They had no way of looking at the books of that company, but an investigator hired by Cord had done some serious snooping, and had documented that four of the deceased "lighting technicians" on the tours, later proven to have connections to a South American drug cartel, had received enormous checks from the straw company Marcus had set up.

"I think we've got enough on…this…fellow…to not only officially remove him from any further dealings with the record company," Cord said at the hastily called meeting, "but from the facts gathered by my investigator, we'd be in breach of our fiduciary responsibilities if we didn't turn our findings over to law enforcement."

Jeremiah loved Marcus like a brother, but was a realist, and was certainly not one with the stamina to do any prison time himself should any discoveries show that he had knowledge of this grave malfeasance and had done nothing about it.

"I agree with you, sir," he said directly to his uncle. "We need to move on this immediately."

Chapter Twenty-one

There was a break in the tour; five days off before another series of shows from the West Coast to the upper Mid-West and then concluding with shows in Philadelphia, Boston, New York, D.C. and Richmond. Things were going great; Siren and Jenkins were counting their days of sobriety, had been joined in regular AA/NA meetings by a number of musicians, technicians, friends and family of each major act, and the professionals secured for the tour by the record label. Jeremiah dropped in on occasion, but everyone recognized that a near ever present Marcus, always one to feign a cool most snidely noted he did not even possess, had been noticeably missing.

He had skimmed $17.9 million from the company, and when one considered that he had legally justified profits totaling more than $34 million this year, one might have thought that Marcus would have been quite comfortable and satisfied. But greed at this level often fed on itself, and much like the cocaine he'd ensured was available to many in his musical empire, Marcus couldn't get enough money to satisfy his expansive dreams.

His palatial home in the Bahamas was flush with luxuries. He had no children; considered himself a playboy and had no shortage of women. There was also the 130-foot yacht he wanted to upgrade from, the penthouse in New York City just blocks from Jupiter Solice headquarters, and the palatial estate in New Canaan, Connecticut. So in real financial terms, he did need a steady and considerable amount of income.

Except for the fact that Marcus did little to actually earn any money. He'd always made his fortune by way of the fortunes, and some might say misfortunes, of others.

When Cord and Jeremiah were made aware of the extent of Marcus's thievery, they had corporate attorneys petition the courts to have a warrant sworn out for Marcus's arrest. Their attorneys also moved immediately to have all of his assets frozen. But that effort failed; there were no judicially recognized malfeasances as of yet, and not until Marcus was found and jailed on the pending charges would any judge even consider weighing in on the freezing of fortunes which were so expansive. And Marcus James Elliot remained, on paper, a founder of the Jupiter Solice recording empire. What the other principles, and their attorneys, needed to do was have him arrested on the thievery and drug charges.

Immediately.

Some of the company's artists were being deposed; Siren and Jenkins about their knowledge of Marcus's involvement with Alvarez, others who could state under oath that Marcus had personally introduced them to the slain drug kingpin, Salvadore Paz. There was enough evidence to bring Marcus in.

But he could not be found.

He knew they were on to him. Cord and Jeremiah had no way of knowing it, but even as they and their attorneys put together a case against Marcus, he was aboard the Precious Cargo, having instructed his yacht's captain to make way for the Cayman Islands. At the same time, massive amounts of both personal and record company capital were being electronically routed to the same location, his off-shore accounts already bountiful with other ill-gotten gains.

They were just along the Outer Banks between Virginia and North Carolina, Marcus just having a good old time with three young women who were looking forward to their promised singing careers with Jupiter Solice but who in truth couldn't sing a lick. They were due to pull into port near Kitty Hawk and refuel, Marcus having paid his captain and small crew handsomely in advance, with assurances that there was greater wealth awaiting them at their destination.

He'd been quite aware of the brouhaha going on surrounding "his" record company; the death of Silver Shadow had served to uncover a considerable drug conspiracy associated with Jupiter Solice, and in press reports he had been personally named as a conduit to an elaborate drug scheme feeding cocaine to moneyed, music industry customers.

Few names were mentioned in the reports within the music industry besides Marcus's. Most of the drug dealers mentioned had all died recently, under circumstances which, news stories emphasized, had actually sparked the expanding investigation.

So Marcus was on the run, and didn't believe there was any way that he could be caught. But law enforcement wasn't the only group after him. It had been proven that he'd been ripping off some of Jupiter Solice's premiere artists, and some of them, born and raised on hardscrabble streets, were not going to sit and wait for the law to level justice.

Chapter Twenty-two

Siren and Jenkins were getting it on.

"Damn, girl!" he said, whispering in her ear as they enmeshed as one on her massive bed. "Aw, shit!"

He came, and the warmth filling her was a heated reminder that he had convinced her that a condom wasn't necessary. He'd been tested for HIV as a measure of course for his recording contract, he lied, and any concern about a pregnancy? He'd welcome a child by the young woman he was beginning to express his love for, though she assured him that she loved him too but that a child would seriously blunt her renewed career. There was a prescription to assure that that didn't happen, she let him know, and after a good measure of foreplay, they had at it.

Another thing which was frowned upon among alcoholics and addicts was sex between members engaged in the same recovery program. It was viewed as a conceptual replacement for the previous get-high, and might lead to a heated exchange among those with something in common considering a joint revisiting of their previous mind-altering explorations. Often recovering addicts used sex as the heated seat to replace the one which had them soaring with some drug or alcohol and, already personally associated and in constant proximity to one another, Siren and Jenkins began having sex whenever they could steal away together.

They lay together on a Wednesday night, having put on a dynamic show the previous weekend in Atlanta, flown home, put in time with family and business associates before taking off, alone but for Marvella and Freddy, to the McLean estate. Although Freddy was her prime security person, there were others on contract to watch over the popular songstress, on the road and at home. So Freddy, having been asked to New York for a business meeting with

Jeremiah and Cord, had seen her home and immediately taken off. Marvella had her own business to attend to in her generous quarters on the estate, an adjunct to the fine home she had long wanted, and Siren had paid for fully, in her old neighborhood. So until Friday, when yet another leg of the tour would commence in Boston, Siren and Jenkins were pretty much left to themselves.

"You know I love you, baby," Jenkins whispered, a dim light glistening off the sweat on his upper lip inches before her eyes.

"I know you do, Jenks," she smiled. "I know you do."

"You know I want to marry you one day too, don't you?"

"Umm..."

"Don't you?"

She smiled, turned over and eased back into him.

"I know..."

He draped an arm over her small waist, pulled her tighter. He was limp, but positioned so that his penis was flush against her buttocks. He began kissing on the nape of her neck.

"I love you, girl. Love you..."

He grew hard again, and she rolled over to accept his kiss, his warmth. His passion reignited and in an excited poster he moved atop her, in her, sweats again mixing and him extending into a position propped on outstretched arms just above her. He believed that he was showing the love he had for her with the feelings he'd stated but with words no longer necessary. A pleasurable joining, a rhythmic excursion and an utterance from her that was incoherent. Exhaustion overtaking him yet again, he eased down to rest so lightly upon her. He rolled to the side after completion of the ride with Siren flush against his side.

"You know I love you too, Jenks," she said. "I do. Really…"

Chapter Twenty-three

"I ain't no goddamn bounty hunter!" Freddy blasted the other two men in the boardroom. "That's what the goddamn police are for!"

Cord didn't feel too comfortable upsetting the huge, muscular man. It was evident as he twitched around in his leather chair at the head of the conference table, looking over his wire-rimmed glasses to Jeremiah. He would sneak a peak at Freddy when feigning as if he were looking at the folders and papers before him. Freddy was seated three chairs down from him on the left side of the conference table, which seated twelve to each side. Jeremiah was in the right chair closest to the director, and he wouldn't look at Freddy either.

"We were....prepared to offer you...twenty percent of what we're seeking to recover from him," Cord said, shuffling through the papers, peering into a folder. "That would be somewhere in the neighborhood of $1.79 million-"

Freddy then appeared to freeze in place, cutting eyes between the two..

"One point seven-nine million dollars?" Freddy said, quickly doing the math. "He stole around $8.9 million from the company?"

"A conservative estimate," Jeremiah said.

"And you say your electronics people got a GPS reading on exactly where the boat is and know where he's heading?" Freddy said, calmer now.

"They fitted his yacht with the systems. On the company's dime and probably the bastard expensed the yacht to the company too," Cord said. He leafed through one folder, slid a ream of printed papers to Freddy. "He was refilling and taking on stores near the Outer Banks this morning. Will have to make another stop somewhere along the east coast of Florida before heading into the Caribbean. Perhaps you can intercept him there."

Freddy looked through the papers. They contained current tracking of the Precious Cargo.

"Sheeee----yit," Freddy said, leaning back in the leather chair and rubbing his chin. "If you gentlemen are ready to write me a check for half of that bounty now, other half upon completion, you got yourselves a deal."

Cord picked up the phone on the table before him. "I'll call Finance now. You can pick up the check on your way out."

"And we should add a measure for expenses," Jeremiah said.

"Certainly," said Cord.

"I'll want somebody thorough covering Siren when the tour resumes tomorrow," Freddy said, rising. "I'll make a few calls. They'll be in touch with her and Marvella and Georgia about the pay and arrangements."

"I'll talk to Georgia and Marvella also myself," Jeremiah said.

"Alright, gentlemen," Freddy said, moving around the table to shake each man's hand. "I never really liked that sucker anyway."

* * *

He had told the captain and First Mate that he was not to be disturbed, and with Belle, Shantelle and Carole Ann, was stretched out in the yacht's master bedroom butter-ball naked, snorting cocaine, drinking scotch, watching Carole Ann do her turn on the pole he'd had installed in the bedroom as if it were a club for exotic dancers. The boat, moored in a rented space near Nag's Head, rocked a little on generous waves. Night had fallen, but the small crew, the captain, First Mate and cook, had gone ashore and were given the night off. As an added incentive he'd given each $2000 cash and told them to not return until the following noon, earliest. Marcus was having one hell of a time exercising his hedonistic pleasures.

The ladies had already been given lump sums of cash, and an astute Shantelle, his acquisition to sate his desire for dark meat, had watched him retrieve the bounds of cash from a store in a closet which she was certain had additional mounds totaling in the hundreds of thousands of dollars. A native New Yorker, Shantelle couldn't help but mentally form a plan to rip off her current sponsor for all the ready cash; she knew that she and Belle and Carole Ann couldn't sing that well, and a native of the hardscrabble streets of Brooklyn, she knew that a bird in the hand...as the old saying goes.

They had sang for him. Sure. But from the outset of this wayward voyage he had let it be known that he wanted much more from them than song. So each in her own turn had fucked him, sucked him, and engaged in such raunchy displays of sexual debauchery that even Belle, who once made her living as a prostitute, appeared somewhat embarrassed.

The cocaine had him paranoid. Or was it the marijuana he toked on occasionally? The scotch didn't help the matter much when it came to Marcus making any sense of what was going on outside his heightened physical senses, and he didn't even notice that Shantelle had been gone for about an hour after Carole Ann had teasingly tormented her with an expert tongue, while his own tongue flitted and flattered clitoral sensationalism from Belle. She was planted firmly upon his face now, Carole Ann kneeling near the foot of the round bed with mouth bobbling about his penis, when Shantelle and a strange, wiry black man crept into the room.

"Now ain't this a sight," the black man said, moving up behind Carole Ann's upraised rear and slapping a hand between her ass cheeks. "Make me want some of this shit my damn self!"

Carole Ann sprung upright, still on her knees, twisted around and scooted to the head of the bed. Belle looped a leg off of the side of Marcus's head and slid back to the head of the bed also. Groggy, his face sparkling with vaginal juices, Marcus propped himself up on his elbows, shook his head somewhat then looked to the stranger alongside Shantelle standing at the foot of his bed.

"Fuck you want, fella?" Marcus slurred. "And who the hell invited you aboard?"

The man reached to the small of his back, retrieved a large, ominous-looking pistol and pointed it directly at Marcus."This invited me aboard, motherfucker," he said, aiming the gun angularly.

"Whoa whoa whoa!" Marcus said, sobriety seemingly taking over him in an instant. "There's....there's no....no need...no need for that, fella! You want...what? Cash? Take the fucking cash, man! No need for violence! I got plenty for you! Just put...put the goddamn gun away!"

"It's over there," Shantelle said, motioning towards the oak doors to a closet.

"Shantelle? Sweetheart? So this is how you're going to repay me after all the trust I put in you?" Marcus said.

"Trust my ass, motherfucker," Shantelle said. "Recording contract. All that...that bullshit about making us famous! Look at your ass: Eating goddamn pussy. Getting your dick sucked. Smoking weed and snorting the fuck outta some yayo. Fuck you, Marcus! I'm getting paid! Now!"

The gunman wrenched open the closet door with such force that it tore off its hinges. He saw the safe inside, turned and again aimed the gun at Marcus.
"Open this motherfucker, yo."
His naked form shaking from both the drugs and the unexpected visual trauma being visited upon him, Marcus

kneeled and crawled to the edge of the bed, arose on weak legs and wobbled over to the closet. He fumbled at first with the combination, but the man placed the gun close to his temple and demanded that he calm down.

"I ain't gonna shoot your ass, bitch," the gunman said. "Just open this motherfucker and me and ol' girl will be on our way."

"Y'all get dressed," Shantelle said to Carole Ann and Belle. "This motherfucker got mad bank in there. We gonna split this shit up between us, and you know with that kinda cash, and what he already gave us, he ain't get this shit legally, like. Won't be no po-po looking for our asses, you know? Ain't no need of continuing on with this game of his and going down to the Caribbean and shit and serving his ass and do. Fuck this motherfucker! Let's just get paid right now and roll out."

The ladies gave her a hard look, but began quickly dressing.

"Well shit, since we ripping his ass off, I want that stash of coke and weed he got there in the side drawer," Carole Ann said, slipping on panties and hobbling over to a bedside table.

She retrieved what appeared to be a plastic bag containing a few grams of white powder, and a larger, freezer-size plastic bag bulging with apparent marijuana. Marcus twisted the handle on the four-foot tall safe, opened it. The gunman took him by the shoulder and easily flung him back into the room.

"Bingo!" the gunman said, kneeled and began pulling bound, three-inch thick bundles of cash from the safe. "You wasn't lying, baby girl! This motherfucker is loaded!"

The visage of a cold, abused, dark Brooklyn girl stood beside the grinning gunman, hand slowly easing into the oversized purse she had strung over her shoulder. As the gunman continued bobbing about joyously on his knees, piling the mounds of money back behind him, Shantelle took a silent step until she was standing just above him, pulled her own pistol from the purse and squeezed off one round to a point just behind the gunman's left ear.

"Oh, shit!" three voices rang out in the cabin as one, shock draining the blood from the faces of Marcus, Belle and Carole Ann.

Shantelle paid them no mind. She bent and retrieved the final wads of money from the safe, took a foot and pushed the dead gunman upside the partially disengaged closet door. Placing the money in her purse, she then moved to the mound the gunman had amassed behind him, began tossing them onto the large, round bed.

"Well," she said, looking from Belle to Carole Ann. "Finish getting dressed and put the goddamn money in your pocketbooks! What? Y'all asses better get to it!"

"You think," Belle began, tightening the belt around her khaki dress, "that people in the boats around here....heard that?"

"Heard what?" Shantelle said, stepping to the bed and securing more bounds of cash.

"That...gun...that gunshot?"

"Fuck," Shantelle said. "This fool had music blasting down here and we couldn't hardly make it out coming down the dock. What boat it was coming from and shit. Plus people down on that bigger yacht partying their asses off! With that rock music shit! Ain't nobody hear nothing."

"But what...," Marcus was at a loss for words, evidently scared, setting near the head of the bed and easing into a pair of tight, colorful shorts no grown man should ever be seen in. "What..what are you going to do....I mean...with me...urr...Shan...Shanteen?"

"Fuck you!" Shantelle blasted. "Motherfucker don't even remember my name and just hours ago me and my girls were gonna be your next big stars! Fuuuu---uuuuu---ggg you!"

The ladies were dressed, each securing bundles of the money Marcus had amassed, had stolen, and had planned to use as operating capital to get him to the Grand Caymans, where the true bulk of his stolen wealth lay.

"Fuck you!" Shantelle said again, nodded to Belle and Carole Ann.

The women left the boat together, leaving Marcus with a corpse and with quite a mess on his hands.

Chapter Twenty-four

From Boston the tour returned to New York City for one night then put on two shows in Charlotte before going to Atlanta and then Miami. All the while the stars were required to make appearances on radio shows, television shows and for a few, at book stores for signings and promotions of CDs. Siren was quite content, and it showed in her performances. With her man Jenkins always near at hand (Keepin' It Easy was always the second-billed act on the tour, and quite a draw themselves) and having on payroll good friends Sunshine and Genese, she began to feel that there was no longer any need for her to attend the AA/NA meetings embedding in the tour and, indeed, felt that she could again indulge in the occasional few glasses of champagne. By the time the hectic tour reached Miami, Siren was self-assured that she could engage in a celebratory bottle of a once-favored cognac. Her birthday was that Friday, and in the past she had gone all out in throwing a most expansive celebration.

Freddy wasn't around during the Atlanta leg of the tour, nor had he been for the previous performances on the upper East Coast. She did have security specifically chosen by her long-time bodyguard, and Jeremiah mentioned in passing that Freddy would be back among them in Miami. He was already there in fact, Jeremiah said, taking care of some urgent business for the record company.

She was about to turn 26, and after the current tour, would be given a well-deserved break and do nothing more than studio work for the coming 14 months. Dr. Samuelson looked in on the tour ever so often. He was, after all, paid an exorbitant retainer of sorts to provide specialized care to Jupiter Solice artists and employees, and on the Thursday before Siren's birthday and the last concert of the tour, he'd been asked to fly down to Miami to look into the complaints of the tour's star.

Antsy about the tour ending and mentally anticipating a spurt away from sobriety in celebration of her birthday, Siren had been feeling nauseous, throwing up shortly after meals, experiencing periods of chills and had begun sweating profusely at other times. Dr. Samuelson gave Siren a brief examination an hour before the show, and told her in private that her medical condition was fine. She was, however, seven weeks pregnant.

"Oh, snap!" was her immediate response. "For real, doctor?"

"I'm most certain," the elderly gentleman smiled. "And as I've been informed, you're supposed to be off the road for the next year or so. Timing couldn't have been better."

"Umm huh."

Dressing, she seemed a bit melancholy, and the doctor was confused.

"So, about the father…"

"Ummmm…."

"Somebody….someone I know?"

He knew that Jeremiah and Marcus kept their acts formed into such a tight knit, familial group that, more than likely, the father was someone also within the organization. He'd noticed her being particularly cordial with the boy from the group Keepin' It Easy…Jenkins, he recalled. Jenkins was another member of the group who had been under his watchful eye for his previous indulgence in illegal narcotics.

"You know him," Siren said finally, smiling. "But I want to tell him in my own way. And doctor? Please don't tell Marvella, Jeremiah or Freddy or anybody! I don't want anyone to know just yet. Okay?"

"Okay."

Chapter Twenty-five

He'd had $300,000 wired to a bank in Port Wentworth, Georgia from his Cayman account, and had managed to get the body of the lanky black man up to the rear of the yacht that dreadful night without any help and without anyone seeing him. Weighing it down with barbells (he did not work out; the captain did) he eased the body into the chopping waters and it sank immediately. Rushing just before sunrise, he found a mop and bucket, toiled at erasing away the bloody trail he'd left dragging the body aft. It took a while before he was able to completely clear the bloodstains; handling a mop was not something he'd ever done, and getting on his knees with a sponge and bucket to clean the pool of blood in his bedroom cabin made him feel uncharacteristically servile.

Quite nervous after the ordeal, he found himself in anxious need of the cocaine, which had been taken by "that black bitch," as he mentally identified Shantelle. He had bars stocked with the finest liquors, refrigerators in three locations stocked with a variety of imported and domestic beers capable of serving a party of 30 or more.

But not until this very moment had he even considered that the powdered cocaine, which he kept and snorted with regularity, had him addicted. Those addicted to cocaine smoked it in its converted, crack rock form, he believed. And after all, he was an affluent white male; his mental depiction of a drug addict was invariably of a black man or woman, downtrodden and skulking about on some inner-city street corner.

He moved to the well-appointed galley, looked in the double-wide stainless steel refrigerator for sustenance. Marcus hadn't so much as boiled an egg in his privileged lifetime, so although he wanted ham, bacon, even a portion of the roasted chicken he saw covered within as a menial breakfast, he didn't even consider placing any of the leftovers in a microwave oven that was affixed atop the sink to his left. Yet he knew he had to place some food in his stomach, for he was surely going to put a serious dent in that bottle of scotch by his bedside, and wanted to be a bit lucid when the crew returned so that he could instruct the captain on a slight alteration in their course.

Spotting the microwave out the corner of one eye while still perusing the selection in the refrigerator, he reasoned that the appliance couldn't be too hard to use. He'd never even had to operate one before, not even during his college years, when family money afforded him off-campus housing with a full-service staff. He'd seen Arlene, the black cook and housekeeper provided him during college, use one when he happened into the kitchen for beer. Hell, it couldn't be that complex, he thought, if that old bird could use it efficiently.

He took the remainder of the roasted chicken from the refrigerator, peeled back the clear, cellophane covering, centered it on the expensive, shiny silver serving platter and, with a self-satisfactory smile, pushed a button that allowed the microwave door to open.

"Piece of cake," he grinned, shoving the bird and platter into the eye-level oven. "Now, let's see..."

One button was labeled "Express Defrost."

He pushed it.

It was the light from within that bedazzled him, wrenched in the focus of eyes that hadn't slept for a while and a brain still suffering from the trauma of the heist, the murder, and certainly the overconsumption of cocaine and impassioned climaxes bought on by women professional at invoking such. The crackling sound further captured his warped mind and it was only seconds but seemed like eons when he eased his face closer to the light and the crackling sound and the sizzling and smoke and BAM!!!

The microwaves reacted harshly to being catapulted in a zillion arching patterns off of the silver platter and the internal chaos sought immediate release by blasting out the glass front of the microwave along with dozens of chips of plastic shards travelling at twice the speed of light accompanied by bone and meat from the chicken, all spat viciously into the inquisitive face of Marcus James Elliot.

The blast forced him back a small measure, but the body went limp and pitched to the floor, the face in a mask of grisly disarray: pink and shredded, with blood slowly making its way to the surface but unassisted by a heart which no longer pumped blood through a suddenly useless, lifeless body.

Chapter Twenty-six

Of course the young, primarily black and female administrative staff saw that word about Marcus's death spread throughout the core of Jupiter Solice. The secretaries in New York got wind when Cord, Jeremiah and other members of the board were summoned to a conference also attended by the investigators who'd been dispatched to find Marcus's ill-gotten gains and those who'd been examining the corporation's finances. Freddy had been rerouted from Florida to exercise his skills with law enforcement officials. He was privy to information aboard the yacht which even others in the Jupiter Solice hierarchy might have had problems accessing.

The boat's captain had discovered Marcus's disfigured corpse. It appeared that he had died as a result of a quite unfortunate accident, and since there was little money on the yacht, no evident indication of any drug use, it was quickly assumed that Marcus, surely under the influence of alcohol, had died as a result of a fatal mishap. Freddy spoke with on scene investigators for a moment, was rebuffed when trying to retrieve the hard drive from Marcus's computer, but otherwise was allowed to do a cursory examination of the yacht's living quarters. Of course he was accompanied all along the way by locals, who'd immediately vetted him, not trusting the credentials he'd presented, and found him on the up-and-up.

Freddy was first to notice the tell-tale signs of some sort drug use. The remains of powdery trails on the glass top of a bedside table caught his attention first, and further indications pointed out by him to the investigators to study the possibility if the presence of more persons other than the deceased on the yacht, and for a time immediately preceding his death.

"He had himself some whores up in this piece," Freddy pronounced in his gruff, analytical voice. "Doing cocaine. Drinking expensive liquors. And the open safe: Appears as if someone made off with his ready cash, or something else, before departing."

"Got signs of blood over here too," a forensics investigator said, examining the floor outside the closet containing the empty safe. "Attempt was made to clean it up. Perhaps by the deceased."

Freddy immediately telephoned his findings back to Jeremiah, and was asked to fly back to New York and deliver a presentation of facts to the record company executives. Immediately, Jeremiah and Cord had their legal and financial experts begin a search of the financial transactions of Marcus, and soon discovered the deposit which had been awaiting him in Port Wentworth. Tracing the source to the Cayman's account was quite easy, and before Freddy even arrived back at headquarters a few well-placed requests (though not all legal) had turned up the amounts and the accounts of Marcus Elliot in the Cayman Islands.

The lawyers immediately filed an injunction to freeze the accounts in case any of Marcus's heirs laid claim to them, easily proving that the funds had been diverted from a Jupiter Solice account and were actually company monies.

Word of Marcus's death moved quickly into the ranks of the artists, many of whom had been suspicious of him and his constant citing of "contractual obligations" in forcing them to make unpaid appearances at social events later discovered to have been held with exorbitant admission fees. Those monies, and many other funds pouring into Jupiter Solice, never found their way to the artists largely responsible for generating them.

"Operational expenses," Marcus usually categorized expenditures from the leasing of spaces to the leasing of buses to the paying for of catered dinners. A joke among the artists was that Marcus's renowned stock of expensive wines and liquors, stored in either his 5th Avenue penthouse or the New Canaan, Connecticut manse, were all financed entirely with "operational expenses."

Marcus was gone now, however. And as repulsive as his business practices were among artists and company personnel, he had been a major part of the Jupiter Solice family.

Siren and Keepin' It Easy were finishing up their tour, with Siren just about to tell Jenkins about the pregnancy, when they received word of Marcus's demise. They were all spending some down time in Miami before returning to their individual homes, and as the celebratory champagne poured well into the next day, both Siren and Jenkins begged off consuming anything but spring waters and fruit juices. Both appeared to be comforted in their short period of sobriety by one another, and even Sunshine and Genese felt safe going about celebrating themselves and leaving the two obvious lovebirds alone at the spacious suite Siren had been put up in.

Marvella had been in a private meeting with Freddy before he left abruptly, and it was she and Georgia Whitefield-Johnson, Jupiter Solice's manager of the tour, who broke the news to little groups and individuals about Marcus.

"Day-yum!" Jenkins said upon receiving the news, speed-walking down the hallway to the penthouse suite with Siren. "That's some fucked-up shit!"

"Marcus," Siren said quietly, reflecting on the man who had been for a large part responsible for her career. "Yeah...that's fucked up..."

Tears welled, in both their eyes. They entered the suite and moved slowly to the spacious view out onto the calm waters of the Atlantic, viewing the towering condo units aligning the shores left and right. Siren stood before the closed glass doors to the balcony, the air conditioning blowing a cool silence which contrasted with the heat evident out on the Miami afternoon.

Following the previous night's final show, they had been feted at a most healthy late night social event, had appeared together at an afternoon meeting of the tour's principles, and were now both crestfallen, memories of Marcus, even with all his suspect shenanigans, serving to mellow out any celebratory airs.

Jenkins stepped up behind her, placed his hands around her and clasped them upon her exposed midsection. She took a deep breath, as his warm hands served to remind her that beneath them lay a life forming for which he was responsible for initiating.

"Yeah, that's sad," she said, gazing at their 40th floor view.

"You know it," he whispered, inches from her ear.

"Freddy ain't say how it happened, just an accident on his yacht."

"Freddy knows more than he's telling."

She took a deep breath, leaned her head back into his shoulder.

"He did some messed up stuff with the money and all," she said. "But the man did get you and I and your boys rolling big-time."

"Yeah. But that was one slick motherfucker, know what I'm saying?"

"I know, Jenks. I know..."

"Still don't know if Jeremiah know all that dude stoled from the company. From us, even."

"Yeah. But from what I hear from the girls in the front office, they was on to something. And that's why he was rolling out, down south, I hear. Heading to the islands or someplace."

"Caymans, what I heard."

"Yeah. That's where them slick boys be hiding cash they don't want nobody to know about."

"Probably half of it was our money..."

Jenkins moved to the nearby kitchen, pulled upon one side of the massive refrigerator and retrieved two bottles of fruit juice. When he returned, Siren had moved to the expansive sofa, kicked off her shoes and stretched out lengthwise. He sat before her, twisted the top off of one drink and handed it to her.

"I know you was cool with Marcus and shit," he said. "But you know that was one scheming white boy. My legal peoples say he was taking us for bad for quite a while, yo. I mean, may he rest in peace, but ol' boy was ripping on us hard about the capital, know what I'm saying?"

"I know, baby. I know."

"Thieving ass mother—" But he stopped himself, as Siren cut cold eyes to him which communicated that he should not speak ill of the dead. He opened his juice, took a long pull from the bottle and placed the other hand on Siren's exposed midsection. She twisted away, onto her side, back to him, cupping her stomach and burrowing her head into a mound of lush pillows at the head of the sofa.

"What's wrong, baby?" he asked, placing his drink on the coffee table before the sofa.

"Ain't nothing wrong," she said without turning. "You know: Just   sad   about   Marcus...and...a little...something something..."

The sofa was deep enough for him to stretch out along side her, to her back. Again, he looped an arm over her, palming her stomach. Moving a measure of her hair out of his face, he snuggled up to her and placed his lips near her ear. She could feel his sudden erection pressing up against her, and attempted to push herself further into the back of the sofa.

"What's wrong, baby," he whispered. "You know you like this..."

She twisted around slowly, face inches from his, looked into his smiling brown eyes.

"Maybe I like it too much," she said, allowing a slight smile. "You know what, Jenks?"

"What?"

"I'm pregnant."

It seemed as if he was allowing what was said to sink in. He looked into her eyes as she again smiled, and he twisted onto his back, sat bolt upright, looked down upon her.

"You're pregnant, girl?!! For real?!!"

"About two months."

"Aw, snap!!"

He leaned into her, embraced her, kissed her lightly on the lips then sprang to his feet as if about to do a jig.

"Aw, man!" he shouted, threw his head back to the ceiling then cupped his hands to the side of his head. "Baby!! That's...that's...aw snap!!"

Chapter Twenty-seven

It did not take a whole lot of legal maneuvering to prove that a good volume of the funds Marcus had presumably secreted into the Cayman Islands accounts were in fact Jupiter Solice monies. Cord and Jeremiah waited until Marcus was given a proper burial before informing his immediate heirs, his mother and father, that their inheritance was not as expansive as first reported. Certainly Marcus, single with no children, had amassed a considerable fortune. But the amounts he had on paper were subject to the intense scrutiny of Jupiter Solice accountants and legal staff, and his fortune, though in actuality in the tens of millions of dollars in cash, stock and property, was considerably whittled down when his ill-gotten gains were extracted.

The monies generated an auditing of Jupiter Solice's books by outside accountants, and even though the company as a whole benefited through the recovery of monies stolen by Marcus. The audit also revealed the way in which company monies had been diverted, and as a result Jupiter Solice's top earning acts, Siren and Keepin' It Easy, each received a sudden infusion of funds which amounted to tens of millions of dollars and substantially wiped out the recovered amount Marcus had redirected.

Of course Siren's personal entertainment attorney, and the attorneys for Keepin' It Easy, participated in a monitoring of the audit and thus earned their third of the pilfered millions. But still Siren and Jenkins, already having personal assets well over $100 million in cash, stocks, property and other investments, received an additional infusion of cash which would keep both wealthy if either never sang another note.

Performance was in their blood however, and even as her pregnancy progressed, Siren was writing new music and collaborating with her "fiancé," Jenkins Shorter, while both she and Keepin' It Easy were on a hiatus from live performances.

For strictly business reasons, both the wedding of Jenkins and Siren and their pending parenthood were kept from the public. Siren sold millions of records worldwide to a young male demographic that envisioned the sultry, beautiful songstress singing personally to them, studies showed, and her being single and available, if only in their youthful fantasies, fueled a good 40 percent of record sales.

Similarly, the lead singer of Keepin' It Easy, Jenkins, was the heartthrob of millions of young female record buyers. Jupiter Solice had spent a pretty penny contracting studies which showed that other marquee performers, previous sellers of millions of dollars in CDs, experienced a serious drop in sales and concert attendance when viewed by their key demographic as no longer single and available.

Five groups from Jupiter went out on the "Reconciliation Tour." This tour was put together by Cord and his friend Jackson Ferdinand over at Star Status Records after two of their rappers were wounded in a gun battle with Shaky Stick and Possum from Jupiter at a New York City nightclub. Although the incident had been quickly hushed up and relegated to the local section of an all but obscure Harlem news weekly, Cord and Jackson knew that the parties involved had a long-simmering beef which went back to their days as unsigned artist doing dollar-party rap battles in the Bedford-Stuyvesant section of Brooklyn.

With a professional control which made some of New York City's finest public relations firms take notice, Star Status and Jupiter Solice first corralled the feuding posses, made each individual sign an agreement to squash the beef and work in a coordinated, and quite lucrative, effort to formulate a joint recording and live performance venture: The Reconciliation Tour.

Integrally involved in the Tour, and with a substantial financial investment in it, were Sirena and Jenkins Shorter, newlyweds when the tour began, the parents of a fresh baby boy and joint owners of Short Siren Music Corporation, their new management and production company. Their wedding, held the previous summer, was made public in the fall, just before the gun battle.

Jenkins was friends with rappers Shaky Stick and Possum, and was present at the nightclub when the melee erupted. Siren, who'd grown more serious and business-minded following the birth of little Troy, had an immediate sit-down with her new husband and told him point blank that his gallivanting around with record-industry "posses" was over. They sat down the following day with a common entertainment attorney, and the Short Siren Music Corporation was formed.

Freddy had meanwhile formed a posse of sorts himself, a security apparatus which served Siren primarily, Jupiter Solice Records in general. He managed a team of 14 full-time, armed special officers, licensed to carry concealed weapons while often in plain clothes, dressed in black for the most part and each of the 12 men and two women wrapped in black protective vest emblazoned with the word "Security" in bold yellow letters.

On most occasions the 9 mm pistols were scarcely concealed, stuffed in holsters tight up on the officers' hips. But on occasion, and in a manner designed to keep potential ne'er-do-wells guessing, Freddy, Carmella, or James would be dressed to the nines, the bulge under their suit coats only evident to the astute observer.

Jupiter Solice Records, in conjunction with Short Siren Music Corporation, mounted the Reconciliation Tour with great fanfare. Press conferences were held presenting artists from Star Status and Jupiter Solice who had been at one another's throats just months earlier. Shaky Stick and Possum, two huge, rotund figures who "spit" lyrics together and developed a sort of tag-team approach to rapping that won them huge acclaim, dominated the conferences as well as the tour.

They were the current most popular and bestselling rap duo to hit the national airwaves, and had been central in the conflict, and gun battle, with Gold Plates and Romello, Star Status's top-selling and competing rap duo. None of the central figures had been harmed in the by now widely reported gun battle, nor had any of the central figures been hurt. But a member of each team's entourage had been voluntarily handed over to New York City police to face gun and assault charges, though members of these boys' families, living in public housing project when the incident occurred, were even now moving into spacious new digs in an upscale New Jersey community.

Siren had meanwhile gifted both Sunshine and Genese fabulous homes of their own choosing, and both remained steadfast friends and constant companions. They were on the payroll and were each having a good hand in managing the young acts Short Siren Music Corporation had signed.

As a couple now, Siren and Jenkins had acquired another massive home on a bluff in McLean, Virginia, overlooking the Potomac River. Siren had unofficially given over the other McLean home and property to Marvella, who by now was known to be "seeing" Freddy. He and Marvella, the eldest among Siren and Jenkins's close circle of friends, remained "set in their ways," as Jenkins's mother put it, and although everyone knew they were a couple, they acted as if all but stranger when happening upon one another during some company business activity.

Keepin' It Easy rarely performed, live, as a group now, though they collaborated in the studio on occasion. The all appeared as if content that each member was well-paid to the point of wanting for nothing. All the members were now either married, with children, or some combination of the two, while Jenkins was quickly becoming an overbearing father to little Troy.

Siren showered the boy with love also, but having secured the services of two well-paid nannies, and with Sunshine, Genese and their own children almost demanding time looking after Troy, Siren took to her new role in management, rarely going into the studio anymore or writing her own materials. She was quickly becoming a stern taskmaster, and with three groups signed to her and Jenkins's label, and investments in major live productions, Siren the renowned songstress gave way to Sirena Lavesque-Shorter, the consummate businessperson.

She stood backstage quietly, observing the goings on as technicians went about preparing for the opening night of the Reconciliation Tour. Genese and Sunshine, strict in their roles as personal assistants, stood nearby. But no one said a word to Siren; when she was involved in the management of a production, everyone close to her knew when she wanted to be left alone, left to simply observe what was going on. And God help the technician, the musician, the artist, who caught her eye while involved in some action perceived by Siren to in any way detract from the professionalism of a production she was integrally involved in.

"Have Gold Plates and Romello been out here yet to get a feel for the stage, the space they have to work with, the placement of the DJ?" Siren asked Genese, not looking to her but standing stoic, arms crossed, the blue pinned-striped suit she wore making her appear as if she were fresh from some Wall Street office.

"Shaky Stick and Possum been out," Genese said. "That's their equipment to the rear of the stage. Gold Plates and Romello down first. That's their's midstage there."

"And where's that boy spins for them?" Siren asked.

"That's him there, on the equipment," Sunshine pointed out a young man standing behind two turntables with one side of a set of headphones to one ear. "The one they call High Roller."

Siren was even more beautiful in her maternal maturity, and although everyone knew that she was the Siren of superstardom, even those who were fresh to come upon her noticed that the former girl singer, the one time young lady songstress, the once troubled cocaine addicted singer, was now a statuesque woman, tall and confident, glowing with self-assurance.

"He's the one does the double-clutch with the bass line on that jam Hurtin' Somebody," Siren said, smiling at the very thought of one of the most popular songs in radio play rotation worldwide. "Them boys Shaky and Pos' don't watch out, we're going to make him an offer and pull him over for the Young Warriors. Now that would be one hell of a match right there."

She was seriously giving an appraisal to her musical suggestions, and both Sunshine and Genese knew it. Siren wandered back towards the dressing rooms, trailed by her assistants, and only gave a cursory nod to a few performers, quite renowned themselves, who appeared overwhelmed by her presence as she passed them by. A few of them knew that it was she and husband Jenkins who'd been paramount in putting together this tour, and to a man were quite pleased with the monetary rewards she, it was said, was primarily responsible for them attaining.

"My manager said it was Siren made sure we got paid, and well, in advance, for doing these joints here,"

Raquan, an underling in the posse of Shaky Stick and Possum, said to another from their entourage. "Boy, if she wasn't with that fool Jenkins, boy...."

"Yeah yeah yeah," his friend said while both focused on the receding rear ends of Siren, Genese and Sunshine. "Like that fly-ass babe would even consider giving you the time of day."

"Naw, son! But still man, can't help but wish, know what I'm saying? That's one fine-ass babe there, son! Fine!"

"Finer than a mug!"

They watched as down the rear hallway, Siren stopped and exchanged brief pleasantries with their own fresh act: Shaky Stick and Possum. The two huge bodies seemed to overpower the tight hallway, but even from a distance it appeared as if the duo was assuming an uncharacteristic passive demeanor while addressing Siren.

"Time to get it on!" another of the group of young men announced, joining in a clutch of seven and moving to the rear of the stage into the shadows.

"Let's turn this motherfucker out!" another said, as the lights came up and a heavy bass reverberated and the crowd roared, surging forth in anticipation in the massive auditorium.

Chapter Twenty-eight

"Banked big-time, and no problems whatsoever," Siren whispered to Jenkins, the baby Troy between them as they sat propped on elbows, backs on overstuffed pillows, in the massive bed which was their primary sleeping place in the McLean mansion. "Even that crazy-ass Romello behaved himself."

Jenkins laughed lightly. "Much money as that fool's making on this tour, he better act like he got some sense."

The Reconciliation Tour had been selling out each venue minutes after the shows were announced. Along with the principles at Jupiter Solice and Star Status, the business entity that was Siren and Jenkins was slated to rake in millions in ticket sales, the sales of marketed items related to the tour and sales of a live album, with songs from the tour already in heavy rotation on urban radio stations across the nation, in London, in France, in South Africa and Nigeria. A measure of drugs, combined with volumes of alcohol, fueled some tiffs after shows in Los Angeles and Washington, D.C. But Freddy and his tight security apparatus had been monitoring actions all along the way, and squelched a few bouts of fisticuffs before they erupted into all-out melees.

"I'm doing a little studio next week," Siren said to her husband. "Some pieces I've been working on in our own studio I want to expand on with some live musicians. But other than that, baby, I'm going to stay with my little baby boy here and just love me some little Troy!"

Her concluding words were part song, part cooing. She nuzzled her nose into the baby's stomach, and the buoyant little brown bundle kicked chubby legs into the air and emitted what for the parents sounded as if a joyful giggle combined with an attempt at the formation of a word.

"Agaaa—eek!" the baby gurgled, smiling lips and eyes directed at his mother.

"Aww," Siren said, kissed Troy on a chubby cheek then looked to Jenkins. "He already wanna be a singer like his daddy!"

At seven months, the baby had been in the care of either one of a pair of nannies, Sunshine or Genese while his mother and father were spending inordinate time ensuring that their considerably new corporation gelled with initial profitability.   Three groups signed to Short Siren Music Corporation needed considerable attention at this point, and together the company had poured three million dollars up front into the Reconciliation Tour. The returns were almost immediate however, and with the greater percentage of investment in the tour being provided by Star Status and Jupiter Solice, the couple's accountants projected that, following the Atlanta show the coming weekend, Short Siren would be in the black and anticipated additional proceeds, in the words of the principles, would be considered "gravy."

Jenkins, wearing a pair of the massively popular "Siren Sounds" headphones his wife had lent her name towards the manufacturing and marketing of, was listening to some tracks the freshly reinvigorated members of Keepin' It Easy had been working on. He rocked and smiled while taking in the warm glow emanating from the baby beside him, the magnificently glorious wife swaddled in a black silk negligee which had cost him $1245 during a stopover in Paris a few months back. His loins began to dance along with the heavy bass being pumped into his ears, and he creased his eyes in a way that Siren knew all too well.

She nodded lightly, smiling herself, and saw that Troy had fallen asleep. Carefully, she folded the sheepskin blanket around him, lifted him and moved quietly across the carpeted floor of the massive bedroom, eased through the gold ornate doors, which were already ajar, and down the hall to the nursery. In minutes she was back, closing the doors behind her and moving to the bed, allowing the black silk robe which matched her negligee to fall to the floor. She climbed in the bed beside her husband, who removed his headphones as she eased up to him.

"The monitor on?" he asked, looking at the device on the bedside table which fed a remote audio signal from the nursery.

"It's on," she said. "But Henrietta was already in her bed in Troy's room waiting for us to put him to bed. She's gonna be there till in the morning at least."

"Good," Jenkins said, taking Siren in his arms and maneuvering her atop him. "That boy wants to be a singer, let's work on giving his ass a little sister or brother or something to harmonize along with, baby. Know what I'm sayin'?"

He flipped her unto her back, mounted her.

"I know, Jenks. I...I...know..."

Chapter Twenty-nine

"As soon as this tour is over," Shaky Stick said to Possum, "I'm gonna bust a cap in that little squirrel-ass motherfucker!"

The two 300-plus pounders were on their own special tour bus, plopped down upon dual massive lounge platforms to the rear of the bus as it sped 60 miles per hour west on Route 40, somewhere between Memphis and Little Rock. There were twelve young men, including the rappers, their entourage and the driver, on the specially-designed bus, along with four young ladies. Two of the females were variously between Shaky Stick's ham-like legs, giving him head, and straddled atop Possum's overextended gut, riding him as if he were some rodeo apparatus but struggling to maintain a posture that kept him hard within her.

"I hear ya, homes," Possum said, easing a thick leg skyward and locking a heel behind the woman atop him. "How that fool think a motherfucker gonna roll on twenty thousand for each show, between us and we the ones. Oh shit! Damn! Uggh....uhh...and...ohhh...damn!"

He repositioned himself, struggled to continue.

"And......like...and....uggh....uggh...and..we....like...we... the...the..we......the....ones...niggas...uhh...uhh...all them niggas...be coming to see?"

Possum was having one hell of a time catching his breath while also attempting to be a maneuvering participant in the sex act. The pliant young lady was plastered onto his thick penis, the lounge quite large enough to allow his spacious form room to lean back into an amassment of pillows. Yet his generous gut was proving to be a bit much to navigate, and although he did have a considerably nice operable nine inches of penis, he wasn't as blessed in the health department.

His Type-2 diabetes often contributed to negating his ability to gain full solidity, and at present his penis struggled to draw hardening blood from a body suffering under the weight of too much cognac, cocaine and bucket after bucket of the Admiral's grease-laden fried chicken.

"Twenty thou," Shaky Stick said. "Bet you Gold Plates and Romello gettin' twice that."

The accounting for the Reconciliation Tour could have been a case study at the Wharton School of Business in how *not* to manage finances. Those at the top were paid up front: Siren, Jenkins, the corporate accounts of Star Status and Jupiter Solice had massive certified checks received and deposited well before the tour was halfway over. But the artists, the technicians, the sundry operational personnel, security? Well, they all seemed to fall into the "get-paid-as-you-go"-category. Some in this category didn't even have bank accounts, and demanded cash. And cash was dispensed only by a person identified as the tour's certified accountant, and only on the morning after each individual show.

These, however, were never amounts of more than a few hundred dollars, two thousand tops. The performers, often with a manager in tow, were paid 20, 30, 50 thousand dollars. They had to have accounts, and of course were paid by check.

Rarely, but on a few occasion, checks would bounce.

It was not as if the corporations sponsoring the tours didn't have millions in assets, millions in the accounts presumably from which the checks were drawn. Quite often, and in the case of the Reconciliation Tour, habitually, the "actual" sponsor of the tour was some promotion company in the host city of each individual concert. And if Jupiter Solice, Star Status or, as they quickly learned, Short Siren Music Corporation delayed, by even a day, remuneration to the local promoter for funds already laid out to secure a venue and the funds were not immediately accessible, then a whole lot of "juggling" went on with payments overlapping output and outputs being delayed and so forth and so on and....an MBA from Wharton would find some of the accounting manipulations a challenge. If not all out financial trickery.

"Motherfucker from Appreciantics Concerts gave our ass a $30,000 check that bounced before we even finished that second show at that joint in Seattle," Shaky Stick said, struggling to his feet and positioning the girl on the edge of his platform so that he could enter her from the rear. "Then tell Simon that was the fault of the people from Star Status and Jupiter Solice. Fuck that shit, man! I'm ...I'm gonna...bust a...bust a...aww shit!!!"

He exploded into the girl not 30 seconds after entering her, the oral deliverance evidently a precursor which had him already on climax's doorstep. He folded his massive frame down upon her, and she wiggled and jiggled her way to the side before fat and flatulence completely enveloped her.

"That's....that's why," Shaky rolled onto his back, struggling for breath and words. "That's why...I'm gonna...gonna...b...bust a cap in that.....bust...bust a cap...in...that...that...that...damn... Freud...he...he don't have....all....a...a....said....ALL...my...goddamn....money when...this tour...is...over...."

"I...hear ya," Possum said, pushing away the young lady who attempted to cuddle up to him. He grabbed a chicken breast from the bucket on the table beside the platform, devoured it as if some nuclear vacuum, sucking every bit of meat off the bones and tossing aside the skeletal remains. "I hear ya."

Chapter Thirty

Freud had been left holding the bag, as it were, a newcomer to the concert promotion arena and considerably fresh to the recording industry. Born Steven Willoughby, "Freud" imagined himself akin to the acclaimed Austrian neurologist whose last name he'd taken on as some sort of mantle in an industry where labels were everything. A wiry, rail-thin nerd of a fellow, Freud was indeed a cerebral sort, very well educated and from a New England family which traced its roots back to the landing of the Mayflower. His bright red hair, wire-rimmed glasses and frail, hunched countenance made it appear as if he should be wearing a lab coat at times, comfortable in a room full of test tubes and beakers emitting clouds of smoke. In an attempt to overcome his...well, comely appearance, he'd borrowed a pretty penny from his father and at the age of 25 set out to make his mark as a concert promoter.

Of course the idea had not been something he'd given much thought to: Just three years earlier, just hours after graduating Magna Cum Laude from a most prestigious Boston university, his equally nerdy co-celebrants had decided to secret a tab of LSD into the Swiss Alpine spring water Willoughby favored and, not knowing just why he was in an hour soaring amongst the clouds, the intellectual graduate came down from his high a few DNA strands twisted away from what might be considered sanity in his stoic upbringing.

Soon thereafter Steven Willoughby put aside his collection of Bach and Beethoven symphonic CDs and began tuning way, way down the FM radio dial to a New England acid rock station. He started referring to himself as Freud and, happening upon an urban rap station one day, came up with the bright idea that he would be a whiz at the promoting of music popular among the nation's black youths. Indeed, he reasoned, he'd once befriended a young black during a summer internship working at a school for troubled youths in Harlem, New York City. Perhaps that experience was the subdural implant which blossomed the idea in his head that this newly formulated Freud persona was destined to become a rap impresario on the level of the famous Snap Dog Diggity, or the equally renowned Turbo Traffic the Terrible.

In actuality though Willoughby never really gained a sound mental foothold after the acid trip. He never truly understood what had fueled the psychedelic astral voyage, and instead of borrowing the $3.5 million from his billionaire father to start a misdirected concert promotions company, he should have just given up the keys to the Porsche and Cambridge brownstone and checked into a mental institution for an extended period of observation and recovery.

Now he'd been left holding the bag: Financial responsibilities for the Reconciliation Tour, on the ground level.

Appreciantics Concerts, Freud's addle-brained promotions company, had been contracted by the bigger wheels at Jupiter Solice and Star Status to handle the logistics for the Reconciliation Tour. Freud and his staff of two, a coke-head former brainiac from Baltimore and the skinny, air-head girl he'd been dating since Boston, formed the sole staff of Appreciantics, and with the considerable endowment from his father, he had jumped feet first into a concert promoting business neither of them had the faintest idea of what the logistics entailed.

Of course astute businessmen Cord and Jeremiah of Jupiter Solice saw this immediately. But as merely the providers of the "talent," they stood to reap enormous profits while having to do little of the grunt work that lies at the feet of the actual promoters. Appreciantics, as required, had put up the necessary bond at each concert venue, also using on-line ticket sales as collateral, while associated tour proxies, Jupiter Solice, their temporary partners at Star Status, and investors Siren and Jenkins stayed home and electronically reaped the lion's share of the tour's profits.

Freud, and some of the touring artists, were left to divide crumbs either forwarded to the account of promoter Appreciantics Concerts by the record labels, monies from meager day-of-the-show ticket sales or, as it turned out in more than one city and venue, from the quickly advanced additional funds provided by McArthur Viscount Willoughby, Freud's father and, as it would turn out, primary financier of the tour.

"We need some more gas up in this motherfucker," Sheffield, the driver of the tour bus for Shaky Stick and Possum advised as they pulled into a rest stop outside of Little Rock. "I'm not coming out on this road again unless one of your boys got one of them credit cards that ain't got no maximum. Some black or gold or platinum shit or some shit!"

Sheffield, a 60-year-old who'd retired from driving Metro buses in the nation's capital, had been handsomely paid to drive the rap artists around the nation and, for another few thousand dollars every other day or so, keep his own counsel about the random stops off route to some less than pristine community outside one or another urban venue. An extremely dark black man whose own substantial girth was a slightly miniaturized version of his famous clients, Morgan Sheffield was quickly growing tired on this particular tour after having to remind "the boys" quite often that this massive, customized bus virtually drank petrol. To put $500.00 worth of gas into the behemoth would to be considerably miserly.

"We got you, Sheff," Shaky Stick said, wobbling to the front of the bus as it was being parked to the rear of a spacious truck stop. He handed the driver 20 hundred-dollar bills. "That dude Freud gonna meet us in Little Rock at the hotel. Replenish our cash stores, know what I'm saying?"

Sheffield had heard such many times before, and as a native of a hardscrabble section of D.C. himself knew well that, when a young black man ended a sentence with the common "know what I'm saying?," it was almost certain that the speaker was only seeking confirmation and didn't know exactly what he himself was saying.

"Alright, big man," Sheffield said, killing the engine and motoring the door open. "I'm going to take me a piss off this joint. Stretch my legs. Y'all don't be getting into no simple shit back there, you hear me?"

"Hear ya, boss!" Shaky Stick said, then secured the door between the driver's compartment and the rear, moved back to snort some more cocaine and sloppily salivate over the little skinny girl's vagina.

A distance across the parking lot, Arkansas State Trooper Terry Broadneux used a pair of binoculars to follow the trail of the fat middle-aged black man who'd left the colorfully decorated bus and moved around to outside the driver's window, reached in and motored the door shut. Broadneux picked up the patrol car's radio microphone, keyed it and spoke to Trooper Stan Foreman, who was seated in a marked sedan just inside the roadway leading out onto Interstate 40 West.

"It's the one, alright," Broadneux said. "Same painting on the side of the half-naked black bitch and the boy with the dreadlocks. Same tags our boys over in Memphis transmitted."

Jointly, they watched the apparent driver move into the rest stop's men's room. The bus seemed docile, quiet, even serene setting in the midmorning sun. In moments, seven additional state trooper vehicles rolled slowly unto the parking lot, navigating around tractor trailers, a few tour buses and the forward area near the restaurants where a number of cars were parked. Broadneux and Foreman slowly rolled their own cruisers towards the bus, joining the seven others until the bus was virtually within a belt of law enforcement vehicles.

"Where in the hell is Johnson?" Broadneux said to himself, looking around at the familiar officers and not seeing the female with the drug-sniffing dog. "Bitch give more attention to the fucking mutt than she does to her fellow officers."

He'd been trying to get Johnson, a 29-year-old sergeant with the K-9 unit, to date him for over three years and, though married for 17 years and father of five children, Broadneux still felt that his standing on the force endowed him with the power to have extramarital sex with any of the number of fresh, younger female officers who'd become state troopers in recent years.

He radioed her again, and looked up to see her pulling into the rest stop off Interstate 40.

"About time, bitch," he grunted, climbed out of his own vehicle and joined the phalanx of officers inching their ways up to the tour bus.

Broadneux took the lead, banging on the bus door while Johnson and Maxx, the drug sniffing dog, stood beside him.

"What tha fuck?!" Shaky Stick said, arising from his sexual perch and peering through glass which, covered with the painting on the outside, only allowed those within to see through it. He looked down on the ring of uniformed officers just as Possum struggled upright and took in the same scenario.

"The god-damn feds all over this joint!" Possum shouted, alerting those in various seatings to the front of the bus.

Attempts were made to flush powered cocaine down the toilet in the cubicle to the rear. Marijuana was thrown haphazardly into a bin under the sink in the small kitchenette. PCP was rushed to the rear of the bus, where the users of that psychotropic substance believed its strong chemical odor might not be detected. One roadie simply snorted a generous portion of the heroin he'd been using throughout the tour, while all became acutely aware that the driver was no where in sight yet the front door was being motored open.

"Let me see your hands!!"

Officer Broadneux, pointing his gun, stood just inside of the door between the driver's perch and the passenger area. He could see at least seven young men and two young women in a spacious front area of the tour bus, but could also see that there was a petition of sorts three-quarters ways down the vehicle. Tight up behind him, Officer Johnson and Maxx awaited his instructions.

"Everybody on this goddamn bus, out!" Broadneux instructed, and then backed down the stairs as the trail of lethargic occupants filtered to the front and out of the vehicle.

"Let me see your hands!" he repeated to the tall, lanky man who was first to descend. "Up against the bus, shithead!"

Other officers encircled the bus's doorway, guns drawn. One by one, short, tall, dark, light, men, then two women, then a third woman descended and were lined up against the bus, frisked, cuffed. Lastly, a humongous form filled the doorway, took the stairs one at a time as the entirety of the bus groaned with the weight, tilting the front exit further towards the ground. The huge man was ushered by two officers to a trooper's vehicle parked to the front of the bus, frisked and handcuffed. The officers who had Shaky Stick were forced to use a pair of handcuffs, interlinked, to secure his hands behind him. His beefy arms would not otherwise come close to one another when pulled to his rear.

A secondary massive form filled the bus's doorway. Possum, hands clasped atop his head, eased off the bus with an awry grin, shaking his head.

"What up with this, officers?" he grinned upon being corralled and cuffed by the state troopers.

"You in charge here?" Trooper Broadneux asked him, nodding to Officer Johnson, who followed two other officers, pointing guns into the interior, onto the bus with the dog Maxx.

"Yeah. This bus is our joint," Possum said.

"Who is 'our'?" Broadneux asked.

"Me and my boy and our posse, yo."

"Posse. What are ya: Some sort of musicians? Rappers?"

"Yeah, Joe. We holla. We spit. We roll like that and this and that and shit, know what I'm saying?"

Broadneux shook his head. "Young man, I have no idea what you're saying."

"Oh, it bes like that, huh?"

"Yeah, it bes like that. Anyway, we have a warrant to search your bus. Got word out of Memphis you were in contact with some known drug dealers there, and that it's possible that you're transporting."

"We ain't transporting shit. Maybe my boys got a little something-something for personal consumption, know what I'm saying?"

"Still," Broadneux said, rifling through the big man's pockets. "In Arkansas, we don't even abide a little 'personal consumption' if it's of something illegal. And especially not from some interlopers coming into our state with some of that bullshit you might be allowed in the city. Do you know what I am saying?"

Possum smirked, threw his head back as if in submission.

"I hear ya, Five-0. I hear ya."

Chapter Thirty-one

"Damn! They were busted?"

"Busted, if that's what you want to call it."

"Shit!"

The show must go on, Jackson Ferdinand, principle owner, Star Status Records, said in conclusion, cut his telephone conversation with Freud and made a hasty call to Jeremiah at Jupiter Solice.

"Outside of Little Rock," he told Jeremiah about as much as he knew about the situation. "Found all kinds of illegal shit on the tour bus. The stupid fucks thought they could flush the shit down the toilet on the goddamn bus and it was going, oh, I don't know, into the local sewer system? Simple fucks!"

Officer Johnson and Maxx had poured over the tour bus, and found such an array of illegal substances that most of them couldn't be actually identified until they were examined in a forensics laboratory. The pharmaceutical diversity was such that Maxx, the drug-sniffing dog, even appeared dazed at one point; he "hit" on drugs in every part of the bus except for the driver's compartment. And even after directed to sniff out drugs on the handcuffed members of the entourage, Officer Johnson was dumbfounded when the dog appeared to be discombobulated when sniffing about the obese forms of Shaky Stick and Possum. A later, detailed search of person and body cavities at the police station still turned up no illegal substances on the persons of either of the two. A forensic pathologist finally concluded, quite correctly, that the two had been consuming such volumes of drugs and were continuously sweating profusely as a result of the bust that the drugs were actually leeching out of their bodies along with the perspiration.

The Little Rock show was sold out, and was a boisterous yet uneventful occurrence until it came time for the headliners who languished in a downtown jail cell. A youthful crowd of 7,840 had been smoking marijuana blunts, guzzling 16-ounce beers from the concession stand and generally engaging in mind alteration but for the most part behaving themselves. The crowd was dancing, singing along with Gold Plates and Romello, the co-headliners who, unbeknownst to the crowd then, would be the last act to perform. Disastrously belatedly, Freud had convinced Romello to announce, after his and Gold Plates' last song, that Shaky Stick and Possum would not be performing.

When he did so, the crowd went berserk.

Celebrants had secreted in bottles of a popular brand of cognac in response to the lyrics of Gold Plate and Romello's Number One hit, "Sippin' that 'Yak' and Hollering Like Dat." Many in the crowd ignited a number of padded seats in the venue using the flammable liquid, though quite sparingly as video footage reviewed later showed revelers hoisting the bottles, passing them around all the while dashing just enough onto the seats to easily ignite them with butane lighters.

The fires, sporadic throughout the venue at first, also ignited a stampede, as smoke quickly filled the place. Many rushed the stage, seeking an exit there. Freddy and his security apparatus knew they'd be overwhelmed, and their primary responsibility was protecting the acts. They rushed Gold Plate, Romello and the opening, lesser known performers out of the rear and into limousines, leaving venue staff and a befuddled Freud and company to fend for themselves.

Madness ensued. Musicians, if they could be called such, rushed to secure their personal items while roadies tried to pack up the thousands of dollars of speakers and other equipment. Freud, with his always shaky countenance, didn't know quite what to do. Hundreds of angry black youths were looking for someone backstage on whom to vent their frustrations, and the white boys who were regulars on rap tours had sense enough to get their essentials and make way for the rear exit seconds after Romello made the announcement. In an attempt to appear casual cool to his youthful hires for the concert, Freud had worn a fine, three-piece gold suit without a dress shirt, his frail, hairy chest exposed behind the vest and sporting at least seven platinum chains and pendants. He also wore the top-of-the-line gold Rolex watch in such a way that it hung prominently just at the joint between his wrist and left hand.

"That's the mother fucking promoter right there!" a dreadlocked, muscular young man who stood over six and a half feet tall shouted, heading an angry mob that flowed unto the stage and to the backstage area like an angry tidal wave. "Bust that motherfucker!"

Freud tried to dash for the rear exit, but stumbled over a large turntable case just discarded by a fleeing DJ. The dreadlocked man was first to reach him, took him by the throat and effortlessly hoisted him, tossing him back into the surging crowd. Those in the crowd who were seriously under the influence of alcohol, drugs or a combination of something or other took to beating the helpless figure, while those close in, and among the more lucid and astute, ripped off the chains and gold watch. Freud was little more than a rag doll in the hands of the mob, and unconsciousness took over as if a blessing to save the pummeled figure from experiencing what had to be tremendous, excruciating pain.

By now fire companies had been summoned, police in riot gear leading the way into the auditorium. The scene was nothing short of pure madness, those not heading to the stage and rear exit forced to fight towards a number of doors to the side of the venue, and to the rear entrance, where they were met by baton-wielding police in riot gear.

The fires were not spreading, with most confined to the chairs on which they'd been set. But the smoke generated by flaming foam seat cushions grew toxic, and in minutes even the police were fighting their ways out of the place.

As the area backstage grew eerily silent and deserted, Freud eased his eyes open and tried to roll onto his side. A broken clavicle made it feel as if his shoulder was detached. Two broken femurs and the left tibia disabled both legs. He found himself unable to move without generating daggers of pain. All he could do was lie there and give thought to the mess he was in both physically and financially.

He certainly wasn't getting back the $300,000 bond he'd had to put up to the venue's owners just in case something disastrous occurred. And from the smell of the smoke and the caustic haze that appeared through the tears in his eyes, Appreciantics Concerts was probably on the hook for much, much more extensive expenses.

Chapter Thirty-two

"That was a hot mess!" Jenkins said to his wife, driving into D.C. to visit acquaintances   displaced from their old Barry Farm neighborhood.   "And Freud: That fool is lucky them young'uns didn't kill his ass!"

For their investment in the aborted Reconciliation Tour, their money was already banked and according to the contract, nonrefundable to the tour's principles. They had made a wise investment, along with Jeremiah, and their primary concern now was little Troy, and sobriety. It had been over two years since either had touched any drug, though Siren had slipped and indulged in a glass of champagne a while back. In "the meetings," they'd learned that alcohol was almost always the initial "drug" any addict picked up, and after that initial relapse, Genese, Sunshine and Jenkins had been watching her like hawks. Both had been tempted regularly though, with the way celebratory champagne flowed (along with other tempting morsels!) at near every event they were part of or attended. But as a couple they were one another's "sponsor," though officially each had a sponsor, an AA/NA guide with years of experience, to guide them through the program.

"He's not geared for this business anyway," Siren said, reflecting on the little pipsqueak, as she laughingly referred to Freud. "I told him from the get-go this business was going to eat him alive."

They were in his Bentley, the gold one, crossing the Woodrow Wilson Bridge which carried the Capital Beltway over the Potomac River between Northern Virginia and a portion of Maryland that abutted the southeast section of Washington. Marvella had insisted on minding little Troy, though the boy had a cadre of nannies and even a security woman from Freddy's group. Over the past three years there had been at least four attempts by hoodlums to snatch the child of a recording artist or movie star, and Siren and Jenkins spared no costs in seeing that their child was secure.

"Sanford's been right tight working with the peoples from down the Farms," Jenkins said, recalling his childhood friend and fellow singer from Keepin' It Easy. "They closed them joints down without giving the peoples no place else to go, like that. But I told them that was coming before we made it out of there. Back when they started building that Homeland Security joint up on the old St. Elizabeths grounds, wasn't gonna be no more Barry Farms like that down there right next to it, hear me, baby?"

"I hear ya."

It was said to be the nation's first public housing project: Barry Farm, literally a farm owned by one James Barry until 1867, when the Freedman's Bureau purchased the land for freed slaves. Jenkins, Sanford and all the other boys from Keepin' It Easy grew up there, as had Siren's father Raymond. Though the neighborhood was among one of the most hard-scrabbled, drug-riddled communities in the nation's capital during the latter 20th Century, the boys from Keepin' It Easy, as did most others who grew up there, had fond memories of the two-story, clapboard houses stuck hard against Suitland Parkway and in clear visual distance from the U.S. Capitol Building.

By 2010, however, the land just up the hill from "The Farm," as it was locally called, had been set aside for the headquarters of the Department of Homeland Security and new Coast Guard Headquarters.   And when completed in the first quarter of 2013, the new developments on the land of the old St. Elizabeths Mental Hospital next to the Farm was a major draw of both housing and commercial development to a section of previously-neglected Washington. Certainly, prime land flush against the new Coast Guard Headquarters was not going to continue to be occupied by a population which was 100 percent black, 99.9 percent of whom were living below the poverty level.

"They're just closed down the Farm," Siren said, shaking her head. "And with the economy all fucked up, they know them people didn't have no way and no means to go nowhere else."

But many of the residents had long seen the writings on the wall, and had desperately made plans to relocate. Ushering many out was the influx, more than had been historically available in most public housing projects, of even deadlier illegal drugs. The Farm had been flooded with crack and heroin in public volumes over the past few decades, and the associated deaths, mostly from shootings, had only mounted.

"Sanford was good at hooking some of them up with that new place over off of Suitland Parkway," Jenkins said, even as he cruised down Route 295 in southeast and could see the drab colored dwellings of Barry Farm off to the right. "Those properties we bought out in Landover won't have the houses done till late this year, my man Anderson said. But from what Sanford says, there's still about forty families from the Farm moved into homeless shelters."

"Those the ones supposed to be at the meeting," Siren said. "Sunshine and Genese and Sanford should already be there. But look, man: Don't be committing no more than we already have with the Landover project. You know how our people can get sometimes: We give 'em the hook-up, next thing you know they're living good but taking their little extra ends and buying crack and smack and shit. Be all up in joints we help 'em get and next thing you know they're rolling around in Lexuses and Benzes and shit. I ain't work my ass off to be doling out for some niggas ain't even thinking about getting no job or nothing and not helping they're goddamn selves, hear me baby?"

"I hear ya," Jenkins said, but really wasn't in agreement with his wife nor really pleased with her changing attitude.

Chapter Thirty-three

They were looking at hard time. Wayne "Shaky Stick" Williams and Antwan "Possum" Taylor had laughed off the drug bust in Arkansas and had made the requisite calls to get attorneys and have bail set for them and their crew. But only the bus driver had escaped unscathed, allowed to return on his own to Washington while the bus was impounded and Shaky Stick, Possum and their posse were carted off to jail. And in jail they remained. All of the tour's producers were doing all they could to legally distance themselves from the boys, who for months before had been prime financiers of their meal tickets.

Once the media got a hold of the story, Ferdinand and Cord put all of their own public relations apparatus to work. They lambasted the very use of illegal narcotics in America, shouting the company's disapproval of any drug use and further announcing that they were severing any ties with the rap duo. And although they certainly didn't announce this fact, Shaky and Poss were still generating hundreds of thousands of dollars hourly through international CD and electronic download sales of a joint venture production. Sales only surged after word got out of their legal predicament. This fact the label ensured gained wide exposure.

Down in Little Rock, a case was being made charging the rappers and their posse with being part of an elaborate interstate drug distribution ring. The variety of the drugs found on the bus, more so than the volume, was the basis of the case. A judge had been convinced to hold the entire entourage without bond. Certainly, the keen minds of a few New York City attorneys would have easily compiled facts and findings and filed motions to have the judge set bond, if not throw out some of the charges all together. But fine legal minds cost money, and although Shaky Stick and Possum were worth a few million dollars apiece on (record company) paper, neither had much in the way of liquid assets other than a few thousand dollars each. This was in the form of personal savings accounts, considerably cash levied expensive homes under sundry contracts through the conversion of equities into cold cash by relatives, and a few expensive cars in the driveways of the heavily mortgaged homes.

Royalty checks coming in from the millions of dollars in sales currently being generated would not be legally due the artists until the quarterly distribution agreed to by them in their contracts. And even in anticipation that the duo was going to be due checks soon, record company executives and their legal teams were already amassing records showing overdue "studio expenses," "promotional incidentals" and "operational tour costs" so that, on paper, Shaky Stick and Possum actually owed the record companies a few thousand dollars.

"No need to throw good money after bad," one company executive said to his attorney in writing of the rap duo. "We need to spend any operational funds now on our producing acts, and write off this...this 'Reconciliation Tour' as a bad investment."

"Are the other tour principles satisfied?" the executive asked.

"They're legally detached from any further obligations, according to the contract. His boys Gold Plates and Romello have no further obligations either, since it was those bastards Shaky and Possum, who negated their obligations through the drug bust."

"Good," the executive said. "Short Siren? That girl Siren's involvement with her husband?"

"It's detached them also. And they were crafty enough to get their investment paid at the tour's kick-off. Shouldn't hear any complaints from them."

"Good," the executive said. "Now, let's erase any indication that those punks down there in the Arkansas jail ever had anything to do with our company."

"As good as done," one attorney said. "As good as done."

Chapter Thirty-four

Sirena Lavesque-Shorter didn't want the heralded star Siren to ever make an appearance anywhere near her old neighborhood without Freddy and at least five of his more robust security team members. Not that she had done any ills or mistreated anyone in the Southeast Washington area where she had grown up. It was just that she had extracted the only friends that mattered to her from there, Sunshine and Genese, and was certain that any other "old friends" who gained access to her were only going to be about "begging," as she so derisively considered it. Playing on their casual childhood association to hit her up for some money, some favor, some "hook-up" which might open a door for them into the music industry. After all, poverty was a lifelong state of being for many in the Barry Farm, Parkside, Garfield communities she'd been born and raised in. It was to be expected that an old school friend, an old neighborhood acquaintance, might hit up the multimillion-dollar recording artist for something, if only for a few hundred dollars. And Siren, with a persona somewhat steeled from her brush with addiction and a waltz with poverty and near death herself, didn't need any reminder that, but for the grace of God, these "beggars" might well have been her lifelong compatriots.

Now, through the insistence of her husband, the two were attending a community meeting with little more than Jenkins's personal 9 mm pistol in the Bentley's glove compartment to protect them. She loved and trusted her husband, but without Freddy's reassuring presence, she was approaching this meeting with a measure of foreboding.

"Man, I don't know why I let you talk me into this shit," Siren said to Jenkins, her voice quivering as they pulled into the packed parking lot of the Greater

Abyssinian Baptist Church in a section of Maryland just across the D.C. line. "We're helping to build the damn houses in Landover. Man, you could have just sent the Barry Farm Community Group this damn check."

"It's good to show though, baby," Jenkins said, parking and nodding at a group of men paying strong attention to the Bentley and its occupants. "Sanford's already out here. So is Rev. Palmdale. We're talking about people who need immediate assistance, baby."

"Yeah yeah yeah," she said, loosened her seatbelt and hesitantly climbed out of the car.

"Jenky Jenks!" a man called out from a group of seven, stepped over to Jenkins and shook hands, embraced.

"My man Low-Rider!" Jenkins said. "Man, I ain't seen your ass in...what? Ten, fifteen years!"

"At least," the lanky, dark man smiled, his teeth shiny, white beacons in the early evening darkness. "I ain't think y'all asses was gonna show, you know, like my boy Sanford said y'all was!"

Siren joined her husband's side, and the other six men on the parking lot sauntered over, as if hesitant to approach.

"Sirena! Hey, baby. You probably don't remember me," Low-Rider said, extending a hand to Siren.

"Bookie Johnson," Siren smiled, taking the proffered hand. "We were in the sixth grade together up at Garfield Elementary. Then in the seventh down at Hart. Yeah, I remember you, with your nasty self."

She smiled, hugged the man.

"I didn't think you'd remember a brother!"

"Yeah, I remember," Siren said. "Nobody will ever forget when your ass got locked up with that stolen car on Ballou's parking lot. Trying to run from 5-0 and have the nerve to be around the school trying to show off."

Jenkins laughed. "Yeah, I remember that time too."

The other men began introducing themselves, and either Siren, or Jenkins, or both of them knew the young men, or some of their relations.

"The meeting started a half hour ago," Low-Rider/Bookie Johnson said, nodding and stepping off towards the church entrance. "Sanford had me and my boys here waiting out here in the parking lot....he said, just in case y'all showed. Come on! People will be glad to see y'all asses!"

Inside the massive facility, the gathering of around 250 people seemed small in a church that seated 15,500. Rev. Harold Palmdale, who had built the mega-church but had grown up in the Barry Farm housing project, had been called upon by the Barry Farm Community Coalition to host meetings about the plight of those who had remained in the Southeast Washington project until the very end. It was now slated for redevelopment into what officials termed a "mixed-use, low- to moderate-income" housing and commercial development. Rev. Palmdale was going over current stages of developments in the placing of former residents when all turned to see the bustling accompanying the entrance of Siren and Jenkins.

"Praise the Lord!" Rev. Palmdale shouted. "Praise the Lord!"

There was applause as the couple, backed by the seven young men, came down the long aisle. This made both Jenkins and Siren uncomfortable; they were used to generous accolades when on the stage before thousands, but were ill at ease, bordering on shyness, when generating acclaim in small, informal settings.

Sanford, Jenkins's band mate from Keepin' It Easy, moved down the aisle to meet his childhood friend.

"I told them you would show!" Sanford said, leaning over to give Siren a kiss on the cheek. "But I thought you'd be busy with little Troy, Siren. But thanks for coming! Thanks for coming!"

Rev. Palmdale, a most colorful orator and, all of his 80 percent female congregants agreed, a most handsome, athletic figure, flashed that 1000-watt smile that had guided at least 5,550 women to the baptismal basin. Sirena Lavesque had attended his storefront church some 10 years earlier, ushered into the small facility by her mother, who'd been temporarily "saved" from a serious heroin addiction through the Narcotic's Anonymous and Alcoholic Anonymous meetings held in the small, shopworn facility from which he'd eventually build this quite popular mega church.

"My my my!" Rev. Palmdale said, reaching out to embrace Siren. He did the same to Jenkins, who'd also attended Greater Abyssinian, in its former incarnation, when a young boy out of Barry Farm. "The most blessed of my children! Welcome home!"

"Thanks, reverend," Siren smiled uncomfortably.

"Thanks, Rev. Palmdale," Jenkins smiled sheepishly.

"Well," Rev. Palmdale said, sensing an urgency among those gathered. "Have a seat among the folks here while I finish up my report on the current developments around Barry Farm, and the status of the families that haven't found suitable homes as of yet."

Dozens of once familiar faces in the pews nodded to Siren, to Jenkins, broad smiles of recognition penetrating Siren's thoughts, punctuating past memories in flashes in Jenkins's mind. It was as if they were back among family, and Siren, having shunned any inklings of memories of where she'd come from upon stardom, felt a bit uncomfortable. She glanced around the crowd as the reverend droned off the names of families which had resorted to homeless shelters when the Farm was shuttered. A tingling vibration coursed through her temples and she locked eyes with a young man she'd known, quite intimately, as a teenager. She looked down, embarrassed, and slid a little closer to Jenkins.

"Now, it wasn't a matter that they weren't members of this congregation," the reverend continued. "You all know I've made it known that Greater Abyssinian was trying to provide a leadership role to those facing homelessness all over the city. And particularly in Barry Farm, in Kenilworth Parkside and Greenleaf Gardens. And it didn't matter if you were Baptist, Catholic, Muslim or of no religious affiliation at all. Greater Abyssinian is trying to do the Lord's work. And we certainly put the word out to the former residents of Barry Farm. My very own childhood home!"

He looked to Jenkins, Siren and Sanford.

"Now I know you all are all anxious about some of our old-school family done come back out here after making us all proud, singing all over the world and putting out some good, good music that wasn't about all that cussing and the 'N-word'-this and the 'N-word'-that and calling women the 'B-word' all over the place! You hear me, brothers and sisters?"

"Amen!"

"You all know that young Sirena and Jenkins have put up a tremendous amount of funds to develop, along with Greater Abyssinian, the Glades Manor Development of finely built, attractive and affordable homes on the land the church purchased in Landover. I invited the two of them out, along with Brother Sanford, to give you a personal update on how that project is coming along. Brothers and sisters, Sirena Lavesque-Shorter and Jenkins Shorter."

The crowd stood as one, and to tremendous applause Jenkins, and a quite hesitant Siren, moved to the place before the pulpit where a table, some charts, a podium and microphone had been set up. Again, Rev. Palmdale embraced the two.

"Hi," Siren said into the mike, a reticent persona which made some in the crowd feel embarrassment for her. This was not the superstar all had seen on stage, on television awards show, in news reports both positive and negative. The tall, still strikingly beautiful young woman, was the introverted Sirena Lavesque many in the crowd had predicted would go no further in life than to be, perhaps, some moneyed gentleman's trophy wife. It was as if she'd lost all of her dominating stage presence in the moments it had taken to step before this considerably small gathering, and was reticent as if it were they who were the stars and she but a meaningless fan seeking their approval.

"Hey girl!" one young lady shouted from amidst the crowd, breaking what had been a miniscule but awkward silence.

"Siren, babe!" a young man shouted.

"Jenky Jenks!"

"Sanford the Man!!!"

"Hey Siren!!!"

"Siren!!!"

There were whistles and more applause, and the reverend sensed, in his acute way of gauging a crowd, that he needed to regain control. He leaned into the microphone before Siren.

"Alright! Alright, good people! Let's settle down! This is a business meeting!"

"Amen!"

"Thank all of you for all your support," Siren said. "Me and Jenkins have been...well, you know...we have a new baby and all."

"Amen!"

"And little Troy is doing just fine. Neither one of us have been doing anything on the road, musically, over the past few months. But we are going back out there, you better bet it!"

"Go on, girl!"

"I want tickets!!"

Laughter roiled, then as immediately calmed. Siren continued.

"When Jenks and I heard about what they were doing with Barry Farm, and some other joints around the city, well, we were all up involved in the studio. Him with Keepin' In Easy..."

"Those my babies!" a female swooned.

"And me, well, you know after I overcame my little...problem....I got back on the road and in the studio. Matter of fact, I have some new joints I'm working on now."

"Can't wait, baby! Can't wait!"

"But with y'all now...you know me and Jenks and Sanford and some others, including the church, have been working to find people other places in the city. But, you know, not paying all them high prices for rental joints. We figured, after talking to Sanford, who's been more involved than me and Jenks, after talking to Sanford, that it would be better to invest in properties people can own. Know what I'm saying?"

"Yeah, baby girl! Go 'head!"

"So, while the places in Landover, the Glades Manor Development, is going up, from what I understand, Rev. Palmdale and Sanford and some others have funded some temporary rental places still in the city for those of you who needed immediate help after they closed down the Farm. And me and Jenkins want to contribute whatever more is needed to help in that effort also."

She retrieved a check from her oversized designer purse, presented it to the reverend. He looked at it and flashed that Colgate smile to those gathered.

"Good God almighty! Bless you, child! Bless you, Jenkins!"

He held the check out to the crowd, waved it around slowly.

"Five-hundred thousand dollars!" Rev. **Palmdale** said. **"My goodness!   Bless you, Sirena!   Bless you, Jenkins!"**

Chapter Thirty-five

Shaky Stick and Possum finally managed to put together enough money to secure a well-heeled attorney and have bail set, but not before having wallowed in the filth and survived on the disgusting food of the Pulaski County Jail in Little Rock for a little over a month. And the source of the $70,000 in attorney fees and the cost of bail wasn't exactly digging them out of their hole, but perhaps descending them deeper into a sordid tar pit they'd find themselves harder and harder to extract themselves from. With both men's families hard pressed to put their hands of the required amount of cash, Shaky had directed his mother to Frankie Ferello, the wholesale cocaine distributor in their native Brooklyn from whom they'd detached themselves when rap careers took off and their own drug dealings were deemed no longer necessary or feasible.

Frankie ensured that they had the best attorneys, and just seven days after their release from the Arkansas jail they stood before a judge and were informed that four members of their entourage who were on the bus had filed sworn statements taking sole responsibility for all the drugs found on the tour bus. Shaky Stick and Possum were free to go.

But they were not free, in a sense, because of the tremendous debt owed Frankie Ferello. And Frankie had dreams of leaving the sordid drug distribution business and starting his own rap label. They'd already been summarily dismissed from their record label, so Shaky Stick and Possum, still an anticipated duo among American rap fans, would be perfect fodder for the premiere of Ferello Entertainment and Promotions, LLC.

Within a month the return of Shaky Stick and Possum to the concert tour circuit was being played up on dozens of urban radio stations. Still licking his wounds from the serious beat-down in Little Rock, and still owing a large sum of money to his father, Steven Willoughby, again using his "professional name" of Freud, was determined to revitalize Appreciantics Concerts and hold Shaky Stick and Possum to the contract he had penned with them prior to the Reconciliation Tour. He'd taken a huge financial loss with the ransacking of the venue in Little Rock, lost the $300,000 bond and, aware of the returned checks which were supposed to have secured Shaky Stick and Possum for the tour, believed in his addled mind that the two still owed him.

The beat-down, apparently, had rekindled micrograms of embedded acid from days of yore. Or perhaps it was the hydrocodone he'd been taking in volumes to relieve recurring pains from the serious Little Rock wailing he'd taken. But he couldn't have forgotten that, prior to the Seattle leg of the Reconciliation Tour, Shaky Stick had confronted him about a $30,000 check that bounced. Little solace could be gained from the considerably paltry $10,000 cash delivered to the duo prior to Little Rock. He was wanted, considered among some in the rap game in a phrase borrowed from death-row prison parlance, a "dead man walking."

With the media still playing up the fact that the rap duo had barely escaped unscathed from the drug bust and had just spent a month in jail, Frankie and the upstart Ferello Entertainment and Promotions would have been fortunate to have been able to fill a phone booth for the pair. They didn't have any new music out, but did have a considerable following in New York, Brooklyn in particular, and in Baltimore and Washington. Frankie had tried muscling the former record label of the two into have him signed over all future proceeds for CD and electronic download sales from Shaky Stick and Possum, but even his gangster background failed against the astute legal minds afforded the previous label. So he had to settle on starting from scratch with the boys, playing small venues while forcing them into the newly-built Brooklyn studio to come up with some material that might initiate their climb back to million-selling artist status.

Things seemed to be well on their way, the duo selling out a 3,000-seat auditorium in Washington, D.C., until Freud and two associates, quite evidently drugged up and giving not a modicum of consideration to their personal hygiene, finagled their ways backstage at the District concert hall.

"Oh no that motherfucker didn't show his nasty ass up in this joint!" Shaky Stick, who'd since incarceration added another 20 pounds to his enormous girth, blasted upon seeing the frail red-headed figure. "I been waiting to bust that ass since Seattle!"

Possum, plopped down upon four-foot-tall speaker backstage, seethed at Freud also. But he had a chubby fist revisiting the deeper part of a bucket of his favored Admiral's fried chicken, and the breast he sucked from the bone in one motion didn't allow for him to mouth words of contention. He merely gritted at the grimy trio of white boys, clearly out of place backstage among the newly-formed rap contingent.

Frankie saw Shaky reach to his rear beltline and, seeing a flash of his fresh career as a rap impresario about to face a sudden, vicious demise, lunged for the huge figure just as the gun was freed and leveled at Freud and company. He was a millisecond too late, as Shaky took one step towards Freud, scowled in a fat-faced mask of contempt, and squeezed off eight rapid, repeated rounds into Freud and the two sinewy fellows who'd accompanied him.

Bullets smacked deadly trails through the chest, the arms, the face and head of Freud. His drug-addled cohorts tried to join a sudden rush of handlers, two DJs and five near-naked female dancers for the nearest exit, but were evidently targeted because of their accompaniment of Freud. Bones shattered while teeth gritted and others fractured as the 9 mm rounds spit deadly paths through the two. Freud, already only a measure away from lifelessness, folded to the floor in slow motion, as if in a psychedelic retrospect of his past acid-induced sojourns.

"Shit!" Frankie cried out, looking to his own armed associates for directions.

Artemis shrugged and nodded towards the rear exit. Demitri nodded in agreement, and the three moved out the rear of the facility, into their late-model Cadillac and quickly motored out of the area.

Those awaiting the show in the front of the auditorium were, to a one, quite familiar with the sounds of gunfire. Most were out of the front entrance to the auditorium and causing traffic, even the escaping car of Frankie, to give pause to the stampede. Backstage, Steven "Freud" Willoughby released his last breath, his pal Cornell "Corny" Watkins spat blood, teeth fragments, then last life, while Rob Torres looked through glassy, tear-filled eyes at the last glistening images he'd see before giving up the ghost.

Still seething, Shaky Stick, his massive form shadowy in the backstage darkness, stood above the lifeless body of Freud, struggled to bend down and, with a loud, audible huff, rifled through the dead man's pockets.

"Motherfucker ain't got but...twenty-seven dollars!" Shaky shouted, righting himself and turning to the only other life in the room, the equally massive form of his partner, Possum. "Ain't that a bitch!"

Still quite bedazzled from the effects of the cocaine he'd snorted earlier and the marijuana blunt cigarette he now puffed in place of the devoured chicken, Possum wobbled to one side and pushed his 340 pounds up off of the speaker, looked to Shaky and then to the rear exit.

"Come on, son," Possum said, rolling to the rear exit. "Let's get the fuck out of here before 5-0 be all up in this joint."

Out of pure spite, Shaky squeezed off another round into the head of Freud, spat on him and moved towards the rear exit. On his way, he spotted the empty bucket of chicken and, out of obese disgust and perhaps a renewed intense hunger, he squeezed off a round into the smiling face of the Admiral.

"Fat motherfucker ate up all the damn chicken, yo!" he called to his good friend's back. "You ain't right, Pos. Colder than a motherfucker, eating up all the last chicken and shit!"

Chapter Thirty-six

Police had been out front of the venue all the time, expecting trouble because of who was headlining the show. But by the time they fought through the escaping crowd and cowered in fear themselves at the sound of rapid gunfire coming from backstage, there remained not a single soul in the auditorium, front area or backstage. The phalanx of officers inched behind the curtains, guns drawn, and saw only the three bodies sprawled about, and the rear entrance standing open.

Frankie, in the guise of Ferello Entertainment and Promotions, LLC., had put up the considerably low bond of $10,000 in case of damage to the rental venue. He was sure now, seated in the Cadillac and headed back to New York, that not only would the bond not be refunded, but that he personally would be corralled for questioning in the shootings.

"Them fucking moolies!" he blasted, seated in the rear behind Artemis, who was driving, and Demitri. "God damn moolies!"

Shaky Stick and Possum, meanwhile, were at a 24-hour chicken joint in a section of D.C. many citizens avoided after midnight. They'd been there with some remnants of their newly-formed "posse" for over an hour, exchanging pleasantries with locals who well knew them and were pleased to have them in their company.

"They say three motherfuckers got shot down at The Complex, yo," an 18-year-old excitedly delivered a report to the rappers. "They say 5-0 looking for y'all, know what I'm sayin'? Yo, but y'all asses cool out here in Southeast, yo! Motherfuckers know snitches get stitches out this bitch! Ain't nobody 'bout to holla 'bout where y'all at, know what I'm sayin'?"

"Y'all can come on up to my crib," a slightly dressed, rail-thin young woman sang, trying to ease into the booth the two rappers occupied where no true additional space existed. "And I know where they got that good butter around my way, you hear me?"

Both Shaky Stick and Possum used a variety of drugs, marijuana blunts and powdered cocaine among those they favored. But the offer of the girl of some "butter," crack cocaine, turned them both off.

"Ain't nobody 'bout to be smoking no fucking crack, bitch!" Shaky spat. "Now, I done bust a few motherfuckers already tonight, you hear me, bitch? Get the fuck away from us before I bust a cap up in your skinny ass too!"

"My bad!" the skinny crackhead said, then immediately sashayed out of the chicken joint to seek her pressing needs elsewhere.

The two quite imposing figures, and the crowd they drew even at this late hour, didn't go unnoticed long by police from the 7th District, who were overtaxed and somewhat annealed to the violence, most drug fueled, which permeated this section of Washington far from the marble halls of Congress. The massive, custom SUV out front with New York tags was also a draw to the overnight law enforcement squads. It had been identified in radio reports as carrying some people wanted for questioning in the earlier concert slayings, and also had been identified as carrying the two stars of the show. Police had also been told that it was most likely that Wayne "Shaky Stick" Williams and Antwan "Possum" Taylor had been backstage when the shootings occurred, and were now perhaps armed, drug-addled and dangerous.

Shaky had already gotten rid of the gun on a stretch of road crossing a bridge into the Southeast section of the city. He had thrown it off a bridge crossing the Anacostia River, motoring into an area familiar to one of his posse members who had done time with a native of this D.C. community and who had visited it on a number of occasions. So when the police, in a pack of seven, entered the chicken joint, Shaky and Possum merely looked up from their mounds of French fries, 40-ounce colas and baskets of chicken wings and acknowledge the approaching cadre.

"Officer Friendly!" Shaky said derisively to the lead officer. "What can we do y'all for?"

"ID," the officer said bluntly.

"No problem, po po," Shaky said, swiping Mambo sauce from his lips with a napkin then leaning heavily to the side, pulling a knot of hundred-dollar bills from a front pocket and snagging a driver's license and two credit cards from between the fold of bills.

"You too, big man," the officer said to Possum while taking and looking over the license from Shaky.

"You got it," Possum said, reaching into a breast pocket of the flowing cargo shirt he wore and retrieving a license.

The lead officer repeated their names, then asked them both to stand.

"What up like that?" Shaky asked, wriggling out of the booth.

"Yeah, man. What's the dealio?" Possum asked, near upending the table as he used it for leverage to arise.

"We'll be asking the questions, buddy," lead officer said, nodding to the other officers who surrounded the big men, three on each. They frisked and handcuffed them both. "And we'll be asking them over at the station."

Chapter Thirty-seven

"They locked up Shaky and Possum about that shooting at The Complex last night," Jenkins said, watching with a smile as Siren breast fed six-month-old Troy. "They say three dudes got killed backstage. And guess what? One of 'em was Freud."

"Freud? How you know it was Freud?"

"His real name was Steven Willoughby, right?"

"Yep."

"They IDed his ass as one of the three killed. And remember that fool was writing bad checks to Shaky and Possum on the Reconciliation Tour. Glad we detached from that mess right from the get-go. And that dude Jackson from Star Status tried to convince our legal peoples to get us to keep our money into that shit for the long haul. Told you when I seen Cord and Jeremiah tentative in getting involved any length of time with Star Status, we made the right move just doing that quick investment. Now look at them fools..."

"I'm surprised they beat that rap down in Arkansas," Siren said.

"They ain't beat it. From what I hear, they got bought out by some of them New York gangsters, and them was the ones putting on the new show."

"A trip I tell ya..."

"And you know New York probably had to lay out to get them back on tour," Jenkins said, remotely killing the television and picking up his cell phone. "Bet you it's already a bunch of stuff on line about it. And you know damn well if them New York dudes took a loss on the bond and spit-ready upfront money, well, they can lock up Shaky and Possum all they want. Them dudes from Brooklyn gonna be on their asses even in the joint."

Thirty miles away from the couple's immaculate home, Shaky Stick and Possum were being ferried across an intersecting river, the Anacostia, in the back of a paddy wagon and on their way downtown to police headquarters, where forensics were more precise than the mediocre equipment at Southeast's 7th District substation. Within the hour it would be determined that Wayne "Shaky Stick" Williams had fired a gun within the past 24-hours. Witnesses (those snitches who didn't fear stitches) had been found, and from the other side of a two-way mirror at headquarters, Vermillion Shast, a dancer booked to perform on the aborted Shaky Stick and Possum show, and Calvin Ambrose, the duo's DJ, identified Williams as the gunman and Possum Taylor as an accomplice.

The statements of the two, however, were extracted by an official who'd been called in especially for investigation of the shooting at The Complex. Detective Lawson had years of experience and considerable pull in the department, and he gathered every officer involved in the investigation thus far, and the arresting officers, to inform them all that this case was special, and involved a lot more than the murders of three men deemed of miniscule importance to an overarching interstate, possibly international drug investigation.

"You fellas leave these guys, Shaky Stick and Possum, as they are well known, to me," Lawson instructed his cast of underlings. "This is a far-reaching investigation. And the chief would not be too pleased if any of you fucked it up."

He dismissed the officers, ensured that his lieutenant took custody and control of the evidence and the two portly prisoners, and moved to his private vehicle in the garage, using his cell phone in privacy where he could be assured that no one else could eavesdrop.

Comfortably at home in Brooklyn, Frankie Ferello was relieved to receive the call from Washington, and was reassured that, regardless of the evidence, Shaky Stick and Possum would be released from police custody within the hour.

Chapter Thirty-eight

"I don't get it, my man," Shaky said to Possum, breath labored after having descended a series of twenty-four steps from police headquarters. "They had me dead to rights about firing the gun, and know our asses was in the joint."

"I don't know either, man," Possum, equally breathless, replied. "But who gives a fuck: Dude says they had the ride outta the impound lot and waiting for us, and there it is."

The sleek black luxury SUV sat sparkling across from headquarters, squat in a zone where any other personal vehicle would have been ticketed and impounded. It was centermost amidst a line of marked police cars, and at the far end, an unmarked one with tinted windows. This one was occupied, but the shadowy figures could not be identified except for there being two dark silhouettes inside viewable through the little light seeping in from the untinted front and rear windows.

Shaky and Possum crossed side by side to the SUV. A speeding, approaching car appeared as if it was not going to slow, careering directly towards the two. Shaky and Possum did a little hop-skip, the closest either had come to a run in recent years, and cursed the passing driver.

"These D.C. motherfuckers don't have no respect," Shaky said, pushed a button on the key fob and unlocked both front doors.

They struggled into the seats, each breathing an audible sigh when planted into the plush leather.

"New York with the quickness!" Possum said, extending the seatbelt and shoulder strap fully, struggling to secure it.

"I know that's right!"

They headed east from the police headquarters, unfamiliar with the area but in a few blocks spotted a sign in the blue and red interstate colors directing motorist to 95-North. Possum punched in a CD of new music not yet released, by the group Keepin' It Easy. He'd managed to get a bootlegged copy of the new music featuring the smooth voices of a group of young men he'd met and wished that he had the vocal talents to emulate.

"My boy Jenkins!" he said as the new slow ballad came up. "This joint right here is tight!"

Shaky was a bit tired, having been up all night at the callous behest of law enforcement. Morning traffic was coming into the city, and the route leading out was lightly travelled at this midmorning hour. But he was determined to put as much distance between himself and events at The Complex, and still couldn't believe that police had not kept him and Possum locked up until the investigation was completed. He was straining to keep his focus, then remembered that there was a gram and a half of powerful cocaine in a secret compartment he'd had put into the passenger's door panel.

"Pos. Man, look in that joint in the door and fix me up a snort of that yang yang in there."

Possum knew exactly what his friend was talking about. He tapped a fist on a spot in the door, and it revealed a small cubicle that was previously undistinguishable from the patterned leather surface.

"Nice little piece of shit here, yo," Possum said, tired himself and feeling a couple of toots might enliven his spirit.

He fixed a generous mound of the cocaine onto a small golden spoon that had been secreted in alongside the baggie of cocaine, leaned over and held it under Shaky's right nostril. Expertly, Shaky vacuumed the powder up, creating a sudden, crystalline wonderland within. The powerful dose was immediate in bespeckling his sinuses and delivering the substance to the bloodstream. A straggling, almost caustic drain of the drug slid slipshod down his throat, and his eyes began to water.

"Damn that's some good shit!" Shaky said, as Possum fed a generous amount into each of his own nostrils.

Shaky swallowed hard, creased his eyes and could see a sign pointing out the Baltimore-Washington Parkway. He wanted another hit, but the constriction in his throat found him struggling even for air. Beside him, Possum was heaving, similarly struggling for air. The two men in the unmarked vehicle following them noticed that the SUV was beginning to weave between lanes, and they allowed a greater distance between their car and the SUV.

Possum vomited, spewing forth a gush of digested and undigested fried chicken, pork rinds, cola, French fries, quarter-pound hamburger leavings, potato chips and apple pie. Shaky began heaving also, but folded forward unto the steering wheel, his girth in such an unaccustomed compilation of fat and internal blockage that he lost control of the vehicle, lost consciousness, and careened off the highway, into the woods and slammed into a thick, 100-year-old oak tree.

The SUV burst into flames. Only the two men in the unmarked police car witnessed the horrendous accident. But they kept on driving by, cruising onto the Baltimore-Washington Parkway before taking an exit, making a loop back towards Washington, and passing by the scene of the carnage just as a Park Police cruiser was pulling over to examine the wreckage across the interstate divide.

Chapter Thirty-nine

Siren and Jenkins, along with dozens of well-known recording artists, attended the funeral of Wayne "Shaky Stick" Williams and Antwan "Possum" Taylor. Since the two had been nearly inseparable since toddlers growing up in Brooklyn, the families of both considered it only fitting that the young men who had died together be memorialized in a joint funeral. There was no viewing of course; the two had been cremated, in a sense, burned beyond recognition in the fiery crash.

Investigators did question why there was a secondary explosion, one which was above and beyond that generated when the gas tank caught fire. But that investigation went nowhere; District police were belatedly issuing a warrant for the arrest of the two on murder charges, and this information, though certainly null after the deaths, was nevertheless leaked to the press, further besmirching the characters of yet two other young black men who'd lived fast and died young.

Frankie Ferello, along with his bookend henchmen Artemis and Demitri, made a showing by moving before the crowd of mourners and placing one red rose on each of the closed coffins. Behind dark glasses, few knew who the man in the tailored black suit was, except Shaky's mother. She remembered him as being the kind gentleman who had come forth to free her son from the Arkansas jail, and was receptive when he paid his respects to her personally. Yet Frankie was not there for any altruistic reasons: He was scanning the mourners for others in the music industry who were close to his lost patrons.

He laid eyes on Siren, and having read that she and her husband had extracted themselves from Jupiter Solice and were part of a growing catalogue under their own label, made a mental note to pay her a personal visit in the very near future.

"The girl and her husband and his group, they've formed the core of a company I understand is pretty prosperous, pretty well placed organizationally in rap and soul music," Frankie said to Demitri as they cruised out of Brooklyn towards his New Jersey home. "She used to be heavy on coke a few years back. Used to score from a guy our late friend Salvadore Paz had inserted into the ranks there. Alvarez, I believe it was."

"He's...he's unfortunately...gone on also," Demitri said.

"Yes," Frankie continued, mentally scheming. "What I want you to do, Demitri, is see who the girl has around her, close to her, a sister, close friends, family. And the boy Jenkins. I believe one of the guys in his group was said to have been replaced for a while because of heroin use. Artemis?"

The driver, Artemis, looked to the rearview mirror at his boss, slowed for the coming exit to Frankie's home.

"Yeah, boss?"

"Get back in touch with your cop friend in D.C., the one that helped...dice up...the coke in the car of our late fat friends," Frankie said. "Have him find out what he can around there, around Virginia where the girl and her family lives. You know if you throw a rock in D.C. into a crowd of them moolies, you're bound to hit at least one that's on either crack, heroin or something or other. We need to find someone close to the girl who has...certain...problems...you hear me?"

"I understand boss."

"I want to have something to bargain with before I pay her a visit, understand?"

"I understand, boss."

"Even if it takes you going down to D.C. yourself, you do that for me, OK?"

"OK. I'll find...something...you can use, boss."

By the time Frankie reached home and moved to his study to further design his devious plans, the funeral of Shaky Stick and Possum had moved to the cemetery, where both were laid to rest side by side. The crowd from the Brooklyn church had lessened in number for the graveside rites, but Siren and Jenkins, along with a number of other major rap and recording artists, had joined the families as a continued showing of solidarity among the East Coast rap music community. Also, Siren and Jenkins planned to spend a few days in their New York music studios after the funeral, comfortable in that their child Troy was not only in the care of two well-paid nannies, but was also being seen regularly by his godmothers, Marvella, Sunshine and Genese.

Siren's mother, Jocelyn, had been recently told to stay away from her grandson; afforded all of the luxuries, and money, available through her daughter's success, Jocelyn had rekindled her association with Sirena's father Raymond, who'd feigned sobriety after stints in and out of jail but, given his druthers, still used heroin with regularity. And after seven years of sobriety, it only took a weekend back in the arms of Raymond to have Jocelyn scowling, nodding in that familiar dopefiend nod, hypodermic needles filled again with a heroin now paid for through the generous offerings given her by Siren.

Both Siren and Jenkins knew well the mannerisms of a heroin addict; Jenkins had been a user until he did the "Titanic waltz" and switched to cocaine until finally seeking treatment. And Siren certainly remembered Jocelyn and Raymond as a child, when they were often about in a near comatose existence before little Sirena was given over to Marvella and, after gaining stardom, falling into the deadly travails of addiction herself.

Jocelyn had been given a nice home in the community she desired (mother and daughter had serious problems residing together), not far from the Barry Farm area where she had known familiar heroin scoring grounds with Raymond. Just weeks earlier she'd come to Siren for yet another infusion of cash, and both she and Jenkins knew that she'd "gone back out," in the common NA reference to a person in recovery who'd returned to using. It was akin to the AA descriptive of falling off the wagon, but by the very nature of their addiction, NAs required a more precise, specialized description. "Back out" capsulized it more precisely: Jocelyn had joined Raymond back out on the heroin strip, where one knew where the sale of heroin took place by the plethora of leaning, frowning users gathered about like so many black flies. Teetering on weak legs and appearing as if they were barely even breathing.

It wouldn't take Artemis long to find Jocelyn. Everyone in the heroin underground knew just who her daughter was, whereas many addicts, short on funds, would occasionally seek her or Raymond out to be "blessed" with a complimentary dose. Artemis, accompanied by Demitri, had Jocelyn's pattern marked within days of being dispatched to Washington. Frankie received this and other information two days after the funeral of the two who'd been slated to form the core of Ferello Entertainment and Promotions, LLC.

He was also given some back-up information, about the carrying-ons of one of the children of a young woman named Genese Taylor. Genese, Frankie was told, was closer to Siren than perhaps her own mother.

Soon thereafter, Frankie called the headquarters of Short Siren Music Corporation and demanded a meeting with the company's principles. They denied him a meeting when it was first mentioned that Ferello held the last contracts of Shaky Stick and Possum, and retained the rights to recordings by the duo yet to be released. The emissary for Ferello then mentioned he also wanted to discuss with Siren, particularly, his company's "association" with Jocelyn Lavesque, and with a certain Rock Taylor. Siren immediately got in touch with Genese, who tearfully told her that her brother Raquan "Rock" Taylor, an unrepentant crack dealer in their native Southeast Washington, had recently gone missing.

Chapter Forty

So what the fuck you want me to do about it?!!"

Siren had told Genese that "Lil'' Rock," as her 19-year-old brother was known, would come to no good end selling crack in their old neighborhood. Indeed, she had asked her best friend to offer the young man a position with her record company, to no avail. And now he was missing, to all who knew him. He had, however, made a cryptic phone call to Genese, asking her to pass on a message to Siren: Lil' Rock was now "employed" by Ferello Entertainment and Promotions, LLC, and was seeking her and Jenkins's cooperation in a proposed "joint music venture."

"I really don't know, Sirena," Genese said tearfully. "But he didn't sound like himself. And then he said his…his 'new boss' said to tell you also that they had a 'target audience' around 14th and Good Hope Road in Southeast D.C. with your mother and father as the 'principle targets'. Girl, what's that all about?"

"That don't take a lot of deciphering," Sunshine, the more cerebral of the two friends, interjected. "They're talking about messing with your mother and father. Fourteenth and Good Hope is around a dope strip. That's where my big brother hangs out, and that fool has been shooting blow for 20 years."

The three were in the 46th floor offices of Short Siren Music Corporation in midtown Manhattan. Sunshine was office manager for the recording and concert promotions company, commuting between her suburban Washington home and New York weekly. Always the most studious of the three best friends, Sunshine remained single, focused on business but content not to have many personal goals of her own. Deeply religious, she felt that things were going to occur regardless, attended the Greater

Abyssinian Baptist Church regularly, but not religiously. She was seeing a young man who also attended the church, but pronounced it as nothing serious to Siren and Genese. Her salary at Short Siren, and previously as an executive assistant to Siren, was $340,000 annually, and she was quite content and extremely professional in assuming her varied and critical duties with the organization.

"They sound like mobsters," Genese said. "They had Shaky and Possum under contract, and from what some of the guys with Keepin' It Easy say, Frankie Ferello's been trying to sign a lot of rappers to this candyland ass label he's got. But talk around Star Status is that they financed that joint through drug money, so Mr. Ferdinand over at Star Status cut ties with anybody have anything to do with Ferello."

"I'm not getting Short Siren involved with that motherfucker either!" Siren said, setting upright in the high-back leather chair, behind her oak desk and looking seriously to Genese, especially, and Sunshine, seated in matching leather chairs before her. "Why is he bringing us this shit about Lil' Rock?"

Genese teared up. "He knows you and me are close. And he knows I love my little brother!"

"And mentioning your mother and father was just his way of bringing family into the situation, just in case you...well, you know...don't have the love for Lil' Rock that Genese does."

"So," Siren said, locking fingers and placing two before her lips in a pose each of her friends knew as one assumed when she was in deep thought. "I want both of you here when I discuss this with Jenkins after him and the boys finish up in the studio. But in the meantime, Sunshine, see if you can get Freddy on the phone."

"Security?" Genese said, sniffling.

"Yeah, security," Siren said. "But Freddy's got skills. I want to run this by him. Face-to-face."

"Freddy," Sunshine smiled.   "Yeah, girl.   That's who you need on top of this."

Chapter Forty-one

They had to continue with their business plan. Even before the deaths of Shaky Stick and Possum, Short Siren Music Corporation had scheduled rolling out a number of radio announcements to coincide with the Black Music Artist and Agents Annual Awards. Both Siren as a single artist, and Jenkins, leading Keepin' It Easy, were scheduled to perform at the BMAA event which was to be telecast live that spring. Frankie Ferello had demanded a personal meeting with the two of them, but Freddy, Siren's most trusted security manager, warned against it, forbade it in fact, and asked that they leave the matter in his hands.

"I have some contacts in Brooklyn who know this guy intimately," Freddy said, in New York after Siren had given him a telephonic overview of the situation and asked that they meet in her office. "Some of his own people, and they aren't too happy with his ass anyway."

So Freddy made a few telephone calls himself, scheduled a meeting first with an old friend from his days in the boxing arena and sat with him over espressos at a little spot off Washington Square. This contact arranged for Freddy to meet with a man simply known locally as "Mr. M," at the restaurant the mysterious man owned in Little Italy. That meeting gave him the precise information, and the authorization to use the source of the information, in a meeting with Frankie Ferello.

At first Frankie refused to meet with the "special investigator," as Freddy had been identified by the secretary at Ferello Entertainment and Promotions.

"Why the hell would the girl hire a special investigator?" he asked Artemis and Demitri, setting in the rear of the storefront/townhome, which he used as the office headquarters of his varied business enterprises. "The little crack dealer we got back there is not going anywhere until she and her husband meet with me.

Personally! She can go to the fucking police for all I care. We'll just disappear the little fuck!" He chuckled at the thought. "No fucking evidence, no foul, no crime!"

"But Dorelle said this guy said he had some words for you from Mr. M," Artemis said. He'd been the one approached by the secretary, Dorelle, about the special investigator.

Frankie sat bolt upright in his office chair, stopped rocking back and forth.

"Mr. M? *Our* Mr. M?"

"Didn't say," Artemis said. "But alls I can figure, must be Mr. M from midtown. Don't think anyone else in the whole damn city would have the nerve to go about calling themself Mr. M."

"Um-huh." Frankie grew reflective.

There was silence in the small, cramped office for close to a minute. Both Artemis and Demitri knew not to bother the boss when he was in deep thought. Artemis grabbed a copy of GQ   magazine from a coffee table, Demitri leaned forth in his chair, twiddling his thumbs.

"Dorelle get this guy's full name?" Frankie asked finally.

"Freddy Glover," Artemis said. "If I remember correctly, he headed up security for the girl when she was on tour, started a security firm of his own later on but stayed on contract with the Siren girl. On with her and her husband's new company, I imagine."

"Um-huh..."

Again, Frankie had to let the information marinate.

"And this guy knows Mr. M?"

"Apparently."

"Well, what the hell," Frankie said, exhaling audibly and arising. "Arrange a meet with this son-of-a-bitch! See what it is the fuck he wants."

Chapter Forty-two

Freddy had a collection of guns which would have been looked upon with envy by any gun enthusiast. Although he had never had to fire one outside of the many practice ranges he visited, he was nevertheless an expert marksman and could dismantle, clean and reassemble any weapon in his extensive collection. He was licensed to carry small arms, open and concealed, and had a selection from the Walther PPK made famous by James Bond, to the .44 Magnum favored in film by Dirty Harry. The M16-A2 was a rifle he favored for its light weight and long distance accuracy. The Mac 10 120309-1 M 11-9 for its ability to do extensive damage in case one was facing down a mob.

Yet the former heavyweight boxer was a peaceful spirit if untroubled. He had a serious demeanor when on a job, was a large, cuddly lion when in the sole presence of Marvella, his continuing companion now to the point where theirs could be considered a common-law marriage. He took his security responsibilities seriously though, and had been protecting Siren for such a period that he had come to look upon her as if she were his own daughter. He had no children himself, after all, and ever since she was 18 he'd been directly responsible for Siren's safety. For anyone to threaten that safety would be a serious mistake on their part.

He received a call on his cell phone while still in the offices of Short Siren, speaking with Jenkins, Genese, Sunshine and Siren about the disappearance of Genese's brother, the cryptic message from Frankie Ferello, and exactly what the message and disappearance of Lil' Rock meant.

"Personally, I believe Ferello's trying to weasel into the company, get Siren and 'Easy under his umbrella. A little asking about shows how he got those fellows Shaky

Stick and Possum out from under their previous contract," Freddy said.

They were all seated around a conference table that had space for 24 seated on both sides and either end. Siren and Jenkins had leased the 46th and 47th floors of this midtown Manhattan skyscraper and outfitted the 47th with nothing but state-of-the-art studios and recording spaces. The 46th was corporate offices, all overseeing specific operations of Short Siren Music Corporation. The conference room, fitted with the long cedar table, red leather chairs and video and conference equipment throughout, was where both Siren and Jenkins preferred to hold their most serious meetings. Small, informal sessions were often held in either's spacious and elaborate offices. But the current matter seemed to call for discussion in the conference room, if only to emphasize its seriousness.

"What's this dude supposed to be: Some kind of Mafia motherfucker or some shit?" Jenkins asked, upset that his wife, through her best friend, appeared to have been threatened.

"He got some connects," Freddy said. "But most in the business, those you might formerly have associated with organized crime, have long since put that sordid past behind them. Present…'family members'….if you want to call them that, are truly your family type. They run legitimate businesses, though their grandfathers and great-grandfathers used to engage in methods frowned upon and debased as organized crime. And from talking to a few…associates…here in the city, many of those whom this guy might seek associations with frown upon his tactics. Not to mention that, from all I hear, he's still deeply involved in the mass distribution of illegal drugs. That's something my…associates…aren't particularly pleased with."

Just then Freddy's cellular phone rang. He arose, took the call while moving to the exit, ended it and returned to those gathered, spoke directly to Siren and Genese.

"I got this, ladies," he said. "You folks go ahead and get ready for your concerts and recordings and such."

Chapter Forty-three

He wore the Walther in a concealed shoulder holster. It was less cumbersome than the Magnum, but just as effective, if needed. The storefront/townhome wasn't particularly distinguishable on a street consisting of small cafes, mom-and-pop stores on the corners, a genteel haberdashery next door to it. The floor-to-ceiling windows fronting the street were covered with curtains, and the only indication as to what kind of business operated from within were the gold letters emblazoned on the curtained, full glass door: "Ferello Entertainment and Promotions, LLC."

There was a discreet doorbell inlaid in the metal frame of the doorway. He pushed the button and could barely make out the shrill ringing of the bell within. A few locks clanged, and a short, dark haired man in an ill-fitting suit held the door open.

"Freddy Glover?" he asked in a course voice.

"Freddy Glover for Frankie Ferello."

"Come on in."

The front of the establishment was set up as if it had once been a supper club. Little light defused the interior, and that was coming from a huge mirrored beer advertisement behind the bar. The little man in the lilac-colored suit walked slowly to the rear of the club area; he didn't have to ask Freddy to follow him.

Through a pair of swinging, padded doors was a kitchen. Stainless steel tables and refrigerators aligned this room, but it was evident from the dust and dank odor that this hadn't been used for food preparation for some time. The little man pushed through a door at the rear of the kitchen, moved into a hallway which was better lighted and had two closed office doors to either side. At the end of the hall was another closed door. The man tapped on the office door to the left, then entered.

"Your guest, boss," shorty said to a better dressed man seated behind a wooden, generic desk. Two others sat in chairs to his left and right.

The man behind the desk stood, extended a hand.

"Freddy! Freddy Glover! Security man to the stars!"

Freddy took the hand firmly, looked deep into the man's eyes, glanced at the two others and back at the short man who'd escorted him here.

"I take it you're Frankie Ferello. Can't say it's a pleasure, my man. Seeing as to the reason that I'm here."

"Well," Frankie said, motioning to a chair before his desk. "Have a seat! Can I get you something? A drink? Water? Perhaps a beer? We have that malt liquor you people like! Want a 40-ounce?"

Freddy's glowering eyes could have cut steel.

"Let's cut the crap, fella, OK?" He sat at the seat before the desk. "Now, I don't give a damn about your...dealings...when it comes to your drug distribution, your trying to play music impresario, the...damn mess you put together that got them two young men killed, the fat rappers. I'm here for one and only one purpose: You've tried to wriggle your greasy ass into the affairs of my good friend and young charge Siren, through her good and dear friend Genese. Now, I'm here for the boy, and to hear you state out of your own vulgar-ass lips that you received the message loud and clear, and that your little...threat...about Siren's people in D.C. was...well, let's just say, a misadventure of some misguided fool."

Frankie leaned forward, elbows on desk, and looked between Artemis, Demitri, his little henchman who bounced about, antsy to Freddy's rear.

Who in the hell do you think you are, coming into my place making demands?! You got a serious pair of cojones on you, you black—"

Freddy raised a hand, palm out to Frankie, then eased back the left side of his jacket, exposing the holstered Walther.

"Now, Mr. Ferello, I'm going to get my smartphone out of my breast pocket. I think there's someone on the other end of an open call I've kept active that you might want to speak with before you make a serious, bad, really, really fucked up move!"

Artemis and Demitri were already standing to each side of Freddy, the little man behind him so close Freddy could feel his breath on his neck. Slowly, Freddy retrieved the smartphone, placed it on the desk before Frankie and pushed a button, activating the speakerphone feature. A female voice arose from it.

"Frankie? Sweetheart? I'm at the place with this Mr. M, and the guys who picked me up said that you'd be meeting me here? Where are you, sweetheart?"

All the color drained out of Frankie's face.

"You black bastard!"

Another voice, older, rugged, arose from the phone.

"Frankie. Do us all a favor and take care of Mr. Glover's wishes. I understand there's a boy from Washington doing some sort...work for you there? Mr. Glover has come to escort that boy back to his family. And the boy's family, and all of their kin, have expressed to me that they no longer wish to do any business with you. Do you understand?"

Frankie, crestfallen, motioned his head left and right, directing Demitri and Artemis to back off of Freddy.

"Do....you...understand...Frankie?" the amplified speakerphone voice asked.

"You can just speak into it, my man," Freddy said, smiling directly at Frankie.

"I understand, Mr. M. Artemis is going to get the boy even as we speak."

"Good," the telephoned voice said. "Now, when Mr. Glover has the boy, and your reassurance that your interests in D.C. are no more, he will give me a call. And this little...luncheon...with this lovely wife of yours, will be concluded and my friends here will see her home safely."

"I understand, Mr. M. I understand."

Chapter Forty-four

They took a cab to the offices of Short Siren Music Corporation, but with traffic thick Freddy spent the time schooling the frail, dreadlocked young man on current events. He looked to the Plexiglas partition and the driver, who had on headphones to an MP3 player. He didn't want anyone to hear the conversation he was having with Anthony, known by many only as "Lil' Rock."

"Here's the deal, son," Freddy said. "Your sister is a very, very close friend of my primary employer, Siren. I know you know her and I know you know that."

"Yes sir," Lil' Rock said sheepishly.

"If it wasn't for your sister, and the love she has among Siren's people," Freddy continued, "we'd have left your tail there with Ferello and his boys, not met their demands, and let them do what they planned on doing with you. And to tell you the truth, even if we had met their demands, they weren't going to let you walk out of that place alive, young man. Hell, last thing they want is a live kidnap victim walking around able to put a finger on them. You listening to what I'm saying, son?"

"Yes sir."

In his element, Anthony "Lil' Rock" Taylor was an often feared, known to be gun-totting young man, a drug dealer in the hardest part of Southeast Washington where, even during summer's heat, neither police nor drug dealers dared move about without the wearing of heavy, sweat-inducing bulletproof vests. But the very shock of having been snatched up by a bunch of true, New York City gangsters had melted away the young man's hard core persona and had him as peevish and coy now as some little jailhouse bitch.

"Now, we're going up to the headquarters of Siren's recording and production company, and your sister Genese is office manager of a business she, Siren, Jenkins and even I am quite proud of. The young lady is making millions, has just signed four new acts and is about to release new material and go on tour. Your sister has a job for you; you are not going back down there on Southern Avenue in D.C. selling your crack. Those days are over, hear me?"

"Yes sir."

"You ever even think about going back there, feel you have a need to get back with your boys, just get that out of your way of thinking, understand?"

"Yes sir."

"I work closely with your sister, with Siren. If I even hear an inkling of you messing up, even on the new job, well, I'll just tell you straight up what's in store for you: With a word from Genese, I'm not going to see no harm done to you. But you fuck up just once, just once, and I have a good friend who has a ranch out in Wyoming. You know where Wyoming is, young man?"

"No sir. Out...out there in the west I think..."

"Yeah. Way out west. And with one word from Siren or Genese about you not getting serious and taking care of business, I'm going to personally escort your ass out there to my friend's ranch. For a year. At least! We'll call it rehab. And after a year working ....I mean real, real hard ranch work out there, I'm sure you'll realize that you're receiving a blessing not many black boys your age get. You hear me?"

"Yes sir."

"If I have to take your ass out to Wyoming, Anthony, the only other black face you'll see for a year, besides yours in a mirror, will be on a buffalo. We understand one another?"

"Yes sir!"

They arrived at the midtown skyscraper, and Lil' Rock seemed surprised at all the people rushing about. He followed Freddy into the building, took elevators to the

20th floor and transferred over to elevators, which ascended from there to higher levels.

"Man!" Lil' Rock said. "New York is crankin' like a mug!"

They were alone in an elevator, the digital notification counting off floors with an audible "ding" at every passing.

"Never been to New York before, huh?" Freddy asked.

"Naw, man! And this time, dudes had me all in the trunk of a car and mess, I ain't even see how I got here!"

Freddy laughed lightly. "You hang in there tight with big sis. You'll see so much of New York you'll be begging to get back to the calmer scene down in D.C."

"Yeah..."

The elevator opened to a reception area warmed with inlaid neon lighting which showed off the matching deep red carpeting and similarly designed wallpaper. A semi-circular desk of finely carved ebony sat before the cursive gold letters announcing Short Siren Music Corporation headquarters. A smiling young lady who could have been a professional model sat on a high chair behind the desk, in indiscernible conversation with one of two armed, uniformed guards who stood stoic on each side of the desk. They all looked to the man and youth stepping into the lobby, nodded to the familiar face of the head of security.

"Diane," Freddy said, stepping up to the receptionist desk. "Dequan. Ellis. How's it going?"

The two looked to the dreadlocked youth accompanying their boss, smiled.

"All good, chief," Dequan said.

"Mission accomplished, looks like," Ellis said.

"Mr. Glover. Ms. Shorter will be so glad to see...," she looked at Lil' Rock, smiled directly to him. "I take it this is her brother Anthony?"

"Anthony Taylor, Diane Franklin." He introduced the young man formally, determined to get him started into a business frame of reference he certainly was unfamiliar with. "And these two gentlemen are Sgt. Johnson and Lt. Massey."

Attempting to present himself in a manner only seen before on television, Lil' Rock stepped to the officer on the left, shook his hand formally, reached over the receptionist's desk and took the young lady's hand lightly, and then shook the officer's hand on the right.

"Nice to meet you," he said to each. "Nice to meet you."

Diane picked up a phone. "Mr. Glover? You want me to let Ms. Taylor know her brother is in the lobby?"

"Is she in her office?" Freddy asked.

"In conference with Ms. Lavesque and Ms. Melody. In Conference Room A."

Freddy stepped off towards a pair of glass doors to the left of the receptionist area.

"I'll take him back," Freddy said. "The girl's been waiting to get the good news. Don't want to keep her waiting any longer."

Lil' Rock smiled to the receptionist, nodded to the officers and followed Freddy through the glass doors. He stood a little taller now, his be-bopping gait of the past suddenly gone. His chest was held out with a measure of pride previously elusive, and his chin was held a little higher.

"I ain't going back out on them corners, Mr. Glover. For real, yo!"

Freddy smiled, nodded. He opened the heavy wooden doors to Conference Room A and watched with satisfaction as Anthony left "Lil' Rock" behind and rushed into the welcoming arms of his older sister.

Chapter Forty-five

"Ladies and gentlemen, put your hands together for nine time BMMA, three time IMRA and seven time AACRC award winner, SIIIIIIII-----REN!!!"

Tickets to all three shows at the downtown D.C. arena had sold out on line within minutes, and for Siren the first show was something of a homecoming. She had personally reserved a block of tickets in the front and center of the arena for the former residents of Barry Farm, many of whom were now purchasing homes at the newly-premiered Glades Manor Estates. She and Jenkins had underwritten many of the purchases at a loss, but through a number of financial maneuvers by their expert accountants, other real estate investments were being deducted from their enormous incomes as business expenses. The three condos in Manhattan were short-term dwelling places for clients of Short Siren Music Corporation. The spectacular house in Las Vegas was listed as property exclusively for any from their roster of artists performing in that city. The properties in Jamaica and the Bahamas? Owned by Short Siren Music Corporation as short-term relaxation sites for clients, staff and artists alike.

Siren was in rare form for the opening night, and her new material dominated the charts of recording industry periodicals and overwhelmed the playlists of a variety of stations nationwide. Not far behind her record-breaking numbers, Keepin' It Easy had released new material on their new label, Short Siren Records, and with Jenkins in top form also, the group was in perfect shape to headline shows themselves.

There was a combination of love flowing along with well thought out joint business decisions. The members of Keepin' It Easy had been promised (and had in contractual form) that they would be paid as if headliners along with Siren, and the group was the only other act besides Siren to appear on the "Return to Victory Tour."

To say that Siren was in fine form vocally and physically would have been a serious understatement. Since her brush with addiction she'd been convinced that only by assuming a good, clean diet and physical fitness regimen could she avoid the calamity often brought on by those first few sips of champagne. And with little Troy beginning to demand more time from his mother, Siren was determined to run her personal and business lives with the utmost efficiency.

Always slender at 5' 9" and an attraction since a pre-teen, Siren had insisted that Jenkins put over space on the 47th floor in New York for a fitness center, and of course had one, and an Olympic-sized swimming pool, in their McLean home. She strutted about the stage energized, and Freddy's security ranks had their hands full keeping surging men, and some women, from trying to climb onto the stage when she broke into her latest hit, "Come Get This."

This was the first show to kick off a 12-week tour, and besides venues in 10 other American cities, the Return to Victory Tour was already sold out for leagues of fans in Berlin, Paris and London. Georgia Whitfield-Johnson, whom Siren and Jenkins had teased over from Jupiter Solice with a $1.7 million signing bonus, was managing Siren and the tour exclusively now. Georgia had initially wanted to extend the tour to 18 weeks. But even as she watched from backstage with Jenkins, Marvella, Sunshine, Genese and Anthony (the former Lil' Rock, now a well paid equipment manager), only Georgia and the other women knew why an extension of the tour would have been inadvisable: Siren was six weeks pregnant with her second child, and beside not wanting to chance her high-energy act well into the pregnancy, she would surely be showing by the end of an extended tour. With Troy, she had been a considerable balloon at five months.

She made her bow to tremendous applause, danced off the stage to the uproarious demands for an encore. The band feigned as if they were going to dismantle their equipment, then as planned in rehearsal after rehearsal, Siren glided back unto the stage, made a show of motioning to her band to prepare for a reprise, then eased into the funky, upbeat, bass-driven song "You Ain't Seen Nothing Yet."

The song was just weeks into rotation on national radio stations, and was especially heavily played in her native Washington. But the song had a moving bridge where superstar rapper Too Good had provided the rapid-fire lyrics in the recording studio. Still, Siren and the band broke into the song, and at the point where the rap lyrics were set to come up, none other than Too Good, contracted by Short Siren Music for only the cameos in D.C., bounded onto the stage.

The crowd went berserk.

After another fifteen minutes of a most exciting and heated performance, Siren finally bid her hometown audience a good night. In joyful celebration, Siren, Jenkins, group members, band members and others turned the entirety of the backstage area into a party. The corks on rich champagne bottles were popped, dressing room doors were propped open for any to flow in and out and, in a few bathrooms, a few individuals fired up marijuana blunts while an even more limited few snorted cocaine or heroin. There were no secrets in this touring group, and Siren and Jenkins, and even security overseer Freddy, knew who was doing what and, more than likely, how much.

Yet the roadies who favored cocaine kept it within their small number, and it was certain that there was no one actually peddling marijuana, coke or heroin on the tour. Nevertheless Siren and Jenkins, the ultimate decision makers, let it be known that personal, private use of whatever would be abided. Indeed, Siren, with her past experiences with cocaine, knew well that some of the musicians, much like her lost beloved guitar player Silver Shadow, performed with such a passion because they knew that, after the show, they could wind down with their drug of choice. For many, it was simply champagne, beer, liquor. But for others, the creative juices seemed dampened if they were not left to their own devices after, and sometimes before, shows that often had them operating and pumped for 18-hour days.

Siren and Jenkins knew they could not even so much as drink a beer, lest they chance being sparked back into, first, itsy-bitsy teeny-weeny tastes, then just-a-hit ingestions before, finally, returning to full-blown addiction. Even now, watching joyous employees/colleagues engage in controlled imbibing of champagne, both were being needled internally to partake. Thus, the nature of an addict's lifetime struggle to stay sober, and the accomplishment of realizing that staying sober is as necessary as breathing. One breath, and one day, at a time.

"Baby, you were on tonight!" Marvella said, easing up beside Siren as she again thanked Too Good for his participation. "Very good, young lady!"

Marvella went off to speak with Freddy and a few of the "senior" members of the tour. They had their own little posse, the seven or so regulars over the age of 40. Siren had a tight little group of her own, and most were keenly aware of her and Jenkins's past problem with drugs. So Genese, Sunshine, makeup artist/hair stylist Shonda and now Georgia joined her in her spacious dressing room, sans alcohol. Too Good gathered with Jenkins, Sanford and the rest of the Keepin' It Easy group. Some sipped champagne, some cognac. All were reassured seeing Jenkins limiting himself to his favored apple cider, quart of acai berry juice and other natural elixirs of one type or another.

"Two more shows down this joint, man!" Sanford said joyously, "the boys" gathered around a spacing of speakers backstage, which now doubled as seats and tabletops. "We're sold out here and in Baltimore and in Atlanta already!"

He looked to his childhood friend Jenkins, clasped his hand and gave him a hug. "Man, you and your wife making it happen, yo! First I thought Keepin' wasn't gonna get back together like this, know what I'm saying?"

"I hear ya, man," Jenkins said.

"Yo," Too Good cut in. "How come you and ol' wifey don't hook me up with the show in Atlanta. Or she ain't gonna do 'You Ain't Seen Nothing' after the D.C. joints?"

"You know she can't do it without your part, young'un," Jenkins said. "I'm gonna holla at her about that, yo. For real though: That was the best part of her set, that encore, closing it out like that and you coming out like, ain't nobody even think that was going to happen. Crowd went off, man!"

"Loved it," Sanford said.

"For real though," Jenkins said again. "I'm gonna holla at Siren about that, Too Good. You show for the same deal we inked for D.C., plus, you know, we'll handle your travel and expenses. I think she'd sure like to have you on in Atlanta, and probably the L.A. shows too. Man, that joint was tight when you came in with your part man! Crowd went cold-blooded off!"

"Alright!" Too Good said. "Talk to Siren about me doing the damn thing in Atlanta. And maybe even Baltimore too. My schedule's open like that. Alright?"

"Alright, bro. Alright."

Chapter Forty-six

Everyone on the dope strip knew that Jocelyn Lavesque and Raymond Carter were the parents of the acclaimed vocal artist Siren. In heroin-induced reflections, both would surface from near comatose nods to grumble on about how their "baby" was making millions. Dopefiends had a cadre all their own, and unlike crack addicts, who would knife another addict in the back over the last "hit," heroin addicts were known to share dope, needles, and any other requisite information or utensil to aid in the acquisition of their common "get-high:" Heroin. Joogie. Blow.

A dopefiend didn't need a lot of money. Ten dollars could purchase a "sack" which, when cooked up and injected directly into a vein, would place the user in a near unconscious abyss for a few hours. What a dopefiend did need was consistent funds. On a good day a heroin addict might shoot four or five dimes, starting at sunrise and ending at sunset. Fifty dollars could last a daily heroin user all day. Whereby fifty-dollars in the hands of a crack addict wouldn't last as many minutes. Siren had blessed her mother with a nice comfortable home; nothing extravagant, and a serviceable car, one which wouldn't attract a carjacker but would serve to get her around to get her dope. She'd also ensured that her mother had a little cash on hand; nothing extensive. Three, four thousand dollars. In twenties. Also an attempt to keep her mother out of the sight of fiending marauders, usually crackheads, sometimes just young'uns who never worked and wanted a pair of the latest $250.00 tennis shoes.

Among the dopefiend cadre around Good Hope Road in Southeast Washington, Jocelyn and Raymond were most beloved. The two could be counted on to "bless" a member, who'd come up short of funds on any given day, with a complimentary shot.   So everyone watched their backs, and as most were seasoned users, in their 30s, 40s, they did have a measure of respect among the young guns who robbed and killed with regularity in surrounding communities. Many of these young hoods, to be sure, were the children of lifelong drug users.

Jocelyn and Raymond had been invited to the opening show downtown the night before; Siren knew they wouldn't come. Dopefiends began their days early, and by nightfall the comatose nod was no longer drug-induced, but generated by a necessity for actual sleep. Out of respect, however, she'd had a pair of front row tickets delivered to her mother's home, and pointedly noticed that the two seats had been occupied by a young flashy dresser and an equally overly dressed young woman. The young man had smiled at her at one point during the show, and the glistening gold front tooth had convinced her that the seats reserved for her mother and father had been sold to a dope dealer. Or more probably, traded to the dealer for a hefty amount of heroin.

Her second assessment was on point.

On the morning after her daughter's show, Jocelyn arose with a nod and a smile. Sunrise was an hour off, but this morning she didn't have to make the trek down Good Hope Road and stand, like a bunch of farm animals awaiting feeding, among the pack of dopefiends anticipating the arrival of the dope man. She had enough smack to keep her off the streets for days, the dealer having been quite generous, and quite appreciative, of the pair of tickets to see Siren and Keepin' It Easy.

Raymond was on the first floor of the home. He'd spent a few hours with her in the master bedroom the previous evening, oversaturated with dope yet solid enough to deliver a climax-inducing penis into the woman he'd been doing so to for over 27 years. Sated both sexually and with narcotics, she'd gone to bed and enjoyed yet another dream of herself in star lights; Jocelyn was a gifted singer in her day. But a then-19-year-old Raymond had spirited away both her virginity and social innocence.

The former church girl and the "bad boy" from Barry Farm entered the death march that is heroin addiction hand-in-hand, and although parted periodically when Raymond was jailed for one crime or another, the two had spent all of their adult lives together. Both were proud when Jocelyn gave birth to little Sirena. And when she eventually gained stardom, after being voluntarily handed over to Jocelyn's own guardian/godmother Marvella, the two were relieved that they had done the right thing and not raised the girl with noticeable vocal talents in their often whirlwind world of heroin addiction.

After a nice, warm shower, Jocelyn dressed and moved downstairs to the savory aroma of fried bacon. Raymond was on the sofa, shoveling scrambled eggs and cheese into his mouth, following it with a scrap of bacon and a swig of orange juice.

"Wassup, baby?" she said, her course, gruff, dopefiend voice now common even when sober.

"Gettin' my chow on, girl," he said in a similar, uninspired voice. "You know we both need to put some food on our stomach, good as that shit is ol' boy blessed us with."

"I know…"

She dragged her way into the kitchen, spooned the extra eggs and cheese from the frying pan and took the last three strips of bacon off the countertop, placed them in the microwave and heated them for 40 seconds. Retrieving a fork from the dish rack beside the sink, she began eating the breakfast fare while walking back to the living room. She took a seat in a lounge chair beside the sofa where Raymond sat. His breakfast finished, he was dipping a measure of heroin out of a plastic baggie, placing it in a tablespoon. He drew water into a hypodermic needle from a glass on the coffee table, carefully injected the water into the spoonful of heroin, raised it and took a cigarette lighter, held it below the spoon until the heroin and water mixture just barely began to boil.

Carefully, he sat the spoon down on the fold of paper towel before him, grabbed a cigarette from a pack and, with teeth, pulled the cotton-like substance out of the filter end of the cigarette. He further toothed apart a small segment of the cotton, rolled it between index finger and thumb, dropped it into the cooling concoction of dope. Easily, he put the head of the hypodermic needle into the now-saturated cotton, filtered up a good thirty cc dose.

A belt around the upper arm, tightened, he was fortunate to find a vein. Many of his had collapsed, and those in the crick of his elbow were now virtually useless. Veins on his hand stood out, however, and in seconds the plunger was pulled back, filling the mixture with his blood and assuring that he was going right into a vein. Injected, he eased the plunger back once again, filled it again with his blood, eased in forward to expedite the flow of heroin into his body.

He just rocked, scowled, removed the needle and took water from the glass into it, squirted it into an ashtray, cleaning his "works."

"Good shit, ain't it?" Jocelyn said, easing down beside him on the sofa and commencing to prepare her own dose.

"No shit," he said, leaning back, eyes aflutter.

The veins in her arms were long rendered useless through years of use. She had on a loose, flowing dress though, particularly because of the way she had to inject her heroin: On a vein in the upper inner thigh. It was precariously close to her vagina, and she wore no drawers. But when engaged in shooting dope, even among a number of men and women in close proximity to one another, female modesty a foreign consideration. She saw blood fill the needle, assured that she had a vein, and engaged the motions towards heroin-induced obliteration.

"Damn!" she said, taking in a deep breath and cleaning the needle.

They sat there, each to his own world, nodding, scowling, satisfied that the amount of dope before them meant they would not have to go out onto the streets for a long time. He nodded to near unconsciousness, jerked himself back up and went for a second hit. She eased her eyes open and, having her own personal set of works, took her needle, got another spoon and fixed a secondary hit also.

Most dopefiends ran out of money, out of dope, before they ingested enough to overdose. Raymond and Jocelyn had been afforded an abundance of dope on a number of occasions since tapping into the wealth of their daughter. But the volume they had now, combined with the overall wear and tear on their hearts, their livers especially, and their bodies as a whole, over nearly thirty years, compounded as one disastrous mix on this morning.

It would be four days before a mutual dopefiend friend, seeking a blessing from the two, checked on them at the home and found the two, dead and stinking.

Chapter Forty-seven

It was Freddy who broke the news to Siren. A friend of his on the police force had been contacted by a dopefiend and told that the two dead users were the parents of the acclaimed star. He subsequently phoned Freddy, and on a two day break following the conclusion of the D.C. leg of the tour, he found Siren and Jenkins at their McLean mansion, joyously at play with little Troy and the two Afghan hound pups Siren had recently purchased.

"Bad news, baby girl," Freddy said in his serious, almost morbid tone. "Your mother and father: ODed."

Siren stopped playing with the boy and the male pup Rascal, looked up to her security man.

"Both of them?"

"Both of them."

"Damn..." Siren and Jenkins said simultaneously.

The main thing that bothered Siren was that she really wasn't that bothered by the deaths. Sure, she loved her mother and father, in a sense. But she'd never really known them, having been put in the care of Marvella as a toddler and only visited by her mother on occasion through her early years.

"Well," she said to Freddy, arising and taking a now walking Troy by a small hand. "I guess there's nobody but me close enough to them, or care enough like that, to make the arrangements. Freddy, if you don't mind, let Marvella know. Is she at...home?"

She knew of their intimacy, but felt uncomfortable addressing her beloved security man about her even more beloved guardian.

"She's at home," Freddy said simply, turned to leave. "I'll get with her, Siren, and we'll claim the bodies and make the initial arrangements. I believe Marvella knew them about as much as you, maybe even more, comes to your mother. I think she can ID the bodies, save you from that nasty chore."

"OK, Freddy. And...thanks."

"You got it, baby girl."

Jenkins came up beside his wife and baby, took Troy's other hand and walked jointly with Siren out of the play room, through the kitchen and into the living room. They were trailed by the two puppies, tails wagging and playful, in a sense, until they neared the three and appeared as if emotionally rebuffed when dancing up and stretching front paws onto Siren and Jenkins. Both crouched down and began to whimper, as if sensing that there had been a death in the family.

Siren sat on one of the long sofas in the living room, took Troy upon her lap. Jenkins sat a few feet from her on the same sofa, patted his lap and called for the puppies to join him. They reacted excitedly, hopped on the sofa and gave themselves over to Jenkins's petting and fluffing of their coats.

"Baby, I hope you don't go blaming yourself for your mother and father," Jenkins said. "You know as well as I do that there wasn't nothing you could do that would have mattered, with them doing what they were doing. Know what I'm saying?"

"I know baby," Siren said.

"Know goo!" Troy garbled in.

Siren laughed, kissed him on a cheek. "I know you know too, sweet thing! I know you know!"

"You should have heard him the other night, baby. Marvella had him on the phone, after the second shows. Boy was trying to sing! I swear! Sounds like he was trying to do my jam, 'Sweetness.' Talk about 'weee—weeee---nees'! Wee---weee-nees'! I ain't lying, Siren. Ask Marvella!"

He fluffed around the dogs roughly, until they both appeared irritated and began growling at him.

"Yeah, buck, suckers!" Jenkins teased them.

"Leave them babies alone!" Siren smiled. "You so mean!"

Siren stretched out on the sofa, Troy cuddled beside her. Jenkins stretched out towards the other end, kicked off his slippers and stretched his feet up to and behind Siren. He began rubbing on her rear end with his toes.

"Stop it!" she smiled. "This little girl inside of me is ticklish..."

He stopped, pulled the leg back and sat up on an elbow.

"What you talking about, girl?"

"Just what I said: This little...girl....inside of me...is ticklish!"

"Aw, baby! You serious?!"

"I'm serious, Jenks. We're having another one. You've been so pumped about the shows, and then, when you've been all up in me like that, it's been like, a quickie. You ain't even noticed?"

He was a bit embarrassed.

"Naw, girl. I just thought, you know? I ain't want to say nothing about you putting on a little weight. Like you girls always be tripping a brother say something like that, so..."

"And I know it's going to be a girl."

He dropped off the sofa onto his knees, and the puppies, sensing playfulness, bounded up to him and began pawing and licking at him. He brushed them aside, did a little wiggle and crawl up to beside his wife and son.

"Aw baby! I'm just glad that you finally decided to say something." He reached over Troy, who was about to doze off beside her between his mother and where Jenkins now kneeled. He turned her head to him, kissed her fully on the lips. "That's why you wouldn't extend the tour like me and Georgia wanted to, huh?"

"Right that."

"And who else knows about this? And how many..how far along...you know...weeks or months, are you?"

"Six and a half weeks. And only my girls know, and Marvella. You know I had to talk it over with them first, cause I know your ass would have made me cancel even the first D.C. shows if you knew I was pregnant."

"You damn right, girl! The way you be bouncing around the stage and shit! Up there with my baby all up in you shaking your ass and dippin' and slippin' and shit! Yeah, you damn right I would have called you out on that like that!"

"But now come on, Jenks! We're going to finish this tour! Then I'll just be about five months, and won't do nothing but studio work and maybe I'll put in a little time in New York at the office. OK?"

"You talk to Dr. Samuelson?"

"Yep. And my OBGYN. I ain't doing nothing on stage that could possibly harm our baby."

He kissed her again, more intimately.

"Better not," he said, smiling.

Chapter Forty-eight

They held what could only be called a dopefiend funeral. Siren had met with her PR specialist Georgia, with Freddy and with Marvella, and all had agreed that Jocelyn Lavesque and Raymond Carter would be feted at a home going celebration of life among their friends. And those, to a man and woman, were the drug addicts they palled around with off Good Hope Road.

Their obituary would mention that they had a daughter, Sirena Lavesque, but there would be a concerted effort made to play down any celebrity association. They organized a simple ceremony, at the small black-owned funeral home not far from the Good Hope Road haunts of the deceased, and through word-of-mouth all of their drug associates were informed of the funeral and all attended.

Most acknowledged Siren and Jenkins with solemn nods, and all were aware that the repast would be held at the home Siren had gifted her mother. Marvella thought it a bit morbid to have a celebration of the lives of the two at the place where they had departed, and suggested that Siren, with all her wealth, could at least have rented a hall at one of the many churches along Good Hope Road. But after the funeral, and viewing the close to morbid state of the dopefiends who'd attended, she could see where Siren was on point in having the post-burial gathering at the home where her mother had herself entertained.

Freddy was along for support; no problems were expected from the draggle of heroin-using men and women who attended. But all felt a little more secure with the security head and one of his most trusted associates along for the duration of the event. At Jocelyn's home there was an extravagant layout of catered foods; unlike crackheads, whose very element was an appetite suppressant, the heroin legion savored a good meal with regularity. Indeed, the mainlining of poison required the body to thirst an equal or better ingestion of healthy sustenance, and Siren was quite pleased to see her mother's friends enjoy the abundance of foods and non-alcoholic drinks.

Misery, a downtrodden, 17-year addict and close friend of both Jocelyn and Raymond, had met Siren on a number of occasions during her pre-stardom years.   A dark-skinned man further blackened by dope, Thomas "Misery" Alonzo had overdosed on so many occasions that other drug users had given him a secondary nickname: Zombie. He represented the descriptive quite adequately the afternoon of the funeral, drip-dragging through the living room of Jocelyn's home. He was one of the few dopefiends visibly high at the funeral, but anyone else present could tell you that he just couldn't help himself.

His left hand was swollen morbidly from years of punctured veins in the armpit, upper arm, hand. He was of course right-handed, yet that one also was showing signs of an elephantine misshaping; out of necessity, sometimes pure desperation, he'd managed to wield a hypodermic needle with his left hand, and any medical personnel could predict that in a few years both hands would become useless. To be sure, there were others at the repast who'd already passed that point, and were dependent on others to shoot them up with heroin.

Bobbing, scowling, eyelids adroop, Misery shuffled over to where Siren stood with Freddy, Marvella and "Quality" Jones, a close female associate of Sirena's mother. He nodded further, opened his eyes a bit.

"My con...dolences, baby...girl," Misery said, bowing somewhat and figuring, quite correctly, that the bereaved would prefer to forego the more customary embrace. "That was my girl there...Jocelyn...and my main man there...Raymond. My...con...dolences to you baby girl, and to the....rest...of the family."

Misery looked to Freddy, Marvella, nodded and then turned and took a zombiotic stroll towards the bathroom.

He knew exactly where it was, having been here many times before.   And it was also clear to everyone in attendance that Misery was in possession of some pretty powerful heroin.   He was heading to the bathroom, certainly, to fix himself another hit.   Formalities and situational respect aside, three junkies, including Quality Jones, delivered secondary condolences to Siren and stepped off to follow Misery.

"I understand," Siren said to Quality's back.

On many occasions as a young girl, she'd seen her mother, Quality, and countless others secret off into the bathroom, and knew that when they were so cloistered, should not ever be disturbed.   At one time Quality was considered her mother's "ace boon coon," as Jocelyn had described her once-attractive friend.   They were the same age, had actually grown up together and in their early twenties, started shooting heroin together after boyfriends then hesitantly allowed them to do so.   Quality had been a striking beauty from a very young age, a "red bone," in the familial description of a light-skinned African-American woman with naturally long, flowing hair and crisp features. But her skin was now something akin to tanned leather, and the hair, still long and flowing if allowed, was more commonly tucked into a bun under the back of some baseball cap.

"That's the nature of that shit," Freddy said, sipping a ginger ale.   "Every since the riots, after they killed Dr. King, ain't been no shortage of one drug or another in the black community.   They saw how ni---how black people would tear up some shit, they knowed best thing to do was keep them sedated.   Been sedating some peoples for damn near 50 years or more.   Evil sons-of-bitches."

"I don't know, Freddy," Siren said, moving over to an elaborate buffet and filling a plate with jumbo shrimp. "Nobody made my mother or any of those people in there shoot no dope. Just like nobody made me smoke no coke back then. So, who're you blaming?"

"I know who I blame," Marvella said, always supportive of Freddy. "I blame them god-damn peoples always getting the kids outside our doors to sell drugs for them. Know them kids, wanting them $200.00 tennis shoes and mother on welfare, ain't gonna turn down a chance to make a thousand dollars a night selling dope." She paused, took a small dish of shrimp, dipped one in cocktail sauce and began chewing on it. "Just like that damn Marcus had that Spanish boy Alvarez selling coke to you and them crew members. Just like that fool girl y'all called the Silver Shadow played that guitar, always walking around smelling like a mortuary with her chemical-smoking self."

A few more dopefiends passed by, heading to the bathroom, while others came out, including Misery, and plopped down in near comatose abyss on sofas and lounge chairs.

"Still," Siren continued, "nobody put that pipe in my mouth."

"You wrong there, baby girl," Freddy said, finishing off his platter of ham and potato salad. "Alvarez, Marcus, and most of all this guy Salvador, they put the pipe in front of you so often, kinda like, it was almost certain you'd pick it up. Hell, they knew of the money you made. They knew of the way you, quite a bit back then, baby girl, would kill a fifth or two of champagne all by yourself. Believe me, they all know that a mind addled by one drug would be easily reeled into trying another. And you should have learned this in those AA and NA meetings you go to: Alcohol is the first drug most all eventual users of others start off with. And you know damn well alcohol is a drug, don't you, Siren?"

"I know," Siren said. "I know."

Chapter Forty-nine

Before the tour concluded, Siren appeared driven as no one had seen her before. Wardrobe assured that her pregnancy, nearing five months by the eleventh city on the roster, was cloaked in loose designer's fashions, which were already in production for her new clothing line. These outfits would be marketed to the masses, and would generate unanticipated millions worldwide. As planned by her finely tuned public relations apparatus, she would announce her second pregnancy right after the tour, and the increasingly astute businessperson would roll out her design of a line of maternity wear. This line would unfortunately have many of her young fans looking forward to a time, in the immediate future, when they too could wear the fashions over a protruding belly.

Ever the proud papa, Jenkins was as driven as was his wife, leading Keepin' It Easy on stage and, along with Siren, taking to the New York studios to compose new music in between shows. The accountants for Short Siren Music Corporation, Sweet Siren Clothings, Easy Going Music and Troy Boy Youth Styles were well-paid and among the best in their field; Siren and Jenkins received reports and on occasion looked over the books. Georgia Whitfield-Johnson, tour manager turned general manager and COO of the overarching corporation, was well deserved of her seven figure salary.

Siren had decided to rid herself of any past associations which in any way, she believed, hindered her creativity. The housing development for the former Barry Farm residents was spun off as a real estate development, with more extensive projects, financed to stability and gifted over to a corporation operated by a few of the residents but overseen by a board set up in Greater Abyssinian Baptist Church and chaired by Rev. Palmdale.

The "dopefiend house," as she thought of her mother's former abode, and one next to it that Siren had secretly purchased some time ago, were deeded over to the Anacostia Youth For Life Corp., an AA/NA group which previously held meetings in a ramshackle storefront hardly a block from the Good Hope Road dope strip. The meetings were moved into the former home of Jocelyn Lavesque, bore her name and, a measure away from the actual strip, grew more successful in weaning many area alcoholics and drug addicts off the draw of the corners.

Not long after the Jocelyn Lavesque Memorial Hall was established, a ravished Misery, stricken with AIDS and on his last leg, spent a few weeks there, sober, before succumbing to the duel effects of AIDS and heroin. Joining him there was his longtime friend Quality Jones, who found sobriety also attending meetings at the memorial hall before succumbing to similar ravages a year after Misery.

By her eighth month of pregnancy, the successful tour was long behind her. She and Jenkins split their time between the family home in McLean and one of the company owned penthouse suites in Manhattan. The home studio was not as elaborate as the one in New York, and both were working on new music.

Just before Christmas the couple returned home with both their new productions completed, in the can as they were wont to say, allowing Sirena to relax among familiars until, on Christmas eve, she went into labor. Just after midnight on Christmas morning, Sirena gave birth to an eight-pound, three-ounce baby girl. Her glistening hair and generous cheeks made everyone who looked down upon her in the hospital smile with joy, and the baby's seemingly pert, sculptured lips made it appear as if she was smiling back.

With Jenkins, Marvella, Sunshine and Genese at her bedside, she announced that she was naming the baby right then and there.

"Starr," Sirena pronounced, receiving a nod of agreement from her husband. "Her name is Starr, with two 'Rs'. Starr Acosua Lavesque-Shorter."

"And I bet you she's going to be a star too," Marvella said.

"And you know it," Jenkins said, glowing.

"There you go," Sunshine said. "Mapping out the girl's future already. Suppose she wants to be a schoolteacher?"

"Then she'll be a schoolteacher," Sirena said. "But you know what my mother and Marvella always told me: You tell a child she's smart, and she'll be smart. Tell her she's a dummy, and she'll grow up to be a disappointing fool. At least that's how Marvella put it."

"Self-fulfilling prophecy," Marvella added from the foot of the bed. "My mother and grandmother put it to me that way, anyway."

"But she's destined to be a star," Jenkins said, leaning over, kissing his new baby and then his wife. "Look at his mother."

Chapter Fifty

Young Starr Lavesque-Shorter was center stage even before the age of eight. At the prestigious primary school she attended, where classmates were the sons and daughters of diplomats and executives and that boasted of having educated the children of former presidents, she was a sparkling presence in every recital, every dramatic production and, on occasion, the central figure in some most unacceptable antics.

She was certainly going to be as tall as her mother, dark as both mother and father, and with a tendency to be adventurous as both of them were in their earlier years. On Halloween it was Starr who lead a contingent of prissy little girls into the third-floor bathroom overlooking the playground, armed with a dozen balloons. Smart and tactful even at a young age, she instructed others to fill the balloons with water, knot them and, in a barrage, toss them down upon unsuspecting teachers and classmates. While her misguided cadre watched the scurrying below in hysterical laughter, Starr had secreted out of the bathroom and was exiting the study hall when the headmaster and the despoiled victims rushed up stairs to the bathroom and confronted the culprits.

They were caught red handed, as it were, and looked with evil eyes to the instigator, Starr, who stood innocently among the headmaster and victims. But not a one of the accused would dare snitch on her, for besides being mischievous to a fault, the girl was a frightful little scrapper. One of only a handful of blacks at the exclusive school, Starr often regaled classmates with tales of unimagined hardship on the road with her well-known musical mother and father. Once a little girl, the daughter of a famous golfer, had challenged her telling of one story, and the pretty persona of Starr suddenly converted to a glowering, threatening little witch.

"Don't make me steal you!" Starr said, stepping to the girl with a tight little fist.

The golfer's daughter had no background, no clue, which would have told her that a "steal," in a part of the city far, far on the other side, meant to sucker punch another. But Starr's glower, and the clutched fist, quickly had the girl's bright, active mind considering but one possibility. From that point on, baby-golfer was one of Starr's closest friends, and was standing forefront to take the blame following the water-balloon fiasco.

Her older brother Troy was two years ahead of her in the same school, and excelling academically at such a pace that his parents were already weighing offers from a number of prestigious secondary schools who wanted him among their ranks at no cost to Siren and Jenkins. And the parents were close monitors of their children's academic progress; Siren was often in the studio recording new material, but making few on stage appearances besides the occasion appearance at a prestigious award's show. Jenkins and Keepin' It Easy had temporarily disbanded, and outside of frequent trips to his expansive corporation's headquarters in New York, Jenkins worked out of a home office and was an almost smothering presence over the lives of his children.

Siren's latest album, simply titled "Starr," had been selling in the millions over the past year. For an artist who didn't make any live appearances following the album's release, the sales were unprecedented. She and Jenkins had long since established trusts and corporations and sub-corporations to further supplement their tremendous incomes, and to allay exorbitant personal income taxes both she and Jenkins had sat with advisors and agreed to have all of her earnings from "Starr" go directly to Short Siren Music Corporation. She merely drew a $300,000 annual salary, as did Jenkins, although their true assets consisted of sole ownership of fourteen corporations, including the record company and clothing lines corporations.

Outside of their Virginia home and a few cars, they personally owned little real properties but held enormous amounts of stocks, bonds and company ownerships on paper. The penthouses in Manhattan belonged to the music corporation, as did corporate "getaways" in the Bahamas, Jamaica and Los Angeles. The ranch in Arizona with adjoining golf course was where retreats were held for members of the various boards of directors of their companies, and for artists who may have required some sort "rehab" out of the public eye.

All in all, the couple had the freedom to do as they pleased, and for the most part Jenkins spent inordinate time with his son and Siren, usually along with Marvella, Sunshine and Genese, doted on little Starr and Troy. Siren's two best friends and business associates, Sunshine and Genese, had children and, for Genese, grandchildren. None in the extended family went wanting, and quite often the McLean home was filled with three generations, enjoying the best that life had to offer.

There were, nevertheless, the occasional bumps in an otherwise smooth, well-paved and well-financed road.

Sunshine had always wanted to marry Elvin, who was the father of her two sons. But he'd insisted, after over a decade, that his "finances" weren't right. Always a no-nonsense woman and a perfect balance between Siren and the flighty, outspoken Genese, Sunshine was treasured by her childhood friends as level-headed and not one easy to impress. But she did have one weakness, at least one which both Genese and Siren always warned her about: Elvin. Or more to the point, Elvin's sexual prowess.

In conversations strictly among grown folks, Siren and Genese would often tease their friend about her inability to wrench herself away from the man who was widely considered, in their old neighborhood, as the consummate "player." More than a few women who occasioned into their tight circle told of having experienced Elvin. He was nicknamed "Donkey Dick" by the girls, and Sunshine, having considered herself his "boo" for over twenty years, could only giggle in agreement when that assessment was made. It was the rare time when their stoic friend seemed quite coy, almost blushing and at a loss for words when the girls discussed men.

"Child, I've been with that fool so long, he ain't going nowhere," Sunshine would explain away word that Elvin, seven years her senior, was living off her six-figure salary and secretly building a family elsewhere.

"But how come he ain't married your ass after all this time?" Genese asked, setting in Siren's living room on a day when the good friends were forgoing any work and simply relaxing.

"He comes home...every night," Sunshine said, embarrassment evident.

"Yeah," Siren said. "When you didn't even have a home and was still staying with your momma and pregnant with your first, he was still working that job at the Department of Justice, making good bread, and still that fool wouldn't even try to get y'all an apartment."

"Word," Genese interjected.

"And now you're making ten times what he makes, twenty, got you a nice house and shit, and now the fool comes home every night?" Siren said. "Nigga please... He comes home every morning, from what you tell me. Five a.m. ain't no night!"

"And we know why you let him come in there like he owns the place," Siren said, stretched out on a sofa a distance across the room.

"Donkey dick!" Siren and Genese sang at once.

"Y'all a trip," Sunshine said, now visibly blushing. "Y'all ought to quit..."

"So," Siren said, setting upright and leaning into the conversation. "You say he said his job is sending him to Atlanta for a conference and he'll be gone for a week?"

"That's what he said."

"Girl, what Freddy tell you when you asked him to do a background on ol' boy back when? He's a, what? 'Property Maintenance Supervisor' at Justice."

"So?"

"Girl," Genese said, sniggling. "That's just a fancy way of saying your old man is a janitor! And since when a janitor's job send him away for a conference? Girl, you just whipped! Believe anything that fool tell you, long as you can get that--"

"Donkey dick!"

"Y'all a mess," Sunshine said, again embarrassed.

Just then her cell phone rang, and she looked at the luminous display of Elvin's smiling picture.

"Speak of the devil," she said, and took the call.

Chapter Fifty-one

Genese was driving the car she and Sunshine had come out to Siren's together in. Sunshine cherished the latest model Mercedes Maybach and wouldn't even let Elvin drive it. But she was too distraught now, tears still flowing in a deluge, as the three friends sped back into the District from Virginia. Elvin had called to tell her that her eldest son Demarquis, 14, had been shot in a drive-by in a section of Southeast Washington where his mother believed he had no business being. In fact she had warned him about some of his so-called friends from the very area, and had afforded him all of the things a boy his age could want or need in their luxurious Ft. Washington, Maryland home. Everything he could possibly want at 14 except, she now belatedly realized, friends and companions in his own age set and, his own words now resurfacing, with "street creds."

"That damn boy!" she sobbed in the back seat. "Lord, why someone want to shoot my baby?!"

They were travelling well over the posted speed limit, and as they hit the Beltway and headed south-southeast on the highway that circles the entirety of the District and its close-in suburbs, three state trooper vehicles with flashing lights sat behind a car on the side of the road. Its hood was up and smoke poured from the engine. Many slowed down, "rubbernecking" to take in the scene. Genese, a long experienced driver, whipped quickly into the far left lane, barely avoiding the slower vehicles, and gave pause to Siren in the front seat beside her. The maneuver also temporarily blunted the grieving of Sunshine directly to her rear.

"Alright now! Alright now! We want to get there in one piece, OK?" Sunshine shouted.

"I got this, girlfriend. I got this."

"Scared the shit out of me too, Genese" Sirena said. "Take it easy, girl. They say he's at the hospital out there on Southern Avenue. They deal with a lot of trauma out that way. He's in good hands."

"Jesus!" Sunshine said, again assuming her mournful wailing. "Oh, my baby!"

She dialed Elvin again.

He was at the hospital with his son, and said that Demarquis had been shot in the stomach. Apparently he'd only suffered a considerably minor penetration wound, the bullet entering angularly at the front midsection and exiting through the right side. It was more than a flesh wound, he told her, but not as serious as a full on frontal penetration. Both parents could not help but envision the dozens of young black men in wheelchairs navigating the streets of their native Southeast Washington. Catastrophic spinal injuries from bullets fueled an entire industry from that and other urban landscapes.

"We're almost to Indian Head Highway," Sunshine said into the cell phone, her tears still flowing but the sobbing now reduced to a controlled sniffling. "We'll be there in about ten minutes."

She paused, apparently receiving an extended talk from the man who'd fathered her two boys.

"OK baby. See you then and tell my boy I'm on my way," she said, disconnected.

She leaned forward, taking to the edge of the plush leather seat.

"He's going to be fine," she said, retrieving a tissue from the inlaid dispenser before her. "It didn't go into his back, thank God! Don't want that boy to be like my little brother, never able to walk again and tied to that wheelchair for the rest of his life."

"Thank goodness," Siren said. "I have one of Jenkins's cousin be calling us all the time for help, paralyzed after getting shot way back in the day down the

Farms. And three guys from out Gladys Manor been put in wheelchairs since them joints opened up."

"These black young'uns always shooting one another," Genese added. "One in a wheelchair or grave, one in jail. No wonder black women up in this piece starting to go with each other. All the guys either in jail, immobilized, got some deadly disease or some shit, or a little faggot-ass bitch-ass nigga. What the fuck…"

"For real, though," Siren agreed.

The Southeast Regional Hospital was the only medical care facility in the farthest, southernmost section of the nation's capital. It was a busy place, serving an area where, even in good times, 24 percent or more of the population was unemployed. This afternoon was no different where the bustle was concerned; when the Maybach pulled into the parking lot, it had to idle for a good ten minutes while ambulatory patients were rushed up to the trauma entrance.

"They're always shooting out this mug," Genese said.

"No joke," Siren added.

"You talk to Jenkins?" Genese asked, craning her neck to look for a parking space.

"Not yet," Siren said. "He's in New York, in the studio with that new group Cream of White. I hate to bother him when he's working, especially with some rookies to the business."

"I heard that," Genese said.

"Genese," a recomposed Sunshine said. "Let me out and I'll go on in while you find a parking space."

Genese idled outside the lift arm to the paid parking lot. "Go ahead, girl. Sirena, you go ahead with her and I'll find y'all."

The two left the car and immediately there was a rumble of whispered voices arising from the dozen or so gathered at a bus stop outside the hospital's main entrance.

One middle-aged man, quite evidently on the rough side of a drunken binge and wearing a blood-stained bandage over his head, rocked over to Siren and Sunshine as they approached the entrance.

"My girl my girl!" the drunk slurred. "Ain't that my girl Siren there? Lord ha' mercy it is you! How you doing sweetheart and, if I may, I don't think you want to get what's ailing you fixed up in this joint! Naw girl! Naw! I know you can afford Georgetown or George Washington Hospital, girl! Don't let these fools cut up on that fine, fine body of yours, girl! Let me holler for a few dollars, sweet thing!"

They kept a fast clip, Siren nodding to a few at the bus stop who spoke respectfully to her. Through two automated doors a receptionist desk with an armed guard beside required guests to check in. The receptionist, who spent most days with little to smile about, perked up when recognizing Siren and stood from a seat she rarely left and greeted the two.

"My goodness! Siren! How you doing, girl?" the robust woman heaved, as if the very act of speaking was physically torturous.

"I'm fine, ma'am. We're looking for Demarquis---"

"Melody," Sunshine cut in. "My son, Demarquis Melody. His father said he's here. Been shot."

The receptionist's demeanor clouded, smile faded, eyes looked to Sunshine with a practiced measure of pity, then down to some papers on the desk as she flopped back down into the office chair.

"Um...sorry to hear about your son, Ms. Melody. Umm...here. He's out of surgery, in the recovery area, not in a patient's room yet."

"Where's the...recovery area?" Sunshine asked.

"Go through those swinging doors there," the receptions pointed past the desk and guard to a set of doors 30 feet down the hall. "Keep straight to the end of that corridor and make a right. The recovery area is the first door on the left."

"Thank you," Sunshine said, stepped off followed closely by Siren and certainly followed by the eyes of receptionist and security.

"I told that damn boy about running around with that crowd over there in Parkdale," Sunshine said, as Siren struggled to keep up. "Always talking about how boring it is out at our house. Now look at his dumb ass!"

They made the right, moved another 30 feet and turned left through another pair of swinging doors. The site before them was reminiscent of some trauma center outside a war zone: A distant wail of a young man impacted the overall pain most in the room were experiencing. Sunshine saw Elvin at the same time he reacted to the tumult of hushed voices that greeted Siren's arrival. The two walked to Elvin, who was standing over a bed with a rail thin boy stretched out on it, his hands clasped behind his head as if he had not a care in the world.

Sunshine walked up to the boy, looked at the smirk on his face and smacked him with a forceful, full on blow.

"You think this is some kind of game, Demarquis?! Huh?!"

"Aw, ma. Chill…"

She smacked him once again, reared her hand back again but was refrained by the equally tall and lanky Elvin.

"Alright, Sunny babe. The boy's hurtin'," Elvin said, wrapping his arms around Sunshine.

"He hurting, alright," Sunshine said. "Look at him, Elvin? Look at him?"

The boy smiled. "Ma, ain't nothing but a flesh wound, basically. Dag…"

"You're lucky it ain't more than that!" his mother retorted. "What I tell you about running around Parkdale with them boys slinging that mess? Somebody's shot over there every other day! You keep on, you hear me? And your father must think that's some sort of....man thing! Getting shot make you a big man, Demarquis?"

"Dag, ma! Chill..."

"Chill my ass!" she turned to Elvin. "And you right here like it's no big deal either, huh Elvin?"

"Sunshine, come on, sweetheart," he said, clearly not as concerned as she.

"Ms. Sirena," the boy looked to Siren, smiling. "Thanks for coming out here with Ma. Thanks a lot. But like I say: This just a little something happen to a man, know what I'm sayin'?"

Siren looked disgusted, glowered at the boy. "No, Demarquis, I don't know what you're saying. And you know what: All you young'uns always spitting off some nonsense, and finishing up with that 'Know what I'm sayin' mess, really don't know what you're saying so you're seeking some sort of clarification that you're understood by the person you're talking to. Don't none of y'all know what the hell it is you're saying, or you wouldn't need confirmation. Do – you – know – what – I'm – saying?!"

The room had grown hushed when Siren began speaking, and now even the distant wailer was on his elbows, silent, looking to the scene midroom with Siren the focus of all of the withered and weary eyes. The silence was palpable for a moment, and then to the surprise of Siren and Sunshine, weak hands came together in a round of applause the two usually only heard after one of Siren's performances.

Demarquis was visibly embarrassed.

"I'm sorry, Ms. Siren. I'm sorry, Ma," he said weakly. "Sorry, Pops."

Genese came into the room as patients settled back into indiscernible conversations with one another. Out of 34 fresh patients, only Demarquis and one other had a family member there to check on their well being. Genese moved to the side of the bed opposite Siren, Sunshine and

Elvin and, having been a part of Demarquis's life since he was born, merely leaned in for a familial hug and kiss.

"You gonna be alright?" she asked him.

"I'm gonna be alright, Ms. Genese. I'm gonna be alright."

Elvin looked to Genese and nodded his greeting, then spoke directly to Sunshine.

"Doctor says they're going to keep him overnight for observation. Said the bullet missed any vital organs. I don't know about him, baby, but my stomach is as vital an organ as there is."

"No joke, son," Demarquis said, the matter of his using the common street slang "son" in response to his father's statement meaning little to a 14-year-old for whom books were foreign items.

"Well," Sunshine said, "some of us have 'grown-folk's business' to take care of, son! Siren, Genese, sorry to have to ruin our day like this behind this boy. Demarquis, your father will come and get you when they release your sorry ass. And if you don't like it out at Ft. Washington, well, you can come get your shit anytime and go move in with your homies in Parkdale! Know y'all asses will be trying to seek retribution on the shooters before the week is out. But Elvin, don't worry: I have the boy's insurance paid up so the funeral won't cost you anything."

Demarquis shook his head, frowned. "Dag Ma! Ain't nobody thinking about no mess like that! You burying a nigga all like that and stuff already like that! Dag! That's cold, Ma. Colder than a mug..."

She turned to Siren and Genese. "Ladies, let's get out of here."

The three headed to the exit, amidst a few "shout-outs" from a number of the wounded. As they neared the exit, a man with a cast on one leg, sling over a shoulder and cast on a forearm smiled up to Siren.

"Siren! Baby girl!" he said. "Sign my cast for me, sweetheart!"

A few nearby laughed, while Sunshine merely smiled and shook her head, looked to her dear friend.

"Come on, girl! Don't pay that fool no mind!" Sunshine said.

But Siren paused, reached into her purse and retrieved one of the many felt-tip pens she always carried, just for such purposes. She walked over to the man, sat on the edge of his bed and placed the marker to the cast on his leg.

"What's your name, sir?" she asked with a warm smile, then signed the cast with a personalized message to "Sugar Daddy Douglass."

Chapter Fifty-two

Cream of White was the first rock band signed to Short Siren Records. They had a unique musical presentation which infused classic rock with techno-rock and interspersed with a pinch of white-boy rap reminiscent of the widely popular General Spice, one of the few Caucasian masters of the word-swagger originated and dominated by young blacks over the past quarter century. Jenkins had heard "Cream," as the group was familiarly called, playing at a dank club on the revitalized 14th Street strip in the Columbia Heights section of Washington.

"Them boys are tight!" he had told Sanford when the men, along with the rest of Keepin' It Easy, were cruising city venues for talent.

He had met with all the members of the band after that show, along with their manager, at a party where various alcohols and drugs were consumed (with Jenkins proud that he maintained his now-years long sobriety count). The group and manager were convinced that, even though their genre was untested by Short Siren, they should consider the high-quality production skills of the black record label and give them a try at producing Cream. The only thing that gave Jenkins pause was the amount of powered cocaine the band's star and lead singer/rapper, Flatiron, had virtually shoveled into his nostrils that evening.

"That might be why that fool's so hyped and spit lyrics like he's General Spice or some shit," Sanford had told Jenkins on their way out of the city that night. "But let's get their asses up to New York in the studio, and tell them straight up that we don't have that shit going on in and around the business. See how they roll with that."

After a thorough going over of the extensive legalese, Steven "Flatiron" Massey, the other members of Cream, and manager Tim "Shorty" Granville signed a management and production contract with Short Siren. They were quite pleased with the $1.7 million Short Siren presented them as a signing bonus, and went to work immediately on developing new material, "burning" masters of their old songs, and preparing for a true coming-out tour in a manner Jenkins, and later Siren, agreed would mark them as another premier act for the ever evolving corporation.

Jenkins was personally overseeing their initial studio hours; these were of course billable towards future earnings, per the contract his attorneys had masterfully crafted. However, these cost were considered minor when it was taken into consideration the potential millions the group would generated with the experienced craftsmen Short Siren was providing.

Jenkins and Sanford, who'd by now demanded and gotten a considerable share of stock in the corporation, were now as dually involved in production as they'd been involved in making mischief as teenagers in their old Barry Farm neighborhood. Both saw tremendous potential in Cream of White, and were working together with paid back-up musicians and Short Siren house musicians to highlight Flatiron's extensive skills as front man for the band. They had been in the studio for seven hours going into a Friday night, and although they had five exceptional numbers "in the can," Jenkins still felt that he did not have that one unique song from Cream that he could roll out as a prelude to the release of their first Short Siren album.

"I want y'all to work that piece 'Shadows and Sunshine' with that track of horns under Flatiron's slow dialogue," Jenkins said, speaking into a mike which allowed him to be heard in the soundproof studio area where the band was located. He looked directly through the expansive glass above the soundboard, nodded at Flatiron, who nodded back to him with a smile. "Let's do that one from the top."

The song was what could only be described as a rock ballad, a soulful tune which Flatiron had written and played lead guitar on. The bridge, repeated seven times throughout an extensive arrangements of heavy bass, guitar solos and soprano saxophone solos, had Flatiron rapping off an almost morbid dialogue, in his gruff, coke- and smoke-hardened voice, with words that were both crass and thought provoking at the same time.

And he'd written the entire song and suggested the musical arrangements during the half-hour afternoon break.

That was the song Jenkins and Sanford instinctively knew would be branded as the trademark Cream of White signature, and they were going to stay in the studio this evening until the song was perfected in its presentation.

Flatiron, however, was paramount to them pulling off this production and putting it in the can. But the droopy, bedraggled talent, all six-foot seven-inches of his wiry frame, began spending more time in the "can" himself with each passing hour.

"My boy stop snorting that shit for a minute," Jenkins said to Sanford, the mike off now, "we'll have this thing wrapped by midnight and can haul-ass back down to D.C. for the weekend."

"For real, son," Sanford said. "The boy is good, but I'm kinda worried that, without that coke, his ass wouldn't be putting out magic like that in a New York minute."

"Yeah," Jenkins said, then, noticing Flatiron grimacing and straining at the guitar while being urged on by his band mates, Jenkins put on his headphones, as did Sanford, and were treated to the exquisite, unique and melodic sound they'd been reaching for.

"Yeah, boy!" Jenkins cried out, motioning to his sound engineer to make a few adjustments. "Do that shit, man! Do that shit!"

They were sure that what they had recorded was going to be the album, and hit single, which would dominate the national charts for weeks after its release. Just before midnight the band finished reviewing the master recordings along with an exhausted Jenkins and exuberant Sanford and asked the two over to the company condo on Fifth Avenue, where the band had been put up for the duration of the recording session.

"Shit, why not," Jenkins said, looking to Sanford for his agreement. "Ain't no need of driving down to D.C. this late on a Friday, right? It's Saturday morning damn near. I'm about to pass out, or either put my face down in some of that pumping-up shit ol' boy Flatiron been skeezing on all night."

Flatiron, slit-eyed, tight-jawed but quite evidently fully alert, showed a little smile and a nod.

"Got a truckload of some torturously exquisite boutique substance, brother," Flatiron said. "You know you're my man, Jenkins. Put a lot of faith in these guys here, and in me. We put together something nice there tonight, right?"

"No question," Jenkins said, leading the group towards the elevators while Sanford secured the main entrance to the studios.

"I'll break you off a little piece, we get back to the apartment," Flatiron said. "You down?"

Jenkins flashed over his years of sobriety, but was more so mentally revisiting the time when he snorted cocaine, in a manner some described as "recreational use." Immediately he flew over the mental landscape that showed the wasteland that was his life when powdered cocaine turned to the smoking of crack cocaine and when snorting heroin was assumed as a presumed salve to get him away from crack. And all the madness and flashes of the symbolic Titanic with its band playing and him being the only passenger moving from chair to chair and---

"Naw, Joe!" Jenkins said as the elevator arrived. "You can do what you want, Flats, but this brother can't hang. Been there! Fuck that!"

Chapter Fifty-three

Siren, Genese, Sunshine and Lil' Rock/Anthony were in the first limousine, followed closely by one carrying Jenkins, Freddy and Marvella. A Bentley behind the second limo rounded out the caravan, and was driven by Sanford, with his wife Michelle beside him. They were all going to the mega-arena in Western Virginia, for the summer's most anticipated rock concert, featuring Cream of White. Siren was listening to the group's hit "Shadows and Sunshine" on the limo's top-of-the-line stereo system. It was the long-playing version of the song which had been dominating the chart since its spring release.

With the supervisory production skills of Jenkins and Sanford, the band had produced a version of the song that lasted 17 minutes 30 seconds. Siren knew that this version had been produced the Saturday morning after the initial tracks had been laid for the No. 1 selling album. It was also why, in a round about way, Siren and Jenkins were going to the show in separate limousines.

She knew he'd gone "back out" when he arrived from New York that Sunday, a day and a half after he'd phoned excitedly and said that Cream of White had put a "masterpiece" in the can. He'd phoned from the penthouse where the band was staying, and by his voice Siren could tell that he'd been using. At minimum, he'd drank some champagne or other alcoholic beverage. Yet she knew, as well as Jenkins, that their history of drug addiction required that they avoid any mind alterative. Certainly he'd broken the covenant and, she was certain also, had been sparked to use any additional "get high" present at the time. And as she knew a little about Flatiron and quite familiar with his cocaine use, she was sure that, after a little champagne or whatever, her husband had taken up the illegal substance again also.

"You're fucked up!" Sirena had shouted to her husband that early morning on the phone. "Aw, Jenks! Man! Please don't go back out like that! Please!"

But it was already too late.

When Jenkins was driven to their McLean estate by Sanford, Siren immediately knew that he'd been doing cocaine. She'd known his best friend Sanford for as long as she'd known her husband, and as they entered the home that Sunday she looked directly to Sanford with accusatory eyes and received the answer to her question even before it had been asked. Sanford immediately looked down, wouldn't meet her eyes, then nodded to Jenkins, said goodbye to Siren and quickly left.

"I hope your ass didn't go so far as to be back smoking that shit," Sirena said, brushing past Jenkins and moving to a room where the voices of children could be heard.

"I'm aiight," he said, moved to the arching staircase and ascended to the master bedroom.

Siren comforted herself with Troy and Starr, taking her daughter in a hug the girl seemed to find uncomfortable.

"Something wrong, mommy?" Starr asked, twisting away and seeing tears forming in her mother's eyes.

"It's your damn daddy," Siren said, letting the tears flow.

Troy, always uncommonly serious where his mother and her career was concerned, sat down his portable video game and moved to embrace Siren.

"He's going to be alright, Ma," Troy said. "He's probably getting too worked up about the new group and their album, that's all."

Siren realized that Troy, diagnosed by school officials as intelligent beyond his years, was probably on point. As she reflected on that Sunday evening, in the limousine now with her good friends and young Anthony,

she couldn't help but frown when they were admitted
through the arena's gate by security and the driver pulled
up adjacent to the tour bus Short Siren Music Corporation
had provided to Cream of White.

"I'm going to check on the logistics, Ma, Ms.
Sirena," Anthony said, relishing his role as a music
professional. "Ms. Sirena: Mr. Shorter and them are in
the ride behind us. You need me to pass on anything to
him?"

For a minute, Siren didn't know to whom Anthony
was referring. Few in the close-knit group called Jenkins
by his last name, and upon gaining clarity, she couldn't
help but smile.

"Yes, Anthony. Tell Mr. Shorter that Ms.
Lavesque-Shorter has instructed that he assume no
corporate duties while on site. Give him and
his...associates...backstage passes and tell them to not get
in the way."

"OK, Ms. Lavesque-Shorter," Anthony smiled, left
the limousine.

"Day-um!" Genese said. "He done really fucked up
this time, huh girl?"

"You damn right," Siren said.

"What?" Sunshine asked. "Don't' tell me he done
got with that wild-ass Flatiron and them and done gone
back to using? Aw, girl..."

"Yep," Siren said. "Not that he's been...like...back
out like that since they finished the album and we set up the
tour. But...well, it's just that I can't trust his ass out
around...you know..."

"I know," Genese said, leafing through papers.
"But you and Georgia and legal were responsible for
booking this tour, girlfriend. And in my capacity as your
executive assistant, and because I love you girl, I'd advise
you to just do like you told Anthony to do: Keep him in the
capacity of an observer. Right now, he's not even signed on

as a producer with the venue management or any of the other managers of the other venues. You feeling me?"

"I'm feeling you."

OK then. Let's go rock with these crazy ass white boys!"

Chapter Fifty-four

The company grossed millions from the *White-on-Rice Tour*. Cream of White, with five acts on the undercard, toured for a month and a half, skipping across the United States, filtering into Canada, then back into the States before flying off for a week in Europe. Flatiron was an immediate superstar, his antics during interviews on camera constant grist for the highlight reels of industry-related television shows. He was wont to wear tattered, cheap tops on stage and off, never buttoned up and always exposing the bunch of nappy, red hair on his bird-chest. His facial hair and the scraggly, shoulder-length mane was always unkempt, but his don't-give-a-care attitude, along with his unique, gruff voice, was what attracted him to the group's millions of fans.

Short Sirens Productions was reaping tremendous financial rewards from their fresh act. Primarily from record sales, but a good piece of change, as Jenkins had put it, was being garnered from the tour. And more recordings, and more tours, were being planned.

"Them boys bringing in a rack of cash!" Jenkins said excitingly to Siren, both in the New York headquarters for other business while the tour was on its European and final leg. "Long capital, baby! Big bucks!"

Siren wasn't impressed. Oh, she was impressed by the black figures in the electronic accounting ledgers. What she was not so impressed with was her husbands clear reversion to his old "street-wise" self. The words. The demeanor. Clear indication that he was again using.

"They're doing alright," she said from behind her elaborate desk, checking figures on her computer. "But I think we need to reign in Flatiron from making the talk show appearances. Not a few of the hosts let it be known that he was seen doing coke in the Green Rooms. And it was evident by his appearance on Tony Aaron's that he was higher than a kite."

Jenkins sat in one of the high-backed, Italian leather chairs before his wife's desk. She remained a striking beauty, but had begun wearing reading glasses, albeit in $700.00 frames, since assuming office business nearly full-time. Her always well-maintained hair remained natural, all hers, whereby most of her friends, girls in the company's acts, even Sunshine and Genese, had required expensive weaves to obtain the locks Siren had naturally. She worked out daily when not on the road, and maintaining a mature attractiveness that warmed Jenkins yet bothered him at the same time.

"You knowed that boy was fucking around when we signed them," Jenkins said, sniffing from his own guilt and also from the after flow of the caustic powder he'd snorted half an hour earlier. "Long as it's coming out of they're own pockets, and don't interfere with business, it's alright with me."

He'd taken to wearing sweat suits over the past few months, although certainly expensive designer brands marketed by Short Siren Sportswear. But Siren didn't like this one bit; he was no longer a "boy-band" lead singer and idol of teenaged girls. The father of a pre-teen girl and teenaged boy, Jenkins was well into his 30s, although Siren did a cursory review of their time together, their addictions, their sobriety and the building of a multi-million dollar business, and thought it seemed like a lifetime.

"I know it's alright with you, Jenks," she said, glancing over her glasses at him. "His connection on that powder must be pretty good, the way you've been all flighty of late. But I just want to tell you one thing, Jenks: I don't want you all buzzed out around the children. Bad enough you up here in the offices like that. You know some of the guys in the acts used to look up to you. And some of the girls....but now that's a whole nother story, isn't it?"

She knew. And now he knew that she knew.

"I know you don't think I'm messing around with that young hottie Fredericka," he said. "Baby, please! She's all over me like that trying to get a single's contract away from Holiday Candies. But you know she ain't all that by herself. I ain't paying that young'un no mind."

Fredericka Sands, a 20-year-old with the group Holiday Candies, had been quite noticeably visiting Jenkins's private office after studio sessions. He'd thought the other three members of the group were keeping a lid on his liaisons with Fredericka, but now apparently Siren was aware of their regular "sessions."

"You're fucking the little bitch," Siren said, swirled around in her chair and began typing an email. "Came by your office the other night and you and her were leaving. Didn't even see me down the hall by reception, talking to Diane. I go up in the place, joint smelling all like booty. You're fucking her, Jenks. I know damn well you are. With your tired ass..."

"Baby..."

"Jenks, I have work to do. Please..."

"But baby..."

"Please, Jenks. We'll talk at home. You going down for the weekend?"

"Yeah, baby. I mean, Marvella and Marie spend more time with our kids than we do. I want to spend some time with my boy and Starr."

She stopped typing, turned and leaned on her desk, looked him directly in the eyes and removed her glasses.

"Starr's going in the studio with Sammy this weekend," she said. "Her teachers says she well beyond those productions at her school. She wants to be like her mother, and I'm not going to stop her. Sammy is writing some new music, especially for her."

Jenkins was taken aback, sprung out of the chair and leaned forward on both arms on her desk, frowning down upon her.

"What about you checking with her father before you go making a serious career decision on my daughter without talking to me?"

"You've been busy..." she said, returned to her email.

"I ain't been that busy, Siren."

"Yeah yeah yeah...."

He was steaming, the cocaine sizzling synapses and sparking a need for more.

"You're starting to turn into a real bitch, Siren," he said, took a deep breath, felt the tingling of residual cocaine in his throat and stormed out of the office, heading for a refill.

Chapter Fifty-five

Troy had his mind set on attending law school. Jenkins wanted him to join his father in the music business, and was by now convinced that he was not going to have another son. Siren told him point blank that she was using birth control, "pharmaceutical avoidance" was the way she had put it in a mannerism which was increasingly annoying to her husband.

"You're still putting that powder up your nose," she told him one evening during "down time" at the family home. "My babies Starr and Troy were conceived when we were both clean. I'm not taking any chance on getting pregnant again, as long as you insist on putting that poison in your body."

As he did often in recent months, Jenkins stormed out of the room, into his basement "man cave," where 300 square feet of luxurious games, pool tables, bar, refrigerator, movie studio and television viewing room kept him in a satisfactory state of solitude and avoidance. It was here where, just recently, he'd reassumed a habit he still frowned upon, but which was a remnant of his past and which now, well into snorting cocaine in abundance, he torturously resumed: Cooking up the powder into pure, rock form.

No one bothered Jenkins when he was in his "Fortress of Solitude," as he so called it. Only by invitation did anyone besides him even come into this part of the house; the mansion was quite spacious, and there were extensive rooms, even a pool, in other parts of the lower level. But Jenkins's spot, occupying a subterranean southeast section of the home, was avoided by both family and housekeepers.

Siren knew that he was devolving back into heavy drug use, and spoke to him about it on a number of occasions before she called "legal" and met to put into place injunctions removing Jenkins from any hands-on involvement in any parts of the Short Siren empire. And surprisingly, he had no problems with the legal restrictions. As long as he had access to his extensive personal fortune, he reasoned, he was quite willing to forego any involvement in the businesses.

He had to admit to himself, though, that the drug use was indeed making him extremely lazy.

"Fuck all that shit," he'd spat when asked to sign over power-of-attorney to his position as chief operating officer of Short Siren Music Corporation, Short Siren Music Holdings, Short Siren Sportswear and Troy Boy Youth Styles. "See how you run them joints without me, hear me, Siren? You just watch!"

That had brought her to tears. Before her was no longer the sweet, dark young man who sang like a gifted bird, who showered her with passions and warmed her heart from their teenaged years and through the tumultuous days when both were addicted. He was crass now, paying little attention to his personal hygiene, and even frowned upon by his own children. That was whenever he surfaced from his man cave, exhausted and simply too tired to do any further consumption.

"He's back on it hard," Sanford told her as she broke down into his arms on a Saturday afternoon while he was visiting out of concern. "We need to get him some help."

"He has to want help," Siren said. "You know how that is, Sanford."

"I know," he said, enveloping her in a warm embrace. "I know…"

Jenkins remained his best friend, though he certainly stopped seeing him as often when he saw that his friend was no longer attempting to hide his drug use. When Jenkins attempted to repeatedly get Sanford to join him in consumption, Sanford, an astute businessman and owner of a good percentage of the Short Siren empire, backed off and lambasted his friend for even suggesting that he join him on the deadly voyage. His own wife and Siren were fast friends, though his wife shunned participating in the fast-paced, high strung world of music production and concert promotions. She did hold a position overseeing Troy Boy Youth Styles, but was a fervent Christian, and really had little in common with Siren and her friends. So she was rarely around when the core of Short Siren meld, either professionally or privately.

Sanford thought of his wife first, and then Jenkins, as Siren meshed her warm body into his and cried on his shoulder.

"It's going to be alright," he whispered, stroking her lush mane of hair. "Baby girl: It's going to be alright..."

They were in the spacious kitchen of the mansion, Sanford having come out at Siren's insistence to attempt to talk some sense into her husband when he surfaced from an extended period of using. Starr was in New York, in the studio with Sammy and with Marvella as an escort. After two recording sessions under her mother's watchful eye, the outgoing girl had demanded that Siren let other professionals guide her initiation into the recording industry.

"Mom, like, OK!" a now 12-year-old Starr said. "You're like, totally micromanaging me from the start! Please, mother, can you be like, a little, like, un-so involved?!"

Siren and Marvella had both agreed, and Siren, still determined to be a hands-on parent while overseeing multi-million dollar corporations, turned her attention to Troy. He saw it coming, and made arrangements to immediately attend a school-sponsored seminar at Harvard, a precursor to some of his college prep training. The help was out for the weekend, and Jenkins was certainly out, upstairs in the master bedroom he'd not occupied for over five days.

"I don't know what to do with him, Sanford," she said, looking through tears into the eyes of one who'd always been like a loving brother to her.

But he wasn't any kin, whatsoever.

He looked down into the tearful eyes of one who'd been like a kid sister to him. He'd met her at the same time, as youths, as had his childhood friend Jenkins. And...he'd always had a thing for her.

"We're going to be fine, baby," he said, and two sets of eyes fluttered closed, two pair of lips met and two tongues did a sensual dance that soon turned feverish.

"Oh, damn, Sanford!" she whispered, felt his exploratory fingers examining her, finding her depths, easing her onto the edge of a bar stool. "No, Sanford! NO... Oh, Sanford! Damn, Sanford... Damn..."

Chapter Fifty-six

That latest cocaine binge had him seriously dehydrated. He felt as if he could hardly breath, throat dry, a dry sneeze tingling in his nostrils but refusing to erupt. He needed water badly, swung his tired legs to the edge of the huge bed and rocked to his feet. The expansive main kitchen was a distance away, a floor below, but he wrapped himself in a robe and directed his depleted body towards sustenance.

He needed to use the handrail to descend the curving staircase. The house was unusually quiet, as if some secrets lay waiting in a distant corner. He knew his children were away, the help was off this weekend, and if anyone were in the massive mansion, it could only be his wife Siren. Or perhaps his wife and a few of her gabby girlfriends. No, that was not possible. Even in a home of such immensity, he would have heard the echoing voices of Genese, Sunshine and Sirena even if they were out back near the pool. The house was too quite. There was no one here but him...and a whisper of a...voice?

He pushed through the swinging door into the expansive kitchen, looked to the middle of the room and saw activity on the far side of the marble countertop. It was his wife, her back to the countertop which occupied the middle of the kitchen. Her arms were resting back on the Italian marble, and she was seated on one of the twelve barstools that surrounded the countertop. Her head was thrown back, eyes closed, but her legs were strangely lifted, as if she were exposing herself, robe open. But to what?

He moved around to where he could gain a view of her from her left side, and what he saw weakened his knees and caused the dry fumes in his stomach to erupt in repulsion. There, holding his wife's legs aloft and tongue flickering her clit like some snake on PCP, was his childhood friend, his best friend, Sanford.

"Aw, snap!" Jenkins shouted, his own tortured eyes, his still-addled mind, hardly believing what he was seeing. "What the fuck is this shit?!"

Sanford dropped the legs and fell back on his rear, looking to his best friend with his face all shimmering with Sirena's juices, eyes bugged out, while Sirena nearly tumbled to the floor, barely maintaining her balance on the bar stool while struggling to her feet and fighting to secure the robe around her nakedness.

"You rotten motherfuckers!" Jenkins shouted, stepping towards the two while looking at the wooden cutlery holder on the countertop and its variety of professionally sharpened knives. He reached for one on the top row, a wooden handled butcher's knife. "God-damn Sanford! My boy! And you...you...damn ho!"

He froze for a moment, and the two misguided lovers seemed frozen also, as if neither knew exactly how to respond to this awkward and potentially deadly encounter. Sanford slowly climbed up from the floor, eyes locked on the butcher knife in Jenkins's hand.

"Man...Jenks man...I'm just...you know...." All he could do was shake his head, tears mounting.

"You ain't gotta say shit to me no more, Sanford," Jenkins said, standing stoic but being blinded by his own tears. "I know you better get your ass out of my house before some ill shit goes down! You hear me, motherfucker?"

"Man," Sanford said, looking between husband and wife. "Don't do nothing you'll be sorry for, man. Put down the knife."

Jenkins took a sudden, threatening lurch towards Sanford, knife extended before him.

"You shut the fuck up!"

He froze, swiped tears, was joined in audible sobbing by his wife.

"And you...you damn ho," Jenkins said, turning towards Siren. "With my boy! With...with...."

He eased over to a bar stool, sat down, put the knife on the counter, and broke down, sobbing uncontrollably.

Siren and Sanford looked to one another, both breathing deeply, Siren using a sleeve of her robe to clear away the tears.

"Sanford, why don't you go on home."

He looked between wife and husband and, certainly, the gleaming knife within Jenkins's reach.

"Sirena...I don't know if...."

"Go home, Sanford!"

He turned to a still weeping Jenkins.

"Bro...main man? I'm sorry, man. I'm...hey: Please don't do nothing stupid. Don't blame Sirena."

Jenkins's head snapped up suddenly, and he looked to Sanford, a gremlin-like smile overtaking his features.

"Don't blame the bitch for letting you eat her pussy? In my goddamn house? Huh? And y'all was about to fuck, better bet it. Huh? Don't...blame...the bitch? And how long this shit been going on behind my back, huh?! Huh?!"

"Jenks," Siren said, stepping towards her husband. But he grabbed the butcher knife again, pointed it directly at her.

"Get the fuck away from me," he said, then pointed the knife at Sanford. "Man, if you ain't out of my goddamn house in ten seconds, I'm gonna gut your black ass, hear me?!"

Sanford, never among the most hearty of the Keepin' It Easy group, began moving towards the nearest exit. He looked to Siren, gave her parting advice.

"Girl, call the police. Just get away from him and call the police."

"Look at you," Jenkins said, placing the knife on the counter, an awry grin replacing the grimace. "You ain't never been nothing but a bitch-ass nigga anyway. Punk-ass motherfucker. And just for the record: I done been up in that fat-ass wife of yours a couple of times, bitch. Yeah. That's why her ass all up in church all the time: Trying to make up for that sinful, stank-ass shit she like that you can't provide for her, punk! Freaking like a common ho and shit! Now, get the fuck out of my house, nigga! And by next week, I want to see you done divested yourself of anything have to do with this business I built with...with this...this stank-ho I call a wife. Now get to stepping, 'fore I fuck your punk-ass up!"

When Sirena cleared her tears and looked up next, all she could see at the far end of the countertop was the swinging door behind her grimacing husband.

"I ain't mad at you," Jenkins said, moving to one of three stainless steel refrigerators and grabbing a bottle of French spring water. "I should have known when I went back out, and stopped sticking it to you like that, that you was gonna get off somewhere else. But the shit that fucks me up is...Sanford? Hey, I know y'all always been close. But...Sanford? He ain't even your type, baby. Little bitch-ass nigga like that. Guess he work that tongue though, huh ho?"

He laughed, sat on a bar stool far from his wife and shook his head.

"Y'all a trip," he continued. "Down here having sex in the fuckin' kitchen like two goddamn kids and shit! Both of y'all can kiss my ass. And you...ho...all you can do for me from now own is suck my dick!"

That hit a nerve. Sirena arose from the bar stool, stormed down to where her husband sat and looked him straight in the eye.

"Fuck   you,   Jenkins!   Goddamn   crack-head
motherfucker!   You got your nerve!   Just....just....fuck
you!"

She stormed out of the kitchen and rushed up to the
master bedroom, locking the door behind her. She needn't
have worried though: With a second bottle of spring water,
Jenkins fumbled through a utility drawer until he found
what he was looking for: A large butane torch, one which
the family used to light fires in one of the fireplaces.

He moved slowly back to the stairs leading to the
lower level of the house, back to his man cave. Once there,
he snorted a tremendous amount of cocaine even as he
separated a couple of ounces from his personal stash and
began the process of converting it into rock cocaine.

He wouldn't be seen by another single person for
twelve days.

Chapter Fifty-seven

Sanford wasn't giving up his percentage of Short Siren Holdings easily. The privately-held company and its diverse subsidiaries were conservatively estimated to be worth $1.3 billion. And that didn't take into consideration anticipated future earnings.

Cream of White was becoming a corporate entity unto itself, but the astute legal minds of Short Siren had the group under contract for ten years and, even if they did leave, the very name of the group was the property of Short Siren Music, LLC. Sanford had a piece of all of this as a minority stakeholder in the overarching corporation, and it appeared as if there was going to be a legal battle undertaken in an attempt to divest him of his interest.

Jenkins could no longer stand the sight of his friend for over 30 years; they'd been toddling around at the age of five, neighbors in the now-defunct Barry Farm public housing project. Approaching 40, both were now multi-millionaires, but each had expansive offices on separate floors of the New York City building where most of Short Siren's operations were headquartered. And Jenkins's offices, on the 46th floor, were in proximity to Siren's, down the opposite corridor from the receptionist's entrance way. Sanford, involved primarily in management of the company's recording studios but more and more just an idled entrepreneur, had expansive offices on the 46th, down from the extensive studios. He didn't even have to come to New York; his participation in corporate operations had been seriously blunted by Jenkins. But he no longer sang, no longer produced any songs for any other groups, and outside of his million-dollar estate on Maryland's Eastern Shore and penthouse on Manhattan's Lower East Side, he had little to do. So he came to the office, to examine operations, yes. But also to needle his old friend Jenkins.

Following the kitchen brouhaha where he'd been caught going down on Sirena, Sanford had disappeared for a while. He levied his considerable cache and booked the company's Jamaican villa for a month, and did not even take his loving wife with him. She remained deeply involved in the operation of Troy Boy Youth Styles, and regardless of her well-considered and personally pronounced Christian devotions, Michelle Jones had been sexually involved with Steven "Flatiron" Massey for the past four months and was slowly becoming accepting, to put it mildly, of his cocaine use.

Jenkins meanwhile had surfaced from that culinary trauma only after his wife grew concerned, summoned law enforcement officers to batter down the locked door to his man cave, and discovered him just short of death from acute cocaine poisoning. He was rushed off to a private medical facility, but not before Maria, one of Sirena's trusted housekeepers, earned an extra $5000 by detailing events within the family mansion to Abby Vann, the intrepid Hollywood Remote television reporter who'd been following Siren since the songstress's own drug-fueled maladies.

In court papers Sanford refused the offer from Sirena Lavesque-Shorter, principle owner, Short Siren Holdings, of $50 million for his share of the corporation. Lawyers for Sanford laughed at the offer; not only were a couple of the music segment of the corporation's holding worth at least that amount, but prospects for the company's latest, freshest young talent, the young lady simply named "Starr," was projected to be worth hundreds of millions after her debut album was released.

"From the papers we were given access to by the courts," Siren's lead attorney in the case advised her, "if Sanford Jones doesn't want to sell his percentage ownership of the corporation, there's nothing we can do to force him to."

"Even if he wasn't a part of the company's expansion?" Siren asked.

"He was part of the initial corporation and all of its holdings. As its holdings were used to further expand the corporation, Mr. Jones is owner of an equal percentage of the profits of the new extensions, just as he is responsible for an equal percentage of any losses of the whole."

She accepted that Sanford was perhaps going to be an inextricable part of Short Siren's ever expanding corporate entity. Of course, she never blamed him for the kitchen malfeasance; he remained an uncomfortable friend. But it appeared that long-dormant feelings had been sparked on that one Saturday afternoon, and both, not to mention Jenkins and Mrs. Jones, who quickly became aware of the sexual liaison, felt they were too well-off to be experiencing unnecessary discomforts.

Especially Siren.

The former singing sensation, former addict, and once caring contributor to the cause of the downtrodden, was quickly becoming a mirrored image of New York's infamous "Queen of Mean," the hotel heiress who lambasted paying taxes as an exercise for the meek and weak. Certainly Siren paid tremendous personal and corporate taxes. But as she neared 40 and was primary head of a billion-dollar corporation, Siren the star grew more and more into a stiff, unyielding corporate bitch: Mrs. Sirena Lavesque-Shorter. And by now, no one in corporate headquarters better ever refer to her simply as "Siren."

"Siren was a business, goddammit!" she was heard to shout when a young visitor to headquarters fawned at her presence. "I'm Mrs. Lavesque-Shorter! Chief executive officer of the Short Siren empire! Get it right!"

She remained beautiful, but ugly in a sense. Close friends Genese and Sunshine were required to make appointments to see her. After he recovered from the shooting, Siren had given Sunshine's son Demarquis a position under Freddy in the company's security apparatus. It wasn't long before she fired Demarquis for failing to provide enough security at a Cream of White concert (throwing him under the bus, as it were, for she certainly couldn't afford to lose Freddy). That opened up the corporation to massive lawsuits when a post-concert stampede ensued, and Short Siren Music Corporation eventually settled, for a total $45 million. Although an astute Siren had taken out an insurance policy covering $50 million in damages, that sealed Demarquis's fate and built an insurmountable wall between Sirena and Sunshine, which forced Genese to have to choose between the two.

"I don't know what's wrong with that...bitch!" Genese said to Sunshine, gathered in Genese's 46th floor offices at headquarters. "I'm damn glad we got our stakeholder's percentages down on paper back when. You know the way that girl is now, she'd probably let either of us go if either of us got on her nerve, and we wouldn't have nothing to show for all the work we put in helping her build this `goddamn empire, as she calls it."

"No joke," Sunshine said. "Look at how she tried to get Sanford to sell his part of the company for little or nothing. That ain't the Sirena we grew up with."

"Sure ain't. Talking about call her Mrs. Lavesque-Shorter in the office! Nigga, please!"

"And that little hot child of hers turning out to be just like her," Sunshine continued, looking out over her spacious view of Manhattan. "I know Jenkins is have problems with his drugs and stuff. But he needs to get over that mess and get more involved in his daughter's life. Sirena is about to ruin that child."

"Giving her full hand in her career," Genese said. "That's the way she put it to me: Giving the girl full hand in her career. Sunshine, the girl ain't even 16 yet!

Marvella's doing good seeing that the child stay out from with them boys from Appreciation. But just barely."

One of Short Siren Music's new acts, Appreciation, consisted of five boys, ages 14 to 16, who were currently tearing up the record charts and being prepped for a concert tour.

"But they're still the opening act for Starr's initial concert tour," Sunshine said. "And my boy Demarquis, before that girl fired him, had them out on the road on the same tour bus. Per Mrs. Lavesque-Shorter's instructions! Talking about saving money, like, Starr shouldn't be 'spoiled' and have her own tour bus. Better off saving her virginity than saving money, that's what I say."

Genese laughed. "Might be too late for that."

"For what?"

"Saving that girl's virginity."

Chapter Fifty-eight

Cream of White's tour bus was pulled over just outside of Richmond, Virginia. Drug-sniffing dogs were called in in response to a "tip," and Abby Vann of Hollywood Remote was all over it immediately. Flatiron was too wasted to even dispose of the three grams of cocaine he had on him personally, and cameras were rolling when the disheveled superstar was handcuffed on the side of the road and carted off to jail.

Of the band and crew of 14 on the bus, only the driver was released without having to go to the Virginia State Police headquarters; the driver, Morton Fitzsimmons, reasoned now that the extra money earned driving for recording artists wasn't worth the headaches. He'd retired from driving Metro buses in D.C., which was often a thankless task. And after the bust of the boys Shaky Stick and Possum in Arkansas, he had been given a ride by the state troopers to a nearby Greyhound bus station, and he determined then and there that that would be his last time on any bus.

Yet here he was now, the money offered him to ferry these Short Siren artists around more than he could possibly turn down. For the second time, he was the only one allowed to go on his way, and went immediately back to D.C. to cash his latest check from Short Siren Music and formally let them know that he was no longer available.

Freddy was dispatched by Siren....Mrs. Lavesque-Shorter...to see if he could work his law enforcement contacts to free Flatiron and Cream in time for them to make the show in Charlotte, to no avail. The very volume of the coke Flatiron had on him, not to mention the three pounds of marijuana and four ounces of methamphetamine found on the impounded bus, negated any possibility of the tour group going free. The cameras of a nationally syndicated television program didn't help the matter, and Virginia's newly elected, get-tough-on-crime governor was already dispatching public relations operatives to ensure that this case, involving an internationally renowned recording artist, be held up as an example that Virginia would not tolerate any transportation of drugs through its boundaries.

This was a major public relations fiasco for Short Siren Music Corporation, and took on a life all its own.

Abby Vann did a feature that uncovered the fact that Jenkins Shorter, one of the company's founders, was in rehab for the second time in his career. Soon, every supermarket tabloid was splashing front-page headlines detailing the drug use deemed "endemic" in the core of Short Siren. Mrs. Sirena Lavesque-Shorter's own background was explored on a Sunday evening news magazine program, including an overview of the lives of her deceased mother and father. Not a single singer or group in the organization escaped scrutiny, and before long law enforcement was scouring the company's associations to see if there were any connections to some national or international drug cartel.

The spotlight only seemed to steel Siren's resolve. She held meetings well into the night, fighting back with her greatest tool: Exceptional music. The boy group Appreciation put out an album of rap/rhythm and blues songs with an anti-drug theme. Blossoming artist Starr did a similarly themed album, interlaced with a couple of soulful ballads, which sat at No. 1, and No. 2 on the music charts for 14 weeks. Siren even called on husband Jenkins and friend Sanford, setting them down together in a conference and pointedly telling them that saving "the business" required them both to shake hands, put the past behind them, and circle up the wagons to battle the media onslaught.

"Everybody's fucked up once of twice in their lives," Siren said in the meeting with the two. "I still love both of you, but of course I have a special love for my husband. And Jenks, you are still my husband and the father of my two kids. Sanford: I love you like the brother you've always been to me. That sexual thing was a serious mistake and, again, I apologize first to you, Jenkins, and secondly, to you, Sanford. Here we have a billion-dollar enterprise going on. We can't let that little incident, or any other, contribute to friction in the company. Especially after the mess generated by that crazy-ass Flatiron and his crew."

Jenkins looked to his wife, standing at the floor-to-ceiling windows overlooking all of Manhattan.

"Yeah, and me too," he said, a bit of contrition evident in his look and voice. "I'm fighting this...this drug thing, baby. But right now, I don't see where there's much I can do to help even by being here. Shit, the damn lady from Hollywood Remote had people hassling the people at the rehab joint. I think right now, I just need to go down to one of the get-aways. Either the Bahamas, or Jamaica."

Sanford, just back from the Jamaica retreat, nodded.

"That Jamaica joint is the shit!"

"I'm sure you think it was," Siren said, turning to face the two men. "Your wife is up here fucking Flatiron, and you, down there banging whatever you could pull from the exotic dance clubs. But I digress: Both of you are officers of this business, and if you can stop letting your drug use, Jenks, and your dicks, both of you, get in the way and exercise some fiscal responsibilities, well, I think we can manage to continue to grow this thing. That damn lawsuit after the stampede didn't help our bottom line any..."

"So," Sanford said, embarrassed that others, beside himself, knew of his wife's relationship with Flatiron, "we gonna let the white boy wallow in jail or, for business purposes, get his ass the finest lawyers and squash this drug beef?"

"Our attorneys are working with other attorneys on that as we speak," Siren said, returning to the seat at the head of the conference table. "We have that fool insured for half a billion dollars. But in the studio, and on the road, he's worth considerably more."

"Future earnings and shit," Jenkins added.

"Yes," Siren said. "We spring him, do a big PR thing about him quitting the road for a minute and going into rehab, whether he does or not, and high or sober, get that guy back in the studio. Short Siren has a seriously invested interest in seeing that he puts as much material in the can as possible. As soon as possible. Because for real, gentlemen, a man engaged in as much heavy drug usage as our friend Flatiron is is really not expected to experience the joys of longevity."

Jenkins and Sanford looked to one another, and then back to the woman both had known for a lifetime. But now, to the both of them, she appeared to be a very different and, perhaps, dangerous stranger.

Chapter Fifty-nine

Fifteen-year-old Starr was the headliner on the "Bubblegum and Braces Tour." The boy group Appreciation was on the undercard, but was more of a draw than the young girl with the current No. 1 hit on the charts. Siren was exercising overall control of the company, but had instilled a solid commitment to her present venture by giving million-dollar bonuses to Genese, Sunshine and Sanford. She still, along with Jenkins, wielded majority control of the expansive corporation. But Jenkins, hard pressed to give up his cocaine, had been dispatched to the company-owned villa outside Ocho Rios, Jamaica, for a presumed extended period of recovery.

The television reporter Abby Vann had suddenly lost interest in members of the extended Short Siren Music family. After Steven "Flatiron" Massey and members of Cream pled guilty, were fined and forced to commit to a period of treatment in a drug rehabilitation facility, Vann appeared to have suddenly lost interest in any other members of the Short Siren organization. Her meeting with security head Freddy, and a shady fellow who simply went by the name of Mr. M, perhaps dissuaded any further studies of Short Siren personnel by the journalist.

For Freddy's part he had his hands full with the up and coming young recording artist whom he knew personally about as good as any other outside of her immediate family: Starr Acosua Levesque-Shorter. The girl was too big for her britches, he said more than once to Marvella, who saw after the teen star even more so than Starr's own mother. Marvella and Freddy were "assigned" to the girl 24/7, and if not for the enormous amount of money each was being paid by Siren, they would have long ago discharged any duties looking after the obstinate child.

She was a handful, to say the least. Bright, intelligent, talented, and tall, leggy and beautiful just like her mother. And she knew it. Couldn't anyone tell the young star a thing, except in the studio, where she put aside playful banter and took seriously the music she created for her millions of fans.

And what a tease! The girl was so flirtatious to a point to where the five members of Appreciation, as tightknit a group as you could imagine, were erupting in an internal rivalry because Starr had allowed, first, lead singer Jason to fondle her and then, within days, she'd been caught making out with backup lead D'Andre. None of this sat well with Rakim, who'd experienced his very first sexual explosion at her hand, literally, and then as quickly been relegated to "my play cousin"-status, in Starr's own coy descriptive.

The Bubblegum and Braces Tour was designed to be Starr's coming-out event. Beginning in her hometown of Washington, D.C., the tour, complete with radio and television station appearances, would go on for seven weeks. Four tutors were ostensibly assigned to accompany the young party, Starr having two personal educators while two were assigned to the members of Appreciation. In fact, however, all of the youths would complete the necessary courses, most through on line computer test overseen by the tutors, to attain high school diplomas mid-tour. Neither Starr nor the parents of Appreciation's members even anticipated at the time that any among them would ever have the need for any higher education.

Antics on the tour bus were kept to a minimum when either Freddy, Marvella, or both of them were aboard. But Starr, with her doe-eyed persuasive abilities, would often convince the two to follow the tour bus in a limousine she'd personally summoned after the completion of shows in any particular city.

"Melvin's got the on board supervisory thing covered, Ms. Marvella," she'd pleaded, pointing out the driver contracted by Short Siren for the tour. "He knows everything's on the up-and-up with us like that, Mr. Freddy! Dag! Give us guys some down town just by ourselves! I mean, we are the ones putting mad bank into your pockets, am I right or what?"

In truth though, the driver was separated by the passenger's area by a partition which could either be opened so that he could see fully what was occurring aboard, or closed off whereby he could, if he strained, barely make out the heavy bass of the music the youths always played when being motored about.

After five sold-out shows in Washington, the tour moved south to Charlotte, where the only two shows there, on a Friday and Saturday evening, were already sold-out. Siren had attended the Washington show; she and a new male friend, along with Genese and her husband, had been seated in the owner's box at the downtown venue, unbeknownst to Starr, the boys, or Georgia. Siren knew that Marvella and Freddy had overall control of things backstage at all of the tour's venues, and didn't want Starr to feel that mother was a constant presence in the daughter's budding career.

Siren didn't have to attend any of the shows; she had exclusive live video feeds from each and every venue at either her New York offices or her McLean home. But she wanted to at least be present at the kick-off of the Bubblegum and Braces Tour, although she'd told Starr that business matters required that she be elsewhere.

Following the D.C. leg of the tour, Siren took a little down time at home, where son Troy was staying weekends while attending law school. Quite independent, he shunned the music business and focused on his education, though Siren tried time and time again to get him to at least keep abreast of expansions in the family corporation.

"I'll perhaps take some of your suggestions into consideration once I graduate and pass the bar," Troy had told her. "Right now though, I'm not even sure I want to focus on entertainment law. Criminal law excites me, mother. I do believe that's the path I'm destined to pursue."

"Yes, Troy," Sirena responded. "That might come in handy if your good-for-nothing father don't straighten up his act after he gets back from Jamaica."

As the tour progressed, Sirena, ever seeking to put another few million in the corporate coffers, spent most of her time in the New York studios. She was working with her team of video professionals to ensure that, when the tour was completed, DVD broadcasts of the tour highlights were marketed, first, to the nation's premier video music channel as a special and, secondly, mass produced and sold on the global market.

Even while trying to cement her relationship with a new, and quite wealthy, male companion, Siren couldn't help but keep her eyes constantly on the goings on related to her expansive corporation. She and her friend were in the New York offices, watching live feeds of the tour from Miami when little Starr took the stage and took over the crowd.

"Bet you were just like that when you were out performing," Ford Terrones, Siren's new, and quite close, male acquaintance said.

Starr was moving across the stage, gyrating into an elaborate dance number, along with three-dozen professional dancers. They were all moving to her popular song, "Hit It and Split It."

"I was still singing in the church choir at that age," Siren smiled, impressed by her daughter on the big screen television.

Ford rocked back in the plush leather lounger before the floor-to-ceiling windows to the left of the screen and a few feet from the similar lounger Siren occupied in the middle of her spacious office. The two had been "keeping company" for over a month, and the 67-year-old, a billionaire in his own right and heir to the Terrones Spirits and Terrones Hotels fortune, had not wanted to leave Siren's side since meeting her.

"You had a good run though, sweetheart," he said. "Not that you couldn't still turn out a crowd like that if you had a notion to return to performing."

Siren watched as her daughter brought screams from the crowd, motioned for silence.

"Shhhhhh! She had problems with this deliverance in Washington."

Starr hit the ending note to the million-selling single with perfection, bringing a smile to her mother's face.

"That's my baby!" Siren said. "Get it, girl!"

"Yes, that was nice," Ford said, arising, moving to the bar and fixing two drinks. He brought one to Siren. "You make a decision on coming with me up to the Cape for the weekend?"

She'd been to the Cape Cod compound once since meeting him, and found herself quite uncomfortable among his staid, high-brow kin.

"I think I need to see a few friends in Washington this weekend," she lied. "We'll get together up there another time, Ford."

"Then," he said smiling, moving over to her and reaching for her hands, "I'll have to blow off the Cape and come to Washington with you."

Oh, hell no! she thought, imagining the impression she'd be projecting to any of the few close friends she still remained in touch with: Genese, Sunshine and Shonda, who already thought that Siren had forgotten where she had come from. Ford Terrones, a tall, white, multi-billionaire, well known to many. And even as she remained married to Jenkins, it would surely be evident to any who observed her with Ford that the two were more than just casual acquaintances.

"I don't think so, Ford," she said, arising and placing her arms around his waist. "Personal matters, dear. Not that I wouldn't just love to spend the entire weekend with you and only you."

He had, after all, lent some pointed directions to her own financial advisors, pointing them to a few investments that had shown immediate profits of seven figures. Siren had more money now than she'd need in two lifetimes, but in her mind she was growing a brand, and even the new fashion line named after her daughter was not going to be rolled out with strictly Short Siren corporate funds.

He kissed her lightly, let out an audible sigh.

"You're just keep a man wanting and wanting for you, sweet Sirena. And then there's that matter concerning your marital status. I thought you told me that, after you'd seen that Starr's show was on the road successfully, that then there would be time for us to have that discussion?"

There was nothing to discuss, she thought, smiling up to him and pecking him lightly on the lips. They'd been intimate on three occasions, and in the short time they'd known one another he'd been quite willing to direct her towards a few tremendous financially successful investments which not only benefitted her personally, but had also been of tremendous benefit to Short Siren Holdings. She saw no need to give in to his personal desires to have her as his woman exclusively, she suspected, and in time, as his wife.

"Ford Ford Ford. A man with all the world and in such, such a hurry. Give me a little time, my dear. There's much, much more you need to know about me. And I about you."

"I understand, Sirena. I understand."

But he was whipped, and she knew it. She'd take him over to one of the company penthouses nearby, give in to his carnal desires and feigned exotic pleasure herself. He'd surely want to have her at one of the family hotel's not to far away, make a showing of escorting this well-known figure up to the Presidential Suite at Terrones Towers for all of those in the know to gossip about. But she'd seen that angle of him, was determined to have him on her terms and, for now, on her own playing field. Ford Terrones was a most desirable "asset," as she thought of their relationship, and she was determined to invest in him wisely.

She took him by the hand, gave him a passionate kiss and then both assumed their professional demeanor as they left the office and bid the receptionist Diane a good evening. They went to the Short Siren penthouse apartment three blocks from the company's Manhattan headquarters, and she spent a good two hours securing her investment before showering, bidding him adieu and taking the chartered jet down to Washington.

Chapter Sixty

"Ooooh! You guys are going to be in so much trouble if Ms. Marvella or Mr. Freddy find out!"

They were on the road to Dallas, and Starr was, as always, teasing the boys of Appreciation. The door between the driver's compartment and the passenger's area was secure, and within the bus was a virtual studio apartment unit: Sleeping quarters including what could only be described as bunk-beds: upper and lower seven-foot long platforms directly opposite one another and to the rear of the compartment. There was a tiny kitchenette midway the bus, with a small refrigerator, wet bar and small round table with two bar stools.
To the extreme rear of the bus, there was an enclosed toilet. Just inside the front door, casual seating areas flush with leather sofa, settee, above a rich carpeted floor. The lighting above and running down the center of the elevated ceiling could be lowered to a cool dimness or brightened to a glistening neon level. Midway the ceiling was a skylight, which was electronically filled with a dimming liquid and could be motored open, allowing for a clear view of the sky.

Jason, the 16-year-old who usually sang lead with the group, was stretched out on a bunk across from Starr.

"How are Ms. Marvella and Mr. Freddy going to find out?" he asked, smiling.

"I know. How are they going to find out?" Rakim asked.

"That stuff smells," Starr said, but was smiling with delight. "How did you get that anyway, the way Mr. Freddy is always watching us?"

"Got one of my boys from Miami a backstage pass," Rakim said. "He slipped me the package when Mr. Freddy and his boys was trying to keep them mad girls from following us after the set. Before you went on."

"Oh," Starr said. "Well, at least go back in the bathroom and smoke it. I don't know if Mr. Williams can smell that up in the driver's seat, but if he does, son, that's going to be your butt. Not mine!"

Four of the boys went to the rear toilet and smoked marijuana. Rocky, 14 and smitten with Starr, had already told his friends in no uncertain terms that he was not going to participate. He sat with Starr, listening to popular rap songs and tip-toeing around the notion that he and Starr should become boyfriend and girlfriend.

"Them my crew," the small, light skinned boy said, fidgeting uncomfortably on the edge of the platform across from Starr. "But you know, Starr, all they want from you is one thing."

Starr, in tight fitting jeans and silk blouse, threw her hair back in a gesture often seen of her when she was on stage. "You cute, Rocky, and all that. But boy, you're only fourteen years old! What are you going to do with....an older lady like your girl here?"

She crossed her legs, retrieved lip gloss from her purse and applied a coat to puckered lips, slowly, then eased her tongue out directly at Rocky.

"You're just a tease, that's all," Rocky said, frustrated and attempting to adjust his seating so that his hard-on wasn't visible. "And Rakim done told us that he got his freak on with you."

She glowered, remembering the hand job she'd given Rakim when the two found solitude in a dressing room backstage in Richmond.

"He's lying! That's just a figment of his imagination! Just like all five of you have those sexual fantasies like I would even consider ever giving any one of you some! Boy, please! You act like you've been smoking that stuff!"

They could tell that the bus was slowing, pulling into a rest stop perhaps. Rocky shot up and dashed to the back of the bus. Starr, sensing that the bus had parked, moved to the door separating the driver from the passenger area, opened the door and looked down to Mr. Williams.

"We there yet, Mr. Williams?"

"Naw, Ms. Starr," the 45-year-old said, securing gears and parking brake. "Unlike you and the boys and your self-contained luxury stuff back there, this fella got to go out to a rest stop and use the toilet and stretch my legs."

"Mr. Williams, you know you can come back here and rest and use the bathroom when you want to," she said, then thought about what the boys were doing back there at the moment, stepped down just as the driver arose from his seat. "But somebody's in the bathroom right now. Come on! I want to go into the rest stop also, maybe get some cinnebons! Is this Texas?"

She looked around, stepping off the bus. He moved down quickly behind her.

"Ms. Starr. They told me not to let you or the boys go out anywhere without no security! I got my...well, I'm licensed, and work directly for Mr. Glover. But it's just me, so if you and the boys don't mind, I'm going to lock the bus up and you and the boys just stay in there while I do my business. Won't be but a few minutes."

"OK," she said, pouting. "We're cool like that."

He watched until she moved through the door to the rear of the bus, Williams moved to the window outside the driver's compartment, reached in and motored the main door close. The small window had a security device on it, and he took a small key and locked it.
seats when she returned.

"You crazy guys are nothing but trouble!" she said, plopping down on the leather sofa between a visibly lackadaisical D'Andre and Rakim. "So, are any of you going to offer a lady a hit or what?"

Chapter Sixty-one

"You gwan offer I a hit or what, brudda?"

Jenkins didn't know this Jamaican girl, but had grown lonely in the luxurious villa and summoned his driver to take him out to a favorite nightclub. They were back now, on the patio of the house in Shawpark, a small village of sorts high in the hills overlooking Ocho Rios and the Caribbean Sea. He had taken a hit of some exquisite "ganja," marijuana grown locally, and for a minute after the first hit had all but forgotten that he was not alone on the arching patio.

"Oh, here you go babe," he said, passing a platter of weed over the table to the dark beauty. "Forgive my manners."

He'd been on the phone with his wife a few minutes earlier, and somehow she'd known that their daughter had been indulging somewhere in Texas. He inquired as to what Starr had been indulging in, was told that it was marijuana, and brushed it off.

"She's still a kid," he told his wife, then rushed to excuse himself and engage the exotic beauty he had at the Jamaican compound.

She was fine, in his common descriptive. A rear end that curved out with a demand that one give it a personal examination. And, after all, she was making a living by being paid to gratify the thirsty Americans and Europeans who came to her little out-of-the-way location outside Ocho Rios just for that. She was an exotic dancer, but at the club where she worked, additional arrangements could be made with a client for a large sum of American dollars and anything else the particular "dancer" requested.

At least she spoke good English, he thought while watching her roll a joint while sucking on his own and feeling the immediate exhilaration. More than just sex, he also was in need of conversation; his mind was a rush of expressions, and he needed an outlet.

"So, what do you do outside of shake your ass on the stage?" he asked.

"I have sex for money," she said bluntly. "One-hundred fifty American dollars and you can fuck I till tomorrow dawn."

"Oh, snap! Yeah baby, that's what I'm talking about!"

"You pay I first," she demanded, rising and stripping. "Then we fuck."

He arose, went to his cash stash and got two hundred-dollar bills.

"There you go, sweetheart," he said, placing the bills before her.

"I finish up this good ganja, then we fuck, OK?"

"OK."

In minutes, they were in one of the bedrooms, and she was even more exciting than he'd expected. Direct. To the point.

"How you want I?" she said, setting on the edge of the bed, legs raised and welcoming.

"From the back, babe," he said, shaking his head at the very thought of her perfectly rounded rear raised, she on her knees, awaiting his entrance. And it wasn't a second before she was on her knees on the edge of the bed, rear end raised and tempting.

"You first put on condom," she said, looking over a shoulder.

He put the condom on his eager, ready penis, eased up to her and took the plunge. After a few dozen strokes, and he exploded. She did too, if her words were to be believed.

"Ooooh! Ooooh! You make I come! You make I come!" she murmured, only exciting him further and inspiring him to push into her harder. "You make I…..come!"

He eased out of her, plopped down on the bed beside her as she turned to lie on her back and leaned over to give him a kiss.

"You know, I also smoke…a little…cocaine?" she said, setting upright and reaching for her purse. "You ever do the crack rock?"

He watched as she retrieved a glass stem, one which brought back torrid memories of a past he'd escaped and sworn never to return to again. The marijuana, combined with the overpowering sex, had his mind engaged in a battlefield, a tug of war between a measure of intense foreboding and one of excited expectations.

"I've been there, babe," he said. "But you know…how much you got?"

He knew it would be a serious mistake to even start. There had been no quitting in the past, and only a torturous period of rehabilitation freed him from the grip of crack the last time. But there it was, on the end of the pipe the girl was now putting a butane flame to.

She held it in, threw her head back, passed the pipe to him.

"I have a little, but I can make a call and get more."

He took the pipe, applied the flame and immediately motioned for more.

"I'll cop some more. Make the call."

"How much?"

He took the rock she offered, placed it in the stem for a fresh hit.

"A lot."

Chapter Sixty-two

Starr was hesitant to take the stage. She was paranoid, the marijuana doing as it often does, having her cautious about those backstage, and certainly fearful of the 7,500 people in the arena who were calling out her name. The Dallas crowd was at the moment a culmination of fears she'd envisioned but never realized before: External realities were now physical prophecies, and she had internalized everything she usually gave to a waiting audience and was now afraid to let it out.

"What's wrong with you, girl?" Freddy said, stepping amidst the group of security men and women he'd dispatched to Texas. "You been messing around with something? Come here."

He took her by the shoulders, looked into her eyes.

"God-damn!" he spat, then looked around to the members of Appreciation, who'd just minutes ago left the stage. "Who got this girl high?"

The boys from Appreciation, all looking sheepish but Rocky, stood to the side observing Freddy and Starr. Guilt virtually poured off Rakim, Tony, D'Andre and Jason, who'd put on a dynamic performance and, Freddy now thought in retrospect, seemed exceptionally energized.

"Marvella!" Freddy called out to his friend. She was on the opposite side of the backstage area fussing about some of Starr's backup dancers. "Marvella! Come over here!"

She rushed over, looked at Starr, who suddenly started giggling.

"What's wrong with you, child?" the matronly woman asked, taking Starr from Freddy's grip and turning her to look her in the eyes. "Oh Lord! You been smoking that shit!"

"I didn't smoke any 'shit,' Miss Marvella. It was some banging weed! Oh, OK. It was some banging shit! OK?"

"Simple, simple child!" Marvella said. She turned to an assistant. "Shirley. Go into the dressing room, look in the refrigerator and get that bottle of pomegranate juice and that bottle of....Oh, I don't know the name! It's a vanilla chai tea juice or something! That vegetarian mess this girl demands be at all her stops! Hurry up!"

She took Starr in a sturdy embrace.

"Lord Lord Lord!" Marvella said, face planted in Starr's hair. She looked up to Freddy. "This child is so picky about eating, about what she drinks, no meat and all that crazy mess. Who in the hell convinced her to smoke some of that mess?"

Both she and Freddy looked to the boys, still standing antsy near the stage entrance.

"Wasn't me," Rocky said, and the glares from his band mates told Freddy and Marvella all they needed to know.

"You little good for nothing heathens!" Marvella spat. "Freddy: Get some of your people to go over that tour bus. From top to bottom! Get the locals to bring in a drug-sniffing dog if need be. And I'm going to call her mother! This child is in a limo the rest of this tour. She is not going back on the bus with them...them little rascals there!"

Aw, come on, Miss Marvella," Jason, the common leader and most forward of the group said, stepping over to Marvella, Freddy and Starr. "She's aiight."

"She ain't all right!" Marvella spat. "And just listen to that crowd!"

The roar from the auditorium was roiling with cries of Starr's name and general rabble that clearly indicated that the crowd was growing restless. It had been 20 minutes since Appreciation left the crowd joyous and temporarily sated. Freddy knew the signs, and was sure that mayhem would erupt if Starr didn't take the stage soon or, God forbid, didn't perform at all.

Shirley returned with two bottles of juice, and Marvella opened the pomegranate juice, forced Starr to gulp some down.

She was then given a good measure of the chai tea drink, one which, Marvella said to Freddy, contained a good amount of vitamins B-6 and B-12.

"This ought to reenergize her," Marvella surmised, whispering her assessment to Freddy. "And it's one of her favorites by this company."

Georgia was managing this tour, and had been fussing about with the bands. The musicians were changing from the backers of Appreciation to Starr's personal musicians. Georgia saw all of the to-do going on around Starr from a distance away and moved over to the group surrounding Starr.

"What's going on?" Georgia asked.

"Damn child been smoking some of that damn weed mess," Marvella said bluntly. "We got her 'bout straightened out, Georgia. Is the band ready?"

"They're set."

"Get them rolling on her opening music," Freddy said. "Crowd's getting a might antsy."

"Child!" Georgia said directly to Starr. "After this is done, we're going to set down and have a talk! And I'm calling your mother!"

That caused Starr to pause midway her intake of the chai tea.

"I'm all right and ready to go, Miss Georgia! Really I am! I'm OK!"

Georgia, more so than Freddy and Marvella, knew that the only person that instilled any measure of fear in Starr was her mother. Her father, absent as he was at the time, had always coddled her, indulged her to a point of spoiling the child who'd never been hungry, never wanted for anything not given her. Marvella, to a degree, had been as coddling as father Jenkins, as was Freddy to an extent, a similarly paternal figure who abided Starr's little rants and periods of devilment. But Sirena had always been determined that Starr would be, in essence, a superstar, didn't indulge her, and would reign in all the luxuries Starr was used to as a matter of discipline. She'd even once had her daughter's cellular phone service cancelled. That had been one of the few times the girl had been reduced to tears.

"Please don't tell my mother I've been smoking!" she pleaded to Georgia. "Please??!!!"

Georgia saw the tears, the fear, taking over the budding star who was used to having everything her own way.

"Get back there in your dressing room and have Shonda redo your hair and make-up," Georgia said, looking at her chromatic watch. "You're on in...four and a half minutes."

Chapter Sixty-three

Siren had a private jet take Starr from Dallas to her next show in Los Angeles. Then she chartered one for herself and a small staff to head to California and be there for the last leg of the Bubblegum and Braces Tour. Figures were already in showing that the Dallas show was a tremendous success; Siren wasn't measuring the financial gains from the box office, but reviewing figures from accounting which showed the uptick in sales of records by both Starr and Appreciation immediately after a show, and by geographic region. Starr's new album experienced a tremendous uptick in sales in Georgia after the Atlanta show, massive downloads and album sales after Miami, hundreds of thousands of units sold after Dallas. Appreciation was generating similar profits.

She took a call from Jenkins while being driven out to Logan Airport; the Boston locale was the closest major airport to Ford's Cape Cod home, and after parrying off his suggestions for a few weeks, she'd finally submitted and spent the weekend with him at his expansive compound there. She had left the billionaire in bed with a smile on his face, and promised that, after business in Los Angeles, she'd pick back up on their torrid liaison the following weekend.

Jenkins was phoning from his extended "rehab" sabbatical in Jamaica. He said he had been robbed of his wallet and all of his credit cards. He needed his wife to express mail him new ones, and more immediately, wire transfer a few thousand dollars to him at the Bank of Jamaica in Ocho Rios.

"Jenks, you still have your passport, right?" she said, watching the seashore soar by as she was driven along the New England coast.

"I have it," he said.

"Then I don't see why you can't just go to the Bank of Jamaica and get some money, sweetie. The company has two accounts there to take care of the property in Shawpark and pay for the upkeep. Accounting set that up last year."

"I know," Jenkins said. "But them accounts...well, you need to tell accounting that all that money has been spent on...you know...the gardeners and the pool guy and...all that kind of stuff."

Siren checked a few figures on her computer pad, the latest mobile device she was never without and which contained applications not even on the general market yet.

"Seventeen-thousand, five-hundred and twenty-two dollars to upkeep and help over...the past three weeks?" Siren said. "And all of the cash withdrawals, by one Jenkins Shorter I see, made on...fourteen consecutive days? Jamaican pussy costing you quite a lot, isn't it, Jenks?"

There was silence. She could virtually hear his addled mind thinking, a few hundred miles to the south, and couldn't imagine what predicament he'd gotten himself into.

"What about your personal accounts?" she asked. "You should have millions in your own accounts here."

"I told you my wallet was stolen! My personal ATM cards and all that shit! Damn!"

She'd known him high, known him sober. Still loved him, but also knew well when Jenkins was lying.

"Don't tell me you're back on that shit, Jenks. Please don't tell me that."

"I....baby...," he said, and there was confirmation of the worse in Siren's thinking. "Just do the wire transfer and have accounting refill the account, dammit! Fuck! Short Siren's my company too!"

"Oh," Siren said, smiling at the beautiful ocean waves to her left, "I might just have to do something about that too, my darling. "I think we might have a case of you being unfit mentally to carry on with any fiduciary responsibilities regarding Short Siren and its affiliates."

"Bitch! You better not!"

In all their years, he had never called her the "b-word," and even during younger years she'd let him know, even as some of their acts used it in song, that that was one thing which she would never stand for personally.

"Oh, it's like that now, dear husband. I'm a bitch now to you, huh Jenks? Well, I got your bitch right here, motherfucker. On the smart pad before me! I'm having finance wire you a few hundred dollars, and freezing the corporate accounts at the Bank of Jamaica until I can change the accesses to our legal rep and our legal rep only down there. Then I'll have the accounts replenished so that our legal rep can see that the help is paid and properties of Short Siren are seen after. You want to play games with me? You know who you're fucking with, Jenks? Before I'll send good money after bad, messing with your stupid ass, I'll see you out trying to hustle dick in Kingston first! And by the way: You haven't expressed any concerns about your son and daughter. Goodbye, Jenks. I have a corporation to run."

She disconnected, speed dialed a banker whom she was personally familiar with in the Bank of Jamaica.

"Mr. Wilson? Sirena Lavesque-Shorter...Oh, fine dear, just fine. Look: I'm having accounting replenish the accounts of Short Siren, Ocho Rios LLC with $450,000 within the hour. I'll also have Oliver St. Sebastian, our attorney in Kingston, come see you and initiate paperwork to place him, and Ms. Sylvia Major of his firm, as sole signatories on those accounts....Yes, to ensure our investments there are seen after...Yes, I was just on the phone with him...Oh, I see....I kind of picked up on that....No, he's not to have any involvements acting in the capacity as a representative for Short Siren there...He can stay at the Shawpark villa...He wants what?....I'm having $500.00 wired there for him, and that's it....I understand...Ummm....Well, then he needs to pimp the whore if she's got him back out like that...I appreciate the insight. Good day, Mr. Wilson."

Chapter Sixty-four

After finding an ounce of marijuana on the tour bus, Appreciation motored to Los Angeles in a virtual vice grip of security. They were very uneasy, with Freddy and Andrea, one of his key security lieutenants, on the bus the entirety of the ride from Dallas to LA. All they could do was concentrate on their music, and the security team was afforded time to get to know each member of the group as individuals.

Jason, at 16, had been initial in forming the group, and was its leader to a degree. Rocky, 14, was a beautiful singer, but pouted a lot, was very introspective, except for when he was in the presence of his beloved Starr. D'Andre, the 15-year-old with a head full of thick dreadlocks, usually followed the lead of his older brother Jason. Rakim, 16, was the more studious of the group and, the son of two African-American Muslims, tended to introduce his friends to literary works as opposed to the ever present Big Apple stereo headsets the others tended to wear whenever not in conversation or being directed by their tutors. Tony, a shy fellow of 15, had a syrupy-sweet falsetto that endeared him to female fans around the world. Together, all five had experienced a generally middle-class upbringing in the Hillcrest community in Southeast Washington, a region of half-million dollar single-family homes where two D.C. mayors had homes and, historically, once was home to the FBI's J. Edgar Hoover.

They were small, yet-to-mature boys to the one, none weighing more than 160 pounds and all between 5-feet 9-inches and 6 feet tall. They ranged in color from D'Andre's coffee skin tone to Tony's light, creamy complexion and, always afforded the best in youthful fashions, were, in their own personal assessment, "fine dressers."

Andrea, the plain-clothed security lieutenant, was strikingly beautiful, and tasked for the ride by Freddy especially for the mission to accompany Appreciation. She was key not only because her beauty never failed to turn the head of most any man, but because she was also a PhD in psychology. That was the main reason Short Siren paid her seven figures to examine, analyze and provide security for select performers. Andrea Mason was always armed, often sharply dressed in a tailored, blue pin striped pants suit, and had requested being part of the security detail even after none less than Mrs. Lavesque-Shorter offered her a salary and benefits which hardly required that she join any security detail.

She was "all that," in the cryptic appraisal of all the boys in Appreciation. They would have been flabbergasted to know that Andrea's likings didn't even lean towards men; she was not married to her partner Svetlana, but as their home state of Maryland had recently passed same-sex marriage legislation, was well on her way to the altar. But her beauty, her demeanor and bright, welcoming smile, always brought the boys, or any in her presence, to attention. When Andrea spoke, the boys removed their headphones and eagerly sat at her feet to hear what she had to say.

"Boys, I hope we are of the understanding that there will be no, shall I say, extracurricular activities on this bus the remainder of the tour," Andrea said, adding a sensuous smile and enhancing the exceptional beauty that had already warmed all of the boys. "I'm not going to ask about how you got the marijuana. I know though that you, Jason, always have calls out to some...let's just say some of your less than upright friends in the business in a few cities before you arrive. Now, I also know that you plan on getting with that boy Black Shadow in L.A."

"What?" Jason said, completely taken off guard. "What up? Y'all tapping our phone conversations or something?"

"Jason," Andrea said directly to him. "For security purposes, we've installed...well, monitors in strategic locations. For your safety."

"Oh," Rakim said, nodding. "You and Mr. Freddy done bugged the bus? Bugged our dressing rooms?"

"We...monitor," Andrea said. "Let's just leave it at that."

Freddy had been sitting on the plush lounge to the side, observing his lieutenant with a smile.

"That ain't right," D'Andre said. "And we ain't make Starr do nothing! That was all on her, yo."

"Starr is with Miss Marvella, and additional security, on a flight to L.A. as we speak," Freddy put in. "It's all business, fellas. You want to show your asses, you wait until you're back home. But on the road, there will be no...shenanigans! You all are familiar with them boys Shaky Stick and Possum?"

They all nodded.

"That was some ill mess what happened to ol' boys," Jason said.

"And maybe what you don't know is that they were busted on the road, on their bus, and only Mrs. Lavesque-Shorter and her legal team saved them that time."

"Dag!" Rakim said. "And the way they went out like that, that was some suspicious stuff!"

"Quite suspicious," Andrea said. "Deserved further investigation, but you know, they weren't under the Short Siren umbrella then, so even though we felt for the boys, it was in our best interest to stay clear and let law enforcement do what they do. And I have to say, just between us, they didn't do very much about them boys dying like they did."

"Damn!" Rakim said. "So, Miss Andrea, you think it was kind of...like...a hit or something? After that thing that happened at the D.C. joint?"

"Perhaps," Andrea said. "Young men: This is a cutthroat business you're in. Siren and...well, her husband Jenkins, to a degree, built a fine company. And you were perhaps...well, to tell you the truth, you were either babies or not yet born. But a little...study...will give you an idea of some...traumas...Siren and Jenkins went through when they were just starting off in the business. But for the grace of God, neither of them would be where they are and, needless to say, I doubt Appreciation would be where you all are."

"My mother told be about that," Rakim said. "Drugs or something."

"Exactly," Freddy said. "Exactly. So they know of what they speak, so to say. Now, you boys want to, how you say it: Make mad bank? Or wind up like Shaky and Possum?"

"Oh, hell no, Joe!" three of the young men said at once.

"Not even," the other two added. "Not even!"

Chapter Sixty-five

There was a big clash at the New York recording studios, and Siren found out about it on a conference call with staff from the suite she, Marvella and Starr were staying in overlooking downtown Los Angeles. It was such a mess, and Siren only wished that she could jet back to New York immediately and take control of the situation.

Flatiron and Cream of White were back in the studio working on new materials. Sanford was the highest level official on site, was being supported by Genese and Sunshine, while in a separate area of headquarters, Sanford's wife Michelle was deeply involved in rolling out a new fashion line for Troy Boy Youth Styles.

Upon hearing that Flatiron and his crew was back in the studios, Michelle, entertaining warm thoughts about her torrid affair with the wild, often drug-fueled musician, decided to pay Flatiron a visit. Memories immediately sparked and Michelle, with quite a measure of cache in the extended corporation, hit up head administrative assistant Diane for the keys to the nearby Short Siren owned penthouse on 5th Avenue.

Within headquarters, the full-time staff of over 140 often joked that, if you wanted to get some unofficial dirt spread around without putting it in hard copy via email, you only needed to tell the dirt to one black woman in the company, and before lunch time came around everyone in the building would be privy to it. Diane told fresh receptionist Dawn that Michelle had secreted off with Flatiron; she also briefed the young lady on Flatiron and Michelle's history. And as that information took shape, altered and moved like an infection through the staff, Sanford got wind of it.

"That raggedy-ass white boy!" Sanford was heard to say as he passed through the reception area, headed for the elevators. "I'm 'bout to bust a cap in his punk ass!"

He descended 46 floors and the time, the changing of elevators, only gave him space to allow the thoughts of his wife of over 15 years engaged with the world-renowned rock star to simmer. He'd known about the earlier affair, and had reconciled with Michelle after she threw up the fact that she knew that Sanford had been unfaithful himself. She knew, from Jenkins no less, that he'd been caught engaged in a sex act with Siren.

But that was a good time ago. She also knew that he'd been taking the younger, much younger Fredericka Sands, lead singer of the group Holiday Candies, to one of the corporate suites after Siren had detached the hot young lady with corporate aspirations from Jenkins.

"I'm gonna fuck his skinny ass up!" Sanford said, armed with a secondary key to the 5th Avenue suite and hailing frantically for a taxi.

A cab pulled over before the skyscraper, and Sanford couldn't believe that fate could be operating with such a cruel sense of irony: The tall, lanky form of Flatiron, chest puffed out with what appeared surely to be a proud measure of bravado, climbed out of the cab and reached a hand back to help Michelle from the conveyance.

Sanford stepped up behind an unawares Flatiron and stole him.

The sucker punch sent Flatiron into Michelle and knocked her back into the taxi. Flatiron rolled onto the rear of the cab, turning just in time to see the second punch as it crashed into his nose.

"Aw, fuck!" Flatiron said, plastering a hand onto his face as blood gushed from his nostrils. "Are you fucking crazy, man?! What the fuck!"

"Yeah, motherfucker! Crazy like shit!" Sanford said, pitching two twenty-dollar bills through the front passenger window to the startled cab drive. He reached in the back and wrenched his wife from the cab. "You still just a fucking ho, stank ass! Jesus ain't even gonna be able to save your ass this time!"

He pushed her towards the building, glared at the gathered crowd, which immediately dissipated. Flatiron regained his footing just as the cab tore off.

"God-damn, Sanford!" Flatiron said, retrieving a handkerchief from an inside pocket and attempting to stem the flow of blood while trailing the two. "It was all business, guy! I wanted to lunch with Michelle to go over Cream's plans for a line of leather goods! What the fuck!"

"Yeah, I'm supposed to believe that shit! Y'all back at it like you was before your raggedy ass had to go into rehab! And on our dime, I might add! Fuckin' raggedy ass, bitch ass motherfucker!"

He turned and went into the office tower, shoving his awe-stricken wife before him. Flatiron just stood amidst a bustling downtown Manhattan, not really wanting to go back into the corporate offices. He'd been threatened by a pistol-wielding Sanford the first time he'd been rumored to have been bedding Michelle. He still had the key to the 5th Avenue suite, waved for another taxi.

He'd give Sanford time to cool off, he reasoned while motoring the few blocks to the suite. And, he thought with a dangerous rush of past thoughts, he sure could use a hit of something about now.

Chapter Sixty-six

The Los Angeles shows were a tremendous success, and on the flight back to New York Siren was reviewing figures already coming in which showed that the West Coast appearance had already generated the sales of 27,789 units of Starr's latest album and 45,634 units of Appreciation's in the same region over the past 24 hours. Starr slept in the leather lounge chair opposite her in the jet, Marvella slept in one beside her, and the makeup artist Shonda and tour manager Georgia were asleep in seats to her rear. Siren had just received reassurance that things at headquarters were under control for the moment, and she was determined to plot further expansion of Short Siren Music after this quite profitable tour.

All the members of Appreciation, along with Freddy, Andrea and the bus driver Wilson, were flying east on a commercial flight, though all in first class. The bus was put in storage in Los Angeles, and would be at the disposal of groups either touring there or out West for other business. Siren had representatives even now scouring California for West Coast offices, and projected to have a full-blown operation there within six months. The business plan called for an L.A. office before year's end, and she was well ahead of schedule.

She took a few minutes during the flight to conference with Ford, thanked him for the latest investment hints and felt an internal satisfaction that her personal fortune had mounted by $4.6 million while she was out West as a direct result of Ford's insider financial directions. She made a note on her calendar to set aside the coming Saturday so that she might thank him in a proper, or on second thought, improper manner. She smiled at her perceived expanding business and social acumen, shut down the computer and napped.

She had failed to turn off the smartphone, however, and just as she was enjoying a dream of herself visiting the White House the device in her breast pocket began vibrating. She looked at the face of the device, was greeted by the smiling photo image of her husband.

"Hey, Jenks," she said lethargically. "What's up?"

"That was some fucked up shit you did, Sirena! Why you have to cut me off from the company accounts down here like that?"

She shook her head, smiled sarcastically. "You're running through money like water down there, Jenks. Fuck up all of your personal fortune if you want, baby. But I'm not letting you fuck up anything involving Short Siren. You're back fucking around with that shit, aren't you?"

He sniffed, the powdered cocaine he was snorting only keep him appeased until Denetia, his latest Jamaican lover, cooked up some into rock form at the nearby dinette table.

"I'm just doing my thing, baby," he said. "But you know I had to sell some of my personal shit, cause you ain't send me but $500.00. What's up with that?"

"You haven't replaced your ATM cards, Jenks? You do have money, baby. And quite a bit, last time I...uhh...heard."

She'd used considerable leverage to monitor her husband's personal fortune. It remained substantial, but the accounts had been dormant for over a month, and she surmised, quite correctly, that Jenkins had been on such a tear that he couldn't take time to do the necessary legwork, and paperwork, to regain access to his fortune.

"Yeah, well, it's a whole lot of shit from the villa ain't there no more," Jenkins said. "You want to be like that. Anyway, I ain't call to get into no argument, Sirena. I just got to ask you, please, at least wire me a few thousand dollars until I can get my shit in order."

"Humph," Siren said. "Your shit won't be in order until you get off of that shit! Now, as long as you're back out and using, I can't do much to help you. You know what we learned in the meetings back in the day: You can't help an addict until he's decided to help himself."

"Fuck you, girl!" Jenkins said, irritation clear. "Just send me some goddamn money, hear what I'm saying? Or I could just lease the Shawpark villa out to some drug dealers or some shit! How would that look on Short Siren if the media got hold of us having a place in Jamaica housing drug dealers?"

That perked up Siren's business senses, and she grew hot. "Jenkins, I'm going to tell you one time and I'm serious as a heart attack: You do anything to put the company in a bad light down there and, well, I still love your sorry ass, but I do have some connections down there that have been keeping an eye on you. And some of them, I mean, for real, would ice their own mother for a hundred-thousand dollars. You understand what I'm saying, sweetie?"

"You threatening me, Sirena?"

"Take it as you want it."

"Oh, you've really got your ass on your back since you've been rolling out them white boys and my baby Starr and them boys and shit. I ain't never thought you'd change like that, Sirena. You've really changed, baby. But that's fucked up, you threatening your husband like that."

"Yeah," Siren said, growing exhausted. "Well, about you being my husband: I'm about ready to end this fake-ass marriage anyway. How are you a husband and I haven't seen your ass in months?"

"Divorce? I know you ain't thinking about no divorce?"

"Yes I am. And as I'm on my way back to New York at the moment, I'm going to talk to my personal attorney about initiating the paperwork."

"Yeah, bi...Siren! Guess you're going to serve me with divorce papers down here in Ochi."

She smiled broadly. "I have attorneys on retainer in Kingston, Jenks. And believe me, my...associates down there...know where to find you 24/7. Now try me."

"Fuck you, Sirena!" he spat. "Just send me some goddamn money!"

Chapter Sixty-seven

Just before Cream finished laying down the last of the new tracks, Flatiron went missing. Siren called a meeting of the board first, and then held an impromptu staff meeting which was attended by 28 of the highest-ranking officials of the corporation. She particularly wanted to call out Michelle Jones, Sanford's wife. In front of many of her closest colleagues, and her husband, Siren fired her.

"Accounting is preparing your separation package and it should be ready for you by noon," she said directly to the confounded woman. "Genese Taylor will be assuming the position as head of Troy Boy Youth Styles."

Michelle, completely taken aback, sprung to her feet.

"Sirena, you're one cold bitch! You've been acting lately like you forgot where you came from! Bitch, I remember when your ass was just another crackhead whore! Fuck you and Short Siren. I just know you better pay my ass generously before I leave this motherfucker!"

"You'll get paid," Siren said calmly. "Now, if you don't mind, remove your black ass from my presence before I have security do it."

"Siren," Sanford said passively, setting a few seats down the extensive conference table. "Come on, lady. Michelle has been faithful to the company since you brought her on board. And Troy Boy has continually shown profits under her lead. You can't be that inconsiderate, Siren. Please, take time to reconsider this move."

"That's alright!" Michelle said, moving towards the closed door. "You act like don't nobody knows that you're fucking that white man up on the Cape. Yeah, everybody knows you ain't all that when it comes to mores, honey!

And I still ain't forgot that Jenkins caught you and Sanford all freaking and shit out at your house that time! So fuck you and the horse you rode in on!"

With that, Michelle stormed out of the conference room, trailed closely by Sanford.

Siren looked around the conference table at an astounded, speechless gathering. She put on the designer glasses she now needed to read fine print, looked over some papers before her, removed the glasses and looked to her gathering of officials.

"Now," she said. "I'm having Freddy and his security people go out and find that sorry-ass Steven Massey, aka Flatiron. He's under contract through the new music Cream is about to complete, and he's going to finish that production. He's in breach of contract if he engages in any further drug use, and I think by now that might be a considered possibility. But when he's found, he will complete the current album. After that, I could give a rat's ass of what he does. Any questions?"

There was a chilly silence.

"Then this meeting is adjourned."

She arose first, everyone else seemingly frozen in place. Genese, dedication barely shaken by the observable change in attitude of her childhood friend, moved up to accompany Siren out of the conference room. Sunshine, not wanting to shake her own personal love and devotion among the key officials, stayed seated, looking around at the dour faces and shaking heads.

"Mrs. Lavesque-Shorter has spoken," Ned, head of accounting, said.

"You know that's right," another official said quietly.

Slowly, all arose to return to their duties in individual departments of the corporation. Most, however, were little inspired to work further for the six- to seven-figures they were earning, and all among them, to a man and to a woman, began formulating plans to leave the business while still retaining some measure of pride and, certainly, a good piece of the considerable wealth Short Siren had afforded them.

Chapter Sixty-eight

He was in a ramshackle joint in the Bronx, and even among the crackheads, everyone knew exactly who he was. He stood out like a sore thumb too: A tall, lanky, still apparently healthy white boy, among a legion where the word health could hardly be spelled correctly.

For three days and nights, Flatiron had sponsored a crack-consuming cauldron of debauchery; naked, frail women abounded, interchanging crack pipes and dicks between parched lips while men, afforded an unusual abundance of rock cocaine, lay variously about with dicks being tempted but most flaccid under the benumbing effects of crack.

Still in possession of the keys to the 5th Avenue condo, he was ready to return there after being up for three days, having eaten little more than some bags of pork rinds purchased by the crackhead whore who'd closely befriended him and bought him to this dank location in the first place. He'd trusted her with his ATM card, unable or unwilling to tear himself from consumption when the supply was running low. And she'd been catering to him with enthusiasm, a 12-year addict who was able to escape the rugged compound on a number of occasions, armed with his card, his PIN number, and periodically withdrawing the maximum amount allowed from the one account he gave her access to.

The receipt for the first withdrawal had nearly given the woman a cardiac: A balance of $768,450.28 showed on the paper, a figure which further steeled her resolve to keep hold of Flatiron (she knew well his stage name and business) for as long as possible.

"I ain't never heard nothing that motherfucker sang or no shit," she said to her equally-addicted male cohort when they jointly moved to make the 14th purchase of crack. "But people say he's big time, and from all the money on this one card, that motherfucker's loaded!"

She had been scheming of a way to access an abundance of the cash, and not spend many more days performing oral sex on him and feeding him crack. But her addled mind couldn't come up with anything, so she committed to just keeping his bank card and PIN number when he did finally leave, get his cell phone or office number, and hope that he didn't eventually come to his senses and see the snaggletooth woman for what she was: A 104-pound crack whore whose front teeth had been punched out by a dealer when she'd been caught trying to sneak into his street stash. The absent teeth, to be sure, enhanced her practiced ability to do what it was she did quite proficiently to feed her crack habit, and at the beginning of her encounter with Flatiron, she'd won him over, temporarily, through her oral abilities.

He was now growing tired, told his newfound friends that he was going back downtown for a period of recuperation, and had to beg up taxi fare. Appreciative, and still in possession of his ATM card (she said she'd lost it, and his addled mind had accepted that), the crack whore gave him $20.00 to taxi as close to the 5th Avenue suite as he could, and he arrived there a stinking bundle of repulsive mess.

The doorman, after escorting Flatiron to the elevators, immediately made the call to Mrs. Lavesque-Shorter, as he'd been instructed by the security guy.

"Put two of your best on him," Siren said to Freddy after disconnecting the call from the doorman. "I want them to sit on him till he's sober. Make sure he doesn't have the wherewithal to return to wherever it is he's been. Give him a few days, but make sure your team doesn't leave the suite. They can take turns sleeping there; it's got five bedrooms. Just get his ass sober and tell your team to bring his ass directly to the studios once he's recovered."

"What about the rest of Cream," Freddy asked. "They've been quite concerned about him."

"I'll meet with them. Have Diane get in touch with all of them and arrange a meeting in my office for tomorrow noon. And thanks, Freddy. You're a Godsend."

"Any preferred backing for your movements this afternoon?" Freddy asked.

"Svetlana and Andrea. They're…discreet as they come, and I'm…well, you know, having a little….assignation…with my dear, wealthy, most valued friend."

She then took the call from Ford, had her secretary cancel any other meetings on her schedule for the afternoon and decided to walk the few blocks from her office to the massive five-star hotel which bore the Terrones family name. Shadowing her every step of the way were two women, each trained in a deadly form of martial arts but still bearing, and authorized to carry, concealed weapons.

Chapter Sixty-nine

Starr was back home, secure in her McLean mansion and following her mother's strict instructions that she concentrate on her studies, obey every word of the four tutors who spent seven hours each weekday at her home. She could only venture out, as discreetly as possible, with the four security personnel put up in the guesthouse by Freddy, and only should the teenager just feel the need to do as teens would do and go scurrying around a mall, along the streets of Washington's Georgetown, or to a movie.

The youngster understood that with her well known face and star status, she just couldn't do all that she wanted to in public. Her mother had certainly seen to it that there was an abundance of food: Starr's preferred natural vegetable and fruit drinks, and a host of distractions to satisfy the highly-energetic girl. Yet what Starr wanted most, and which her mother forbade, was the presence of Rakim, of Appreciation fame, in her lavish bedroom.

After dissing Rocky as being too young for her, teasing Jason in a fondling session which brought him to the brink, and actually delivering a hand job to Rakim which had him experience his first sexual explosion, Starr had determined to stay clear of all of Appreciation. She was currently smitten with 19-year-old Sean Jackson Rogers, newly signed to the Short Siren label and a young man whom no one doubted was certainly destined for stardom.

He was not yet a star though, and as Starr was just short of her 16th birthday, her mother wouldn't hear of it. So for male companionship (of which she heatedly desired, if only in a platonic way) she turned to the only boys with whom she stayed in touch by phone and email and who also lived close to her Virginia home: Appreciation.

She saw them all as what she termed play-cousins. But any young man who got close to the striking beauty, one with a mature beauty and sexual aura well beyond her years, desired more than just friendship.

Except Rakim.

After their initial one-way sexual encounter, the dark, handsome, intelligent boy had shown no further interest in Starr. The fact that he wasn't drooling over her like every other boy was actually what attracted her further to him, and also steeled her resolve to reign him in and secure him as her personal playmate. (She frowned upon the term "boyfriend," considering herself much too important a personage to have so pedestrian an association). In that sense, she was really just like her mother, many around her believed: Above and beyond the strikingly pretty looks, she and Siren were strictly about self-gratification as a tool in their climb to the top.

Outside of security and half a dozen housekeepers and the weekday tutors, Starr had the mansion to herself when mother was in New York or otherwise out on business. Her brother Troy was attending law school, would come home a few weekends a month, but had shown no interest in the family business and seemed to prefer staying well away from it. Her father remained in Jamaica, and as most astute children are capable of doing, Starr knew well that Jenkins was on drugs. She could tell by his brief acceptance of calls from her, not to mention that the Internet was full of past failings, long before she was born, of both mother and father.

Marvella stayed in touch when she was not on the road, but was getting up in age and determined to have a personal life outside of the Lavesque-Shorter family. Starr loved the woman about as much as she did her own mother, who had become more of a business manager than parent. And she had few girlfriends, so even though she'd already amassed a personal fortune of well over $50 million, Starr was quite the lonely young lady.

She stayed in touch with Tiffany, her young school from the exclusive secondary school she'd attended before international stardom made her mother remove her from any regular school attendance. But Tiffany's parents were laying a path for her that didn't include palling around with some "pop star," as they derisively described Starr with a sniff. Also, Tiffany had never really forgiven Starr for allowing her and other friends to take the blame for the water-balloon fiasco, for which all of the accused experienced strict disciplinary action which killed Tiffany's chances at becoming class president and valedictorian.

They talked by phone nevertheless once or twice a month, but when Tiffany refused Starr's request to join her Saturday afternoon for some shopping, Starr disconnected the call abruptly, hung up on a still explanatory Tiffany and, lips stuck out, deleted Tiffany from her speed-dial address book and defriended her on the popular social media network.

She then speed-dialed Rakim, in dire need of some communications with someone similar in age and, more so, in need of some salving of an ego that was usually stroked by the laudatory praises of thousands. Usually the boy, a star of note himself, would allow many of the calls to his main cell phone to go to voice mail if he didn't recognize the name or screen photo as any of the numerous young ladies he didn't mind speaking with. Thirty miles south of Starr's McLean home, he showed the picture to Jason and D'Andre, smirked and let it ring a few more times before answering.

"Hello, sweetheart," the melodious voice greeted her, making her smile.

"Hi, Rakim. What's up?"

"Not a thing, Starr. Me and the brothers throwing around some lyrics, on paper, trying to come up with some new works. What up with you? You trying to motivate a brother?"

She giggled, again the child she truly was and not the young lady who wanted so badly to be.

"What do you mean, 'motivate'?"

"You know," he said. "Inspire a brother to write bomb lyrics. Inspire me, baby."

"How?"

"I have a ride. Where are you?"

"At home."

"Want some company?"

"Yes," she said, wishing she hadn't responded so quickly, so anxiously. "If you're coming by yourself."

She'd never seen any of the group without all of the others in close proximity, and actually thought it was her own mother who forbade her million-dollar act to travel singularly. It was actually written into their contract, the receptionist Diane had told her during a casual conversation about boys.

"Why you think I have to roll out with my boys all the time?" Rakim said, smiling to his friends. "That's just my manager and your mother's way of thinking. I can roll out on my own, and don't need no security like that. Girl, I carry my own protection, know what I'm saying?"

"I hear you, Rakim."

"So, text me the directions to your place. But first, your mother or Mr. Freddy or Miss Marvella ain't around that joint, are they?"

She sniggled, felt a little tingling as she scooted down to the edge of the sofa. "My mother's up in New York, as usual. So's Freddy. Miss Marvella's at her own place. I have some security peeps around this joint, but they and the housekeepers don't bother me. I'm sending you the address and directions, Rakim. And you better not leave me hanging!"

"Aw girl, this is me! I wouldn't leave a sweet thing like you hanging like that! Look, I'm just going to take a shower and get with my ride. You know they don't let me drive yet, even though I just got my license. But look: Old dude who drives me is just going drop me off, then I'll call him when I want a ride back here.   Can I stay for a little while?"

"Sure."

"See you in about an hour, sweetheart."

Chapter Seventy

"No, man! No!" she said, wriggling to get away from him. "And, dag! You didn't even think to bring a condom? Then that must mean you wasn't expecting to get none. So there: You aren't getting any."

Harder than Chinese arithmetic! he thought, playing the words through his mind he'd heard during some lurid conversation among the guys. He grabbed his hardness and slid close up behind Starr, planted himself against her back and nuzzled her about the neck.

"You're always teasing a brother, girl," he whispered, scented breath and the Somali Rose oil he wore warming her. "Why you want to be like that?"

"I can't take a chance, Rakim," she said, breathing heavily. "You should have at least brought a condom."

He reached around, spreading her leg slightly, fondling her. "Yeah...you know after last time...with me in your hand like that...you wanted me inside you, girl. Don't you...want me...inside you?"

"Yes..."

"Come here, girl," he said, twisting her around to face him.

They kissed passionately, tongues just a flailing. She wore one of the short jeans skirts she thought showed off her legs best, and right now, horizontally on her queen-sized bed, it didn't matter. He wasn't looking anyway, eyes closed and tongue darting a path towards her throat. She twisted her mouth away from his, back handing away errant spittle.

"You shouldn't..." she said as he eased her onto her back and knelt up, sliding off her panties with little resistance. "Rakim...no! No! No..."

He leaned forward, planted kisses between her cleavage while at the same time undoing the silk blouse, button by button, slowly, his tongue tracing a path down her chest as each button, freed, exposed more flesh.

"You...Rakim? Rakim no....n...n..."

He let the blouse lie open. She wore no bra, and the perky little breasts looked at him looking at them and demanded savoring. He took one nipple between his lips, then moved over to the other, all the while working two fingers on his right hand in between her legs, generating moistness, then certain lubrication. He mounted her, and Starr's legs flew back as if she had done this a thousand times.

Neither could have known it, but it was the first time for them both. Yet nature was at work, and they engaged a natural rhythm, she most welcoming, he of precision deliverance. The mutual explosions rocked both their worlds, worlds which collided in what could rightly be described as another manifestation of the Big Bang.

"Oh, Rakim!" she said, clutching him tightly to her.

"Yeah, baby!" he said, planting his face in the pillow her head lay on.

The tensions subsided. He eased out, back, to the side, exhausted with eyes closed and a satisfactory smile creasing his dark features.

"That's my baby," he whispered into her ear, only meaning to claim her as his own.

What he could not have possibly known at the time was that that very phrase could actually have comprised an accurate descriptive of what was about to begin taking form within Starr Acosua Lavesque-Shorter.

Chapter Seventy-one

He appeared somewhat embarrassed afterwards, and their conversation in bed was uncomfortable for both of them. She fiddled around with her smartphone, he lay back watching her. After half an hour, he decided he'd spent a proper period after the sex to phone for his ride home. He eased up beside her after making the call, hurriedly dressing.

"My driver just stayed on the property," he said, leaned over and kissed her on the cheek. "You want to do something tomorrow?"

"Ummm," she said, laying her phone aside and reaching over to finger the shirt he was buttoning up. "I want to go to the Georgetown Mall, but you know, I have to have my security people along."

"I'm game," he said.

"And afterwards...." she directed a glowing smile at him.

"Yeah," he said, leaning in for a full kiss. "Girl, you was something else. I thought you said this was your first time?"

Creasing her eyes, she glowered at him. "It was my first time! What do you think?"

"I mean...you was like...I mean...working it, know what I'm saying?"

"Still," she sat up, swung her legs over the edge of the bed. "It was the first time I...you know....had a boy inside of me."

"Aw, aiight," he said, arising. "I told my boys you were---"

He tried to catch himself, but she faced him abruptly, apparently aware of what was to be said to complete the sentence.

"You told them what?" she said. "What, Rakim?!"

"I was just...wasn't nothing..."

"You told them I was, what? A virgin? A ho? What, Rakim?!"

He faced her. "I told them you was just a dick teaser, that's what!"

She moved to the bedroom door, wrenched it open. "Well, you can forget about tomorrow, Rakim. Dag! You talk to your boys about all the girls you mess with?"

"All what girls?"

"You...you....just go, Rakim! You're just a dog!"

He didn't argue, moved to the door, down the stairs and the distance across the foyer to the front entrance. He looked outside; his driver was waiting.

"Bow wow wow yippee yo yippee yea," he sang, walking to the car. "Bow wow wow yippee yo yippee yea!"

While inside, Starr was in tears. She moved to the most convenient computer in her bedroom, one which was on a table top. When in deep thoughts, and when writing songs, she preferred the desktop to the laptop or tablet; it allowed her to sit upright and not laze, as she was prone to do when experiencing emotions still confusing.

She wrote lyrics, poetry at first, then formed the words into a song which would be one of her bestsellers of all time. She titled it, "Lonely and in Love."

Chapter Seventy-two

Ford insisted that she turn off all of her cellular devices while they spent a Saturday evening in the Presidential Suite at Terrones Towers Hotel. They were not to be disturbed, he had instructed the maître de hotel, who'd been on staff for over 27 years and knew that when Mr. Terrones wanted privacy, only a massive fire or evacuation of the city due to terrorist threats would be cause to bother him. And Monsieur De Villfoir, the maître de hotel, saw the way Monsieur Terrones had looked at the stunning black woman who'd accompanied him. Monsieur De Villfoir only wished he could be so fortunate as to be heading to the top of the towers with such a striking, mature beauty.

He knew too that the woman was sort of famous, at least in the African-American community. De Villfoir was keenly aware of the two suited women who'd discreetly accompanied "Madam Lavesque-Shorter" to the hotel and, as a regular host of plenty of rich, famous political and entertainment people, knew that the two women had been providing security for Madam Lavesque-Shorter. They had been discreetly directed to an anteroom of the Presidential Suite, where they were to remain, in considerable luxurious surroundings themselves, until summoned by either De Villfoir, Madam Lavesque-Shorter, or Mr. Terrones.

The Presidential Suite was just that: A spacious arrangement of rooms furnished in priceless period pieces, furnishings which were older than any of the guests and a place where, quite often, the president of one nation or another resided while conducting business at the United Nations or otherwise attending to business in New York City. Ford had reserved the suite for the entire weekend, and planned to spend each and every moment there with the woman who was swiftly winning over his heart.

They sat together on the 18th Century Queen Anne embroidered sofa, Siren tucked into a corner sipping a mixture of acai berry juice and vanilla chai tea. Her long, lithe legs extended from within the red silk robe she wore, crossed pertly at the ankles across Ford's lap.

"And why shouldn't we go public, my dear?" he asked, continuing a conversation that had been carried on from the bedroom, to the terrace overlooking Central Park and now, into the living room before the blazing fireplace.

"Time, sweetheart," Siren said. "Everything in its time."

Ford was not one not used to getting his own way. He held Sirena in high regards, a self-made millionaire who ran a number of affiliated corporations, his research had shown. But her net worth was hardly a tenth of his, and she had been the only woman in recent memory who hadn't jumped at every request he'd made, personal or business wise. He did things at his own pace, but was not one to abide lollygagging when he projected his desires.

"We've already been mentioned as...an item....in Cathy Wharton's column in the Post," he said, massaging her feet with a fragrant oil. "The paparazzi are camped out across the street day and night just waiting for a shot of the two of us together. We can still keep them guessing about the nature of our relationship, honey, while feeding them a few morsels to nibble on. And, I must say, it can't do Short Siren's stocks any harm to have inklings of an association with Terrones Holdings leaked."

She liked his mind; much like hers, he was always thinking of the profit potential of any venture. And certainly he'd seen that she benefitted greatly from his extensive connections on Wall Street and beyond since they'd been seeing one another. By conservative estimate, she figured, Short Siren Music Corporation and its CEO in particular had seen $5.7 million in profits since she'd been getting financial advice from Ford. She had not seen a loss on any investment at all by following his investment suggestions, and although she didn't consider herself greedy by any stretch of the imagination. She had once been an unrepentant cocaine addict, and had long since discovered that attaining vast fortunes was far, far more addicting than any drug she'd ever tasted.

"There's still the fact of my remaining married to Jenkins," she said to the thrice divorced older gentleman.

"Were you not recently discussing a divorce with him?"

"Yes. And I've initiated those actions and have attorneys in Jamaica about to serve him shortly."

"When is that?"

"By Monday, Tuesday latest. As long as he can be located."

"Well," he said, removing her legs lightly and going to the bar. "We can reserve any...public...attention, as it were, until we hear back from Jamaica."

He fixed a glass of his favored bourbon, moved towards the master bedroom. Looking over a shoulder, he held an arm out in her direction.

"Come along, my dear."

He went ahead into the bedroom. Sirena took the time to activate her main Smartphone and view the calls missed and the text messages she'd been left. Only 14 of her closest family, friends and business associates had this particular number, among them Marvella, Troy, Starr, Freddy, Genese and Sunshine. She scanned the "subject" line of the 24 text messages she'd received, and paused at the one titled "URGENT re. Flatiron."

"You coming, my dear?!" Ford shouted from the bedroom.

"On my way! Just freshening up my drink!"

The brief message from Freddy said that Cream of White had finished laying down all the tracks to their new album, with Flatiron putting forth an amazing performance. Sure, he'd taken breaks every 20 minutes or so to visit the bathroom outside the recording studio, and not a person present didn't assume, quite correctly, that Flatiron was taking breaks to consume cocaine.

In a brief, cryptic message, Freddy brushed over the scenario which had followed, and culminated in what could only be described as yet another tragic turn of events for Short Siren Music.

The final session had finished, the band, the backup musicians, the sound techs erupting in joyous celebration. Few had believed Flatiron would make it through the recording of what was already anticipated to be a multi-million selling recording.

As others celebrated in the studio's adjoining lounge, Flatiron, to the disapproval of none of the satisfied celebrators, had gone off into the men's room and had not been seen again for hours. Chauncey, his closest friend in Cream, finally went to search him out in the bathroom just before eight that evening.

Steven "Flatiron" Massey, 29, was found lying stretched out on the marble bathroom floor, dull and yellow/white as a rock of crack cocaine, cold and unresponsive.

Chapter Seventy-three

The headlines certainly didn't do any good for Short Siren Music's public image, and again journalists were dredging up the past drug histories of Siren, Jenkins and certainly, the deceased lead singer of Cream of White, Steven "Flatiron" Massey. His death roiled the rock world, particularly as it followed fresh on the heels of the death of rock legend Diamond Gentry, the 1960s icon who'd been rumored to have been on cocaine for a virtual lifetime. Diamond actually looked like he'd already been embalmed when making a rare public appearance, and per his personal instructions, had been viewed in an open coffin before burial with a slight smile on his face.

This oddity further fueled speculation that extensive cocaine use did indeed twist users' DNA strands into unadulterated miasmic meshes, which didn't allow for the distinguishing between sanity and complete madness. Flatiron, it would later come out in the form of his last original lyrics, claimed that sanity had been ever evasive in his last days and times.

Flatiron's sallow image from recent months was splashed across the front page of local, national and international newspapers. The same image, eyes sunken, hair a ragged attempt at white-boy dreadlocks, accompanied many lead television news stories also. Millions of fans mourned, along with his band mates and personnel at Short Siren who'd grown to love the colorful fellow however briefly. But the person who seemed to mourn him most was the fired Michelle, and it didn't go unnoticed by her husband Sanford.

The couple attended the funeral together, and Michelle appeared as inconsolable as did three young women who'd suddenly surfaced with claims to have been married to the deceased. Everyone knew that Flatiron often lambasted the very institution of marriage, and if not for security, the funeral might have erupted into a full blown brouhaha as the women, acknowledged by band mates as close friends of the late Mr. Massey, maneuvered to get seating among Flatiron's parents, the highest officials of Short Siren, and the band members.

Michelle, in a tearful lamentation, cried out that Siren had abetted Flatiron's drug use in order to attain the million-dollar music he seemingly was capable of dispensing only when under the influence. She shouted out directly to Siren in a vicious, accusatory missive, further casting the already unorthodox ceremony into a heated maelstrom reporters clambered to get recordings of.

"That rotten bitch right there killed him!" Michelle cried out, pointing to a black attired Siren from two pews back.

She was quickly removed from the church by security, Sanford trailing her, since she had pushed him away when he attempted to lend support.

This all didn't go unnoticed by Abby Vann, the Hollywood Remote reporter, who'd been afforded access after being contacted by none other than the billionaire, Ford Terrones. He'd pulled a few strings with officials in the New York police department, had Abby provided a personal escort past the security perimeter ringing the downtown church, and promised her further, exclusive information on Sirena Lavesque-Shorter and Short Siren Music Corporation if she'd only leach out the information per his precise instructions.

Certainly she recalled quite acutely then the stern warning from a Mr. M about examining the company earlier, and mentioned it to Terrones. But he'd assured her that he too knew Mr. M; he placed a call to this mysterious gentleman in Abby's presence, and handed her the phone.

The same voice that had previously chastised her for her extensive coverage of Siren now reassured her that his relationship with Terrones was much more important, and that she should take his advice on "matters concerning Sirena Lavesque-Shorter." Her security chief, Freddy Glover, remained highly regarded by Mr. M, but in the grand scheme of things did not hold as much sway with Mr. M as did the billionaire Terrones.

Once buried, Flatiron became the central focus of energies in the Short Siren Music Corporation. The new music was in the can, and before the grave was closed Siren was setting in her lush office with two men from Legal going over the company's latest contract with the late rock star. It was a revised one, inked just three days before his death, as the initial contract, and a secondary one, had been voided through a clause that cancelled each out in case of any illegal drug use by the artist.

Siren saw vast millions in a release of the "Memorial Tribute Album" that was quickly being redesigned and remastered. The other members of Cream, still reeling over the death of their lead singer, were incensed when told about the plans to rush their latest, and Flatiron's last with them, to market under a new marketing ploy.

"You're a cold bitch!" Jon "Stampede" Stephanos told Siren in a meeting a week after the funeral. "Cold fuckin' bitch!"

"Yes, Jon," Siren said calmly. "And about to put a cool $3.8 million plus in each of your pockets."

She looked between the four surviving members of Cream, a small smile on her face. The glares she received in return did nothing to endear them to the woman who, in essence, controlled their future careers in the music business, if they wanted to continue performing as the entity Cream of White.

Siren, with four attorneys, Sanford, Genese and other principles of the corporation seated along side her at the long conference table, returned the glare of the band members seated at the very far end of the table.

"Well, gentlemen, to put it bluntly, Cream of White is a trademarked operational unit of Short Siren Music Corporation. I'd love to keep each of you on as a part of this unit, and we already have some of our best A & R persons scouring the globe for a voice and personality to replace....our dearly departed brother."

Jon sniffed. His three band mates leaned back, rocking in the comfortable leather chairs, looking to one another.

Siren continued: "I'm as torn by the loss of Flatiron as you are, gentlemen. But we're in a business where precision of timing matched with a quite expensive promotional campaign spells the success or failure of a new product. Our new product at this point is the Memorial Tribute Album. It's shipping as we speak, and A & R...Artist and Repertoire, has the four of you already scheduled for a number of television and radio appearances. Now, we prefer that you talk up the album and Flatiron's great...well, sacrifices...in rolling it out. I understand you need additional time to mourn the loss of our brother. But as I said, time is crucial in this matter. You have before you some talking points A & R and Legal have put together for your...Memorial Tribute...appearances. Go over them, gentlemen, and I for one look forward to continuing our relationship with Cream of White."

Chapter Seventy-four

Abby Vann's latest televised feature hinted at turmoil in the 46th floor suites of Short Siren Music Corporation, and she hinted that the company's CEO, Mrs. Sirena Lavesque-Shorter, was seeking solace in the warm bed of a prominent Massachusetts billionaire.

She didn't have to name Ford Terrones; anyone with any business on the upper East Coast knew of his predilection for black women. Indeed, he had married one, had been seen with a number of prominent African-American females of note during soirees on the Cape and in Manhattan. And anyone who read the New York City gossip columns knew that columnist Cathy Lipford's pen name for him, "The Black Sheep of Scotch," was often whispered about when he was ensconced in one of the family's hotel suites.

Vann's report only confirmed what many in New York and Cape Cod haute couture already knew: Ford Terrones had set his keen sights on Sirena Lavesque-Shorter.   And everyone knew Terrones always reeled in any catch that even dared nibble on his well-regarded fishing lure.

Short Siren had successfully rolled out "Flatiron: A Memorial Tribute, with Cream of White."   Still under contract, the remaining members, led by Jon, assumed the tribute PR tour A&R had designed to accompany the album's release, appearing on seven talk shows and discussing their torrid relationship with Flatiron for millions to hear.

He was most beloved by the group's members in truth, but the public affairs heads within Short Siren had scripted a contentious relationship within the group leading up to his death. It made for good fodder for the planned motion picture on the group, Siren had suggested, and would presumably pump sales of the additional music Short Siren had in the can which Flatiron had produced with Cream but which had previously been deemed not worthy of release.

Meanwhile, Siren was peeved that a lot of personal information about the goings-on in headquarters was being leaked not only to Vann but to the gossip magazines and supermarket tabloids. Her relationship with Ford was by now so well known that she no longer attempted to secret into the Terrones Towers or stay out of sight when visiting him on the Cape. But the publication of one morsel of news, and something that was even news to her just a few months after Flatiron's death, had her flying back to her Virginia estate in a tizzy: In her flaring style, Abby Vann aired a report that said that the reason that young Starr Lavesque-Shorter had been only making appearances in the recording studio after the success of her "Bubblegum and Braces Tour" was that the now-16-year-old was pregnant.

Ford lent her his private jet to zoom down to Virginia. Troy was home for a rare weekend visit, and when Siren arrived at the estate he and his little sister were setting in the main family quarters, snacking on fruits and juices and apparently having a serious discussion. Troy arose, hugged the mother he saw so infrequently of late, and sat in a lounge chair as his mother moved to sit beside Starr on the sofa.

"Tell me it isn't true, Starr. Just...just tell me it isn't true."

Sirena was looking at the loose sweatshirt her daughter wore, as if expecting the girl to be prominently showing.

"What?" Starr said, truly confused at her mother's question.

"Tell me you're not pregnant."

Starr's jaw dropped, and she could no longer meet her mother's eyes.

"Oh, damn!" Siren said, shaking her head. "Girl, how could you?!"

Troy arose, seeming as if he too had been caught off guard and feeling that the mother and daughter should engage this discussion out of his presence. He moved towards the exit.

"I'll...urrr....I'll let you two talk," he said, quickly moved out of the room.

"How could you, Starr?"

The daughter took a deep breath, then regained her common confident air and again met her mother's eyes.

"It was like this," she said, then lifted her jean's-clad legs aloft and spread them as if to demonstrate a sexual position. She immediately dropped them and sat back upright. "Just kidding, Ma. For real though: You know I didn't plan for this to happen, but now...I'm like...and we're going to eventually get married so—"

"Married?! Who, Starr."

"Rakim."

"That black bastard!"

"Ma, don't go blaming him. It wasn't like—"

"It wasn't like what? And where? And...girl, how far along are you?"

"Twenty-two weeks."

"Well, it's too late to—"

"Too late?" Starr sprang to the edge of the sofa. "Too late? Too late for what? If you had known earlier, you would have had me....UGGGH! No way! Unh-unh! Wasn't no way anyway! Ma?!! Dag...Umph umph umph..."

"Of course I would have suggested it!" Sirena said. "I mean, your career!"

"Career? Ma, I'm 16!! I haven't even decided on a career! Singing? Ma, that's mostly fun...and like, something you like so I do it! I'm not going to live all my life like you!"

That stung, and it showed as Sirena seemed deflated and her eyes began to well with tears.

"You're right, you're 16," she said, regaining her composure and again the stern business executive. "And already the media's got wind of your...you being....Aw, damn you, child!"

Sirena arose, left the room.

Chapter Seventy-five

Daniella Rogers, the business manager of Appreciation and mother of Jason and D'Andre, had been on the phone with Genese for ten minutes trying to book some studio time for the group. From the New York headquarters, Genese had deflected the business manager's questions and request long enough to suggest that she talk to Sunshine, who was better suited to answer any questions regarding matters on the 47th floor where all the studios were quite active. Daniella, the business manager, couldn't understand why she could not be put directly in touch with Siren. After all, she told Sunshine, Siren had always been warm and welcoming to the group and their parents when the boys were generating millions of dollars in record sales.

"So," Daniella said into the phone. "The boys haven't produced anything new in months, and Mrs. Lavesque-Shorter doesn't have time for them now? Lady, I'm trying to book studio time so they can work on some new material they've put together. What's wrong? Does Appreciation have to pay to use the studios? If that's the case, we can use a studio down here! I don't get y'all, Sunshine. I swear. What is up with Siren?"

"Appreciation is still under contract with us," Sunshine said. "They can use the studios and we're looking forward to their next production, Mrs. Rogers. It's just that, right now Siren has instructed that the company focus on three new acts that are fresh to Short Siren and have a potential to expand our portion of the pop music market tremendously. Appreciation is...shall I say, on hold at present, in reference to putting out new material."

"Well, Appreciation is ready to put out some new material," Daniella said. "Even if we have to do it with another label."

"I certainly would advise against that," Siren said, and for the first time Daniella knew that the company CEO had been listening to the entire conversation on a speaker phone. "Appreciation remains under contract to Short Siren. Now, Mrs. Rogers, you can tell the boys to continue to work on new material on their own, at home or wherever for that matter. Our studios are booked solid with the groups and individuals we're rolling out in coming months according to our business model. Tell the boys I send them my love, and we'll be in touch."

She nodded to Sunshine, who abruptly disconnected the call.

"Have Genese come join us," she instructed Sunshine.

They were in Sunshine's spacious office, one which was almost comparable in size and view of Manhattan to Siren's own. She'd kept her childhood friends close, rewarded them with continuing high-level positions in the corporation and considered the two the only ones to whom she could share her innermost thoughts, secrets and desires. They were also among the few whom she felt in recent years did not look upon her in a disparaging light. She knew well that, secretly, most among her staff of over 300 now referred to her as "The Queen Bitch." But she didn't care. She was not only wealthy beyond any of their wildest imaginations, but wielded power which generated respect, though often restrained, within the sometimes treacherous music industry.

The three friends sat in comfort, preferring to meet around the carved African coffee table surrounded by four comfortable lounge chairs. The arrangement was before floor-to-ceiling windows which allowed for a sweeping view of Central Park and upper Manhattan, and only Siren's office, being a massive corner one, had a view which even competed with Sunshine's.

"Girls," Siren began the private meeting. "I need to work up a business model wrapped around Starr's pregnancy."

Genese and Sunshine pinned each other with looks of amazement, looked back to Siren and then they both shook their heads in unison. Of course Genese, since their teenaged years, had always been one to speak her mind and call out Siren when, in Genese's caustic appraisal, Sirena "got her ass on her back."

"Sirena: Please, girlfriend," Genese said, releasing a little guffaw. "The girl's album is still generating sales and the tour DVD is getting play from here to South Africa. Now, I know how you raised the girl. Or half raised her. Hell, me and Sunshine and Marvella done most of the raising, to tell you the truth. But the child's getting ready to have a child of her own. Don't be trying to market that shit! For real, Sirena. Step back and take a deep breath."

Siren looked out upon the park, to the cloudless sky. "That girl...."

"So," Sunshine said. "Is that why you're punishing Appreciation?"

"I'm not punishing them boys! Why would you even think that?"

"Because before," Genese answered, "those young'uns could do no wrong. I told you it was a mistake to put them and Starr on the same tour bus. But, naw, you said it made good business sense, and saved money, for them to travel together, get to know one another. That it would enhance their chemistry on stage and shit. Ask me, girl, for real, Starr is as pregnant by you as she is by Rakim."

Siren certainly didn't like that, and let it be known that she didn't.

"Genese, fuck you and all of your flighty thoughts about parental responsibility!"

"Parental?" Genese sniffed. "Damn! I didn't even know that word was still in your vocabulary, girl. Huh! Now you're a parent? Girl, please! You've hardly been anything but a business manager to that child, and here you call us in here, your girls and shit, trying to get our take on your 'marketing' of the damn baby before it's even born. Sirena, I still love you, girl. But sometimes your ass can be a fuckin' trip!"

"Well," Siren said, leaning, elbows on knees, directly to Genese. "I ain't really need your goddamn opinion on shit has to do with my goddamn family, you hear me? You ain't all that your damn self! Look at your child Markesia: Four little rug rats and ain't hardly 20 years old! Don't talk to me about parenting, Miss Thang!"

"Ladies ladies ladies!" Sunshine said. "Let's not get nasty up in here!"

"Oh, it's done got nasty!" Genese said, springing to her feet and stepping around the coffee table to stand just over Siren. "Bitch, don't you ever come out your face bad-mouthing any of mine! At least Markesia's baby daddy did eventually marry her! Only way Rakim gonna marry that hot-ass daughter of yours is if you work some of your okey-doke shit and arrange it! Then it'll probably just be for a reality TV show! You got your goddamn nerve!"

Genese stormed out of the office, and Siren, shaking her head but ever scheming, nodded a goodbye to Sunshine and went to her own office.

She immediately had her secretary get the head of Legal on the phone, inquired as to the company's contractual arrangements with Genese Taylor and then had her secretary contact personnel about finding a suitable candidate to head Troy Boy Youth Styles and extricate Genese from the company with as little financial remunerations as possible.

Chapter Seventy-six

He had finally taken the time to fill out the necessary paperwork to have new ATM cards issued in Jamaica, and Jenkins, down to his last $20.00 American, was breathing a coarse sigh of relief. Millions! he'd told Sassafras, his latest female partner in crack consumption. I'm finally regaining access to my millions!

But once issued the cards and individual personal identification numbers, he was greeted with an on-screen message advising him that the accounts were frozen and that he should go into a bank and see some banking official.

In New York, Siren had been informed by her lawyer that attempts had been made to access her husband's accounts, and further that she should expect a call from Jenkins within hours. Her lawyer advised her to avoid any conversation with him about his accounts, and to transfer the calls directly to Millicent Gerhardt in the offices of Gerhardt, Wonder, Finch, the legal powerhouse which had assigned none other than the esteemed Millicent Gerhardt to the case of Sirena Lavesque-Shorter v Jenkins Shorter.

After numerous, documented attempts to serve Jenkins with divorce papers and other legal documents in Ocho Rios, Gerhardt had easily won an injunction from her friend of over 40 years, Judge Terrence Ransom, freezing all the American assets of Jenkins Shorter and, in absentia, ordering him to present himself to a court official in either Jamaica or the United States within 90 days, or be declared in contempt. Thereafter, all the petitions for divorce and the assumption of "fiduciary responsibility" over his estate would be granted to Siren. In simple terms, all of his moneys and other assets were frozen, and in 90 days would become sole property of Sirena, who at the same moment would be legally divorced from him.

"That cold blooded bitch!" Jenkins cried at the last of seven ATM machines he tried. "I could kill that bitch! I know her ass is behind this!"

He was bedraggled, hungry, his penis shopworn from the meager attempts at raising it to some semblance of solidity by the plethora of girls who still recognized him, or knew from local lore that the villa he occupied belonged to a rich American rap star. Yet now even they were growing leery of the unkempt man, who was often seen bartering furnishings and electronics from the villa for crack rock.

The once luxurious hilltop villa was now threadbare, with even an expensive, king-sized bed having been carted away by the minions of a crack dealer as payment for a few hundred dollars worth of rocks.

He still had his cell phone, though even retaining that had been chancy after he'd loaned it out on a number of occasion to get crack on credit. He called Siren, was informed in a short spiel that he was going to be a grandfather, and transferred to some woman whose legalese really aggravated Jenkins's pressing need for coke.

"Fuck you bitch! Just have that ho release hold of my money!" Jenkins blasted and, a few hundred miles north, Gerhardt hung up and decided then and there to do all within her legal power to divest that nasty bastard she'd spoken to of every asset his wife had requested.

Jenkins hobbled over to Sassafras, who'd been anxious anticipating an outpouring of American dollars from the last ATM machine they'd visited.

"No luck, baby," Jenkins said to the frail woman. "Looks like you're going to have to go book one of them tourist around The Top, you know, get a few dollars...doing that thing you do."

He was asking her to prostitute herself, which she had no problem with. Indeed, she had been selling herself to him for the past few weeks, and watched as his meager funds from sales of household furnishings and electronic equipment dwindled. Now he wanted to pimp her to continue their joint consumption. Sassafras had been on crack for seven years, and if any measure of intellect remained in her addled brain, it was the ability to realize when a "trick" had been drained completely.

"I go fuck and get us some more, baby," she said to him, the fake smile she displayed cracking ashen, chapped lips. "You go back to your 'ome up in Shawpark and I be there in the hour."

Weak and shaking, Jenkins headed back up into the hills, unable even to afford a taxi for the two-mile trek.

He'd sit on the porch of the villa, anxiously watching the road below for some semblance of Sassafras's return, but would never hear from her again.

Chapter Seventy-seven

It was time to meet the parents, and Sirena really did not want the sires of that wretched Rakim in her house. She spoke to them on the phone, arranged to have Andrea and Svetlana provide her security, and was driven to the family's home in their considerably modest community in Southeast Washington.

Starr had strenuously objected to accompanying her mother on this, the first meeting of the two families since all had become aware of the pregnancy.   Mr. and Mrs. Rahman, Rakim's parents, had met Siren on one occasion backstage, at the downtown Washington kick-off of the Bubblegum and Braces Tour, and Siren had quite literally turned her nose up at the couple dressed in colorful African attire.   Later, she'd joked to Marvella that she was certainly going to ensure that the finances of Appreciation, and especially Rakim's, were not finagled with like some of the monies of others in Short Siren Music were.

"Next thing you know," she'd whispered to a trusted Marvella, "they'll have that Farrakhan all up in New York going over our books!"

Now they were in the custom Bentley, being driven into a section of Washington, D.C. Sirena had vowed never to return to after lending assistance to those ousted from the Barry Farm projects.

"Why didn't you tell me you've been talking to that boy's people?" she asked Starr, who was seated beside her on the rear seat facing forward. Two seats, facing back and behind the driver's compartment, were occupied by two silent, stoic women: Svetlana and Andrea.

"I texted you about it Ma, dag! But you never responded so I figured you were totally OK with it. And I said they wanted to meet with you, and probably Mr. and Mrs. Rahman figured, since they didn't hear back from either of us, that you really didn't want to honor their request for a meeting. Or that you just didn't care, with the way you're more concerned about your company than about your daughter."

"Little girl, mind your manners!   And my...concerns...are evident in that I've been working my tail off to build the business so that you, and Troy, will never have to want for anything."

"Ma, we totally don't want for anything now and, as quiet as it's kept, hello?! I've banked enough on my own so that I won't ever want for anything. Peace and hair grease, Ma...."

"And what the hell is that supposed to mean?"

Starr just blew a breath of exasperation, folded her hands before her, resting them just above the stomach that could no longer be hidden below loose sweatshirts.

They motored through a section of Southeast Washington where Sirena had grown up as a young child. She remembered it as being exclusively black when her mother and father and their circle of friends occupied the corners in this area, awaiting some sort delivery, she thought and, in retrospect, recalling how her parents and others spent hours on end in zombie-like states after "being served."

There was a caravan of bikers, all young white men and women, pumping their sleek conveyances up a hill in this stretch of Southeast.   Changes, Sirena thought, where economic realities, for many, had them relocating as close to their work places as possible. Even as close in as this section of the city, where at one time even elderly African-Americans avoided the streets after sunset.

"You and that boy even think about the near future, I mean, when you're both 18, of perhaps...well, it will still be kind of young for the two of you, but you want to be adults, then act like adults and make it legal, Starr. He even talk to you about the future with that baby?"

"We'll be married," Starr said. "But not just because we have the baby, but because we love one another."

It was Sirena's turn to take a deep breath, exhale in exasperation and shake her head.

"Girl, you haven't been around long enough to know true love. And neither has he."

The driver pulled into the gravel covered parking space outside of the address he'd been directed to by the GPS and verbal instructions. He parked behind a late-model SUV, nothing fancy, and a Toyota which had seen better days. A stone walkway led to the modest brick home with the attached garage, and their arrival had evidently been noticed by the home's occupants. A tall, dark man in a white knitted skullcap stood inside the glass storm door, his long arms held behind him, a slight smile on his bearded face. Barely visible to his left and slightly to his rear, a woman a few inches shorter than the man gazed out the door also, her hair covered by a gold scarf which matched the full-length dress she wore.

The driver moved around and held open the rear passenger's door, and Andrea and Svetlana were first to exit. The driver lent a hand to Sirena, then to Starr. All looked to the front of the house, at the man and woman, and the security women stepped aside to allow mother and daughter to approach the home together. The man inside stepped onto a small, circular brick porch as Starr and Sirena neared the entrance, held the door ajar, nodded and held out a hand to Sirena.

"Mrs. Lavesque-Shorter. Mohammad Abdul Rahman, Rakim's father."

Sirena held forth a hand. "You can call me Sirena, sir."

He nodded, stood aside and waved them formally towards the entrance. The woman inside stood a few feet into the entrance on an oriental rug which went well with the highly-polished hardwood floors observable beyond. She bowed slightly as Sirena entered, followed closely by Starr and then Rahman, then stepped to Sirena and embraced her formally.

"Welcome to my home, sister. I'm Atiba. Atiba Rahman. And you're Starr's mother. I was at your show about...well, almost twenty years ago, at the Carter 7 Center. And always loved your music, Siren. May I call you Siren?"

"Certainly," Sirena began to warm.

"Come," Atiba said, moving into a spacious, well-appointed living room. "We have tea, and coffee if you like. Have a seat."

Starr, with Rahman to her side, moved into the living room behind her mother and Mrs. Rahman, as she identified Rakim's mother. She whispered to Mr. Rahman before moving to the sofa to sit beside her mother.

"Is Rakim going to be here?" she asked.

"He'll be coming down shortly," Rahman said, stretching an arm towards the sofa, directing Starr to a seat.

Mrs. Rahman sat in a high back, embroidered chair to the front and right side of the sofa. Mr. Rahman, after all the women were seated, took an identical chair to the front and left. A coffee table between them and within reach of them all was full of tea cups, an ornate pot from which steam poured, and a polished silver platter, covered in a white silk napkin of sorts on which sat a variety of finger sandwiches, cookies and crackers. The crackers were topped with what Siren's practiced eyes knew well to be salmon roe. She just loved the salty, expensive delicacies, and truly didn't expect these "Black Muslims," as she was mentally categorizing them, to have such exotic taste.

"Umm," Sirena said, setting to the edge of the sofa. "Smoked salmon roe and also surgeon caviar. I just so love them all! Do you mind?"

"Help yourself, Siren," Atiba said, pleased at the selection her husband had earlier frowned upon as an attempt by Atiba to "put on airs." "We have herbal teas and coffee. From our little talks with Starr, I would take it that you're more of a tea drinker."

"Thank you, Atiba," Sirena smiled, took a small service saucer and placed a selection of appetizers on it. She sat back, savored a cracker with a mound of salmon roe on it, breathed deeply and smiled broadly. "Very, very nice!"

"I'm glad you enjoy it," Rahman smiled. "Now, before my son joins us, I want to apologize for my entire family for the manner in which young Starr here finds herself in. My son Rakim has taken full responsibility for...this...incident...but at this point, I believe that we as parents need to do whatever is deemed appropriate to ensure the health of the unborn child. Do you agree up to this point, Mrs. Lavesque-Shorter?"

"Please," Sirena said. "Call me Sirena. Let's not be so formal!"

She chuckled a bit, looked to Atiba with a smile, took the tea cup the wife offered and, without sipping, placed it within reach on the coffee table.

"Yes. Sirena," Rahman said. "And I'm certainly of the understanding that you were not at all pleased with...with Starr's impregnation. I tried to instill in all of my children the serious nature of the relationships between a male and a female. I was of the mind to say between a man and a woman, but in our case, and excuse me young Starr for being blunt, but in our case this is hardly the results of an event between two adults. Rakim certainly knows the gravity of what he's done, and has expressed to me that he and your daughter do have an understanding.

Of course, they say it's love, but in my view, they haven't had life experiences enough to distinguish between that ultimate of emotions and, say, passion. Or simply infatuation."

"I agree," Sirena said, reaching for the tea cup.

"I'm of the understanding that Starr has already furnished a nursery in your home in Virginia?" Rahman asked, fixing his own cup of tea.

"Yes."

"And of course, you're going to be around, or at least have some capable hands around, to give this...forgive me, but I have to be blunt: To give this young girl some supervisory assistance in the correct ways of seeing after a baby?"

"I know how to take care of a baby!" Starr said.

"Hush!" Sirena said, turning to her with glaring eyes.

"Forgive me, Starr," Atiba said. "But in actuality, you have no experience in the needs of a newborn, and although there are things instinctive to a mother, well, things, unexpected things, are bound to occur. I and my husband, and I'm sure, Rakim, just want to make sure that the baby, our grandbaby, has the finest of care."

"That's right," Sirena said.

"Well," Starr said. "I'm not going to have a nanny raising my baby, if that's what you're trying to say."

"Not in any way," Atiba said. "As I've been told, you and my son are eventually planning on continuing on with your musical careers."

"Which have been blunted," Rahman said, a bit coldly, "by actions within Short Siren Music, at least as far as Appreciation's production abilities are concerned."

"I know," Sirena said sheepishly. She sipped tea, nibbled on hors d'oeuvres.

"Atiba. Please go and have Rakim come down," Rahman instructed.

She arose, nodded with an excusing smile, moved across the spacious living room and ascended stairs.

"I'm sure that, urr, Rahman, that the new acts we have in production will be making space in the New York studios available in coming weeks," Sirena smiled. "Many are shifting home, back to the West Coast. You know we have new offices and state-of-the-art studios opening up in Los Angeles in three weeks?"

"I didn't know that," Rahman said, still bearing a serious face but now smiling a bit. "Congratulations."

They sipped tea and snacked in silence for a moment, until Atiba returned, followed closely by Rakim.

"Hi, Miss Sirena."

"Hello, Rakim."

He looked to Starr, grinned and moved to sit beside her. His father arose, directed his son to the chair the father had occupied and remained standing behind it.

"Now," Rahman began. "You two children are about to become parents in another few months. Son, you're only 17, Starr here just turned 16. You can't legally marry at this point, but as the father of the child who's going to bear your name, it's only a matter of being upright and honorable that you and your...your girl here, be married at some point in the near future. The child will be born in, what? December?"

"December," Starr said, not looking directly to Rahman or Rakim.

"By the time the child...boy or girl...is a year old, my son will be 18, Starr 17. As soon as feasible after his 18th birthday, Rakim Abdul Rahman shall marry the mother of his first child, Starr Acosua Lavesque-Shorter. I would like to hear an agreement on those terms from the mother of Starr. Mrs. Lavesque-Shorter?"

Of all her business acumen and often insistence that everything was business-related, Sirena was taken aback by the formality of this man's pronouncements concerning the life, the very future, of her child! But instincts told her that now was not the time to attempt to exercise her self-perceived upper hand in the leveraging of most any situation.

She folded, smiled up to Rahman.

"As long as Starr agrees, and Rakim agree, hell, who am I to argue!"

"Then so be it," Rahman said, patting his son on the shoulder and motioning for him to follow. Together, they moved to the rear of the house, leaving the two women, and Starr, to discuss matters among themselves.

Chapter Seventy-eight

Ford knew that she was back in New York City, and was pissed that she had yet to return any of his numerous calls. His plan called for the gossip journalist Abby Vann to "leak" information from "a reliable source" that Ford Terrones was slated to wed super music mogul Sirena Lavesque-Shorter. It had already been reported, by Vann and others, that Siren's divorce from former boy band singer Jenkins Shorter had been finalized, and further reports (at Ford's prompting) were splashed across the front pages of two supermarket tabloids with pictures of a scraggly, near homeless vagabond begging coins on the beach in Ocho Rios, Jamaica. The cutline for the pictures identified the bum as "Jenkins Shorter, crackhead in Jamaica."

Of course, the public relations department of Short Siren was well aware of every bit of news aired about the corporation. They had not managed to squelch the constant paparazzi presence outside of the Lavesque-Shorter family home in McLean, nor effectively block the many telephoto lenses stretching to get a picture of the very pregnant Starr. They had been so omnipresent that even the help was hesitant to take on the assignment of tending to the required upkeep of the mansion, the pool guys having to be paid extra to parry away journalistic inquisitions while struggling their way onto the property.

After the meeting with Rakim's parents, Starr returned to her home escorted by her mother, who only spent the remainder of that weekend there before jetting back up to New York. She was meeting with staff, packing her already extensive schedule with meetings and sessions to hear new talent and arrange singular concert dates and tours for her growing catalogue of talents. The Los Angeles offices would soon be opening, and she was mentally prepared for that grand occasion along with plans to interface Short Siren with Atlanta and Los Angeles based film companies with the production of movies in mind.

She hardly had time for Ford Terrones or even time to consider his proposal of a convenient, though lucrative, marriage between the two.

For his part, Terrones motives were unknown to anyone outside of himself. He had billions, and had always been known as a heated sexual predator. Besides a fine bourbon, Ford's pleasures were simple: Sex, and plenty of it.

His power stemmed from his being able to bed just about any woman he set his sights on. At 67, he kept himself in fine physical form, tall, muscular, a full head of grey hair and a full matching beard, always perfectly trimmed. A hair from his thick, matching grey moustache had better not extend below the fine arch of his thin upper lip. He prided himself on being in fit form. Outside of his visits to the Health Club in one of the family hotels, or the gymnasium in the outer house of his home on the Cape, he relished in his ability to take on younger, virile women in such a variety of sexual positions that might make a seasoned pornographer blush.

He had had his sights on Siren since seeing her perform years ago in an arena he was part owner of and, having years later successfully bedded her, was now determined to make a public display of marrying the well-known music mogul.

She finally returned his call, spoke glowingly to him as if there was no cause for friction between them.

"Hello, Ford. How are you, my dear?"

He frowned, gritted his teeth before answering. "I've been lovely, Siren. Just lovely. I have been, however, concerned about you. Left, oh, seven messages and a prime courtesy would have been to at least phone and say you were busy, couldn't spare me a moment or such, not even to extend me the courtesy of a few words on the telephone."

Oh, this motherfucker is getting on my last nerve! she thought, then again smiled into the phone. "I know you've seen all the public airing of my family's dirty laundry, Ford. Daughter pregnant at 16. My ex out on some vagabond crack mission in Jamaica. Yes, dear, I've been remiss in returning your calls. But forgive me if familial concerns outweighed our little...dalliances, as it were."

Bitch! he thought, then again smiled into the phone. "It's only that I've missed you, my dear. And as you note, I've been keeping abreast of events in your close circle. It appears, from all reports, that you are again a single woman. Quite frankly, that's in a ways what I've been trying to set and talk to you about. Our...agreement...when you did gain your freedom from...that fellow...you'd give my proposal serious consideration."

She'd certainly considered it, and had run it past her personal attorney. There was a sort of passion between the two; his very status excited her, and in bed, well, he wasn't "all that," as she put it, during straight up, vaginal sex. But orally? Well, he was 67 after all, and had probably been wielding a practiced tongue for at least half a century.

She knew too that he particularly wanted her as his wife as sort of a status conquest. Yet she could not denigrate him for that: She would only marry him because of the cache it would bring her in upper crust society, an entrance into the "old money" arena where participants usually had pedigrees which could be traced back to colonial days.

"My dear Ford," she said, mental calculations run amok. "Because of your considerable holdings, and my...well, considerable recent financial acquisitions, our getting married is going to be fraught with all kinds of legal attachments and dispensations on who should heretofore

and how much the party of this and the party of that...my
dear.   I don't want to engage you as a business
arrangement! In actuality, we already have that and more.
So, are you really ready to commit publicly to a
relationship with another black woman after what you've
already told me about your kinfolks' reactions concerning
the past two black women you married?"

"To hell with what they think! I'm sole owner of all
that I have, and none of my holdings interface in any way
with the other Terrones properties, fortunes, businesses.
Fuck 'em. I'm doing this solely for me, and you, of course.
And as a firm showing of my commitment to you, darling,
I'll have my attorneys draft documents designating you as
my sole heir, should I predecease you, with the caveat that
such a document will be null and void if you leave, separate
or divorce me within the first five years of our being
married."

She needed an attorney to look over such a proposed
agreement, but it sounded so good, with his fortune being
conservatively estimated at well over $2 billion, that she
could only smile at the thought of gaining ownership of the
hotels that were his and his alone, the liquor
distributorship, the Cape Cod manse and other properties
he owned globally. She was just over 40 now, and cruelly,
was thinking that, if nothing else, she'd probably fuck him
to death within a couple of years.

"With such an agreement," she said, smiling
broadly, "how could I ever refuse?"

Chapter Seventy-nine

With the caveat in place and contracts signed after a team of both their lawyers had poured over them, Sirena Lavesque-Shorter dispensed of the Shorter appendage and became Mrs. Sirena Lavesque-Terrones during a beachfront ceremony three weeks after becoming a grandmother.

Ford was immensely satisfied with the arrangement, and although he had warm feelings for Sirena, he certainly didn't love her. This was merely a culmination of his grander quest to attain the finest of things on the planet: Race horses, oceanfront properties, five-star hotels, and now, the ultimate of trophy wives.

To be sure, the contracts which preceded the actual wedding one was tilted in his favor: He had no intentions of leaving the Terrones fortune to this African-American woman and her kin. Indeed, he had a son and grandson whom he considered "thoroughbred Terrones," and had a will leaving near all of his fortune to this son. Sirena knew nothing of this, of course, and the estranged son, who'd disassociated himself from father after Ford divorced the boy's mother and "took up with" the first of his black women, had recently made amends and been briefed on the financial dispensations of the Terrones holdings by his father's attorneys.

Before five years had passed, his given span for spending singular time with any woman, Ford planned to divorce Sirena. He'd certainly been enjoying her, and planned on ravaging her, sporting her about global gatherings, for the next 48 months. But the caveat in the pre-nuptial contracts specified that she would get all of his fortune if he died before she did and of course, as long as she didn't divorce him within the first five years or their marriage. Deep, deep down in the contract, and not pointed out to Sirena by her attorneys (who, unbeknownst to her, were secretly awarded $2 million cash each to engage in this legal oversight) was a clause which gave Ford the right to divorce Sirena at any time and void all other parts of the contract. She'd essentially be left with what she brought into the marriage, and nothing of the vast Terrones fortune.

He was flying high, even going down to Virginia to visit his wife's new granddaughter and make nice with his stepdaughter Starr. The consummate professional, he sported Sirena around and visited her business headquarters, invested in a few concert promotion tours and underwrote the expansion of Short Siren Music Corporation in establishing its London offices. He was certainly making quite tactful investments, for he felt an investment in his wife was an investment in his own future. Even after divorcing her and moving on to the next conquest, he was certain, they would remain friends, business associates, but certainly he'd be holding on to all of his investments and she, well, she'd have benefitted from his astute financial advice but certainly, probably disappointingly, have no right to any of the vast Terrones fortunes.

Fifty-nine months, and he'd have accomplished yet another widely-publicized conquest. He never considered that the pre-nuptial contract failed to cover one possibility, for Ford had always considered himself invincible: If he, Ford Terrones, should die within the 60 months, the specifics of the contract, leaving all of his extensive holdings to his present wife, would be enforceable.

Sirena knew this. She'd actually reviewed it over and over on the copy of the contract she'd taken back to her office before signing. And with a little digging by some fine investigators she'd asked Freddy to assign the task, easily discovered that two of her own attorneys had been part and parcel of the attempt to deceive her.

She had the attorneys fired, secreted a message to the mysterious associate known only as Mr. M, and was assured that the attorneys in question would never again be inspired to even try and make contact with any Short Siren business entities or members of the corporation.

Then Sirena determined to put Ford to rest, within 59 months, and hopefully through means that might be determined as being "natural causes."

Chapter Eighty

Sirena had argued but a few minutes about the Muslim name. She relented when Starr and Rakim told her that their daughter would be named Sayeeda Hasna Rahman, and Sirena immediately envisioned a wealth of financial possibilities in clothing lines and other products under the name "Sayeeda's Simple Things." Loosely translated by Rakim from the Arabic, the child's name meant beautiful, happy servant of Allah. Sirena just knew that the name would be quite acceptable to Rakim's parents, and was almost certain that the new parents would certainly frown upon the grandmother's wishes that the girl be named after her deceased mother, Jocelyn. And Jocelyn Sirena Lavesque, since the two had not yet married and Sirena was already envisioning a career in the business for the child.

For the most part, Sirena was living now with her new husband, either ensconced in the Presidential Suite at the Terrones Towers Hotel, or at his expansive estate on the Cape. The two made countless public appearances together, Ford having nothing better to do than socialize and make the occasional suggestion to his league of financial planners, accountants, business associates. Others handled his business almost fully, and he devoted most of his time in the handling of Sirena. Before they had married, his sexual appetite had seemed insatiable. Now it appeared as if he had assumed the mantel of ownership, and rocked and pumped and socked it to Sirena in every conceivable position and in any location that he wanted.

She visited the Virginia estate only occasionally now, having already suggested that Starr, Rakim and the baby assume the McLean estate as their own and begin living together as a family. The Rahman's had a problem with that arrangement, but when Sirena got wind of their objection, she dispatched Sunshine to meet with Appreciation's managers and had them return to the New York studios and begin laying down tracks for a new album. She had the group put up in another 5th Avenue penthouse the company had acquired, and had Marvella assigned, along with a professional nanny and the continued league of housekeepers, to see after Starr and the baby.

Sunshine was performing the duties of Chief Operating Officer for the corporation, along with Sanford. He still had a problem with Sirena and the way she had fired his wife, and Sunshine still was not pleased with the way Sirena had fired their mutual childhood friend Genese. In fact, Sirena had since asked Sunshine to iron out problems between her and her dispatched friend, to no avail.

Genese, who left Short Siren Music with a separation package totaling $7.92 million, was luxuriating on her suburban Washington estate with seven grandchildren and three of her four children still around to fuss over. She did not miss the New York corporate scene one bit, and told Sunshine to tell Sirena thanks but no thanks (she had actually said "Tell that bitch to kiss my black ass!"). Sunshine put it mildly though, saying their friend had said that she would never return to work for the corporation.

With many of her primary duties handled and always with fresh young talent at hand in both the business and musical sides of her corporation, Sirena decided to focus her attention on leveling the playing field with her new husband. Ford seemed as if the marriage comprised a game of chess, with Sirena his opponent. And whenever he plunged himself forcefully into his wife doggy style, and they both succumbed after mutual, exhaustive climaxes, she could have sworn that she heard him whisper, under his breath, "Checkmate!"

Siren did not play chess. But she had always been intrigued by the mystical tales Marvella had spun ever since Sirena was barely ten-years-old.

Marvella's own mother and grandmother were said to be refined practitioners of "root-working." It was a scarcely talked about part of life in what was then considered old Southern Negro families that certain members of the community, near exclusively female, had extensive knowledge of herbal potions which, combined with spiritual incantations, gave them the ability to sway events surrounding the lives of targeted individuals or groups. Sirena grew up knowing that Marvella could "work roots," had never doubted it, for she'd witnessed even some of the woman's friends petition her for assistance when some man, or some other conflicting personality, needed what the older women referred to as "a readjustment of they're attitude."

She was taking a break from the company and, surely, from the increased ravaging of Ford, spending some time in Virginia with her child, grandchild and Marvella. For now she was at peace, able to help Starr out in the home studio as she prepared new material and glad to see that her daughter was at last comfortable with Rakim being away and back at work himself.

"They're putting down some bomb joints!" Starr told her mother excitedly, seated in the comfortable video room of the mansion with the baby and Marvella nearby. "You should hear some of the tracks, Ma!"

Sirena had a satisfactory smile on her face, so pleased to see her own daughter now mastering the challenges of being a mother herself. The baby was a plumper version of Starr when she was a baby, but other than weight was a near mirror image of a child Starr. Sirena tried to parry away a rush of business projections for Sayeeda, and was still trying to get comfortable with the name.

"Daniella attached a couple of cuts to me by email," Sirena said, referring to Appreciation's manager and the mother of Jason and D'Andre. "I really, really like what they've come up with thus far."

"And what about the concept of Rakim and I doing that jam 'Daddy's Little Girl' together?"

Starr had written the lyrics to the ballad, and had video conferenced with the musical director in New York on the instrumentals. Siren knew that the song would be well received by the public, but was bothered by the seemingly undercurrent expressions in the lyrics which in her view seemed as if Starr had some deep-seated longing for her own father.

"It's beautiful, Starr. Just beautiful. But it surely made me wonder if you were writing that especially for your father. You know it was by his choice that he's no longer in the picture."

"I know. I know. He still calls me now and then."

This was news to Sirena. "Oh? From Jamaica?"

"That's where he says he is. But he's always asking for money, Ma. He doesn't—"

"What?" she cut her daughter off. "You're not sending him any money, are you?"

"Ma, why not? Dag, it's not as if I were broke or anything, I mean, a few hundred dollars, a grand or something, like, wow! He is my father and, like, wow Ma, as they say, I got it like that!"

"So you're sending that...fool...money? You know what he does with that money?"

"I really don't care," Starr said. "Yeah yeah yeah I know: All that stuff you talk about teaching a man to fish and not abetting an alcoholic or addict in his addiction and blah blah this and blah blah that. But Ma, you also said you can't help an addict recover until he wants to help himself. Well, if Daddy wants to continue like that, then who am I to judge? And also, he said you cut him off from all his money when you married Mr. Terrones."

"Ford! You heard him time and time again say that he wants you to call him 'Ford'."

"Yeah, that's just so it will not make him feel like the old fart he is, always after something younger and fresher. Like men and cars: always wanting the latest model when their own engine is all fucked and transmission all worn out."

"Watch your mouth, young lady! That's my husband you're talking about!"

"Yeah, Ma. Sure you're right. He's, what? Ninety-nine? And you're 42?"

"Ford is not any damn 99! He's only 68."

"Sixty-eight, divorced four times from two black women, one white and one Japanese. He's all over the Internet," Starr said. "Only...only 68, Ma.   But who's counting?"

Chapter Eighty-one

"Girl, why don't you just pray on the matter?"

Marvella did not like dabbling in the "dark arts," as she referred to them, and had been a fervent Christian and worshipper of Jesus Christ with a deeper and deeper commitment as she grew older. She was now well aware of the fact that, in not so many more years, she would be finding out first hand just who her maker was and exactly what He thought of the life she'd led. She was 77 now, and long before she'd taken on the task of raising the daughter of two unrepentant dopefiends, she'd not been so upright herself.

For countless generations, back to the tribal areas of Ghana, women in Marvella's lineage had been, when translated from an archaic term into English, could be described as "practicing priestesses of medicinal healings and attitudinal adjustment therapies." Old folks in Louisiana, Georgia, Haiti and Jamaica capsulized the description into one word: Roots.
Marvella's grandmother could work roots with such assuredness that it was well known that a woman, about to lose her husband to another woman, would approach the grandmother, often with some belonging of the soon-to-be-absconding husband (often, a pair of his drawers). Soon thereafter the man would be displaying a newfound commitment to the wife, and would only have any further desire to leave home either for work or when in the company of his most beloved wife.

What happened to the woman the man was about to abscond with was something never discussed in the presence of children, and rarely within earshot of any fervently upright Christian adherents.

Sirena had never put much faith in religious teachings, and praying on the matter concerning her relationship with Ford was out of the question.

"Mami," she pleaded. "Just do this thing this once for me! Please!!!"

"Girl, you don't go messing around with no spirits and incantations against somebody unless they done done you wrong in some manner," Marvella said, seated across from Sirena as the two sat alone in the spacious kitchen. "There's an old saying that if you go about digging one grave for someone else, you might as well dig two. And you know who the second one is for."

"Yeah," Sirena said. "Me."

"Correct. Now, if that fella done done you some wrong, or done done you some harm, or threatened you in some way to plan to do you some harm, then that's another story."

Sirena brightened up, sat a little more erect on the counter barstool. "He did threaten to do me some harm, Mami! And I swear, that man's just been a whole different person since we were married! He helped me a lot in business, but you know, it's not that I was suffering or anything anyway. But, Mami, I think he wants to take over Short Siren and all of its affiliates! For some reason, and he's got more billions that anyone could ever want, for some reason I just think it's a power grab. Even...well, you know...when we....do it? He's always assuming this powerful, dominating stance. And it was just all lovey-dovey until we were married."

"I'm gonna tell you what," Marvella said, leaning on the counter and looking deep into Sirena's eyes. "We'll do some protecting of you and yours from him. But I'm going to tell you right now, if his intentions ain't as you say, and you come at him messing around with black arts against him, well, I'm just gonna tell you up front, ain't no good gonna come of you if'n you're wrong. You hear me?"

"I hear you, Mami. I hear you."

Chapter Eighty-two

They definitely had a winner. And Sirena was back in headquarters working 12-hour days to ensure that the new release by Appreciation garnered the attention she so believed it deserved.

It was a masterpiece, she told the boys and their family members, and she was going to throw an enormous amount of Short Siren's considerable resources behind it to see that it gained the airplay it deserved. Already a tour was being designed, designed being the operative word because this was not just going to be a series of concert performances. Starr was putting the finishing touches on her own new album, and public relations, A&R and an additional contracting out to one of the nation's most prestigious public affairs organizations was combining to make the roll-out of Appreciation's new album, and Starr's, nothing less than a stellar occasion.

Siren had let her husband in on the revised business module for the as-yet unnamed tour, which was already being slated to go on for two months. It would hit 24 cities in the United States, make a stop in Europe, two locales in Africa and conclude as the featured event at the popular Sunny Days of Jah Reggae and Rhythm and Blues Festival in Negril, Jamaica. Ford could see the excitement in Siren's eyes, hear it in her voice and see it in the faces of those moving about in Short Siren headquarters. He was virtually absorbing the excitement himself, and realized this was one of the prime reasons he had married this particular black woman: The excitement inherent in her people when they were exercising creativity, well financed, well fed and happy. He wanted to be an integral part of this excitement.

He limped into the 46th floor office of his wife, hobbled after a freak accident on the 9th hole while golfing the previous weekend. It was the strangest thing, he'd tell Siren later: He was 30 feet from landing a bogie, scoring well under par with his regular golfing buddies, when he made the putt, stepped to the hole and bent to retrieve his ball and all of a sudden the greens appeared as if they were on an incline. Viewing the landscape as if through a fish-eyed lens, he tried to use the putting iron to balance himself, but instead twisted sideways on the left ankle and was hurled to the greens as if catapulted by some unseen force.

Siren was awaiting him with a glowing smile.

"Hello, my dear!" he greeted her, stabilized by a custom-carved walking cane. "How are ya?"

He moved over to where she sat behind the custom desk, leaned and gave her a kiss.

"I'm fine, Ford. Just fine. How's the ankle, darling?"

"Oh, it's nothing," he lied. The pain was excruciating, had been even after he'd taken the pain medication prescribed by a doctor Siren had summoned for him. "How's progress on the new tour?"

"Moving right along," she smiled. "Starr's putting the finishing touches on 'Daddy's Little Girl'. Were going to roll that out as a single next week, generate a little buzz for sure, play up the fact that she and Rakim are to be married after the tour, all the bells and whistles of a major production."

"Good," he said, taking a seat in the conference area by the picturesque window. "And your legal team is in agreement that Terrones Holdings will underwrite the European leg of the tour?"

"It's all yours but the management, darling. You know we have Georgia Whitfield-Johnson under special contract for the entirety of this tour, and she has full authority to place personnel of her choosing in the technical and management positions throughout."

"I understand," Ford said, smiling. "I've had others vet her, even when she was primarily working with Short Sirens exclusively. Received nothing but praise for her all around."

"Good," Siren said, paused at the writings she was doing by pen on the desktop, removed her reading glasses and smiled to her husband. "Darling, I'm kind of busy here this afternoon. You want to arrange something....say...around eightish this evening? At the Terrones Towers?"

He wanted for nothing less, loins throbbing at the very thought.

"Sure, sweetheart. Sure." He arose, limped over and bent and gave her a full kiss on the lips. "I'm going over to McInnerney's for a bourbon with the boys. I'll be expecting you at the Presidential Suite around eight. Good day, my love."

"Good day, Ford."

Chapter Eighty-three

Troy showed in the offices just as his mother was getting ready to roll out the premiere event of her lifetime. Starr was the star, Appreciation almost as popular. Together, they were an event that was already generating spectacular public raves and a demand for more shows. Each announced one sold out on the Internet in record time.

Starting the concerts was Holiday Candies, with Fredericka Sands leading that all girl's group. There was Cream of White on the undercard, a unique mix of white rock and soul. All of the announced venues in the U.S. were already sold out. And many were anticipating the performances globally. It was a unique undertaking: rock and soul and rap united.

Troy had shown little concern about what was occurring; he'd just graduated law school, and only wanted familial support for his own newly conceptualized organization in the hard-scrabbled region of D.C. he was determined to serve as a community organizer.

He greeted his mother and Ford, whom he had heard about but had avoided meeting. Troy wasn't particularly pleased that Sirena had divorced his father and taken up with a white man, in a most public display of what he deemed to be a most obvious business transaction. Without her knowledge, he'd convinced her lawyers to let him review the pre-marital contract, and found it lacking in favor of Ford. So he really had no love for the new stepfather, and greeted him with little warmth.

"Troy!" Ford said, smiling broadly. "So, we finally meet!"

He stepped to the young man, who was as tall as he but a stark contrast: Dark, suited and sporting shoulder-length dreadlocks. It was evident that Troy wasn't as receptive to the meeting; he smirked and twisted his full lips to the side, looked into the warm blue eyes of Ford with cold, brown ones and peered deeply into the very soul of his step-father.

"Hey, fella," Troy said. "No disrespect, man, but what's up with you? You trying to take over my mother's company or what?"

Siren sprang up from her seat behind the desk, stepped to between the two men.

"Troy? Baby?" She took him in a warm embrace. "You have no idea of what is going on in my relationship with Ford. Please, baby, don't go there."

"Relationship?" Troy said. "That's how you describe a marriage? Ha! The answer lies within the question, and I haven't even asked it yet. You just answered my question, Ma."

She held him at arms length, looking him up and down.

"Baby, we're in the middle of something big here," Siren said. "Don't come in here throwing rocks and stuff. Now, congratulations on your passing the D.C. bar. We were set to have a little to-do for you, but as you know your sister and our top acts are rolling out this tour, and you...well, congratulations, baby. But right now, we have an enormous amount of logistics to take care of. Are you staying in New York for a while? Going with us on some of the tour?"

"No, mother. I just stopped by to see Starr."

"Oh, you didn't stop by to see your dear mother?"

"I love you, Ma." He kissed her lightly. "But apparently you and Mr. Big here got business to take care of. Where's Starr?"

"She's up on 47 laying down some backup tracks. You know where the large studio is?"

"Sure. I've been here a few times, Ma. I know where it's at."

"Good. Then go on up there and see Starr. She'll be glad you stopped by."

"Alright. Nice to meet you, step-dad."

He   glared   at   Ford,   who   seemed   to   be uncharacteristically at a loss for words.

When Troy entered the largest of studios on the 47th floor, he came across the members of Christmas Candies. Fredericka, the group's lead singer, was first to catch his eyes: She was dressed as if for performance, long, chocolate legs protruding from a silk skirt that would have been thought pornographic in the public. He'd seen her on videos, knew well of her highly-publicized relationship with Wordsmith, the rapper who was also a member of the Short Siren musical family. She locked eyes with him, arose and sashayed directly to him.

"Troy?" she said, extending a manicured hand. "My goodness! I've seen your pictures in your mother's office! Hey! Nice to finally meet you!"

She embraced him, purposely pressing her warm, lithe frame into his midsection.

"Hello, sister," he said with little warmth.

"My goodness!" she said, taking both his hands and stepping back to view him totally, at arms length but with sensuous eyes. "My my my! You are fine!"

She took him by the hand, introduced him to the other members of the group. The girls knew Fredericka well; knew that she was already maneuvering to get closer to Troy, and through him further endear Christmas Candies to his mother.

"Nice to meet you all," Troy said, looking through the glass-enclosed studio separated by the common area to his sister, who had finally opened her eyes mid-song and seen him. She smiled, motioned for the engineers and musicians to pause.

Fredericka was still nuzzling up to her brother when she bounded out of the studio, jumped into his arms.

"Troy!!!"

"Hey, Starr!"

The sister cast cold eyes to Fredericka, an unspoken warning that the heated singer stay away from her beloved older brother.

"What's up, Troy?!"

"Ain't nothing, Starr. Just stopping by. You know I passed the bar."

"I heard! But I haven't been home for a minute, getting ready for this tour. You talked to Ma?"

"Yeah. And that old white guy she married."

"Oh. I can't stand that fool either."

"Billionaire. And still wanting more. But he's not getting his hands into Ma's business like that, know what I'm saying?"

"Not even! But he is lending financial support to the European leg of the tour. That's probably going to take a little of the financial weight off of Ma and the company. You know she's banking that part in the red, and hoping that the residuals from record sales make up for it."

They moved away from the members of Christmas Candies, seeking privacy. The girls gathered and moved into the studio, but not before Fredericka shot a sensual gaze at Troy, licking her lips and twitching her little ass in retreat.

Troy and Starr took a seat on the vacated leather sofa.

"You ever talk to Daddy?" he asked, growing serious.

"I talk to him. Send him some money now and then."

"He's still in Jamaica?"

"Yeah. And from his voice, still into that stuff he's been smoking."

"Damn. I was thinking about flying down there and seeing if I can…you know…kind of get him to come back to the States and go into rehab."

"I don't know, Troy. You know Ma used to be on that mess and got straightened out. Long before we were born even. And she knows. Says that if a person doesn't want to get right, there's nothing anyone can do till they want to straighten out themselves."

"I know, Starr. I know."

"But hey!" she sprang to her feet. "You need to hear this new jam I did anyway, called 'Daddy's Little Girl'! It's for him, you know."

"Like he's going to hear it…"

"He might. And anyway, I didn't do it just for him to hear, know what I'm saying?"

"I know. Money. You and Ma…"

"It's not all like that, Troy. I like the business. Like making people happy with my music. You never did like the business. But that's all right. You do your thing, big brother. But don't knock me and Ma for doing ours."

"I don't have a problem with that. It's just that…you know…her marrying that guy. Probably only because he's got the connects and billions and all. Starr, I just hate to see Ma pimping herself out like that."

"It's not like that, Troy. I think she, and he, they like, truly enjoy one another."

"Mixing business and pleasure, huh?"

Probably. But that's how them old folks do. That's how them old folks do."

Chapter Eighty-four

The tour was a financial success for everyone involved in it. Christmas Candies was the new "it" girl group. Appreciation rekindled its love by millions of new fans. Terrones Holdings added a few million dollars more to its holdings and became a public darling for its support of black artists. Starr's light shined brightly on an international scale, particularly with the new single, "Daddy's Little Girl." It was the song she was slated to close out the show with at the Sunny Days of Jah Reggae and Rhythm and Blues Festival in Negril, Jamaica.

On the flight to Montego Bay on his private jet, Ford was experiencing yet additional medical traumas. Seated across from Siren, he was pouring sweat, seemingly unable to catch his breath and still using shots of bourbon as a perceived remedy to what ailed him. Siren was not in the mood to assist him in any way. She'd just disengaged from a heated confrontation with Fredericka following a most inspired performance by Christmas Candies at the London stop in the tour. Wearing one of her designer earrings, Fredericka was regaling her band mates backstage when Siren stormed up to her, presenting her with the match to the earring, one which she had found on the bedside table of the suite she and Ford shared in London. She'd already lambasted the singer for her unscheduled departure from to the tour during performances in D.C. and, having dispatched one of Freddy's investigators to trail her, had been told that Fredericka had spent a night at her McLean estate. And only her beloved son Troy had been in residence there at the time.

Siren had insisted then that Marvella fly over to London for an urgent meeting, sat down with her for a few hours and, once receiving the sought after reassurance, sent her life-long guardian back to Washington by private jet.

Marvella, nearing 80, was no longer willing to trail along with Siren in her present, hectic itinerary, but had been convinced that Ford was not doing right by Siren, and was well deserved of whatever ills befell him.

It was the extensive flying, the long periods in the high altitude, which sealed his fate.

Still within the window which would see all of his vast holdings passed over to Siren should she remain married to him for at least the agreed upon five years, Ford was feverishly trying to raise his primary attorney on the phone. Heart racing, he was now in acute realization that, should death overtake him within the coming months, Terrones Holdings would fall, lock stock and barrel, into the coffers of his African-American wife.

To be sure, she was by now a billionaire in her own right. But pride and historic familial dedication would not allow Ford to have the generations-old conglomerate passed on to someone not of blue-blood, Terrones stock. And the very thought of this, the very trauma of its consideration, made him pour on more bourbon and surge his blood pressure fatally when his lead attorney could not be reach.

Twenty-two hundred feet above the Caribbean Sea on approach to Montego Bay, Ford Xavier Terrones slumped his head to the side, looked up at the cloud ceiling, and was at once spiritually one with them. He exited the plane in a last exhale of breath, and Siren, not even lifting a hand to verify that he was dead, leaned back in her chair and followed the pilot's instructions to secure her seat belt and return her comfortable leather seat to the upright position.

Taxiing to the private aircraft region of Sangster International Airport, Siren undid her belt and went forward to inform the crew that Ford had passed away. She was so nonchalant about it that the pilot and co-pilot pinned one another with quizzical gazes.

"Well, Mrs. Lavesque-Terrones," the pilot said. "We need to inform the proper authorities in the terminal and make arrangements to have the body removed. And after the officials confirm your...your findings, Mrs. Lavesque-Terrones, would you like for us to...urr...return the remains to New York? To Boston?"

"Boston," she said. "But actually, I need you to stay here. Can't we just have him...ahh...boxed up and sent back in the cargo hold of a commercial flight?"

The men were momentarily speechless, engaged in parking the plane and killing the engines.

"That's...a distinct possibility, ma'am...if that's what you want."

"Exactly what I want," Siren said. "Besides, you flying him back and then returning here in time to get me after the concert would be extremely costly, wouldn't it?"

"Ahhh...in all probabilities, quite costly."

"Then arrange to have him boxed up and put in the cargo hold of a commercial flight."

The co-pilot moved to the exit, lowered it for his remaining passenger. She stepped to the exit, looked over her shoulder with a smile.

"Good day, gentlemen. Enjoy you stay in Jamaica."

Epilogue

One of the two nannies on board to see after baby Sayeeda had her bundled and held to where her body was clasped tight to the nannie's chest, her little head over the nannie's shoulder and looking to the crowd gathered near the beach. The area was backstage of the concert platform, fenced off from the throng gathered between the rear of the stage and the beach. Those who had not been able to afford the costly tickets and be among the thousands who stretched well into the business region of the resort town of Negril belted the area, just to get a taste of the sounds, if not a clear view. The nanny watched as Mrs. Lavesque-Terrones appeared as if she were arguing with the lead singer of the girl group which had just left the stage, tossed what appeared to be an airline ticket into the girl's face and stormed off.

In actuality, Siren had just fired Fredericka, giving her her walking papers in essence, which consisted of a one-way, commercial, coach ticket back to the States. She was fuming, having been told by security that Fredericka had snuck into the exclusive quarters of the members of Appreciation the previous night. Upon further investigation, the security woman had discovered that Fredericka had secured a separate, private suite at a Negril hotel, and had even gone so far as to play social butterfly with the headliners, Starr, and her fiancé Rakim. Later that evening, Rakim had been observed leaving the suite where he and Starr had been staying, taking a taxi and motoring over to the hotel where Fredericka had moments earlier secured a suite. He did leave within an hour, returning to his betrothed. But Siren knew Fredericka well, and was almost certain that the girl had slept with her soon-to-be son-in-law.

"You're just one low down, nasty ho!" Siren had blasted Fredericka before hitting her in the face with the airline ticket. "Your ass is no longer in the group! You know damn well that Rakim is the father of Starr's baby, my granddaughter! And your stank ass have the nerve to sleep with him!"

Fredericka just smiled, tossed back a mound of the $750 hair cascading down upon her shoulders.

"Mrs. Lavesque-Terrones, you have your nerve!" Fredericka said. "Your high and mighty ass was all up in Mr. Terrones jock while you were still married to that crackhead husband of yours. And for your information, I don't think your dear husband Ford, would kindly on you treating me in any manner that's disrespectful. He and I have...let's just say, we find that we have mutual likes, if you get my drift."

"You...you...you black-ass bitch! And just in case you have to wonder about it later on, you and your little....dalliance...with my husband, is one of the reason he proved himself to be a no good son-of-a-bitch and got what he deserved, OK?"

"Huh? What in the hell are you talking about, old lady?"

"For your information, young ho-ass bitch, Ford is no longer with us. My dear husband had a heart attack or some kind of medical emergency on the flight down here. He has passed away."

She then tossed the airline ticket directly into Fredericka's face. The singer bent down and picked it up, and before stepping off, looked over a shoulder and sneered at Siren.

"We'll, you have my condolences, Siren. I thought that maybe me and...Ford...might have found something there. But still, I think you and I are going to have to be on better terms, Siren, since in a few days I'm going to be your daughter-in-law."

Siren was floored, reached to a stage railing for support. "You...you and...my Troy?! Aw, hell naw! Bitch I'll kill you my goddamn self before---"

Security stepped in, restraining Siren just as she removed her earrings and kicked off her heels.

Fredericka reached into her pocketbook, retrieved an engagement ring fitted with one of the largest diamonds Siren had ever seen.

"Yes, mother. Me and your dear son Troy." She took a few steps, turned and pinned Siren with a cold glare, flashed the ring and wiggled her fingers. "Ooops!"

Siren was flushed, began to speed dial New York but was distracted by the crowd as they roared in anticipation of the final act: Starr. Appreciation had opened, with Christmas Candies placed between the two most popular acts so that, in closing, Rakim could reappear and do the most popular duet with Starr. Cream of White had been well received in London, but was not anticipated to be much of a draw in Jamaica and had been sent home.

Siren had arranged this, the last show of the tour, with perfection: It was also being simulcast to millions around the world, at a cost of $49.99 per viewing to what was already calculated as a paid audience of 758,500 viewers in America alone. The matter of Fredericka would just have to wait.

Starr took the stage to a rousing ovation. She didn't disappoint, shifting through a number of tunes from her first album to new material currently occupying four spots on the U.S. Top Ten chart. Siren was feeling a measure of pride, which suppressed the range of thoughts grinding on her: the matter with Troy was foremost, bouncing stride for stride with her determination to put an immediate, permanent grip on the vast Terrones Holding's empire.

She smiled at the thought that she was now owner of a couple of New York City's finest hotels, not to mention the Terrones Spirits liquor conglomerate which, according to common lore, had been around since the initial distillery served spirits to colonialist and still populous Native Americans.

She moved over to the nanny cradling Sayeeda. Rakim was standing there also, making faces and goo-goo noises to his child. He smiled at Siren as she approached, but the smile immediately disappeared when he saw the serious look on Siren's face.

"You get your ass ready to do your duet with my daughter," Siren said. "And I want you happy and gay and shit on that stage like nothing in the world is the matter. But afterwards, I'm going to have a talk with you about your little thing last night with that bitch Fredericka."

The nanny appeared as if she were the target of Siren's rapprochement, rocking Sayeeda and eyes bulging. Rakim appeared speechless, mouth hung open, eyes fearful. He struggled for words.

"Mrs. Lavesque-Terrones, I wa....I..it wasn't...."

"Aw, shut the fuck up!" Siren spat. "She's getting ready to do that closing number. Get your ass over there and get ready to join her."

Other members of Appreciation, along with the remaining members of Christmas Candies, had been observing from a short distance away. They could hear the words being exchanged, but none even dared move in that direction. When Mrs. Lavesque-Terrones was on a tear, even some of her security personnel went out of their way to avoid her.

Siren displayed a tight smile when she reached to cup her granddaughter's head, bent to give the baby a kiss, then turned to the gathered group around the rear of the stage. She walked over to them, and all conversation among them ceased.

"Sharon, you and the girls should meet with me the beginning of next week in my New York office to discuss the search for a replacement for Fredericka. She is no longer a part of the group or part of anything under the Short Sirens umbrella. And Jason, D'Andre, Tony, Rocky: You boys will be having a new member also. After this show, Rakim Rahman is no longer a part of Appreciation."

"Whoa!" Jason uttered.

No one else said a word.

Starr moved into her practiced transition, which consisted of some light banter about the joys of entertaining on the beach in Jamaica as the music play softly below her. She did a brief take on what inspired her to write the song, "Daddy's Little Girl," and explained that it would not have been the million-seller that it was without the smooth, additional voice of Rakim Rahman.

The music came up, she broke into the opening lyrics while stretching out a hand towards the rear of the stage. Rakim, smiling and in true professional form, strolled out onto the stage, mike in hand.

The crowd went wild, but backstage, the mood was all but joyous. The only gleeful face there was that of Sayeeda, who was again being held on the chest, head over the shoulder, of the nanny. The baby smiled, took the pacifier out of her mouth and held it out towards a man at the rear gate who was being barred by security from entering the backstage area.

The man was pleading with the huge security officers, to no avail. He then locked eyes with the baby holding forth the pacifier; it seemed as if the baby was offering it to him particularly. The smile was familiar, reminding him of the young woman who was then on stage, belting out a song which he knew had been penned especially for him.

Convinced that he would never be admitted without a backstage pass, Jenkins walked to the deserted beach, sun setting to the West above azure waters. He sat crying, the strains of "Daddy's Little Girl" washing over him much as did the cool waters as he sat much too close to the incoming tide. Sobbing uncontrollably now, he reached into the breast pocket of the tattered tropical shirt he wore, retrieved the worn crack pipe, a lighter, and his last chunk of cocaine rock. It was of a size which he'd usually break into pieces, forming three, four individual hits. But he feared that parting the rock with his dirty, crusted fingernails might cause a good portion to pop out of his hand and amidst the sand, hardly distinguishable from the thousands of small pebbles which, through his tears, looked like a thousand crack rocks.

He put the entirety of the rock into the stem, raised it and applied the butane flame.

"Always daddy's little girl," the voice of his daughter rose above the roar of the crowd. "Always daddy's little girl."

He shook in a convulsing fit of tears, trying to hold in the fumes of the crack for maximum effect but finding himself unable to. Jenkins arose, dripping wet now, still tearful and pulling again on the crack pipe.

"Daddy's little girl!"

It seemed as if she was calling out to him.

"Daddy's little girl!"

He began weeping uncontrollably, started walking into the Caribbean Sea.

"Always daddy's little girl...!"

The waves pushed him back, but he kept on out to sea. He kept his footing until waist deep, lost it for a moment, arose and continued further and further into the waters. Willfully, he let go of the crack pipe, and let go of the lighter.

"Always daddy's little girl..."

The waves washed over his face now, seawater mingling with saline tears. He could no longer feel the floor under his feet, and had never been a swimmer.

"Always daddy's little...."

He was pushed towards the shore, could feel sand beneath his feet again but would not cooperate with the motion of the waters. He gave in to the outgoing currents, shut his eyes to the tears and could no longer find his footing.

"Always daddy's..."

And then the sea claimed him.

THE END

www.ingramcontent.com/pod-product-compliance
Lightning Source LLC
Chambersburg PA
CBHW030811260626
47169CB00001B/278